GARDEN OF INK AND ANCIENT STONE

INK OF THE FAE BOOK 1

N. Z. NASSER

Silver Sea
Echohold
Lunaria
Etherbrook
Frostfang
Umbra Depths
Strange Tides
Frigid Basin
COURT OF SILENCE
Stellvick
Greystorm Ridge
Shadows
Ravenwing
Oakenspire
Elv
Cerulean Strait
COURT OF SILVER SEAS
FAERI REAL
Glimlyn
Ashenvale
Soulforge
Eventide Highlands
Murkthorn
Surenne
Lacrima Lake
Gloomhaven
Aurora Lowlands
COURT OF CHAOS
Elyssian Edge
Whalesong Estuary
Frenzi
Fallen Gulf
Ebonspire
Spellmyst Shore
Broken Sea
Disputed Territory

COURT OF BONES
Marrowreach
Runeth
Wyvern Reach
Loch Bare
Wilvoria
Moltenkeep
Dead Man's Ridge
Loomveil Lake
Pale Reach
Nightblaze Isle
Blackbrine Ocean
Duskmire Glen
Scattered Craggs
COURT OF EMBERS
The Wastelands
Scorched Plains
Merwine Hills
COURT OF NEBULAS
Feylight Marshes
Shrouded Forest
Wraithwoods
Celestiva
Sylvanturm
MORTAL REALM
inelight
COURT OF LUMINOSITY
Serennor
Ebonmere
Riven Cliffs
Larkspur
N
W
E
S

PRONUNCIATION GUIDE

YSADORA: *EE-suh-DOR-uh*
ZEPHYR: *ZEH-feer*
KAZIMIR: *KAH-zih-meer*
CAIRN: *KERN*
LUNARYS: *LOO-nah-ris*
MAREN: *MAR-en*
FERRITH: *FEH-rith*
DANAË: *duh-NAY*
THIAGO: *tee-AH-go*
CYPRIAN: *SIP-ree-uhn*
WYLDA: *WIL-duh*
SEQUOIA: *seh-KWOY-uh*
GABOR: *GAH-bor*
LOXLEY: *LOX-lee*
ROWENA: *roh-WEE-nuh*
VEDA: *VAY-duh*
MYTHROS: *MITH-ros*
XAIRE: *ZAIR*
ELOWEN: *EL-oh-wen*

YSADORA

*May you find the courage to trust your inner voice, the discernment to see through silver-tongued lies
and a love that is steadfast and true.
—The Binder's wish for the youngling Ysadora.*

Our bookshop had once been ordinary across the realms. Back then, bookshops were ten a penny, each with a unique essence. Every villager could read, and most could write, although not in the beautiful cursive of Father's calligraphy. A home without books on the shelves warned that something had gone terribly wrong, either in circumstance, intellect or optimism.

My memory didn't stretch back that far, but Father assured me it was true.

He mourned those days. *The days of plenty,* he called them.

Although it was our business to deal in books, Father and I didn't need words to understand each other. When his eyes misted with memories of happier days, he didn't just mean streets dotted with bookshops. He meant food and coin. Most of all, he meant my mother's love. Mother had been gone for nigh on twenty orbits, and my memories of her were mere wisps: gentle lips curving, thick blonde hair scented with lavender, and the croon of her silken voice when she sang me to sleep.

Sometimes, the swell of grief in Father's brown eyes made me catch my breath, but it wasn't in his nature to loudly lament. Sorrow was best buried in the past, he said. A tall man, Father had learned long ago not to make ripples in the world. Instead, he preferred to fade into the background and live out his days as best he could. I didn't dare to poke at his pain. He couldn't abide fussing. Our life in Larkspur had a ticking inevitability about it. We perfected our routine, and neither of us deviated from it. Father was a staunch believer in practicality; in his view, emotions were for stories. life depended on everyday tasks done quietly. So we tended to our bookshop: organising the shelves, attempting to replenish our stock, contributing to the trickle of literacy amongst uninterested villagers, and feeding the reading habits of distant courtiers.

It wasn't always enough to keep broth or bread in our mouths, let alone meat.

But we had each other, and coin would sometimes appear in our bleakest moments as if by magic. Father would smile wistfully, then, as if the gods themselves had blessed us. With a ladle of five-day-old stringy lamb stew remaining for tonight's supper, I prayed the gods would see fit to fashion coin for us today.

Father turned off a lamp, casting the small stack of coins he had been counting into shadow, and pushed his half-moon spectacles up his nose. "I am tired, Ysa. I will walk to clear the cobwebs from my mind."

I set aside the letter from a scout with its dizzying promise of an unheard-of text. It was Father's habit to take a short walk once a week at dusk. He always returned with a bitter tonic for us to drink, a life-giving elixir, as he always called it. Like I was a four-year-old who didn't eat her greens and not four-and-twenty. It was a ritual that hadn't been disrupted by Mother's disappearance and provided comforting continuity. "You'll avoid the forest?"

He pocketed a few coins and brushed the rest into a lock box under his desk before easing himself to his feet. "It is not a daughter's job to worry about her father. The Shrouded Forest holds no fear for aged men, Ysa."

"Of course, Father." I wondered for the thousandth time if—like me—he was thinking of Ferrith's sister Vixora, who had ventured into the forest before she knew how to tie her shoelaces and whose bones had never been found.

His placid expression gave nothing away. "Did you and Maren train today?"

"Anja needed help at the bakery, so she could not spar with me today. I practised drills." In truth, my rumbling stomach had prevented much practice. He had always insisted that it was important to be strong in both mind and spirit. Sometimes, when there were tussles over valuable texts, it helped that I had practised drills until my body acted on reflex, that I was nimble and strong despite my slight stature.

He skimmed tender fingers over my cheek. My mind

flashed back entire orbits to when those same fingers were blotchy with a myriad of inks in indigo, emerald and silver. I resisted the urge to smooth his rumpled cardigan as he ambled past under the golden orbs of vintage lamps, footsteps heavy on the tasselled rugs underfoot. Father's willowy body cast long shadows on dark panelling as he paused at the dwindling fire with its reading nook and peered mournfully at the painting of a dragon he had commissioned long ago. A dragon with iridescent bronze scales, its wings outstretched as it soared over a mountain range, its flaring nostril and golden eyes turned towards the viewer of the painting. Sometimes, he stared at the painting for so long that it seemed he wanted to fall into it. Sighing, Father continued past a shelf once stacked with leather-bound encyclopaedias, now replaced by picture books for adults. Then he lifted his chin and walked stiffly into the twilight. Out, out towards the forest, where no villager dared to tread, where the silvery bark of birches merged with the inky black of yew trees.

The door thudded shut. Not for us the brash bell of an apothecary or common grocer's.

With a sigh, I returned to my letter, carefully noting details about the owner's situation that would influence whether we offered coin or an exchange for the book. The stillness of the bookshop cocooned me. I was so engrossed in my task that, at first, I didn't register the approaching footfalls.

A voice rustled like leaves in the graveyard. "The ages pass in a blink."

I lifted my head and met a cerulean gaze akin to the blue ribbons on the maypole at the village fair. My stomach tightened. Our paths had crossed no more than twice, but she was not easily forgotten. The woman's violet robes hailed from bygone times and carried the faint scent of burning wood and dewy moss. Silver hair shone under suddenly buzzing and winking shop lighting. Her skin was grooved, and her fingers knotted.

The woman met my scrutiny and returned it. I weathered her keen eyes as they drank in every detail of my visage—the dark tumble of my hair, brown eyes flecked with gold like Father's, unpainted bow lips that the fashionable village women tittered at—then drifted to the plain dress barely hiding the bird bones of my thin body, and finally to my ink-smudged fingers and the reams of notes before me.

"The written word comes easily to you. Almost as if it is innate."

I shrugged. "I grew up in a bookshop. Words are as familiar to me as breathing."

Her voice hummed like a distant song in the night sky. "As they should be. You know who I am?"

"You're Lunarys. Father went out to meet you." She was dangerous, despite appearances. I had always known it, and I always wondered why Father risked crossing paths with her. I wondered what tied him to this particular woman when he preferred the company of books. When there were any number of medicine women he could have bought the elixir from.

"Careless of him to divulge my name." Frowning, she extracted a familiar frosted flask with its black wax seal from her sleeve but didn't hand me the clove and cinnamon concoction.

I reached for the small pouch at my waist. "Let me settle your payment."

Her smile did not reach her sea eyes. "A bargain was struck. No coin is required, Ysadora."

Shivers snaked up my spine at how my name danced on her tongue. I wasn't sure of the etiquette—whether Father would expect me to insist on payment or ask her to stay until he returned, although my every instinct fizzed with the knowledge that it would be better if she left. I hesitated. "Perhaps I may find you a book for your trouble?"

Bookshops held a certain magic. A tiny nudge to browse our shelves, and she would no doubt return with a small stack of treasures. If I made some coin, I could make Father some salted trout, and we could wash away his displeasure with some wine. I liked him drunk. He'd tell me stories that brimmed with magic that felt so real my skin tingled. Then he'd snore loudly enough to mask the sound of my footsteps as I snuck down to the cellar.

Lunarys straightened her back. "I came merely to survey my handiwork before…"

I gave her an uncertain smile and gestured to the armchair next to the dying fire. "I could bring you some elderflower tea while you wait for Father?"

"That wouldn't do. He won't be pleased with me for coming here."

Then why had she come? Gnarled fingers tattooed with tiny moons toyed with the flask and uncorked it. Her brow clouded, and then, with a sharp movement, she poured the contents onto a spider plant on the counter and set the flask aside.

I cried out at the unexpectedness of it. The plant, chosen for its purifying nature in the dense shop air, had survived my persistent neglect. But as the liquid seeped into its cracked soil, the cascade of tapered leaves lost their lustre, edges browning, the plant hissing. It was still alive, I thought, but inexplicably altered in form, as though drained of its essence.

My heart pounded. "Was that poison?" My nose told me the concoction smelled as it always had. What had it done to me if a healthy plant had withered when exposed to it?

The light in her eyes blinded me. I had to look away. Who was she? *What* was she?

She huffed in disapproval. "He was a fool for not teaching you our ways. Still, with a little luck and a little bravery, you might salvage the situation. You must be ready."

"For what?"

"You will know when the star unravels." Lunarys gave the plant a rueful glance. "My sisters will lament this choice. The old laws forbid this path. But it's hard to let things die when you have cared for them."

I might have laughed if she had been sweet, mad Annie or the prankster Soren, but her tone was serious, and I had seen with my own eyes what the liquid had done. The liquid that I had taken into my belly week after week since I was a babe. The shop lights flickered, a morbid thinning that mirrored my internal ruminations. Cursing myself for not keeping a decent weapon closer to hand, my fingers inched towards the letter opener on my desk.

Lunarys looked at me in disdain. "Enough of that. Listen carefully. Convince your father that you drank the elixir. An outright lie won't work. You'll have to be cleverer than that. It might make all the difference to your survival. And his." She pulled up her hood, casting her face into shadow. "Tell Kazimir I have no regrets."

My mind scrambled to process the prickle of my skin, the elixir that had been intended for me but had devastated the plant, and her strange request to lie to Father. What did she mean by survival? "Wait—"

She walked into the night before I could ask her who Kazimir was.

2

———

YSADORA

Names are power.
Some fae hoard their names like jewels.
—Danaë Everreed's annotations
in her Faerie books

T stared at the destroyed plant and the lanterns the woman had extinguished in her wake. The bookshop was our haven, but Lunarys had turned my perspective upside down with the ease of a cat toying with a mouse. With the finesse of a preacher at a pulpit.

I didn't want to trust her. I wanted to throw the unnerving assertions to the wind.

But what choice did I have?

I couldn't risk anything happening to Father. Lunarys was no stranger, and neither was she a fool. So I carefully removed all evidence of the withered husk, grateful that Father had always shown more passion for his garden than indoor plants. A glance at the grandfather clock told me that Father wouldn't return home for another half hour. Enough time to sneak down to the cellar to soothe my rattled nerves. As long as I didn't get caught.

I swept my research into a drawer, taking a little more care with my ink pot and quill. Although fewer than one customer a day graced our doorstep, I turned off the lights to dissuade any further interest. Then, from force of habit, I tiptoed down the sloping stone steps situated in the hallway between the bookshop and our home, my fingers tracing the familiar pockmarked wall. The air grew cooler and heavier as I descended, and the darkness wrapped around me like a coat. The cellar was my place of comfort.

At the bottom of the stairs, a worn door creaked open into a small, claustrophobic space tucked beneath the house like a forgotten pocket. Lichen covered patches of the stone floor as though the earth reclaimed this hidden space. A single, perpetually lit lantern hung from the low ceiling, casting a dim, thin light that barely reached the corners of the room.

Against the back wall stood a single wooden bookshelf, narrow but sturdy, made from dark oak. Father had installed it himself after Mother's disappearance when he'd brought her favourite books down here. To me, they were worth more than all the treasures in our bookshop combined. The books were our last tie to Mother. Maybe that was why he couldn't bring himself to part with them. He couldn't bring himself to come down here—his expression grew sad when he passed the stairwell—and I would make sure that he never discovered my own visits.

We forged ahead after knocks, Father and I. We didn't dwell.

There was no seating in the cellar and I didn't dare to bring anything bulky downstairs, with the exception of a velvet cushion Mother had made and a woollen blanket. With a slow exhale of breath, I settled myself onto the cushion, pausing to marvel at her embroidery: a medley of notes from a musical score. Then I turned to the real treasure in the cellar.

The sole bookshelf was crammed with old tomes and scrolls, some bound in leather, others in cloth. Their bindings were worn, their parchment yellowed. Delicate gold leaf, now illegible, adorned the spines of the books. When I gingerly opened the books, the sweet scent of honey and sharper notes of something metallic—almost like iron—twisted my stomach. The pages were thick and smooth, a golden shimmer running along their edges. The text was written in a flowing script, precise, yes, but with the unmistakable irregularities of work inked by hand. My curiosity sparked at symbols from long-forgotten languages—from *the days of plenty*, my bookish mind told me. Reams of illustrations could be found in the books: creatures and plants, both strange and familiar. Winged creatures, fiery sprites, ethereal beings blurring into the very air around them.

But it was Mother's annotations in the margins that captured my attention, mind and soul.

Spiky scrawl captured her observations about the text —small clarifications and thoughtful questions—that revealed how much more she was than my mother or even a singer. My mother had researched. My mother had deciphered this forgotten language. My mother treated these texts like they were more than stories. She decoded them as if they depicted something real.

Perhaps her obsession could be explained by madness. My instincts told me otherwise.

I liked that I had this mystery to tie myself to her when she was long gone. It made me feel less alone. It made me feel like her passions lived on in me.

Only, for once, the cellar was cold comfort tonight.

I hunched in the dim light and wove together my half-truths for Father.

"SHE CAME HERE?"

I lied to him on the whim of a stranger. "Yes."

"You drank from the flask?"

I dropped my gaze. "There wasn't even a sip left."

There was a challenge in his voice. "You didn't leave any for me."

Foolish to get trapped in my web. "I'm sorry."

He stilled, thumbing the bronze necklace he wore around his neck, like he sometimes did when he was lost in thought or memories. Then, the hardness of his expression softened like a rock eroding. "I'll be in the garden."

Maren huffed at me, distinctly unimpressed, and tugged a reed from the earth. "We waited for nearly an hour, Ysa. Now you're here, you're distracted. I wouldn't speak to you for a week if Ferrith weren't leaving. You had your nose in your mother's books again, didn't you? If your father catches you down there, he'll have you dusting shelves until your lungs are full of spores."

"I was careful," I assured her. I almost told her about Lunarys and the spider plant, but there was so little time before Ferrith left. Maren's mossy eyes narrowed as she read the tightness in my lips. For once, she held her tongue and turned her freckled complexion to the afternoon sun. "I'm sorry, Ferrith. I forgot it was your last evening."

Ferrith's lips quirked, and he ran a hand through his curly blonde hair. "I'll be gone for a year, maybe two, not a lifetime. Although it reminded me why you and I would never have worked. You must have read those books a dozen times, and you still choose them over your best friends." He peeled off his shirt as if to show us what we were missing.

"Don't blame it on me. You moved onto Maren soon after."

"Lucky me," said Maren, but underneath the prickles there was warmth. As sexual experiences went, Ferrith had been a gift, she'd told me: never demanding or rough. In a village of peacocking oafs, he'd been gentle. She'd put a distance between them eventually. He'd accepted it, hidden his yearnings under bravado.

He held Maren's green gaze, and she squirmed. "Oh, I remember."

This time, it was Ferrith who was putting space between us all. I shook my head, scattering my thoughts like feathers in a gale. Along with Father, Maren and Ferrith were the reason I called Larkspur home.

My tone came out sharper than intended. "Will you feel the bigger man once you are carrying steel?"

Ferrith shrugged. "I can't stay here forever."

That stung. "Why not?"

"Nothing changes in Larkspur. I need to see the world."

I understood that feeling only too well. In the decades since Mother's disappearance, I sometimes dreamed of leaving the village and turning a new page somewhere further afield. But that hadn't come to pass.

Maren shoved him. "You will write? A few lines, at least?"

He held up his square hands. "These are made for cruder fare than a quill."

Maren and I exchanged glances. We remembered the boy who had written poems. Ferrith's trajectory had changed when Vixora had gone into the Shrouded Forest. He had lived half his life without her now, but which thirteen-year-old boy could be unchanged by such a happening? He had been a farmer's son who'd one day take over the reins of the family farm. But after Vixora, Ferrith wanted to prove his bravery and strength. He had delayed his soldier's training the summer his mama had passed, but now he was more determined than ever to return with his colours or perhaps even as a general.

We'd all lost someone: my mother, Ferrith's sister and mother, Maren's father. Maybe that was why we were drawn together.

Maren and I knew that Ferrith's tender heart was made for nurturing, not for battle.

We knew that King Azeem rallied troops in the northern realms because the crops had failed for a second year, and the people grumbled that the *days of plenty* would never return. The king couldn't keep his throne if he sat on it idly. Like other monarchs in my history books, he'd choose war against an imagined enemy to rally support for his reign.

Don't go, I wanted to tell Ferrith, but our friend had no

desire to watch his shell of a father deteriorate further. Not when the old man himself resolved to send his remaining offspring into the world so he could drink himself into his grave. Ferrith scowled at the clouds passing over my face, so I kept my tone lighthearted. It would hurt too much to part on sour terms. He'd made up his mind. "It's not like you need the challenge. You can best all the village men with barely a bruise."

"Blindfolded, I reckon," said Maren. "As long as he's not downed a barrel of ale."

Ferrith drawled, "Someone has to defend your honour, ladies."

Maren rolled her eyes. "We can take care of ourselves, as you well know."

"It *is* fun to watch you two put morons in the dust. Although how Yalvir's beard ended up on fire, I'll never know." Once, it had surprised him that we could best him in a fight, our agility a fair match for his brute strength. Now, he revelled in our skill. He raised an eyebrow in challenge. "Are you two coming? I'll be surrounded by hairy-arsed soldiers soon enough. Let's swim, for old times' sake. Just like when we were carefree teens."

"You don't need us." Maren laughed as Ferrith jumped into the creek in his breeches and surfaced a moment later, his pale torso gleaming with water rivulets. "You know very well that there'll be a queue of women willing to give you a pleasurable goodbye at Bloomtide tonight."

Ferrith grinned, teeth chattering. "But it's you I'll pine for. Come on. It's not as cold as it looks."

"Liar," I retorted, but I kicked off my shoes and pulled off my dress all the same. "Shall we?"

Maren—dressed always for practicality with a touch of

whimsy—shrugged off her tunic and fuchsia scarf and pulled her rusty hair into a messy bun. "I'm blaming you, sunshine, if I look like a rat at Bloomtide," she called out to Ferrith.

I pulled her towards the creek, teasing, "You'll look hastily put together and pretty as sin, like always."

She clung to me as we ventured into the bracing waters in our undergarments, the white cotton quickly turning translucent. There was no shame in being naked around Maren and Ferrith. We'd known each other our whole lives. They had been a couple more than once. Even Ferrith and I had kissed on occasion, for practice or when tipsy with liquor during revelries, but there was no jealousy or recriminations between us. Just the comfort of childhood bonds with all their quirks and contradictions, of meaningless quarrels and dandelions heavy with whispered longings, first loves and shared griefs, fumbled dances and night swims under the stars. But most of all, friendship. They were family to me.

We glided through the water like otters as the sun dipped below the horizon. The sounds of villagers preparing for Bloomtide drifted over the creek. Men grunted as they rolled a meagre count of barrels, given the rationing of wine and mead. Ponies—thinner than last year—whinnied as they were saddled up for children's rides. There was a heave-ho of the maypole being hoisted. Maren's husky laugh echoed off the banks of the creek as she splashed Ferrith, and he retaliated. I floated on my back, staring up at the sky through gaps in emerald foliage. The fading light painted the clouds in hues of tangerine and candy pink, but I couldn't help noticing dappled shadows in my peripheral vision. The light seemed colder than it had yesterday, the shadows deeper. The reeds at the creek's edge whispered of change.

I didn't spoil Maren and Ferrith's fun with my gloomy mood. Neither did I tell them of Lunarys or the dream that haunted me last night in which collapsing, crumbling libraries parted to leave me on parched ground amongst skeletal trees under dark skies. How there had been a lone, luminous flower at my feet. How the dream had ended with a crooked lighthouse swaying in a turbulent storm, fire raining down and a stranger's gloved hand enclosing mine in a bone-crushing grip.

I'd hated storms since the night Mother had disappeared.

I dragged myself from the creek, bones heavy, my flesh pebbling. Ferrith leaving had unsettled me, that was all. Plastering a bright smile onto my face, I focused on my friends. "Please tell me somebody brought a towel. If we're late to Bloomtide, Hilda will eat all the toffee. I'd like at least one piece if we're reliving our youth."

Ferrith clambered up the bank in the half-light. "I've decided that youth is overrated. I prefer your bosoms over flat chests."

Maren snorted. "It so happens we prefer your low timbre to the high-pitched squeal that used to live inside your chest."

"Touché," said Ferrith. "How about I treat us to sticky toffee and a glass of blackberry wine?"

Rolling her eyes, Maren wrung out her undergarments and pretended not to notice when Ferrith received a peepshow. "It only took him four-and-twenty orbits to share your coin with us." She frowned at me. "Are you all right, Ysa?"

I stepped into my dress and ignored the wet patches. "Of course. All is well."

They returned to their bickering, masking their anxiety at our impending separation. I listened, my heart aching with love for them. As I did, the shadows retreated, and I almost felt like myself again.

3

YSADORA

Shrouded Forest
Mortals may seek its depths for lost treasures,
forgotten knowledge, or to seek the blessings of
the fae who live within.
Few return unchanged—or at all.
—A Compendium of Faerie Flora and Terrain

Bloomtide was in full swing when we arrived, enveloping Larkspur in a riot of colour. Stringy wildflower garlands adorned doorways and lamp posts, their soft scent mingling with the aroma of roasting meats and artisan bread. The displays grew sparser with each passing year, the weather as unpredictable as the harvest, but the delights of the revelries warmed me, nonetheless. A trio of travelling musicians played folksy music on the fiddle, flute and tambourine. Children zig-zagged the village square with faces painted like tulips or etched chalk drawings onto the ground.

Friends and neighbours called out hellos or bawdy compliments as we cut our way through the throng. I parted with coin to purchase two flower crowns from old Celeste, whose fingers were still nimble despite her old age, and gave one to Maren, and she slipped it onto her tangled head. Young and old alike danced around the maypole, twisting blue, white and red ribbons into intricate patterns. Hilda beckoned me over, but I shook my head. I wanted to check on Father first, keen to smooth over the ripples of deceit between us. Keen to make merry with him to wash away the taste of Lunarys's forebodings.

I raked my fingers through my still-damp hair as Maren and I waited for Ferrith to return with our promised treats. My gaze drifted to the Shrouded Forest. Ancient oaks and firs were draped in thick, emerald moss that hung like old, tattered curtains. Its perpetual mist was now a dense, swirling fog that seemed almost alive, shifting and curling around the trunks like ghostly tendrils. As if the evils of the forest held their breath, watching us from the shadows: a reminder of the unseen that lay just beyond the familiar.

Ferrith narrowly avoided crashing into a tall man with mahogany skin, offered a brief apology, and then brought us earthenware mugs brimming with blackberry wine and sticky toffee wrapped in muslin. "Here you go. Don't drink too fast. I'm off to steal goodbye kisses, then I'm yours for the rest of the evening."

Maren's wine slopped dangerously as she curtseyed in thanks before booting Ferrith on the behind as he strode away. She unwrapped her sticky toffee from the scraps of muslin. Its caramelised edges glistened under the lanterns being lit in preparation for nightfall. She smelt of autumn bonfires despite the spring evening. "You ever think there could be more than this?"

I took a deep gulp of wine under the dusky sky, wincing at its tart taste. "You know I do."

"Yeah." Maren paused. "Will he be okay?"

"If he's not, we'll build him back together when he comes back."

"Deal." Her green eyes glimmered with new fire.

I knew with sudden certainty that Ferrith's leaving had unlocked something new. Maren wanted to be more than his casual lover, more than his friend. Had I been too caught up in my latest book hunt to notice the signs? Pushing her into a confession would cause her to withdraw. My best friend was as tight as a clam when it came to secrets. She would tell me in her own time.

The toffee bundle slipped from my fingers and tumbled to the parched ground in need of rainfall. I cursed and dipped to retrieve it from amongst dry blades of grass before it was trampled by a passerby. But strong hands got there first, scooping up the delicate cloth a fraction of a second before I did. Our fingers brushed. For a moment, time stretched impossibly thin. The sounds of Bloomtide faded, the chatter, shrieks and folk music fading as though muffled by invisible walls. We crouched inches apart. The world narrowed to the man's fingertips grazing mine, my cool skin against his warmth.

I looked up sharply, but he was already watching me. He had the build and bearing of a warrior, though his stance was relaxed, almost effortless. There was a quiet power about him.

I raised an eyebrow and rose to my feet. "I think you'll find that's mine."

He followed my lead, straightening until he towered over me. He had tawny skin and was encased almost entirely in black. His leather clothes hugged his muscled body, and a dark hooded cloak—edges brushing his boots and frayed as though he had seen many journeys—was fastened at his neck with a silver clasp. His inky hair was slightly too long and tousled in the breeze, framing angled cheekbones and a deep sweep of lashes that had no right to be a man's. Shadows prevented me from seeing his eyes clearly, but I thought they might have been grey-blue, a shade darker than a stormy sky.

He felt familiar, like the echo of a dream I had yet to fully recall. Brows bunching, I noted he also smelt like the wilds—of lashing wind, mossy ferns and the metallic tang of blood—like the Shrouded Forest.

His voice was low and velvety, a rich timbre that made me want to lean closer. "Done looking?"

My cheeks burned as I bit back, "Are you done returning the favour?"

The corner of his mouth kicked up in surprise. It was true. Barely concealed curiosity danced in his eyes as if he mapped every inch of me and assessed every reaction. My pulse quickened as his eyes swept my face, taking in the flower crown on my mussed hair, my simple dress, down to the tips of my fingers.

He unwrapped the muslin, pinched a toffee between his thumb and forefinger, and brought it to his lips, chewing thoughtfully for a heartbeat. A silent storm brewed in his eyes as he locked his gaze with mine and sucked the edge of his index finger. "I can't decide whether your birth was a stroke of luck or a curse waiting to unfold."

"If you speak to all the girls like that I imagine your bed is *never* warm." Foot tapping with impatience, I turned my palm skyward for the muslin bundle. "Thief."

A low laugh rumbled through the man's chest as he returned my treat. "You don't know the half of it. I think you'll find that nothing on this green earth truly ever belongs to us." His fingers lingered against mine for a fraction longer than necessary, tracing a small, swirling pattern on the tender skin of my left wrist, where my veins flowed like tributaries. An odd warmth spread beneath his fingers, almost like a pulse.

I flushed, my dark hair tumbling forward as I wrenched my hand back. Stars above, he was cocksure.

A slight smile ghosted his lips as he backed away. "Don't bother to thank me."

"I won't." I stuffed a toffee in my mouth to spite him and thought I heard a gentle chuckle.

The sounds and colours of Bloomtide suddenly surged once more, pulling me back into myself, into what was right and proper, annoyed that I hadn't loosed more stinging retorts. Maren would laugh until her throat was hoarse. Still, I couldn't help glancing up to trace the stranger's gait through the crowd.

He was gone like he had been swallowed up in the revelry.

Oddly disappointed, I turned to Maren. "Well, *he* was something. Arrogant boor."

Maren took a generous slurp of her wine and pulled her gaze from Ferrith, who was cavorting around the maypole to the delight of the village women. "Who?"

I shrugged. She'd missed the entire interaction, which was a lucky stroke of luck given her propensity for ribbing and meddling, like any best friend worth her salt. "Find Father with me?"

"Of course. Can't wait to see what cardigan Cairn is wearing today. Will it be the dusty blue one? The purple one with the enormous buttons or maybe…"

Bloomtide buzzed around us as we threaded through the crowd, my hands still tingling with the stranger's touch. We found Father with Bronwyn, a woman of robust hips and temperament, whom he enjoyed verbally sparring with. Maren patted his purple cardigan merrily and curled into his side for a hug while Bronwyn picked a twig out of my hair.

"It's a crying shame you won't take Rixian's hand in marriage. Being a grandmother is my greatest wish, but Ysa shuns the blessings of marriage. What will you do, Cairn, if she continues this way?"

Maren's lips twitched. Bind me to the maypole? Toss me in a barrel? Stage a javelin contest for my hand? The possibilities were endless. Bronwyn's *real* problem wasn't my bookishness or even Rixian's donkey laugh. It was her son's habit of turning a whole room against him simply because he was too fond of his own voice. The rumour was that the innkeeper kept a mild sleeping draught under the bar so Rixian didn't drive away all his customers.

"Ysa has plenty of time for marriage. No need to rush into anything," said my father.

Bronwyn's eyebrows jackknifed. It *was* a stretch. Most women of our age in Larkspur were married and rearing young ones by now. But Father didn't care for social norms, and Maren's mother was so grateful to have a child when she came along that she didn't put any constraints on her happiness. And given the new developments with Ferrith…

I pressed a kiss to Father's cheek and lingered there, drinking in the faint hint of lavender and sage oil he used to protect his hands each night after long days of handling parchment. He loved me. He wouldn't do anything to harm me, I told myself, closing my eyes to the memory of the withering plant. "I thought we could make merry together, Father, at least for a while."

His lips curved, breaking his usual austere expression. "The young people want to celebrate Bloomtide with us, Bronwyn. What did I do to deserve such jewels?"

Maren basked in his warmth. We were family. I had always felt that way.

I sipped my blackberry wine, and its warmth spread in my belly. "Tonight's our goodbye to Ferrith."

Bronwyn clicked her tongue. "I've heard whispers of weapon forges firing up all over the realm. Of men discarded like wheat chaff from the threshing floor, their worth weighed and found wanting. Thank the gods that Rixian stays in Larkspur to guard my feeble heart."

Father scowled. Behind him, Bloomtide lights flickered like fireflies against the dark sky. "Tell Ferrith to stay alive, do you hear me? King Azeem thinks he has an army of toy soldiers. It won't matter to him when the battlefields are wet with blood."

"We'll tell him," promised Maren.

Father gave us a soft, approving smile just as shouts of alarm rang out across Bloomtide. We froze.

The sky itself split open, followed by a surge of light that cut through the black expanse like a knife. A meteor burned its way toward Earth like a final cry of a fallen star. My breath caught in my throat as it grew larger, its tail of fire stretching out. But then, like a dream fading with the morning, it vanished. Only the night sky, vast and empty, remained.

The trio of travelling musicians faltered before their tune spluttered out entirely. The crowd rippled like a wave, surging away from the forest, tripping and shoving in their haste. Mothers clutched their children, men shouted in confusion, and some villagers muttered old prayers under their breath. Instincts drove me closer, even as dread iced my veins.

Father reached for me. "Stay back, Ysa." It sounded like a prayer.

"It can't be," said Maren.

His voice was strained. "Quiet, child. Or else the darkness will find us."

I flinched at his words, but my eyes were still trained on the Shrouded Forest, my vision pixelating. The crowd dispersed enough for long, jagged shadows verging the forest to be visible. There was a sharp, audible intake of breath, and I didn't know whether it belonged to Father, Maren or me. Father's hand was a vice on my arm, urging me to stay at his side. I peered into the dark, breath ragged. A body lay on the ground. I slipped from Father's grip and darted forward a dozen metres. She was older than I remembered her. Her cheekbones were more pronounced, and her nose flattened with age. But her violet cloak was the same, and as I watched, gnarled fingers tattooed with tiny moons twitched just once before they stilled.

Lie to your father. It might make all the difference, she had said.

But no one could tell the future, or Lunarys wouldn't be lying dead amongst us.

My chest tightened as my perception widened past the lifeless body.

Standing over Lunarys was a figure cloaked in tendrils of shadow. The twin daggers he held were like extensions of his body. They caught the light of the festival torches, blades darkened with blood. Our eyes locked across the distance, even as the shouts grew shrill, as Ferrith barrelled towards the stranger, bellowing words I couldn't discern. Neither of us moved, my heart thrumming so fast I thought it might beat clean out of my chest. Then the man—the stranger who had stood so close that our noses might have brushed—stooped to close the dead woman's eyes with cold efficiency, rose to his feet and melted into the Shrouded Forest.

Ferrith got there perhaps five seconds later, the only one who dared. He didn't slow his run. There was no indecision, nothing but wholehearted commitment. His speed increased, and my heart ricocheted, knowing he would pursue the killer into the forest. His head of blond curls passed the tree line. Our stupid, stubborn friend. As if it would be nothing if we were to lose him like we had lost his little sister long ago. As if he wanted to follow her to certain death. As if justice mattered more than his life.

I'd take self-preservation over unthinking bravery every time.

"My boy!" cried out his drunken father.

"No!" roared Maren. "Don't be so stupid, Ferrith Namara. I will never forgive you."

He reemerged. Fists balled in anger, and shoulders slumped like he had failed, Ferrith returned to the body. As he did, Lunarys's flesh broke apart, flaking, disintegrating like dust caught into a wind tunnel. It happened so quickly, so unnaturally, that my mind struggled to process what we had all seen. One minute, solid; the next, as if she had never existed at all.

Ferrith keeled over and vomited on the ground.

I whipped my head around to look at Father, stumbling over the jigsaw pieces my mind couldn't assemble. *Convince your father that you drank the elixir. It might make all the difference,* Lunarys had said. My vision tunnelled as I focused on the person I had counted on all of my days. A man who valued truth as much as I did. To me it seemed like he was the one doing the lying. My voice was a low throb of hurt and accusation. "What are you hiding, *Kazimir?*" Wasn't that what the dead woman had called him? My pronunciation faltered as if the name itself resisted me, twisting and slipping in my mouth. The syllables came out clumsy, tangled, heavier than any word I'd spoken before, laden with power that my tongue couldn't quite shape.

I doubted myself then, but Father's reaction told its own story. Silt settled over my soul, smothering the light.

"Ysa…" Father's normally ramrod-straight body went slack, his face pale and anguished.

Behind him, Bronwyn was almost feral. "Bloomtide is a celebration of life. But that flash across the sky. And the woman is *dead.* Her body is ashes in the wind. Bodies can't do that. Not without a pyre beneath them. That was *magic.* What will we do? Cairn? What will we do?"

Father made no attempt to comfort her. Eyes widening,

he rubbed his ribs, his mouth gaping, closing, gaping, closing again like he couldn't find the right words. It dawned on me that, for the first time in my life, he looked afraid. Not sad, as he had when Mother had disappeared, but truly afraid. As though he was in free fall with no hope of ever slowing down.

Maren's eyes snapped to Bronwyn. "Find Rixian. Take him home." Then she shook Father, rattling his spectacles. "We have to get Ysadora out of here. You know they'll come for her. We have to execute the plan." She squeezed his upper arms harder. "For Ysa, you must pull yourself together."

My heart pounded like a war drum in my chest. Why was Maren speaking as if she was his collaborator, not my best friend? The Maren I knew would be consoling Ferrith at this moment and perhaps pricking his pride for good measure. Not taking command like this.

Father heaved a breath, and Maren let her hands fall away. There was urgency in his voice as though the spell of malaise had been broken, but he hadn't answered my question and focused only on Maren. "There are things I need to see to at the bookshop. Follow the plan. I will be there as soon as I can."

You know they'll come for her. "Father, please…" I rasped.

He looked at me at long last. I stiffened under the kiss he dropped on my forehead. "Hurry."

Determination flashed in Maren's green eyes. Her scarf —usually arranged in artful disarray—lay forgotten on the ground. "Come with me, Ysa. There's no time to dally." She tugged my hand.

I resisted, my heart pounding like a war drum in my chest. Her behaviour made no sense. Unless my nearest and dearest had been lying to me. I searched my best friend's face for the answers I needed. "The truth. Or I'm not going anywhere."

Maren's lashes fell to shield her expression.

Oh, blistering stars. The shadows on the riverbank hadn't been a glitch of perception or nature's prologue before the curtain of night. They had been a warning.

4

———

KAZIMIR

Kazimir stood in the garden he loved—where he had chased Ysa as a youngling—cursing himself. Not because the garden was another part of himself he had to leave behind but because Ysa would be forced to flee all she had ever known.

A surge of cold ran through him. A meteor. No. No, that couldn't be right. It must have been a hallucination. He'd been around long enough to know that stars did not fall like that, not without design. His mind was fracturing under the stress, the world around him slipping out of focus.

He had been helpless to stop the assassin, unable to call upon the deep well of his now dormant power. The Binder, who had veiled him and his daughter from the monsters beyond the forest, was dead. She who had made him shake with fear with each encounter, despite his gratitude for all she had done. She who was neither fae nor divine but a primordial being who was a stabilising force in the cosmos. Whose lifespan should have surpassed his own. Her body had dusted, absorbed by the universe. She had told Ysa she had no regrets. Such clipped words for a sacrifice so great.

A sharp pain stabbed his chest at her loss. At the disruption to the fabric of the universe.

At the gaping hole in their defences. How vulnerable they were.

The chaos at Bloomtide had erupted too quickly for Kazimir to glean any clues to the killer's identity. His mind raced through the factions, but after all this time, he no longer traded letters with *her*. His knowledge was confined to books and the scraps of information that the Binder had offered. If she was in the right mood.

Fighting to regulate his rising panic, he closed his fist, mistakenly crushing his spectacles. He'd known this day might come, had prepared for it, and here he was as disoriented and clumsy as a dragon hatchling. He let the crumpled spectacles fall to the ground. He didn't need them anyway. They had been a parlour trick, part of a disguise.

It was Ysa that mattered now. Only Ysa.

His beautiful daughter. His reason for living.

As a high-ranking member of the Order of the Glyphs, Kazimir had always been a keeper of secrets. But none as heavy a burden as the secrets he'd kept since Ysa's birth. Sometimes, he wondered how much it changed a male to live each day without revealing his essence, his heritage or his innate skills. Stars above, he missed soaring on Caldoron's back, missed the glorious glint of the dragon's scales as he banked in the moonlight, missed even the pluming smoke rings that had singed his eyebrows on occasion. Their separation was sometimes more than he could bear. He missed the simplicity and shared goals of the Order, but the Order was gone, swept from the board like it had been inconsequential. Like it hadn't been a hub of brotherhood and pulsing knowledge and a home to magnificent fiery creatures so loyal that his chest tightened to think of them.

Sometimes, he missed *her*. The female he wouldn't, couldn't name.

The female whose name was a twisted dagger in his gut.

But Ysa had filled his life with more joy than he could fathom. Despite the dread rising in his bones, a smile tugged at the corner of his mouth. Throughout his long life, a child had seemed an impossibility, an unimaginable gift. But then *she*—it hurt too much to think her name— had brought Ysa into the world. The first time Kazimir had held the babe, she had wrapped tiny fingers around his thumb and had reached for him when he placed her in the crib. He'd known then that he would suffer any humiliation, any pain, so that Ysa could thrive. He'd dared to hope that she could mend the frayed ribbons of his heart.

So Kazimir had agreed to flee with the baby, even as terror seeped into him that he wouldn't be enough. That he wouldn't be able to guide her, that he didn't have the knowledge himself to navigate their new life. But each day that Ysa grew, every small triumph, every new word she mastered at impossibly young ages, every determined step she took in the world, filled him with fierce pride. Like witnessing the blooming of a rare, precious flower. His tenacious, vibrant daughter made even the colourless mortal realm seem wondrous. His Ysa was a sponge for knowledge, a beacon for truth, and one of the most curious minds in all the realms. Like the formidable librarians in the soaring libraries of his youth. Worthy of more than this pitiful land with his shrinking literacy and diminishing thirst for knowledge. Watching Ysa's mind unfold had been one of his greatest joys. She was the best part of him, the only part of him that deserved protecting.

He would throw himself to the dogs if it meant she could live and be happy.

Kazimir blew out a breath. The look of condemnation in Ysa's dark eyes—not quite her own, of course—had cut him to the quick. As a girl, it was him she sought out when she sliced open her knee or when one of the village boys had pulled her pigtails. When she struck a target with her dagger or climbed a tree in record time, she looked to him for approval.

His insides twisted to think Ysa might never look at him like that again.

Accusations had blazed in her eyes. She'd called him by his birth name, a name he had never shared with her. A name he'd dreamt of one day entrusting to her. One day. But instead, when it fell from her lips, Ysa's mouth had twisted as if his name itself was distasteful. As if he were a liar.

But his kind couldn't lie. The manipulations Kazimir had uttered since her birth to Ysa, to his mortal friends and neighbours in Larkspur, had not been lies. They had been omissions, variations on the truth. He was tired, so tired, of finding loopholes and trickeries to mask the truth. That was why he favoured encyclopaedias from the books in the shop. The facts were etched in black ink on white pages.

Secrets and manipulations: two diamond-cut reasons why the task had fallen to him.

For Ysa, he had given life to entire fabrications that held the merest kernel of truth, convinced himself that it was of no consequence, that his soul wasn't blackened by each manipulation. That his fabrications were justified for the sake of his daughter. But no priestess, no spirit of the earth, not even his own faerie king would absolve him. He would beg Ysa's forgiveness when he held her again. He'd palm his hands together and humble himself for veiling her heritage.

But he wouldn't change a thing. The subterfuge had been necessary. He weighed Ysa's safety above all else. Above inconvenient truths, broken promises and the colour of his soul.

Kazimir cut a furtive glance over his shoulder despite the wards that protected their home. He cursed himself for not hiding deeper in the mortal realm. He was wary of the mortal king. His long life had shown him plentiful examples of males who hungered for power. Who sullied themselves in their attempts to wield it, consolidate it, expand it.

Besides, when a being as powerful as the Binder had offered her help, he had been selfish. He couldn't bring himself to carve out more distance between himself and Faerie, even though his once formidable magic was a mere taunting whisper in his veins. A cruel slide into irrelevance. He hadn't wanted to flee even farther from Caldoron, yearned for a return someday. And, of course, there was *her*, their bargain etched onto a hidden expanse of skin.

His flesh had sizzled as the bargain had dissolved from his ribs. Still, the release was bittersweet. One less binding to her. A severing of the tether in acknowledgement that he and Ysa could no longer stay in Larkspur.

Not when they were being hunted.

He thanked the stars for Maren. Though not even she knew the whole truth. Still, there was no one else he would trust with Ysa's wellbeing. No one else was capable of keeping her safe and providing comfort. Maren would know how much to tell Ysa and how much to keep hidden, even at the expense of fracturing their friendship. She knew how much was at stake for them all. He shivered in the coarsening spring air, his breath misting.

Their painstaking preparation would not fail them.

A wave of nausea crushed over him, telling him that the effects of the elixir were fading. Without his full well of power, Kazimir worried he was more a hindrance than a help to Ysa and Maren.

The assassin would lie low only until Bloomtide cleared and the villagers slept. Kazimir dragged in a breath, and because it was pitch dark and he had to make haste, he risked casting magic that younglings at his court mastered before they learned to walk. He raised his hand, and fae lights spiralled into the air like fragments of stardust, glowing with hues of deep indigo and silver, as if he had pulled light from the very stars themselves.

He swept his gaze around the garden one last time, grimly observing that the fire had ravaged the few paintings he had commissioned of Ysa and the one of Caldoron. He swallowed, but the lump in his throat didn't ease. Neither did the tightness in his chest. Only singed corners remained of the canvasses, and the embers would make light work of those. He begged the stars that Ysa remained faceless to their enemies. He'd been reluctant to put a dagger in her hand, but he gave a wicked smile now to know how quickly she had taken to violence. As if it balanced her intellectual side. As though wielding a blade came as easily to her as spooning broth into her mouth. His Ysa was no damsel. Especially when she had just cause to rail against the night. One corner of their garden bore the marks of her gruelling sessions with Maren. Once, he had lamented the churned, uneven earth, marred by their footprints, the ground hardened by repetitive impacts. He had muttered over benches strewn with daggers, swords and staffs, and weighted practice stones abandoned after gruelling bouts. No more.

Kazimir was glad. A dizzying hope dispersed in his chest for a moment that all might still be well. That his Ysa would be fine. That despite his failings, she could thrive. That like him, she had the capacity to live with an open heart but also to be clandestine when her life depended on it.

His lips quirked. Ysa had already shown a nature ripe for secrecy, drawn as she was to the cellar to read Danaë's books from Faerie. Books he'd acquired at great risk to himself back when he wanted to appease Danaë when he thought their marriage would survive. Maybe he should have taken a match to them after all, not pretended that his fae hearing could track Ysa's footsteps and sighs. But Ysa had needed to feel a connection to the only mother she had ever known and so it became just another pretence on his towering stack of failures.

He dipped his head beneath the trailing branches of an ancient willow tree, its delicate leaves swaying in the chilling breeze. Leaves he sometimes glamoured into coin for Ysa or Maren when food was short. Simple tricks that he could still manage if he didn't try too often. The fae lights didn't illuminate the veiled space beneath the canopy, but no matter. His kind had sharper senses than mortals. Besides, he could map this space as well as the shape of his palm. He liked to ruminate on the worn bench here, imagining the wood as an old friend welcoming him. A small inkwell had been carved into an inconspicuous area of the seat, covered by twisting ivy that sometimes bloomed with small white flowers. But it was the small patch of plants adjacent to the bench that were most beloved to him of all the plants in the garden. Plants that could flourish in the darkest places, if tended by a member of the Order. Plants that glowed of their own accord that he'd smuggled from Faerie despite the laws against their migration. That he guarded in memory of his brothers who had fallen that day. Seven species when the Order had hundreds. Before they burned it all to the ground.

His stomach clenched like it had happened yesterday, not four-and-twenty orbits ago.

Envelopes of seeds and bulbs he'd tucked into the mewling babe's blankets, alongside his favourite quill and a scale belonging to Caldoron he still wore around his neck.

In memory. In grief. In hope. In love for his dragon.

A dragon that had likely perished at their separation.

His vision blurred and refocused on the inkweeds,

starbinders and shadeblooms, then the glimmerthorns, veilstems and mistweaves that glistened with dew before him, even under the blanket of darkness. Their colours ranged from vibrant indigo to deep violet, shimmering silver, obsidian black and muted green. But it was the firevein that called to Kazimir as he coaxed the distant hum of his dwindling magic. A magic his father had passed to him and his grandfather before that. The firevein's leaves were like emerald silk. Its veins glowed with a faint orange light, like embers within a flame. The fiery sap produced an ink that burned words onto parchment…and stone. An ink that bound itself to a calligrapher's intent, making it impossible to alter once written. Impossible to erase.

Stars, he needed Ysa to understand.

He reached for a glass vial nestled within the carved inkwell of the bench and extracted a thin, silver needle from its case in his pocket to act as a conduit for the sap. Lowering himself beside the firevein with reverence, Kazimir murmured the old words in the fae tongue. The plant's tendrils curled inwards like a creature bracing for touch. Still chanting, he identified a plump vein and slipped the needle into it. A small hiss of heat escaped as the sap flowed, a stream of molten orange that ran down the needle's hollow core into the waiting vial before thickening into crimson ink.

Murmuring soothing words to the firevein, Kazimir dipped his precious quill in the newly extracted ink and approached a jagged stone, perhaps three feet wide and waist-high, nestled beneath the willow's canopy. A stone that could have been mistaken for the remnants of an old outbuilding. One that looked weathered by time when, in fact, it was weathered by magic. He gave a mirthless laugh, thinking how the stone had, in some ways, become his confidante. It had taken significant skill to prime it to absorb his magic. He'd begun not long after they'd arrived in the mortal realm. From the very beginning, it had been a form of catharsis to spill his secrets into the stone. He'd cradled his youngling to sleep inside, then come here to this sacred space. Kazimir was compelled by force of habit to make one last entry. Compelled to archive the thoughts and memories Ysa deserved to know. Secrets that he could never divulge.

He grunted. Once a librarian, always a librarian.

That was when his magic could achieve magnificent feats. When his calligraphic scrolls maintained the balance of magic across the realms. When it unlocked the secrets of coveted texts and artefacts. When he crafted clandestine correspondence. When he, unlike any other in the brotherhood, created soul-binding scrolls that forged unbreakable bonds between individuals, even unwilling ones, and unmade mating bonds. For his sins.

Now, his magic was a mere trickle. His brothers would despair that his sorry displays were all that remained of the Order.

Fingers trembling around the quill, Kazimir summoned the remnants of his magic like the last flickers of a dying flame. The quill's nib gleamed with the crimson ink of the firevein. He touched the tip to the stone's surface. His written words had always been more proficient, more laden with meaning, than the dull twists of his tongue. Chanting, he fed the crimson ink to the stone, transcribing his final entry in towers of complex runes. Soon, sweat beaded his brow, but he didn't stop.

Cocooned under the willow, he noticed the gathering storm only in passing. Each mark upon the stone was laborious, dragged from his core.

Then, he took the quill to his forearm and winced as he drove its nip into his flesh. He dripped pearls of his blood on the memory stone, replicating a ritual that he had used in the Order, wondering if it would work as well on stone as it did on parchment. Necessary, since he had no choice but to leave the stone in place when they fled.

He begged the stars that the ink he had siphoned from his body was enough to seal it.

The stone glowed faintly, then lost its sheen.

Kazimir laid his head against it, relief washing over him that the work was done. A deathly cold chill seeped into his bones, his body spent from his exertions. All the loose ends were now tied. He would take his beloved plants and join Ysa and Maren. Together, they would make a new life deeper in the mortal realm. He would find someone, another fae, or he thought grimly, a divinity or witch with talents for glamour and magic nulling so that they would be safe.

He was good at ferreting out clues. So was Ysa.

He only hoped that the effects of the elixir wouldn't unravel too fast for Ysa. That her death wouldn't hasten the undoing of the nulling magic. He didn't want Ysa to feel her identity splinter. He didn't want her to attract attention.

A male's thickly accented voice made him jolt. "That must be your gravestone, calligrapher."

Kazimir froze, and fear hit him like a bolt to his chest. He kicked himself for being oblivious to the subtle shift in the air. For failing to discern footsteps muffled with practised stealth against the soft earth. Stupid. Stupid. He should have known and understood that this was a possibility. He should have listened out for the subtle rustling of leaves, the chill air, and the almost melodic hum of energy that accompanied this faerie king courtesy of his wife. But the truth was that the Faerie King of the Court of Silence was a legendary spymaster, even amongst the fae, who were known for their tricks and manipulations. And Kazimir was too out of practice, too accustomed to the mortal realm to survive by the rules of Faerie.

Resolve straightened his spine. Still, for Ysa, he would try.

Kazimir turned, folding one arm behind his back and manoeuvred his quill up his sleeve.

The faerie king had a similar build to Kazimir, tall and gaunt. But whereas Kazimir's skin was olive, the faerie king's was an unnatural ashen white, with blue veins running beneath the surface that resembled frozen rivers. His skin was brittle, akin to cracking frost, his face hollowed. His short-cropped black hair held more silver than the last time Kazimir had seen him. The streaks were sharp and sleek, like the edge of the single blade the faerie king carried at his waist. He wore no armour and was accompanied by two guards as if he didn't deign to get his hands dirty but wanted to be here to witness my humiliation. Kazimir knew the faerie king could snap his bones before his next inhale. He was tenacious. Dangerous.

Long ago, he had managed to steal something precious from Kazimir.

Neither of them had forgotten it.

Kazimir met Thiago's calculating pale grey eyes, noting his goose-pimpled skin, the frost on the ground beneath them and the latent storm that had burgeoned into something ferocious. Worse still was the aura of dread and despair that settled over Kazimir, one of the male's most effective gifts. His hooded cloak—a garment of shifting shadows and mist, worn by all the males in his court over the age of ten—flared as he stalked forward. His was the most magnificent of them all, its shadows deepening with every deception. In comparison, Kazimir's misshapen cardigan seemed almost a humiliation.

Still, he wondered why the faerie king hadn't yet put a blade to his throat. He resisted the urge to edge backwards against the stone as the faerie king closed the distance between them. Fighting against the well of despondency, Kazimir suppressed the shivers induced by the plummeting temperatures. He inclined his head in greeting as if this was a contract, a binding scroll to be negotiated. As if they were equals, when in truth, Thiago was his better in every way. The legendary spymaster of Faerie had access to more information than any other fae, perhaps bar one. All these orbits, Thiago had locked away knowledge of Kazimir's hiding place in the vault of his icy soul and bided his time.

He who controlled information controlled the fate of all the realms.

That much had always been true.

Kazimir forced his body into a relaxed posture. "What do you seek, Thiago?"

The faerie king unfurled a predator's smile. "You. And your daughter."

Shadows swooped around him, binding his ankles,

tugging so hard that Kazimir's feet jerked out from beneath him. His head cracked against the memory stone, and even through the pain, he thought the splurge of warm blood might strengthen the binding he had made. He didn't know how long he lay there. It could have been hours.

The next thing he knew, another male appeared, walking with languid ease from the house. Moonlight flickered over his sharp features, casting shadows that rippled with each step. Recognition hit him then like a blow to the chest. This was the male who had killed the Binder with simple blades. It shouldn't have been possible. Even now, he didn't understand it. To Kazimir's shame, he recoiled and almost released his bladder.

The male paused, and his lips curled into a faint, knowing smile. His attention flicked to the faerie king. "There are no likenesses of her inside the house. He must have destroyed them."

A grunt of annoyance from a guard. "Twenty orbits will have changed her."

Kazimir held his breath, wild hope spiking the depths of his desperation. No one knew what his Ysa looked like, not even the spymaster. Perhaps he had done enough. To keep her safe, at least.

The faerie king's eyes glinted with cold satisfaction. "There are other ways of extracting her likeness."

"No need," said the killer from Bloomtide, the rich timbre of his voice unlike Thiago's thin rasp. "I saw her up close. My group and I will deal with her."

"Keep your mercenary hands off her," said the faerie king.

The male whirred one of his twin daggers. "You think so highly of me, uncle."

Kazimir's bones turned to jelly, and he watched, helpless, as the faerie king narrowed his eyes at his nephew, then turned his attention to his own splayed hands. A whispered incantation brought forth ice, and he fashioned tools of frosted silver from it.

When he had completed his task, the faerie king barked a command to his guards. "Retrieve the plants."

Defeated by his bindings, Kazimir looked up from the ground, one hand to his bleeding scalp. "Please. They won't survive."

The faerie king's magic fizzed, and his thick voice simmered with wrath. "Silence."

Kazimir found that his lips couldn't move, that his jaw was clamped together.

Eyes widening in horror, his fingers traced the smooth skin where his mouth had been, where he had been rendered mute. As he squirmed, the faerie king strode away from under the willow without a second glance, away from Kazimir's beloved bench, away from the memory stone, away from the guards desecrating all that remained of the Order of the Glyph with their crude techniques and their hard hearts, with their ignorance that didn't allow them to discern between the varieties. To know that even if the plants survived, how much cajoling it would require to soothe a plant that should have been harvested during an exact phase of the moon. Or sliced at the base with a starlight-infused dagger. Or tugged from the earth with a moonwater-soaked silk.

Outside the willow's canopy, the faerie king's blizzard

raged. The shadows tightened their noose around Kazimir's ankles and followed their master, dragging Kazimir on his stomach across the bumpy ground into the open. The storm was confined to his garden alone: a demonstration of power designed to turn his one sanctuary into a battleground. The snow-covered lawn was layered with thick, uneven drifts, and the stars had blinked out of the night sky.

He shuddered. His cardigan snagged on the ground, and there was no warmth anymore, only biting cold. With his lips sealed and panic rising, it was difficult to remember to breathe through his nose. But it occurred to him that, like parchment and stone, snow captured every inscription. For a while.

The shadows tugged harder, dragging Kazimir faster. He was almost at the edge of the garden and now could sense that mere seconds remained before he would be lost. With a pained grunt, he fumbled in his sleeve for his quill. His humble source of power. A smile drifted across his face at the firevein ink still engorging its tip. It had been a lucky choice. Firevein was intrinsically stable, less likely to dry out than other inks, and resistant to being washed away or obliterated by the storm's fury.

He pressed the quill against the snow-packed ground, and the crimson ink flowed with brutal precision. Tears trailed his cheeks as he crafted a hurried message to Ysa, his breath rasping, his strokes assured against the icy canvas.

When he was done, he let his quill slip from his fingers, begging the stars that the blizzard would evaporate with Thiago's departure. He prayed that the guards would be too busy with their loot to notice his message. His last thoughts were whether he'd see Ysa again. Whether she'd recoil from him without his human glamour. Then, he gave himself to the shadows as they hauled him after the faerie king into a gaping abyss in the garden's frozen landscape.

The abyss seemed to swallow all light.

It swallowed him.

YSADORA

Maren's cottage, with its thatched roof and integral bakery, was usually a peaceful enclave amidst the clamour of the world. Tonight, it brought me no solace. Maren darted through the bakery, not once pausing to devour a buttered pastry or pinch a slice of cake dusted with powdered sugar, as per our habit. Not even pausing to utter more than a grunt as her startled mother removed golden loaves from the stone oven.

I offered a cursory greeting and then rushed after her. "Why in the stars won't you give me any answers?"

"Soon. When we're safe." Maren took the stairs with a speed that added to my rising dread.

I followed her into the compact living room above the bakery, where dried herbs hung from the ceiling, milky vases of wildflowers cluttered a rickety table, and quilted throws softened wooden chairs. My eyes widened, pulse erratic, as she retrieved two satchels from a hidden compartment in the wall I had not once noticed, though I knew her home as well as my own. I prided myself on telling the truth from a falsehood, and yet here I was, deceived by those closest to me. By someone who I considered a sister.

Maren's flower crown—and my own—were long gone.

Working with quiet deliberation, she checked the satchels. She pulled out two tightly folded cloaks and set them to one side. Next, she rifled through undergarments, tunics and a worn map before adding loaves of bread and cheeses from her own family's store, jars of water and salve. Finally, she secured the straps with a sharp tug, tested their weight, and lowered them to the floor with a dull thud.

I wrapped my arms around my knotted stomach. "What is all this? Who *are* you?"

"I'm your friend." Her mouth was pinched, unhappy, like she'd give anything not to be in this situation. "Please, Ysa. Let's go. We can't stay here a minute longer."

I met her glare as the flickering light from a candelabra cast long shadows across the room. The heat radiating from the oven in the bakery was no match for my burning anger. "I won't follow you blindly. I deserve to know what's going on. Why you lied."

Maren flinched. "I didn't lie."

I huffed, eyes tracing a bookshelf I had always admired. The sort of bookshelf that Father said disappeared with the *days of plenty.* A bookshelf that revealed this family was whimsical and kind and learned by the fairy tales and books on scientific discoveries bowing the wood. But why had I never questioned why this family—from all those in Larkspur—still devoted time to books? Why hadn't their books been used to stoke their fire? Why hadn't they lost interest or the ability to read and digest like so many others in our village? My thoughts fell like crumpled paper, discarded before they had a chance to unfold. I kept circling back to how Father and Maren had spoken as if I were on the outside, and they had all the knowledge between them.

"You're part of this. You know who Kazimir is." Father's name was sharp and foreign. It cut my tongue.

Regret welled in her eyes like forest pools. "I have known his true name since I was a child. Ysa, I'm sorry—"

The air in my lungs thinned. I cut her off, my breath tight and gestured at the satchels. "You weren't surprised by Lunarys's death. You were *ready*. The two of you had a plan. How long have you been tiptoeing around behind my back?"

She balled her fists. "Do you think I wanted this? To keep things from my dearest friend? Everything I agreed to was to protect you. By the embers of my soul, I swear it."

"Protect me from what, Maren? Don't you swear on yourself. I won't have it." Despite my ire, I knew that I loved her more than I loved myself: my companion, my sister, my sparring partner. She was the wild to my calm, the heartbeat beside mine in both joy and sorrow. She was entwined with every memory of who I was and who I'd become. Her betrayal devastated me.

Maren's voice wavered. "You skirted the truth, too. You didn't tell me Lunarys came to the bookshop."

"I didn't want to mess up Ferrith's goodbye." Nausea rolled over me like a fog, but I pushed it down, willing myself to put the pieces together. "But you knew anyway…because Father told you."

Her face crumpled, and part of me wanted to comfort her, even though I had been wronged.

"We had to keep this from you, Ysa. Your father knew that one day, you'd be hunted for what you are and what you could become. Now they've found us. That male will scour all your familiar haunts. The bookshop. This cottage. The creek. Every inch of this village. That's why we have to leave."

My mind blurred with the memory of the stranger's blood-slicked daggers and Lunarys's body, dusting, dusting into the night. I backed away from Maren as her mother's heavy footsteps sounded in the stairwell.

The creak of floorboards punctuated our conversation as Maren's mother came towards us. The lines on her face were like a map of forgotten roads etched by the passage of time. To my surprise, Anja didn't look bewildered. She looked resolute—dignified, even—as she pressed a pouch of coins into her daughter's hands. "With the effects of the elixir ebbing, you'll need to be cautious, Maren. Chewing wormwood might help."

The room spun. "Who else knows more than I do?"

Maren reached out to me. "Ysa, please."

I shook my head. "You've built mountains of lies. I don't know if I can forgive you."

Pain flickered across her face. "I'm not asking you to trust me blindly. I'm asking you to survive. Kazimir's enemies are coming. Hate me if you must, but if we stay here, we won't make it through the night. Your father must almost be finished with his tasks. He'll meet us by the inn."

"You expect me to run from Larkspur without knowing what I'm running from?" My brows pinched together as the weight of her words settled on my chest. "You would leave without saying goodbye to Ferrith?"

A desperate sadness swept over Maren's face. She loved him, and she was giving up one last look at him, once last hug or jest so that we could leave. "Tomorrow, he'll start a new life. He doesn't need to be involved in this." But it wasn't just Ferrith she would be leaving. It was her mother. Her mother, who was alone, and had lost her father long ago.

Anja wrapped a lingering embrace around her daughter. "You and Ysa were always meant to be friends, from the moment we put you on a hay bale together. Just like your fathers before you. When all else tests you, remember your friendship is true."

I jerked my eyes to Maren. "Our fathers knew each other? Yours died before you came to Larkspur."

"A lifetime ago," said Anja. "And yet perhaps the world hasn't changed much at all."

Her tone scared me. "Who am I that my father's enemies would hunt me so?"

"If I tell you, will you come with me?" Maren held out one of the coarse cloaks.

A sharp nod. "Fine." I draped it over my shoulders. The hood billowed as I pulled it over my dark tresses.

Maren blew out a breath. "You are the calligrapher's daughter, Ysadora."

I frowned. She said the words with such meaning. As if I didn't know my father was a calligrapher and bookseller and a man who liked to garden. As if it was something new.

She continued. "Ysadora, daughter of Kazimir Silberquill."

My words were leaden, a last grasp for a reality that had once been mine. "My name is Ysadora Everreed."

Maren flapped a trembling hand. "Everreed was just a mask."

Her mother stooped to retrieve the satchels and pressed them into our hands. "Now you must run."

WE HUDDLED in shadows beside the inn, our backs pressed against the cool stone wall, hoods casting our faces into shadow as if we were vigilantes. As if we didn't know the villagers guzzling from their tankards inside. Occasionally, the door swung open, releasing gusts of warmth, the musty smell of spilt ale and hushed conversation about the events that had befallen Bloomtide. A peep through a half-open window showed me women clutching protection charms. A man boasted loudly about having sent word to the king. Ferrith slammed a tankard of fresh ale in front of the man in approval.

"I can still taste the dust in my throat," said Ferrith. "I gagged, I tell you."

The man slurped his ale. "In truth, you vomited, lad."

I returned my attention to Maren. "Ferrith's in there. We could say goodbye before he heads south."

"He'd only try to stop us. Or to convince us to go with him. Which is why we're going east."

Sweat broke out on my brow regardless of how often I slicked it away.

She peered at me like I'd grown two heads. "Are you okay?"

"Everything's just dandy."

She slipped a blade from one boot. "Go on. Take it. I already have one."

I sighed and stashed the dagger. I felt better holding it. If I saw the man who had killed Lunarys again, I would stick it between his ribs and smile as I twisted it. I scowled at Maren. "Do you expect us to wait here until moonrise?"

Maren's eyes narrowed, and for a moment, I thought embers sparked in them. "You're right. It's taking too long. Come on."

She skittered over cobblestone, avoiding the waning light of street lanterns, past the abandoned maypole shrouded in a curtain of night. The chill air wrapped around us, rustling our coarse cloaks and the satchel bumped against my leg. I ignored the tight drumbeat of anxiety in my veins, ignored the fact that my body felt like it was burning up, ignored the weight in my chest that asked whether I could trust my oldest friend. Part of me wondered if this was a nightmare we'd wake from. If I'd wake back at my desk in the bookshop, having fallen asleep over some letter of note.

When we arrived, the bookshop frontage was unusually dark. Not even a glimmer of light reaching it from our living quarters. The door creaked open with a long, mournful groan that stretched out into a heavy silence. With a curse, Maren palmed the hilt of her knife.

I shot her a sharp look. "You know he doesn't like weapons in here."

Maren held a finger up to her lips. "Hush, lest you coax devils into the world."

I took the lead, suddenly conscious that despite all the books, the familiar warmth of the shop had been replaced by a hollowness that made our breathing seem intrusive. The silence suffocated, and every careful footstep seemed too loud. Fear curled up my spine like a cold draft seeping through the floorboards and settling in my bones.

"That's odd," I whispered, gesturing to a faded outline where Father's painting of the bronze dragon had hung and then a few paces further to a missing miniature of me.

"We shouldn't be here," hissed Maren.

We moved into the house, calling softly for Father, our voices swallowed by the silence. The door to the cellar was open—a dark yawning stairwell into the black—but I resisted the pull to peer down it. There were no snores, no rustling of paper, and no candles to light the tasks he had been determined to finish. I stayed rooted in place for a moment before setting down my satchel and taking my dagger from my boot.

I released a slow breath. "Whenever I couldn't find him in my childhood, he was in the garden by the stone."

Maren nodded. We made our way outside, daggers raised, to the garden which Father had tended all of his days and where Maren and I trained. I swallowed a gasp. Father's sanctuary lay in disarray. Broken pots lay scattered, delicate plants trampled, and thick snow blanketed the earth in patches. Tender spring shoots and uprooted plants lay strewn across the frozen ground as if they had been wrenched from the soil, their petals strewn like confetti. A once-proud trellis sagged under the weight of dishevelled vines as if a storm had torn through. My brow furrowed. A storm confined only to our garden.

And the silence. Stars the silence. No trees rustled. No crickets chirped. No owls hooted their disdain.

My breath hitched. I'd been a child of barely three orbits, but I'd heard the whispers in the village—ones repeated every All Hallow's Eve that stung—that Mother had vanished in a storm like this. A sudden, violent tempest tore through our garden on a night when storms had no place, and in the morning, Mother was gone. I coughed, my skin unbearably clammy.

I couldn't tell if I was unravelling or the world around me.

My pulse pounded in my ears, louder than the quiet around us, louder than my thoughts. I blinked hard to focus, but every breath felt laboured, my head light and disoriented. Maren stood a few feet away, her face pale and drawn in the moonlight.

Was my entire life a carefully constructed illusion?

I didn't want it to be true.

My stomach churned as my gaze landed on the dying embers of a fire, then a few feet further, an irregular shape half-buried in the snow. I crouched in the pale moonlight, fingers trembling as I brushed a layer of snow away to reveal Father's crushed spectacles, the lenses shattered, the frames warped beyond repair. The sight of them was like a punch to the chest. Father wouldn't leave them behind unless…

Then, just beyond the desecration of his favourite flowerbed beneath the willow, a drag mark on the ground, across patches of snow. I darted forward, following the tracks, Maren on my heels.

"Ysa, wait—"

I fell to my knees at a flash of ruby in an otherwise white expanse of snow and pushed back my hood, begging the stars that this wasn't Father's blood. That he hadn't been hurt or worse. My breaths plumed in hot exhales into the icy air.

It wasn't blood. At least, I didn't think so.

Vivid crimson ink stood out against a pristine canvas, like a wound bleeding against pure snow. An unsettling warmth emanated from the ink as if it beckoned me to read. The letters had been formed hurriedly in what was unmistakably Father's hand as if he'd been dragged while drafting it. Heart ricocheting in my chest, I scooted around to read his message the right way up, barely noticing the chill of the snow seeping into my clothes. Barely noticing the flash of a ruby feather as Maren retrieved his beloved quill from the ground.

The ink leapt off the page of snow as I read, each curve and line filled with the echo of Father's voice.

Kazimir's voice.

My darling
Stay away from the dark forest.
Don't look back.
Trust Maren.
Run.

A tear trailed down my cheek. I sensed his love in

every word, every stroke of his penmanship imprinted into the snow. I stood to face Maren, one hand wrapped around the hilt of my dagger, the other cradling the spectacles against me like they were a broken bird. A red welt bloomed where a glass shard caught my skin, but I didn't care.

"He's been taken by force. You know where they've taken him." It wasn't a question. It was a statement.

There was no mockery in her voice, only gentleness. "To Faerie."

To Faerie. Stories swirled in my mind. To Faerie, where there were enchanted forests and endless revelries. Where the air hummed with tangible magic and trickster creatures hid behind every twisted branch. Where there were glittering courts filled with fae who spoke in riddles and betrayed you with a smiling word. Where glass castles perched in the air and fae nobles were as untouchable as stars. Where silver rivers sang you to sleep. Where a day could feel like an orbit and an orbit like a single breath. To Faerie, from where some souls never returned.

The world tilted. Laughter almost fountained from my throat at the thought that the superstitions and fanciful tales told by elderly villagers might be true. That they hadn't merely been cautionary tales to keep children in line. That I had sometimes scoffed at the word *magic*, even though I had been so drawn to stories of enchanted, faraway lands.

I shuddered. Hadn't I always felt in my bones that there had been more to the stories in the cellar?

Why else would Mother have been so beholden to them? I'd been too young to prevent Mother's death, but I had to believe Father was still alive. We had to find our way back to each other, to some semblance of a loving father-daughter relationship. I couldn't live with myself otherwise. Even if Faerie swallowed me whole.

"It doesn't matter what he asked me to do." My fierce lament shattered the silence. "I'm not going to run."

Maren's green eyes sparked. "I know."

6

———

YSADORA

T descended the slanted steps, dagger aloft, already sensing an echo of absence. When I stepped inside the cellar, I bit back a gasp of anguish to find it entirely empty of Mother's library. I found only a desolate expanse of cold, uneven, lichen-covered flagstones. Even her embroidered cushion was gone. It was as if she and her passions had never existed, and this shrine to her was an empty tomb. I missed Mother fiercely then and wondered if anything remained of her in this house at all.

My memories of her were mere scraps, fed to me by Father as though I were a malnourished child.

A steely resolve settled within me. I wouldn't, couldn't fail him.

I lingered a moment, a prickling sensation flickering across my skin like a gentle caress. Darkness clung to the corners of the room, deeper than it should have been, its edges shifting subtly. I rubbed my arms and gave the cellar one last look. Just a few days ago, everything had felt stable and predictable: the warm familiarity of our bookshop, the rhythm of daily life with Father, my nights reading down here, and the joyful comfort of my friendship with Maren and Ferrith. Now, it was gone, like a door slammed shut without warning. The safety of my little life—a life I valued beyond measure—had fallen away.

Nothing felt solid anymore, not even the stone beneath my feet.

I could almost laugh at how naive I'd been.

My bones were heavy as I climbed the stairs to Maren, who rummaged through our kitchen drawers by moonlight. She jerked in alarm at the sound of my footsteps, exhaling in a whoosh at the sight of me. Lips pursed, she returned to her task, her fingers brushing over certain objects hidden in plain sight. She pulled them free: a compass from behind a panel in the cutlery drawer, a soft leather pouch of seeds nestled in the middle of a stack of dishtowels and a small glass vial tucked away at the back of a dark cupboard behind chipped cups. She wrapped Father's quill in a cloth, but dark streaks of ink leaked through like a secret refusing to be hidden. Then she placed all four additional items in her satchel and fastened it.

I was pretty sure I was running a fever, not that I told Maren that. "You already packed."

Maren snorted. "We're not going on a jaunt to the next

village."

"I'll go on my own if you wish to stay behind," I said stiffly.

"Why do you think I agreed? I promised your Father I'd protect you, even from your own stupidity." She sighed and squinted at me. "You don't look great, Ysa… But unless we leave now, we'll miss the moonlit path. Whoever has taken Kazimir will go deeper into Faerie. We won't stand a chance of bringing him back."

I gulped. "Let's hurry then."

She gave a grim nod as she fastened her satchel and slung it over her shoulder. "You must promise to listen to every word I say. If I tell you to be quiet, you will clamp your lips shut and try not to even loose a breath. If I tell you to hide in a ditch, you will. If I tell you to run and leave me behind, that's what you'll do."

I tugged anxiously at the sleeve of my cloak. My fingers wrenched the fabric as if I could ground myself in its texture. I had no means of orienting myself in a world that had suddenly become foreign. Each choice I made felt like wandering through a dream, disjointed and surreal, with no landmarks to guide me.

Without Maren, I would have been lost, so I simply asked, "Where are we going?"

My friend's green eyes shone like the ethereal haze of the galaxies in formation. The corners of her mouth lifted. "To the Court of the Nebulas. To Kazimir's home and mine. To your ancestral home. If they are to reignite the full scope of his power, he will need to put to rest the ghosts of his past."

THE VILLAGE SLEPT as we crept towards the edge of the Shrouded Forest. Warnings clanged in my ears, drummed into me by every caregiver and teacher I had ever had, to beware of the magic that tangled in the roots and leaves of the forest. Nobody wanted another Vixora. Nobody wanted to hear another mother's wails or witness another father drink himself into a grave. Nobody wanted to watch the clearing, hoping that their beloved would miraculously emerge.

The forest took more than it gave, and it had always been that way.

A quiet terror settled into my bones as Maren and I stepped into the forest. An uneasy silence grew between us. My breath was shallow, and my senses were alert to every whisper of the wind. No starlight pierced the dense canopy overhead. A thick mist clung to the ground, curling around our ankles, and the mossy floor absorbed the sound of our boots. Firs towered above us, their bark darkened by age and wrapped in creeping vines. In the dim light, their shapes morphed into eerie forms that flickered in my peripheral vision. The air felt alive, tingling against my skin. Every rustle of leaves or snap of a twig made my heart race, but the dark didn't seem to bother Maren. It never had.

Almost as though she was secure in the knowledge that she'd always find light if she needed it.

After a while, we stumbled upon a clearing. The sight of it stopped us dead in our tracks. It looked as though it had been torn apart by force. Trees on the edge of the clearing were charred, their leaves burnt away, and their bark stripped. Glassy black stones littered the area, fused with the soil by immense heat. In the midst of the clearing was a crater of blackened soil, and in it, a smouldering, roughly hewn stone embedded in the earth as though it had slammed into the ground. The outer shell of the meteor was a solid shell of dark shimmering stone, but an eerie, silver glow pulsed weakly within it, casting a dim light. It glowed with heat. Not just any heat…with power. Old, dangerous power mirrored in the thrumming of my veins.

"The stars don't just fall," Maren whispered.

I knelt at the crater's edge, almost involuntarily, fingers grazing the cracked earth. There was a strange hollowness in my chest when I looked upon the stone. "I didn't think the flash across the sky was real." A soft, rapid scuttling pulled at the edges of my awareness: unseen things drawn to the remnants of the meteor or us.

Maren grabbed my hand, tugging me away from the smoking stone. "We have to keep moving."

We trekked deeper into the dense forest, so far that my feet blistered in my boots. All the while, questions gnawed at me, spiking my fear and resentment. Questions about how my father fared, if I'd see him again, if we went blindly to our deaths, and if Maren would prise open the secrets she had been keeping. The deeper we ventured, the more I yearned for dawn. It was as though the forest held us in a suspended twilight where day and night blurred. Sometimes, I caught the faint outline of bioluminescent flowers or flickers of light darting between the branches, but Maren warned me to look away, lest the object of my attention turned its gaze on us or we were lured into a trap. After a while, the darkness didn't seem so black, and I could make out emerald leaves with shimmering veins, flashes of ivory that might have been teeth and the scuttling of creatures too big to be insects.

I crept closer to Maren then, wondering whether our daggers would be of use if the monsters in the forest decided to hunt us.

I didn't know if my heightened awareness stemmed from delirium or my imagination. It didn't matter as we trudged on endlessly. Nothing mattered except putting one boot in front of the other, except retrieving Father from his captors. Soon, the hems of our cloaks were muddied and torn by thistle and thorn, and my eyelids drooped with sleep. I didn't think the shivers would ever cease, but Maren wouldn't let us stop.

"I know you are tired, but the path to Faerie only appears by moonlight. It vanishes at sunrise." The compass spun erratically in her hands. "This forest is cloaked in illusions and glamour, and we don't want to get trapped in the net of a vicious creature. It's best we keep moving. We will be safe at the Court of Nebulas. Our ancestral home will protect us."

Accepting the Court of Nebulas as my ancestral home meant believing what remained unsaid between us.

That both my Father and I were fae. My mind was clearly addled by fever.

Maren held the compass further from her body as though it might solve the instrument of its indecisiveness. "Just a little further. Kazimir told me the compass had never failed him."

"What if he is hurt?" I blurted out, narrowly missing a protruding root.

Maren turned to face me, shoulders drooped. Her short, auburn hair had pulled free of its bun, causing some sections to stick out at odd angles. "I keep forgetting how little you know. Fae heal quicker than mortals, Ysa. Your Father is too valuable to lose. His kidnappers will have access to healers. Healers beyond anything you've known in the mortal realm. Healers who can purify dark magic, knit wounds together and mend broken bones with the slightest touch."

The tightness in my chest eased. "That's good."

She hoisted her satchel into a more comfortable position and started walking again. "Sometimes the healers can even cauterise trauma and grief."

I frowned and dipped under a low bough. "But that's like taking a piece of your identity away."

"That's how I feel about it, too." Maren dropped back, so we walked side by side. She scanned my face as though she didn't know how to bridge the gap between us. "We need to talk about the past."

The cauldron of my anxiety swirled faster. "Thank you."

She darted me a confused look. "For what?"

I pressed her hand, though hurt lingered like a shadow. "For being here."

"Oh, Ysa." She stopped in a clearing. "Please don't be afraid. I'm going to drop my glamour."

"Your glamour?" My heart hammered as I watched her, aghast, as she changed before me in the moonlight.

Her mossy eyes shifted into a vibrant amber, flecked with hints of gold and green, and her hair deepened in thickness and shade. The freckles on her fair skin seemed to rearrange themselves into the shape of constellations and her skin took on a luminous quality. Her features sharpened subtly: her cheekbones grew more pronounced, and her ears—visible between the tendrils of her errant hair—elongated to graceful points. A subtle strength reshaped her slim silhouette. Her spine straightened, her shoulders broadened slightly, and her slenderness gave way to a lithe, athletic grace. But it was the change in body heat I most noticed. She radiated a steady warmth that contrasted with the cold forest air. It was like she'd stepped off the pages of one of Mother's stories.

I stood rooted to the spot, emotions crashing over me in a relentless tide. It was all a lie, down to the very core of my understanding of Maren. Disbelief tinged my voice. "Was any of it real?"

"The most important part. My love for you. Our friendship."

"How long? How long have you been living this lie?"

"Since we first met," she said quietly.

"We were toddlers." My nails made tiny moons in my palm.

"My mother invoked the glamour until I could do it myself."

"Anja said our fathers knew each other."

Maren gave a soft smile. "Our fathers belonged to an ancient group founded in the Court of the Nebulas called the Order of the Glyph. They were fae calligraphers tasked with maintaining a grimoire that balanced the magic between Faerie and the mortal realm. Days that allowed for the stability known as the *days of plenty*."

I frowned, unsettled about how fae wars could spill into the mortal realm and impact human prosperity. I'd seen that suffering. I thought back to thin broths and stale bread we had eaten for supper time and again. It didn't seem fair that mortals were at the mercy of the fae, even in their own homes, when they didn't have the smallest kernel of knowledge about Faerie.

Her beautiful eyes sparked with joy. "The calligraphers were dragon-riders and so much more. That bronze dragon in your bookshop? That's Caldoron, Kazimir's dragon."

Dragons. For the stars, dragons existed. My father had ridden a dragon. Grief swelled in my chest at all the things he hadn't shared with me. Emotion choked my voice. "What happened?"

She shook her head. "Jealousy. Power games. Wrath. I'm not sure Kazimir ever really knew who was behind it. There was a dark faction who wanted to break the pact between Faerie and the mortal realm for their own gain, seeing humans beneath them. My father and yours treated with the dark faction at the Order of the Glyph. On the fifteenth night of negotiations, the Order burned to the ground. Your father was the only one to escape. Kazimir doesn't talk about that day. I'm not sure he even knows who was behind it."

I froze. "What happened to your father?"

"He died in the flames with his dragon."

Tears clogged my throat. For a moment, I forgot we were in the Shrouded Forest, forgot we should keep moving, that we should keep our voices low. "I'm sorry. I'm so sorry… You couldn't tell me he died so violently. I couldn't help you."

Maren sucked in a breath. "There was nothing left of the Order. Nothing left to protect Kazimir. When you were born a few months later, he escaped Faerie with you in tow and made a home in the mortal lands. Once my mother had weathered the first days of grief, she realised she had no hope of raising her youngling without the Order. But Kazimir had been a friend to her, and so she followed him to Larkspur, and in time, I learned about my past and how important it was to keep you safe. My father would have wanted that, I think." A pause. "I did okay, didn't I? We care for each other, don't we? That's real. We trained together and made each other strong. If I did it again, I would tell you everything."

"You wanted me to be safe…" Her choices had been made in the context of losing her father and concern for me. Could betrayal be honourable? I didn't think so, but I softened all the same. I couldn't throw away our shared history even if I wanted to. Not here, in the midst of the Shrouded Forest. Not when my life was worth less without her in it. I wrenched each heartsore syllable from my lips. "No more lies."

She hugged my shivering body, and her warm strength felt foreign against mine, but her scent was still hers. She smelt of the creek and toffee and the blackberry wine we had guzzled at Bloomtide. "Okay."

I couldn't reconcile the face in front of me with the one I'd known all my life. The one that had pressed against mine when we'd slept in each other's arms as children or fallen over drunk as adults, our bellies shaking with laughter. But I tried to move on for the sake of rebuilding our trust. "Maren? What do they want with Father now?"

"I don't know, but Lunarys warned him that Faerie had changed—" Her eyes flashed wide.

A scream tore from my throat as an enormous beetle lunged from the shadows and clamped its pincers around her waist. The creature was the size of a tractor, its shell a grotesque mosaic of sinister thorns and jagged bark, perfectly camouflaged against the trees. Dread coiled in my stomach as it dangled Maren in the night air, its pincers digging into her sides.

We hadn't trained for this.

I drew my dagger and sprinted forward. With a fierce cry, I lunged at one of the beetle's joints, where the tough shell met softer flesh. The blade sank in with a sickening squelch, and the creature let out a guttural screech. I ducked low to aim again.

"Stay clear!" Violet flames flickered to life in Maren's hands.

Her flames burned with the energy of a collapsing star. They illuminated the forest, forcing back the curtain of night. Their edges glowed with faint hues of indigo and silver, rippling like silk in the breeze, while their core burned with a purple so deep it seemed to absorb the light around it. They shimmered, almost liquid in their movement, casting long shadows that danced wildly across the pine trees.

My breath rasped. "You could have told me you could do that."

"I'm showing you now," she ground out as she unleashed more fire towards the beetle. "Let go, you bastard."

I darted backwards, awestruck. Even from several paces away, the searing heat licked at my skin. It wasn't the comforting warmth of a hearth; this heat was wild, raw, and dangerous, like standing too close to a wildfire. The air around Maren warped, shimmering as waves of heat radiated outward, distorting the forest around us.

The beetle recoiled, its exoskeleton sizzling and smoking where the fire made contact. The beetle thrashed in response, its glossy eyes bulging, legs buckling as it attempted to shake off the fire. Maren aimed for its legs, and the acrid scent of burning wood filled the air.

She was unaffected by the scorching heat that radiated from her magic. Her violet fire swirled around her like a living thing, yet her skin remained unmarred and not a single pearl of sweat lined her brow. She looked magnificent as if she had been born from the flames themselves.

I would have sworn she would best the creature. Would have staked my life on it.

But though the beetle was enraged, its armour was thick, and it was undeterred by the heat. All of a sudden, it lifted Maren higher and pivoted with surprising speed. It surged across the clearing, its many legs skittering across the forest floor with a sandpaper scratching. Thorny, singed legs churned through the undergrowth, kicking up leaves and debris as it bolted deeper into the forest, Maren still clutched in its pincers.

Panic flooded my veins. "Don't you dare let it take you!"

Maren's voice was strained. "Stay back! I'll find a way to get back to you."

"Wait!" I gave chase, my feet slipping over damp roots and moss, branches whipping at my face.

I pushed harder, sweat-slicked, legs burning, lungs screaming for air. But the beetle was vanishing into a dense maze of brambles and towering oaks. The rhythmic crashing of its passage grew quieter, swallowed by the Shrouded Forest. I stopped when I'd lost all sense of them. When I could no longer see the brief flares of her violet fire or hear Maren's muffled shouts. Then I curled over, hands palming my knees, my dagger limp and useless in my hand, tears threatening to choke me. I couldn't breathe, couldn't think.

Even if Maren survived the beetle's attack, how would I find Father or survive the hostile forest without her?

7

YSADORA

*The soldiers are loud and brash, excited about the
king's arrival, but I can't focus. How could Maren
and Ysadora leave without a word?*
—Ferrith's diary

Retracing my steps back to Larkspur was not an
option. Eventually, I walked back to the clearing
to retrieve our belongings.

A hypnotic voice sounded behind me. "I see you met
my creature."

I whirled around to face it, a cold chill creeping up my
spine.

A figure double my height—more tree than man—
stepped out from behind a gnarled oak tree. He was like
the silhouette of a primal, ancient nightmare. Ruby eyes,
the colour of autumn leaves glinting with a cruel
intelligence, sat within a face etched with deep knots and
sprouting antlers half-hidden beneath a crown of twisted

thorns. His skin had the texture of cracked earth, dark and dry, threaded through with green sap-like channels. Vine-wrapped claws tipped long fingers.

Every instinct in my body screamed to run, but there was nowhere to go.

He sniffed the air, which still tanged of Maren's flames. His words held a quiet, hidden fury. "My forest does not take kindly to intruders. Your friend belongs in Faerie, but you do not. You're all alone now. Alone and sick. What will you do?"

I didn't need him to tell me there was something wrong with me. By now, I was certain of it. I was a fool to have ignored my sweat-drenched body and light-headedness, a fool not to have asked Maren for help. My trembling grip tightened around the dagger at my side. "Maren will come back. I'm not alone."

"My creature has taken her to the place she calls home."

To Larkspur? I clenched my teeth. "Who are you?"

"I am the Thorn King, and I do not grant you passage. Not without passing the test that many have failed." His lips peeled back to reveal teeth like jagged stones. The cadence of his speech was rhythmic, like a dark incantation, each word weaving a spell that ensnared. "I hunt them down. I flay them. Snap their spines. Muffle their cries with moss. Grind their bones. Let the roots tangle with their veins. Entomb them in the trees. Feed them to my creature."

The vibrations of his voice settled deep in my bones, and calming my sickly body was impossible when he lumbered towards me, his hulking frame making the earth shake. Impossible when his breath smelled of damp earth and decay, so close that it ruffled my hair. I looked up into the Thorn King's ruby eyes. "I'm not turning back. You can't have me. I will pass your test."

The bramble beetle loomed beside him, pincers clicking, no longer jerking Maren like she was a marionette. It fixed its bulbous eyes on me and emitted a soft, unsettling hum, almost like a purr, as he laid a hand on its shell. Other fae creatures lurked just out of reach, eyes gleaming in the murk of the Shrouded Forest, waiting for my moment of failure.

Waiting to devour me, toy with me, or claim me as theirs.

The Thorn King's voice scraped like bark against stone. "You must offer payment for your passage. Pain. Either of the flesh or of the soul. Choose to spill your blood or share your darkest secret. Choose, or my creature will choose for you."

Bile rose in my throat as the beetle's pincers flexed and clacked in anticipation. I didn't know what was worse: the sting of a flesh wound or the destructive nature of truth when I had already been destroyed by it a thousand times over these past days. The beetle might wound me enough to leave me for dead, and I didn't want to die, didn't want to fail Father or Maren or find myself on the forest floor with monsters fighting over the scraps of my remains. The truth had always been a lighthouse for me. How could I cower from it now?

Thorny tendrils inched towards my cheek as if tasting my resolve. "Your choice, intruder."

My pulse drummed in my ears as the creatures in the forest shifted closer. "Pain of the soul."

The Thorn King snarled. "Speak it then. The secret you

have kept. Bare your soul or perish in the shadows of your lies."

I swallowed hard and allowed the truth to bubble up, a truth that had gnawed at me in the dark of the night when I had crept into the cellar to read Mother's books. A truth that had solidified with Lunarys's visit and Father's pained expression at Bloomtide. A truth that had become a roar in my mind when Maren had revealed her true nature to me.

I wasn't just a woman from Larkspur. I wasn't just the daughter of a bookseller.

I was something more dangerous, something darker. Something that nestled within the pages of Mother's books.

I opened my mouth to speak, but my throat closed in panic. Was it even true? Would the Thorn King and the creatures of the Shrouded Forest kill me for it? The ground beneath me swayed as I wrestled with my thoughts. The creatures pressed so close I sensed flashes of movement: long limbs draped in moss, the glint of bloodied fangs, salivating hunger. I couldn't do it. I couldn't say the words that would hasten my death and prevent me from ever seeing Father and Maren again. I couldn't do it.

A sudden burning hurt my left wrist, and I looked down to see a pattern glowing there of interlocking keys in silver and gold. I frowned. Perhaps the kind of rune spoken of in some of Mother's books. Could Maren or Father have placed it there? Was it a link to them, even in their absence? There was a pull, as though the rune illuminated nagging discomforts buried deep within me. All those truths I refused to acknowledge because they didn't fit into my worldview. That I dodged and weaved around, like avoiding eye contact with something unsettling in the hope that it would fade into irrelevance. Warmth spread from the rune, racing up my arm and filling my chest, and I knew, I knew the words pearling on my tongue were true. I glanced up to see the twitching displeasure of the Thorn King and his hissing beetle as if they sensed something had changed.

"Speak your secret," demanded the Thorn King.

I lifted my chin, my voice steady. "I am fae, born of ink and shadow. And I won't be anyone's pawn."

"True." The creature screeched, and beady eyes waiting in the dark sighed their disappointment until it continued. "But someone interferes." Its spindly legs clicked as it closed in on me.

I barely had time to draw my dagger before its thorny pincers dug into my arm. A sting of ice and fire pierced through my nerves and the sensation rippled up my arm, a burning throb that pulsed in time with my heartbeat. Dark blood welled through my cloak. Even as the pain blurred my vision, I slashed at the beetle's leg, throwing my body weight behind a swift motion in which I took its front leg.

A sickening crunch sounded as its limb shattered beneath my blow. The beetle gave a high-pitched scream as it reeled back, and somewhere, the Thorn King called his wrath, even as he called his creature to heel.

It took me a second to come back to myself. I gagged as I stared at the pus-encrusted leg I had severed.

The Thorn King was not done with me. The weight of his ruby-red gaze pressed down on me, and he bent his face to my own. Anticipation crackled like static in the air.

"You dare harm my creature? You dare cheat in a bargain? Who here has meddled in my domain?"

I refused to cower, though fear seeped into my voice. "I arrived with only my friend to guide me. A friend your creature took… I played your game. I did not yield to pain without purpose. You will grant me passage."

He sifted through my words, searching for lies. Then he bellowed, his voice projecting far beyond the darkened glade to the eerie cacophony of life in the forest beyond. To the writhing shadows, the luminescent eyes, the contorted bodies and scuttling insects, to the faerie wisps and gnarled beasts that lurked in the gloom. "I cannot prove the deception, and so she may pass. For the secret she spoke was true. She is fae by one half or the other, by birth if not by learning, and so she may stay in Faerie. Though I will not harm her, her safety is far from guaranteed."

With that, the creatures of the Shrouded Forest skittered away. They melded into the growing light, past the mottled bark of ancient oaks, into the tangle of roots and brambles. The Thorn King clicked his tongue at the beetle, and together, they faded into the breaking dawn. They left me alone, though my awareness of the forest left me with no peace of mind, and the rich, metallic taste of magic lingered on my tongue.

The adrenalin that had fuelled me since the beetle took Maren drained from my body. I stumbled towards our strewn belongings, a tidal wave of exhaustion coming over me. My heart no longer pounded. Instead, it stuttered unevenly in my chest. Nausea rolled over me in waves, and I wondered how long it had been since I had eaten and whether my tired body could fight off infection without food. I just needed to get to the jars of water that Maren had packed. A few steps more.

But each breath grew harder, shallower, as the burning heat of fever spread across my skin. Each step felt like wading through thick, suffocating mud. The trees blurred together, the canopy spinning. My arm was wet and heavy and grew stiffer by the minute. My hand fumbled for a tree—the rune on my wrist still faintly throbbing—but the rough bark under my fingers didn't anchor me. My head swam before my legs gave out entirely. I slumped to the ground with a soft thud, my back against the bark, knees tucked to my chest. I could feel the fever building, hot and smothering. The world spun. Dark shapes hovered just beyond my vision. My head lolled back, my eyelids too heavy to keep open.

I closed them, thoughts reeling. Maren wasn't coming back.

I couldn't summon the energy to panic. I just needed to rest for a minute to gather my strength. It was good the sky was lightening. The sky didn't seem right without the stars, and I was grateful for the new day to chase away the night's monsters. It was okay to rest. Father would want me to rest.

A woman's voice accompanied a gentle hand on my forehead. "She's burning up." The hand lingered, testing, and then the hand pressed against my cheek, assessing the heat radiating from my skin.

I twitched, my body protesting, but I couldn't peel my eyes open, couldn't shake the hold of the fever.

"Her true nature is fighting back after being suppressed for so long." The woman's voice was distant and muffled like it was coming from underwater.

"Gabe's starlight will help with the infection from the creature's wound, but not with the rest. There's wormwood in her bag, though. We could try that or mundara leaf."

"No, ashwagandha is better. Plus moonshade or willow bark for the fever. Be quick about it," said a man in low velvet tones I recognised. That struck fear into my heart. He knelt before me and smelt of the wilds.

Someone lifted the sleeve of my cloak and grasped my arm. A second man. "I'm sorry. This will burn."

I tried to stir at the searing pain, at the dazzling light, to lift my head and open my eyes, but it was no use. I parted my lips to cry out, to rail against their mistreatment of me, but the words wouldn't form. My body felt like it had turned to lead. I was at their mercy. I didn't think it would stop, and when it did, I latched onto their voices, any foothold to stay conscious.

"You really gave her the rune," drawled the man. "Risky to interfere in a bargain."

"It wasn't a risk. The Thorn King owes me."

"He would have flayed you if he'd discovered it. Tied you for an age to the great oaks."

"Nevertheless, she did well to survive an encounter with him," said the woman.

Something soft and bitter was pressed past my lips. I pushed it away with my tongue, but a delicate hand cupped my jaw and urged me to swallow. The texture was rough, the taste earthy and sharp, with a hint of mint. Next, deft fingers pulled at the buttons of my tunic. A breeze brushed against my burning skin as the fabric parted. A moment later, damp leaves pressed against my chest. They smelled of moss and dew, of something ancient and wild. They dragged me towards a fragile, fleeting peace.

I drifted then, sinking deeper into the darkness, but before it submerged me, strong arms scooped me up and lifted me from the forest floor. My cheek pressed against the hard planes of his chest, and his strong heart would have comforted me had he not been my enemy.

A curse rumbled from him. "She's too light for her frame. Is there no food in Larkspur?"

"None that's fit for our fine palettes." A pause. "You can't mean to take her with us. Thiago—"

The woman spoke, softer, urgent. "She'll be dead by morning if we leave her here, Gabor. She needs care. Maybe, soulstem."

The vibrations of his voice against my ear soothed me. "She's too weak to weather the soulstem."

Gabor grunted. "A blindfold then. At the very least, we—."

The woman interrupted. "She's no threat to us like this."

Provocation rippled beneath the silken voice of the man who held me. "Let him speak, Wylda. Question my command and see what happens." He didn't wait for a response. Shifting me against him, he tossed my cloak away. "She's soaked to the bone. There's a blanket in Mythros's saddlebag."

I wanted to ask who they were, where they were taking me, and if they would bring my father's compass and his quill, but the questions wouldn't come.

Cool air brushed against my fevered skin before someone draped a soft blanket on me, but I was too far gone to feel its relief. Somewhere, horses whinnied. My awareness flickered like a dying flame, fading in and out, losing finer details, until all that remained was muffled voices, dawn's flickering rays across my closed eyelids, the rhythm of footsteps and the steady rise and fall of the chest I was cradled against. Firm, gentle hands hoisted me higher, and the earth scent of horses filled my nose. There was a jolt as my body met a saddle. I moaned. I'd been so comfortable with my cheek resting against his heartbeat. This time, my back pressed against solid warmth. My head tipped back against his shoulder.

"It'll be quicker to fly her there."

"She rides with me, Gabor."

The clip-clop of hooves. The last threads of my consciousness unravelled.

Then, the dark claimed me.

8

YSADORA

Soulstem
An ivy with dark green, pulsing leaves. Found
around ancient, oft forgotten, fae dwellings.
Properties: can be used in healing rituals to mend
emotional wounds. It may drain one's life force.
—A Compendium of Faerie Flora and Terrain

When my eyelids fluttered open, the fever had broken and I was lying in bed with a fur-lined blanket draped over me. I didn't know how long I slept, only that the Thorn King and his creature surged in flashes behind my eyelids, that red ink was smeared on pale snow and that someone shushed me when I cried out and laid a calloused hand against my forehead. My dreams had always been vivid, but the nightmares tangling with reality were worse. So much worse. My tongue was like sandpaper as I peeled the limp leaves from my chest. Their herbal scent lingered in the air, a faint reminder of the sickness they had drawn out.

Fragmented, grainy memories of the night filtered through my mind: us following Father into the forest, Maren pincered by the beetle, the Thorn King eager to grind my bones, the uncanny knowledge that I was fae, my body growing sicker, a horseback ride between a stranger's thighs. I flushed. With a jerk, I remembered the creature's pincers in my arm, but when I checked the skin, there was no gouge there, only pink, newly healed skin. The rune on my wrist was still there, and I scratched it, aghast. The interlocking gold and silver keys etched onto my skin glimmered softly in the dark room.

Clearly, I wasn't out of danger yet.

Pulse racing, I took in my surroundings: a thick silence blanketed a windowless room of stone walls, making it impossible to gauge the time of day. The sturdy door was almost certainly locked. A low fire cast a warm glow across the space, and thick rugs adorned the floor. A small table at my bedside held a pitcher of water and a cup, along with a bowl of strange fruit: plump black oblongs dappled with silver specks. Two familiar satchels sat against the wall, and next to them, my boots.

A softly clipped voice startled me from the corner of the room. "You woke sooner than expected."

I relaxed only a little when I realised it wasn't Lunarys's killer, though I missed my dagger terribly.

The man stretched his arms and legs and stood up from a chair with a yawn. Firelight flickered across his rich, mahogany skin, and I frowned, trying to place where I'd seen him before. His expression was calm, and there was a hint of curiosity in the tilt of his head. "We thought you'd need more time, but you are full of surprises."

My voice scratched with dehydration. "I understand that in Faerie, you have to adapt fast."

"So you do remember the night's happenings, Ysadora." His lips quirked into a small smile as he crossed the room. He had an athletic frame and wore dark trousers, a leather jerkin layered over a long-sleeved shirt and sturdy boots. Almond-shaped eyes changed from hazel to gold as he approached. The fine point of his ears beneath braided, jet-black hair made me tense.

I edged away from him. "It seems unfair that you know my name when I do not know yours."

He gave an easy laugh and placed a hand on his chest. "My apologies. I'm Cyprian." He poured water into the cup and offered it to me, together with a piece of fruit. "Welcome to Ebonspire."

When he didn't retract his offerings, I took them and eyed them warily, considering my options. My stomach was a cavernous hollow, but the faerie tales Mother had collected warned against accepting gifts in enchanted lands. In her books, dangers lurked everywhere. The fae could offer something mundane—water or nourishment, a bauble, a small favour—and in return, an unsuspecting mortal could be bound to a lifetime of servitude or worse. Eating might mean I would be trapped in Faerie forever. A tiny morsel might bring on hallucinations, or I might never be satisfied by mortal food once I returned home.

I didn't even know if Larkspur was still my home without Father, Maren and Ferrith there.

"It's a starshade plum, not poison. If we'd wanted to

kill you, we would have left you in the Shrouded Forest or slit your throat while you were fighting the fever."

I scowled at an ill-timed rumble from my stomach, and Cyprian's smile deepened within his angular face. I huffed a sigh, knowing that I wouldn't stand a chance of escape if I was too weak to get out of bed. Breathing in the honey-sweet scent of the fruit, I squeezed it. Its skin split open to reveal ripe violet flesh. After a moment of indecision, I bit into it, savouring its sharp berry flavour, then gave up any semblance of restraint before drinking water fresher than any I had tasted from the village well.

Despite his hospitality, the looming fae made unease curl in my chest. The windowless walls closed in on me, and the absence of connection to the outside world made the air seem thicker and more stagnant. Without a glimpse of the sky, it was impossible to tell if it was day or night, and the disorienting timelessness heightened my sense of vulnerability. Who knew how long Father and Maren had suffered at the mercy of their captors.

I wiped my hand across my mouth. "Am I a prisoner?"

Cyprian rubbed the back of his neck, clearly weighing his words. "It's complicated."

My eyes narrowed. "The last few days have been nothing but complicated. Either I'm free to leave, or you're keeping me here. Which is it?"

"Zephyr thought it best to keep you out of sight. Bringing you here was a risk. Not everyone agrees with his methods."

Zephyr. The man who I had met at Bloomtide and had buried his daggers in Lunarys within yards of playing children. The man who was their leader. I ignored the frisson that ran down my spine as I recalled his scent and the hard lines of his body. He was dangerous. Perhaps even reckless. I could use the information about dissent within his ranks against him later.

"He's a murderer."

"He's many things."

My eyes flicked towards the door. "What does he want with me?"

Cyprian shook his head. "That's not for me to say."

I rose from the bed, defiant despite his height dwarfing mine, despite being partially undressed, and my tunic skimmed the tops of my bare thighs. Expecting to teeter on shaky feet after my bout of ill health, the fluidity of my movements surprised me. I scanned the room for my clothing, my dagger, and the compass. "Then I'll find out for myself."

Hazel-gold eyes assessed me with clinical detachment. "You wouldn't last a day."

"I don't want your protection."

"I am over a century old. Hear me when I tell you Faerie has never been as dangerous as it is now. I don't know what you are capable of, but I do know you've already drawn too much attention." He gestured to a narrow door swallowed by shadows in the corner of the room. "You'll find fresh bathwater and clean clothes in the adjacent chamber. We will meet at supper."

My brow knitted. "I slept all day?"

"You slept for two."

Anxiety flared in the pit of my stomach. "Maren. My Father. They need me."

Cyprian gave me an apologetic frown. "You are no help to them in your current state."

I balled my fists. "Who is *we*? Who else will be at supper?"

His wicked grin revealed a flash of sharp canines. "The other mercenaries, of course."

Dread slithered up my spine, considering the moral fibre of those I was trapped with. Considering what mercenaries did to women. I thought I'd heard a woman's voice when I had been fevered, thought I'd heard the names Wylda and Gabor, but I couldn't be sure, couldn't tell what had been my fever spiking my imagination. "Are you all men?"

His voice grew gentler. "We are both males and females here. You are safe within these walls, Ysadora." He turned to leave but paused. Concern flickered across his face. "In the bath chamber…do not be afraid of what you see in the mirror."

When he was gone, I tried the door handle, then wrenched it with all my might.

It was indeed locked.

With rising dread, I turned out the contents of the satchels and found nothing had been taken. Even our daggers—presumably retrieved from the floor of the forest —hadn't been removed, as if I was no threat at all. A dark chuckle spilt from me. Let them underestimate me. I would show them.

Yet, as I padded barefoot across the rug towards the bath chamber, Cyprian's words haunted me.

The narrow door creaked softly as I pushed it open, revealing a room arched like the inside of a temple, bathed in warm candlelight. Steam rose lazily from a tub sunken into the floor, a vast pool of shimmering water that glowed silver. The air inside was thick with the scent of lavender and sage, and the rough-hewn slate beneath me was cold against my soles.

But it was the stone walls that caught my breath, not plain like in the bedchamber, but alive with stories flowing in pictures: winding narratives woven into the very structure of the room—figures dancing across the stone, their movements frozen mid-step. Battles raged between warriors and beasts, lovers embraced, and strange creatures roamed across landscapes of stars and shadow. A gilded mirror dominated the far wall, where a window should have been, and I approached it, noticing a thick towel, a comb and a plum gown on a stool, together with flat, silver sandals.

Fog obscured the glass of the mirror. With a deep inhale, I wiped a patch clear with my palm. My heart jolted as I faced a reflection I barely recognised. For a long moment, I looked away. It was everything I feared: a distortion of who I was.

But I had to be brave. Father and Maren needed me to be brave. Even though my sense of self slipped through my fingers like sand. Even though our bodies are maps we live by, and I had no hope of ever finding my bearings.

Hands clenched, I looked again. My olive skin had a luminous quality as if kissed by the moon. The soft lines of my jaw, the gentle slope of my nose and the curve of my rosy lips had been smoothed into something more ethereal. Terrified, I brushed newly elegant fingers over pointed ears framed by dark hair, glossier and thicker than before despite hanging in a tangled mess down my back. But it was the vividness of my new gaze that unsettled me the most. Once brown like Father's and gold-flecked, they were now sapphire with hints of amethyst, like the shifting colours of a twilight sky.

I pinched myself, hard, but when I dared to look at the mirror again, the half-familiar face stared back at me.

I couldn't shake the strange dissonance that gripped me. There was an undeniable beauty in my reflection, yet it felt foreign, like a portrait of someone I could not quite place. I was an echo of the person I had been, wrapped in a transformation that disconnected me from my own identity.

Anxiety fluttering, I unbuttoned my tunic, my movements slow and deliberate. It fell to the floor, and I peeled off my undergarments next before walking trance-like to the bathtub. I dipped my hand into the water and found it warm—almost too warm—to the touch. I slipped in, my body sinking into the basin. Warmth enveloped me and I wanted to give myself to it, to erase all thought and fear, and let myself float away. But that couldn't be. So, I lifted my hands to my face and body, half-expecting to feel the contours I had always known. Instead, I repressed a shudder at my ears, my hair, the subtle gracefulness of my limbs, the almost artistic shape of my fingers, and the interlocked keys etched onto my wrist.

Choking back a sob, I recoiled at the thought that my hands might not belong to me, that I was inhabiting a borrowed body that didn't align with my essence. I yearned for the familiar comfort of my old self, a semblance of a body and world that felt tangible and real. How could I walk the tightrope between acceptance and apprehension without Father and Maren to guide me? Without Ferrith to make me laugh. Without my Mother's books to decode the mysteries around me.

My eyes drifted back to the walls. One section near the bath depicted a spire reaching into the sky, encircled by shadowed creatures. Another told the tale of a faerie queen, her skyward gaze reflected in stars, her hands outstretched.

I was an intruder in a space that knew far more than I ever would.

Though my body craved rest, unless I found answers, my loved ones would be lost.

9

ZEPHYR

Are faerie lords as lonely as mortals?
—Danaë Everreed's annotations
in her Faerie books

T he sun hung low in the sky, casting long shadows across the rocky outcroppings of the landscape. They prowled through sparse underbrush a kilometre away from Ebonspire.

Zephyr loved the old gatehouse, but only now, away from its stony walls, did his lungs expand.

The past months had been a labyrinth of riddled truths and manipulations. His sharp mind, normally able to weave through intricate court politics, had been tested at every turn. Every conversation away from his people had been layered with meaning, every silence a potential trap. There had been moments when he'd questioned his instincts.

In Faerie, the games were never truly over. Not until

the last breath was drawn.

Now, even Gabor, one of their own, questioned his command. Three years as part of the group and Zephyr couldn't shake the feeling that there was an edge to him, something sharp beneath the surface, like the blade of a hidden knife. They were all haunted by things they had done and still planned to do.

Zephyr knew well the rot that stemmed from dissent. How it spread through the ranks. He'd have to nip it in the bud, but his mind was muddy. Even his own shadows were resistant, slower to respond as if the darkness around him had become sentient, pulling him into its depths rather than obeying his will.

As if they would take him over completely.

The calligrapher's daughter had slept for two days. There had been no signs that she'd rouse soon. Cyprian and Wylda had been taking turns watching over her. Zephyr had been in there himself but had taken his leave quickly. She looked so innocent with her dark hair tangling across the pillow, but she'd surprised him. She'd been brought up as a common village girl, uninitiated in the ways of Faerie. And yet, though it was her friend who had wielded flame, it was the calligrapher's daughter who had blazed with defiance when facing a nightmarish foe, the likes of which she had never encountered before.

A foe who had slain far greater beings.

Zephyr was drawn to broken things. Maybe that's why he'd given her the rune, a snap decision that could cost him more than he was prepared to give. He frowned at the memory of her body pressed against his. Hours they'd travelled together, and yet he'd gleaned nothing despite calling on his magic time and again. A residual impact of the Binder's elixir, perhaps.

It had been stupid of him to scoop her into his arms, knowing she was a prize many would kill for. His people came first, always. Who knew how many scuttling forest creatures had hurried to their masters to tell tales of her arrival in Faerie?

He blinked away the image of the Binder dusting before him from his mind's eye. One moment he'd been almost flirting with the calligrapher's daughter, his fingers brushing her wrist, the next, he was blinded by such rage that he'd knifed a primordial being. The Binder had smiled when she had mentioned Veda's name. Why had she smiled? He pushed down the sense that he'd been manipulated when usually he was the manipulator. The Binder had made him a pariah in the midst of a mortal festival, but that was nothing new. He was always an outsider, operating on the periphery, never central to anyone's plans or anyone's love. Except his mother's.

Zephyr didn't particularly enjoy killing, but he'd always been drawn to danger, always been eager to pit himself against the worst terrors of this realm and others. Even more so after his mother had died, when there was no one to worry about him. Oh, his father had pretended, but a male's absence during a youngling's formative years fractured the parent-child bond.

There was an aching void where there should have been feeling.

It did him good to be out here, using the slash of his blade to dull the thorny thoughts in his mind. While Kazimir's daughter slept, he had weighed every scenario. For once, neither Cyprian's counsel nor training provided any respite. His group had been idling over a meal at Ebonspire, taking bets on when their captive would wake when the ward had sounded. Loxley had grinned a challenge. It was a welcome distraction issued by the one in their group assumed to be the most heartless.

But Zephyr knew otherwise. He knew how to read the pain under a male's bluster.

Of course, he accepted. He wasn't one to shirk a challenge. That was how they found themselves bowing westward through the landscape, tracking scattered stones, puddled venom and deep grooves that marred the earth.

Loxley's alabaster skin contrasted with the black leathers he wore. His luminous green eyes and tangled beard evoked the chaotic essence of his origins. "I know you're the strong, silent type, but I'm all ears."

Zephyr scanned the environment. "Stay alert, or its fangs will end up buried in your neck."

Loxley gave a mock salute. "Yes, sir."

The air was damp and still, the scent of earth mingling with the tang of salt from the sea. They crouched, and tension prickled Zephyr's skin like a warning. The disputed land didn't belong to them, but Zephyr knew its shapes and shadows, its gifts and poisons, better than he knew himself. And Loxley was no fool, despite the glibness of his tongue.

A flicker of movement caught Zephyr's eye, and he signalled to alert Loxley.

The serpent shifted against the barren cliffside, metallic scales gleaming like blackened steel, absorbing the dim light before flashing with a hint of deep green. Its body was as thick as a barrel, stretching over forty feet in length as it wound through the jagged cliffs. Sharp ridges crowned its head, and curved fangs lined its mouth. Its tail twined around rock formations with enough force to pulverise stone into dust.

"This could get interesting," muttered Zephyr.

Loxley gave him a roguish grin. "Come now, we've seen worse."

They crept closer, waiting for an opportunity to strike, like they'd done a thousand times before, always in pairs or larger groups. Zephyr had commanded them never to be alone. He had a callous disregard for his own safety but not for theirs. He could never forgive himself if one of them fell, if the future were erased from their story.

When thirty feet separated them, the serpent raised its head and fixed yellow-slitted eyes on them. Its muscles tensed in awareness.

Loxley's voice was playful. "Watch and learn."

He shot forward, boots pounding against the rocky terrain, each step sure and precise despite his rugged physique and the uneven ground. The sword strapped to his back glinted in the twilight, but he didn't draw it. As the serpent reared up its wide, flat head, Loxley ducked beneath its snapping jaws and planted his shoulder into the serpent's form, driving his weight against it. His brute strength was enough to knock it slightly off balance. The serpent hissed, tail lashing, and Loxley swung himself up and over so he straddled the creature, grabbing slick scales with both hands as he clung on. The serpent bucked violently, nearly smashing his skull against rock.

Zephyr cursed. "Do you have a death wish? Subdue him, dammit it." Shadows melded around him as he raced to help, daggers at the ready.

Loxley's muscles strained as he wrestled with it. "Where would be the fun in that?"

Zephyr released his shadows once he was at the serpent's flank. With a series of agile leaps, he danced around it, darting between its coils, taunting it, distracting it from the male who rode it. The serpent coiled and snapped, its massive jaws missing him by inches. A low hiss reverberated off the cliffs with every exhale.

"See," said Loxley. "I knew you needed this."

Zephyr's laughter rang out, exhilarated by the thrill of the hunt. He lived for these moments when his head quieted, and he could immerse himself in the task before him. When he could surrender to instinct and training, test his skill and mettle against an uncertain outcome. His adrenalin pumped. The wind bit against his skin. The primal nature of a hunt enveloped him.

His earlier annoyance faded away. Yes, he had needed this.

The simplicity of battle. A victory. Another notch in his mercenary ledger.

The serpent was capable of crushing entire trees or stone outcrops as it slithered. The scales, dark and metallic, clinked faintly as they slid over the earth, resembling the gleaming plates of a warship, impenetrable and cold. Still, Loxley beamed with delight as it thrashed beneath him.

"Why did you give her the rune? It's all anyone will talk about."

Zephyr grunted, stormy eyes fixed on the serpent. "Not a good time, Lox."

It undulated in sinuous, calculated movements. He would have preferred speed to this careful, hypnotic trap.

A forked tongue slashed out as it turned its head in his direction. Zephyr sidestepped smoothly, spinning one dagger in his hand. He dropped to a knee, ignoring a sharp pain as his knee struck a jagged rock and jabbed the flat of the blade against the creature's jaw with all his strength. The impact reverberated through the creature's length, momentarily stunning it.

"I mean, she's a pretty little thing, but the Faerie King of Silence will have your balls."

"Not helping. Will you get on with it?"

"But you're doing so well without my help. You even look happy."

As the serpent coiled to strike again, Zephyr swirled his shadows around the serpent to disorientate it with an illusory darkness. The serpent swayed, its head bobbing slightly as it tried to discern the source of its sudden disorientation. Zephyr pressed his advantage. Using the flat of both blades—taking great care not to be bitten—he pushed down against the dazed serpent's head, guiding it toward the ground as if it were no more than an inept dance partner.

"Easy," Zephyr soothed, almost as if coaxing it into compliance. He frowned at his split leathers, irked by that more than the two-inch cut to his knee. Then he growled at Loxley, who still straddled the creature whose awareness grew with every passing second, "Now, or I swear to the breathless night that I will tie you up and leave you as bait for the next one."

"No need to be like that." Loxley's legs were now flat against the earth, his cropped brown hair no more dishevelled than usual. He leaned forward and reached into the serpent's mind.

Confusion drifted across its yellow eyes. It trembled as it succumbed to the influence of Loxley's magic. His will took hold, and the beast became as still as stone beneath his touch. Zephyr leapt into action, binding its movements with shadows that wrapped around it like chains: first its jaw, then pinning sections of the serpent's body to itself, entangling it without leaving a mark. The serpent writhed, and Loxley tightened his control, pushing against its instinctual urges.

"Stop taunting it."

Loxley huffed. "Fine."

He released the creature from his mind control. It lay at their feet, yellow eyes filled with malice, subdued but not broken, its metallic scales dulling slightly in defeat. Zephyr leaned against the cliff face, breathing hard, wondering if the serpent had been in this form too long to remember who it was.

Loxley's lips quirked in triumph. "Well, that got the juices flowing. Better than riding a wench."

A small smile crept onto Zephyr's lips despite himself. "Speak for yourself."

"At least I didn't cut my knee open like a youngling."

"You almost got yourself killed. Or worse, bitten."

Mischief flared in Loxley's luminous eyes as they prepared to haul their prize back to Ebonspire. "Admit it. It's good to play outside the sandbox sometimes."

"We're doing that far too much for our own good."

"We could wipe her mind and leave her in the mortal realm or just leave her in the wilds in the path of a monster. Pretend we never even crossed paths." Loxley ran a hand through his cropped hair. "I know what you want for us, but maybe…maybe we just collect our coin. Do what we're trained to do. It's not a bad life."

A bitter taste permeated Zephyr's mouth. He'd always wanted more for them and for him.

She was a piece on the board it made sense to knock down. Yet her history puzzled him. He only knew half of her lineage, and for all his shadows, Zephyr didn't like to operate in the dark. He'd shadowed her in Kazimir's house, but she had given nothing away. Giving her the rune had been a stay of execution to buy him time to think. The calligrapher's daughter didn't belong in Faerie, no matter what the Thorn King had surmised. Once Zephyr had the information he needed, her fate would be determined.

They frowned at the sound of approaching hooves before a mimicked lark call alerted them to the approach of one of their own. Twilight lent Ciprian's skin an almost bronze sheen as he cantered towards them on horseback. In the sky above his friend, flocks of birds wheeled in chaotic circles, their cries harsh and jagged. They filled the sky in a disordered mass of wings, darting like flecks of soot against the pale blue. Many had ragged feathers and smudges of grey, as though they'd been caught in smoke or ash. Beaks snapped as they called out, a blend of frantic chirps and sharp caws. They shifted between tight clusters and sudden dispersals, flight patterns like a moving storm, dark and roiling.

Cyprian drew closer and tossed the serpent a nonchalant glance. His time magic was a clear asset on missions, and he knew it. "There you are. Nice work. Not as big as my one last week."

Loxley scoffed. "Yes, but you returned covered in gore."

Zephyr fixed Cyprian with an impatient look. "News?"

"She's awake." He dismounted from Mythros and gave Zephyr the reins, eyeing the wound on his knee visible through his ripped leathers. "Go clean yourself up, or you'll scare her."

"If a little blood and sweat scare her, she won't last long in Faerie. She'll take me as I am or not at all."

Cyprian gave a heavy sigh. "Just try not to be an arsehole. No need to make things any harder for her."

"I'm capable of charm," drawled Zephyr with a quick look to the sky.

Loxley snorted. "That's new."

"I'm pretty sure by now his cock has dried up," said Cyprian.

"A crying shame, if you ask me." Loxley smoothed his beard. In the sky, the birds darted and veered in strange, dizzying patterns, sometimes diving close to the treetops as though seeking shelter, then rising high with frantic flaps. "You're not really going to leave us here to do the grunt work?"

"I am. Hurry and get home, though. Faerie is telling us to get moving."

"Yes, my lord," said Loxley with a jig.

Zephyr ignored him and approached Mythros. "Hello, old friend."

The sleek, muscular horse had a mane that rippled like liquid shadow and hard brown eyes that only softened when he looked at his master. None other than Cyprian—who had been bitten once—and Zephyr could ride him. His ears twitched in recognition of Zephyr, and though the serpent and the wingbeats of the birds made him skittish, he calmed when his master laid a palm against his muzzle.

"I'll collect his story later." Zephyr slung himself onto Mythros's back and clicked his tongue to guide the horse forward under bird cries that echoed off the cliffs and filled him with foreboding.

They blended into the shadows, their bodies already swaying in sync. Part of Zephyr's mind maintained the hold of his shadow chains, but the rest of him was consumed with the problem of the female imprisoned in the stone room.

Behind him, Loxley and Cyprian dragged the serpent back to Ebonspire.

YSADORA

Whisperroot
A pale, bioluminescent vine that grows
in damp areas and emits soft,
whispering sounds when disturbed.
Properties: compels the user to speak the truth
and can cause digestive discomfort.
—A Compendium of Faerie Flora and Terrain

The bath soothed my muscles, but I didn't relax in its scented waters. Worry and the alienating discoveries of the past days threatened to submerge me. I scrubbed the dirt from my skin, carefully avoiding the tight pink of my healed wound, and washed the grime from my hair.

Facing my reflection again terrified me, so I rubbed myself dry with haste and tugged a comb through my tangled hair. With my own clothes in a sorry state, I stepped into the gown, its fabric like a hue of twilight fading into night. It had the soft and luxurious feeling of ancient craftsmanship. The fabric flowed from my waist, brushing my ankles like liquid velvet. Long, draped sleeves pooled at my wrists. I hadn't worn anything so fine in my four-and-twenty orbits.

I cast aside the sandals in favour of my boots and stashed Maren's dagger into the right one. Once I knotted the silken mass of my dark hair, I slipped Father's quill like an ornamental pin through it and hid his compass in a hem pocket. They were a reminder for me to stay on task and of my own power. Making further preparations would give away my intentions, so I left the rest reluctantly behind. Anxious energy built in me as I waited to be summoned. My stomach rumbled, but I didn't eat any more of the fruit. The fire burned out.

I would escape this prison. I would find a way back to my family.

After some time, the door handle twisted without warning. I stiffened, expecting to see Cyprian. Instead, the leader of the mercenaries stood alone in the doorway, framed in low light like a shadow given form. He stepped into the bedchamber—unarmed—dark clothing blending with the grey flickering light of the room.

Suddenly, the space was too small.

He was taller than my memory of him, standing with a quiet authority that made me want to step back, though I held my ground. Without the hood masking his features, I took in his blue-grey eyes, full lips and unruly dark hair drying over his forehead in loose waves. He wore a midnight blue shirt over dark breeches. A well-fitted tunic hugged his torso, its high collar unbuttoned at the neck, revealing a glimpse of tawny skin still beaded with water, as though he had bathed but not fully dried himself. Bare, corded forearms carried faint scars of battle. There was a predatory elegance to him, as though he was always in command, even in the most informal moments.

The air between us crackled with something unfamiliar that felt too dangerous to name.

Zephyr. Still, I lifted my chin. I would not let him see my fear.

His storm-cloud gaze swept over me with unsettling calm. He assessed my fae ears, the colour of my newly sapphire eyes, how the fitted bodice clung to my curves, my collarbones just visible beneath the demure silver-stitched neckline, the way the light from the nearly gone candle wicks caught my dark hair and the muddy boots peeking beneath the gathers of my skirt.

My fists clenched in anger. I didn't even know myself. Yet here he stood, as though I were a scroll with its seal broken, every secret inked in bold strokes for him to read.

The door was open behind him. But Lunarys had been powerful, and he had killed her as if she had been nothing. If I ran, he would stop me as easily as a child catches and pins a resting butterfly. So I stayed still, waiting for him to make the first move, my heart thundering in my chest.

His voice, when he broke the silence, was smooth and controlled. "You look…much improved."

Disbelief washed over me. "Oh, in that case, I'll forgive my imprisonment."

He tilted his head, a hint of challenge in his eyes, and extended an arm. "I'm here to escort you to supper."

I almost laughed. My hand looped around my left wrist, where he had branded me with the interlocked keys.

Instead of taking his arm, I pushed past him and walked out of the door. He was nearly over a head taller than me, with sinewy muscled arms that promised quick, lethal force. I had no sense of his intentions towards me. But he let me pass.

I took in my surroundings, spine tingling with awareness of him at my back. Ebonspire was grander than any building I had ever been in. The soft scrape of our boots against the floor resonated off the walls, the sound swallowed by oppressive silence. Vaulted ceilings loomed overhead, and corridors twisted out of sight into endless, darkened hallways.

He fell into lockstep with me and cupped my elbow. "I wouldn't want you to get lost."

My breaths came in shallow, rapid rasps as we passed dozens of closed doors. Some seemed permanently shut, others ajar, revealing glimpses of untouched chambers. The building dwarfed us, but it wasn't the size that intimidated me; it was the sense of its untapped, dormant power. Amidst the pressing stillness, the distant boom of waves called to me from a narrow window at the end of the hall. When I went towards the milky pane, the mercenary leader made no move to stop me. The moon hung low over a turbulent sea, its silvery light casting diamond glimmers on the black expanse. The crashing surf was both a lullaby and a roar.

"Blistering stars." Even with the compass, I wouldn't have any hope of navigating this strange world and finding Father and Maren without help. But I had nothing to bargain. No way of convincing my captors to give me aid.

Low tones vibrated in my ear. "Faerie is vast and wild, unlike the village you left behind."

I spun in my ridiculous gown, trying not to notice the scent of the wilds—moss and earth, sea salt and clove—emanating from him or remember how he had cradled me against his chest on the way to Ebonspire. "Why did you bring me here?"

"Why were you foolish enough to come to Faerie?" he countered.

"To find my family."

"You would have been wise to run. Your family put you in this situation. I'm surprised you're so eager to save their necks when you should be worried about your own."

"It's easy to be self-centred when you're hiding in these sea-swept ruins."

"Your father is of Faerie. Your friend fought the Thorn King's creature and survived. They will fare quite well without you."

Father and Maren's betrayal still stung, but that didn't mean I would abandon them. My voice shook with passion. "How could someone like you know about love and regret and bonds that can never be broken?"

He exhaled sharply and glanced away. "Come on. First, we eat, then we talk."

I clamped my mouth shut, anxiety churning, knees buckling, as we descended a narrow stairwell. We veered left, then right, then left again in quick succession, leaving me disoriented despite my careful counting of the lanterns lining the walls. Eventually, the subdued signs of life gradually became more pronounced, and we approached a heavy wooden door. Raucous chatter spilt out from underneath it.

"Stay close," commanded the mercenary leader. "Not all my people want you here."

"Fine," I said, though I wanted to put a hundred miles between us.

My imagination ran wild with what I might encounter. The mercenaries that drifted through Larkspur were heavy-booted, battle-scarred men who stank of smoke and sweat. Men, who were best avoided. They didn't think twice about abandoning a comrade or taking advantage of the weak. I hated their menacing, lascivious leers, hated it when they held court at the tavern with tales of conquests that made my skin crawl. Cyprian had assured me that I was safe within these walls, but the fae mercenaries were likely of a similar ilk. I fisted my trembling hands. What if they saw me as a toy for their carnal desires, to be exploited and then discarded? What if they wielded not only weapons but dark magic?

I needed to learn the rules of this world, and I needed to learn them fast.

Zephyr opened the door, and a wave of warmth enveloped me. Instead of a vast dining hall, I found myself in a cosy kitchen where wooden beams contrasted with stone. Platters of roasted game, fragrant bread and strange fruits crowned a table. My mouth watered at the scent of rich, savoury aromas and something sweet that reminded me of honey and almonds. It was the kind of feast Father and I would share with Maren and her mother at Yule.

The kind that hadn't graced our tables since *the days of plenty* had ended.

But it was the mercenaries that commanded my full attention. Candles flickered on the table, illuminating their faces. There were six in all, including Cyprian and Zephyr.

As we approached, the conversation lost its easy rhythm, and several pairs of wary eyes turned towards me. Zephyr pulled out an empty chair for me and took the adjacent one at the head of the table.

He leaned back, his tone dry. "You can stop pretending not to notice our guest. Meet Ysadora, the calligrapher's daughter."

My gaze shifted uneasily from one face to the next as the mercenary leader turned his attention to piling my plate and his with food. Their features, though still human-like, were twisted by their inherent magic, like reflections in a warped mirror. Their skin appeared as though carved from marble, cold and translucent, and their ears were pointed. Wide eyes glimmered with unnatural colours, like molten lava or darkened suns. The eyes of my neighbours in Larkspur were filled with human emotions: mischief, empathy, envy or melancholy. But here, I saw only cool calculation. High cheekbones lent them an intimidating elegance. Their fingers were too slender, with nails that gleamed like claws. Their perfectly symmetrical lips hid sharp teeth.

A shudder snaked up my spine. These were creatures of the unseen, the monsters from Mother's storybooks, who could twist reality with their will and rip the very fabric of the world apart.

Cyprian caught my eye. Tonight, he wore a charcoal coat with silver fastenings, cinched at the waist over an emerald shirt. "I trust you found everything you needed?"

I became small beneath his assessing hazel-gold gaze, pulling at my gown, chewing my cheek. "Yes."

"Introductions, then." He turned to his companions, indicating the bearded male on his left, with hair like a fallow field and eyes to match his deep green tunic. Then he nodded at a female in burgundy with wild curls pinned up loosely and a second one who was taller and sturdy with thick braids at her back. "Meet Loxley, Wylda and Sequoia." He cocked his head to the stove, where a large male with long dark hair and powerful wings—blended black and silver in colour—sprinkled a pinch of herbs onto a dish. "And that's Gabor. The best cook in residence."

I gawped at Gabor's wings, unable to look away, even after the Thorn King. Even after Maren.

I felt distinctly mortal in their midst. But I was becoming one of them—or maybe this is what I'd always been—and that horrified me.

Gabor brought the bamboo bowl of colourful vegetables to the table, placing it closest to me. "Don't listen to them. There are none here who can compete with me in the kitchen, but Faerie has delights far beyond this spread." His wings folded closer to his back as he sank onto a stool. A necklace made from twisted silver and sapphire hung at his neck, just below a deep scar.

So I hadn't dreamt Wylda and Gabor's names. I darted them a glance. "You helped me in the forest."

The short sleeves of Wylda's dress revealed vines tattooed along the deep brown of her arms. "It was no trouble."

The bearded male called Loxley smirked. "Don't believe her, lass. They saved you, alright. In Faerie, shadows swirl like hungry spirits. Hounds with slithering tongues and skeletal frames hunt the scent of fear. Winged phantoms steal your sanity while you sleep. Duskweavers feed on despair as they pull you into—"

My heart thudded erratically in my chest as chuckles echoed around the table.

"Enough of the bedtime stories." The angles of Zephyr's face sharpened to a point as if they were sculpted ice. His lashes, impossibly dark and long, framed eyes glinting like the ocean under a darkening sky. "Eat, Ysadora, unless you want your flesh to fall from your bones."

"You'll have to excuse Loxley." Cyprian gave a crooked smile. "We don't often receive visitors."

The warmth of the dining hall closed in around me as the mercenaries took their cue from their sullen leader methodically eating. The clatter of cutlery against fine porcelain punctuated their conversation. Even though the mortal realm was within a few days' reach, it seemed time moved differently here; emotions held a different shape, and the rules of survival were written in a language I couldn't decipher. Every so often, their eyes flickered my way—subtle but unmistakable—and the sense that I was prey grew. They were listening, not that the mercenary leader deigned to speak with me. I caught his gaze, but he gave nothing away. There was only an unreadable flicker in his storm-cloud eyes. When he glared at my plate, I picked up my fork and took small bites of stew and golden vegetables and rich fruit that glooped on my tongue.

Every so often, I attempted to glean information. "Are Father and Maren at the Court of Nebulas?"

"He is elsewhere."

I thrust the rune under his nose. "What does it do? I want it gone. Please."

His face flashed with irritation and something softer:

regret. "It's woven into you now. That's not one I can remove."

I hissed in frustration. "I could have died if the Thorn King had discovered it."

His face hardened. "Or perhaps you would have died without it."

Only when I deviated from questions concerning me did he open up somewhat. "Tell me of him. What is the Thorn King?"

He sighed. "He didn't always look that way. He was ancient when I met him, but handsome still. The forest changes you. He was once the Faerie King of the Court of Bones. He was a fair ruler, but even kings are fallible. His most trusted advisor exposed his darkest secret. He had betrayed fae law to save his wayward mortal lover."

"Oh. What happened to her?"

The mercenary leader didn't answer. "After that, they stripped him of his crown and cast him into the Shrouded Forest. He's cursed to guard its borders and ensure mortals do not cross into Faerie. Truth is his obsession, as he failed to confront his own, but pain is an acceptable alternative."

"But they call him a king."

"It's a cruel echo of his former status. He forgot his own name long ago. Sometimes, someone reminds him. He was revered once. Now, his court is reduced to a single beetle bound by loyalty."

The quiet clink of knives and forks didn't drown out the hushed murmurs of the mercenaries' voices. I strained my ears to glean clues that could help me escape or find my family. I caught snatches of words, but they talked in riddles of serpents and grimoires and broken promises. I couldn't make head or tail of it. I needed to know how the power worked at Ebonspire and how I could manipulate it. Who was important, who was expendable and who could be persuaded to give me aid? Gnawing fear grew inside me with every bite of the roasted golden vegetables, their edges caramelised to a deep amber hue. When the mercenary leader's plate was clear, he sipped from a goblet of honey-coloured wine, waiting for me to finish. Only when I had swallowed my last morsel did he speak.

A charged tension took hold as though the mercenaries had been waiting for this very moment.

"There is chaos outside these walls, Ysadora, and I need to know if you will be a help or a hindrance." Zephyr's long fingers encircled the stem of his goblet. "What has your father told you of Faerie?"

My pulse thrummed in my throat. I blinked, trying to focus, but the world felt too vivid, as though the veil between my thoughts and the physical world had thinned. "He told me nothing. He kept me in the dark all my life."

The mercenary leader took the role of chief interrogator. "What is your father's name?"

I was on the verge of revealing everything: my fears, my desires, my secrets. The very things Maren and Father had spent years guarding. "I'm told it's Kazimir Silberquill."

Sequoia grinned at Gabor. "Whisperroot never fails to work."

A jolt of panic seized me. I had been so caught up in the games being played around me that I hadn't noticed the growing warmth in my chest and the faint dizziness swirling in my head. My eyes skittered to the vegetables with the sprinkling of herbs that Gabor had brought to the table. I had been too caught up in the tension of the room to notice that no one had touched it but me. I'd been foolish to let my guard slip, to think I could outwit them when I hadn't even realised the game had begun. They could probe me, unfurl all our secrets, make me say anything.

I turned accusing eyes on Cyprian, my throat constricted. "You said I was safe within these walls."

Hazel eyes softened in apology. "No harm is intended, but we cannot trust you. You were brought up in the mortal realm, where lies abound. We need the truth."

Humiliation washed over me as I scrambled for a way out, but my thoughts moved slowly as though through treacle. I bit my tongue, tasting blood, eyes darting for a decanter of water, salt, or anything to turn out the contents of my stomach.

Every tilt of Zephyr's head, every quirk of his lips emphasised how otherworldly he was. He slid his hand into his pocket and pulled out the soft leather pouch of seeds Maren had packed that I hadn't even realised was missing. "What did the calligrapher teach you about the Order of the Glyph?"

The truth was waiting to pour out of me and the weight of it was unbearable. I balled my fists under the table, nails scouring my palms. My tongue had a life of its own. "Heavenly skies, I hadn't even heard about that damn grouping until Maren mentioned it. I know nothing of Father's talents other than his mortal ones. Nothing of why he pretended we were something we weren't. Nothing of how he could make himself the centre of my world and simply disappear. He tainted the life we built together." My breath hitched, my eyes stung. The betrayal burned as if it had its own heat. "I believed every word he said, trusted every action. Why didn't he trust me? Why didn't he tell me the truth instead of turning me into a stranger in my own life? His secrets. His agendas. He didn't care how I felt about any of it. He didn't care that he involved my best friend in his lies."

Wylda sighed in Sequoia's direction. "I thought our parents were beyond contempt."

Zephyr's slate-blue eyes didn't leave my face. "He told you nothing about Faerie? The factions, the courts, the rules that bind it to the mortal realm?"

The words rose in my throat like water seeping through cracks. "I lived my whole life thinking I was safe in our little village, thinking the world beyond was small and manageable. I didn't even believe the old folk and their fears of spirits and ghouls, and who took…" A sob rose as I remembered Ferrith's little sister. "I didn't even know Faerie existed. And now I'm here, neck-deep in it, surrounded by things I can barely comprehend. But Father…he knew. All this time. He just let me walk into it blindly."

"There is nothing of use hidden in her mind." Loxley scratched his beard. "She's not even important enough to be a pawn, let alone a lever."

Anger flared, hot and sharp. I gripped the edge of the table as though it could anchor me to reality. "I'm not a pawn."

Zephyr held up a hand, watching me intently as if waiting for me to crack. "What is your magic?"

The instinct to free my dagger and hold it to his throat was overwhelming. I spat the words. "I have no magic."

He toyed idly with his gleaming silverware, his eyes like weathered steel. "Who is your mother?"

I frowned. "My mother is dead. My mother was taken. Her name is Danaë."

He considered me for a moment, then gave a mirthless laugh. "The woman you knew as Danaë Everreed is alive and well."

My chest felt too tight to breathe. My body went cold. "You're lying. She can't be…"

The mercenary leader's features were hard and unreadable. He didn't flinch. He didn't look away. "I assure you, it is true."

I stood, knocking my chair to the ground, and he stood with me. Her books were gone, but somehow, somehow Mother had survived that storm. Her books were gone, but maybe I could find her. Maybe we could meet, and we could have the conversations I had missed these years. She could hold me, and I could fill the void inside me. I met the mercenary leader's eyes, confused, not knowing whether he was a demon or a bringer of gifts. "She's in Faerie?"

There was cool distance in his eyes as he breached the space between us. "I will take you to her."

Emotions crashed over me: the pain of abandonment, the ache of being kept in the dark, the fear of the strange world around me. I couldn't trust him. He was wrong. Wrong about everything. Twenty orbits since Mother had died, and still, just the mention of her was enough to set me spinning. She'd never known me in adulthood and would never know how much I had learned and changed and achieved. Yet still, I found myself caught in the wreckage of grief, even as time pulled me further and further away from it. Though I was in Faerie, the world was smaller for the fact Mother wasn't in it.

He was wrong. I couldn't trust anyone here. As if by instinct, my fingers brushed against Father's quill tucked in my dark tresses, the cool weight of it grounding me. Without thinking, I slipped the quill from my hair, and my breathing slowed as I noticed how the crimson of Father's ink had congealed to obsidian black, and a few drops pooled in the channel of the nib as if they had patiently waited for my awakening.

My magic was instinctive as if it had slumbered in the marrow of my bones, ready to pour forth with the slightest breath of recognition, like finding an old journal with pages I had written but seemed to have always belonged to me.

I lifted the quill and swooped it in a circular motion through the air. The ink dripped in tiny, dark drops that splattered with a soft, melodic hiss against the stone. The room flickered, reality warping and bending as the ink danced in the air around me. The mercenaries faded into a blur of colours and sounds. Then, the air around me thickened as if the ink itself was alive. It spread, shifting, swirling, a ripple rising from the floor. The ink spread upward from my feet, curling around my legs, enveloping my torso, my shoulders, and my head.

The room stretched and pulsed, and I was already running before I made a conscious decision to escape.

I darted through the door into the darkened halls, ignoring the snatch of hands and muted shouts behind me. The ink was a shifting darkness, weightless and heavy at the same time. I felt the magic settle, felt a connection to it as if it would hide me, protect me. My fae limbs were strong enough, the thud of my boots fast enough to give me a chance of eluding my captors. My compass was already set in the direction of the Court of Nebulas—the home Maren had spoken so longingly of—where I could reunite with my family and learn the secrets of my heritage and my magic.

I ran upwards on spiral staircases that seemed to climb into the heavens, my cloak of ink around me.

Though I ran, for the first time in days, I felt a lightness of spirit.

11

ZEPHYR

Faerie is alive in a way the mortal realm isn't.
I'd give anything to see it.
—Danaë Everreed's annotations
in her Faerie books

He stood motionless, grey-blue eyes locked on the empty space where the calligrapher's daughter had been moments before. Even without the truth herb, he would have believed her answers for the raw emotion in her voice. She knew nothing of her heritage. That was why his lore magic had failed to unearth the truth of her full lineage: she didn't know it herself. She had been oblivious even to her own magic. That was, until she had taken Kazimir's quill, and her eyes—the colours of a twilight sky—had widened with innate knowledge.

That rune had caused more trouble than he realised.

Pushing her, triggering her, had been part of the plan, but this? He heaved a sigh. At least he had an answer to why the Binder, Thiago, and all the damn players in the entire realm were so interested in her.

Ysadora Silberquill wasn't just an inconvenience. She was a fucking liability.

He came back to his senses, his gaze sweeping over the thoughtful expressions of his companions. They'd weathered battles and storms together, too many to count, and fought their way across lands where no one else dared to go. Yet, in that fleeting moment when Ysadora had pulled her magic out of thin air, they, too, had been caught off guard.

"She's not a lamb waiting to be slaughtered, after all," said Loxley. "Impressive."

Gabor spooned a chunk of slow-roasted starshade plum into his mouth. "Yeah. That was raw, untamed magic."

Cyprian's arms were folded, his mouth set in a grim line. "Whatever you owe your uncle, you can't hand her over to Danaë."

Sequoia grimaced. "We don't have a choice. You shouldn't have told her like that, though, Zeph."

"Oh, I don't think she believed him," said Loxley.

"I like her." Wylda's lips tipped upwards.

Cyprian stilled. "Did you lock the dungeons?"

Loxley tossed him a set of keys. "Of course. What do you think I am?"

"She won't get far, bless her heart. Not in this place." Wylda rose. "I'll fetch her before she tires herself out."

Zephyr's gaze drifted towards the place where the calligrapher's daughter had stood. It was almost as if the air had taken on a heavier weight there–like the room held onto the lingering echo of her presence. She might not get far, but she had made a move, and that in itself had earned her a place in their world.

Cyprian laid a hand on his shoulder. "Zephyr? What are you thinking?"

He rose and snapped his gaze to Wylda. He sounded prickly, defensive. "I'll get her."

However unprepared she was, Ysadora could no longer return to the mortal realm.

Without waiting for a response, he strode out into the bowels of Ebonspire. His senses were honed to a razor's edge through close to a century of training, battle and magic. His ability to track was woven into the very fabric of Ebonspire's wards, bound to his shadows that clung to the stone walls and the vaulted ceilings of the ancient gatehouse. The wards were Ebonspire's first line of defence, attuned to anyone or anything that moved through them.

They were the reason why no one outside his inner circle had set foot in Ebonspire—until Ysadora.

It's not like he had any choice.

He closed his eyes, hands flexing as he absorbed the ambient energy of his home: the only true home he'd ever known. The currents wrapped around him like living threads. Ysadora's magic had left an imprint, faint but unmistakable. A scent. A ghost-like lingering presence. It thrilled him. After all, he was a hunter. He called his shadows, and they became his eyes in the darkness. They whispered to him, confiding to him where the pockets of energy shifted, where the shadows thickened.

Breathless night, she had been magnificent as the ink had cloaked her.

Witnessing her come into her magic was almost enough to shake him out of his world-weary ways. It flared so suddenly that it nearly pulled Zephyr out of the weight of his world-weariness. Almost.

He'd lived in the shadow of magic all of his life, but he'd never quite seen anything like hers. His hand tightened around the pouch of seeds in his pocket. He could have sworn from his understanding of history and lore that the calligraphers from the Order of the Glyph required more tools than a quill and congealed ink. By her own admission, Kazimir had taught his daughter nothing of the talents and rituals that made his brotherhood famed across Faerie and into royal circles in the mortal realm. His brow furrowed. She hadn't so much written her magic into reality as woven a new reality from splatters of ink. Then there was the fact she was female.

By the Order's own rules, it shouldn't have been possible.

But then, her magic wasn't polished or calculated. It wasn't the result of years of training or the staid practices of the brotherhood, tried and tested over time. It had called out to him in some primal way. It was hard to ignore the ripple she had caused. The kind of ripple that could change everything. For a split second, a flicker of hope stirred in him, long buried under the decades of battle-hardened cynicism.

He shoved the feeling down.

Zephyr couldn't afford hope. Not now. Not ever. The reality in Faerie was that power was as much a curse as it was a blessing. Her awakening would only draw more eyes and more enemies. Besides, he was too weary, too worn by the weight of Faerie's endless struggles, to let himself believe in anything or anyone.

Eyes still squeezed shut, he probed further through the wards. He sensed a flicker of change, a pulse of energy that wasn't quite right, where her magic skittered along stone floors at that very moment. He could tell from its ebb and flow that she tired already. New magic was tricky like that.

A smile played on Zephyr's sensual lips as he opened his eyes. His entire being was attuned to her now. He sensed the faintest sounds: her masked footsteps, the brush of fabric against stone, the soft inhalation of her breath, her jerking heartbeat. Her presence was a storm in his bones, keener than the hundreds of times he had done this before. The more he leaned into his magic, the clearer the picture became. He saw her dark hair, the determination in her amethyst eyes, and her parted lips as she ran.

She was brave. Maybe even clever. He had expected her to take the stairs downwards, but she wasn't far from the cliff-hewn door, not that it would open for her even if she reached it.

His hands brushed against the cool walls as he moved. Then he let his shadows take him, giving himself up to innate magic just as she had done so he could catch the female who had turned Faerie upside down.

12

YSADORA

Not all bargains are malevolent,
but all come with a price.
—Danaë Everreed's annotations
in her Faerie books

My thighs burned, and sweat slicked my skin as I climbed ever upwards in a dizzying twist, but I didn't dare stop. There was something unnatural about Ebonspire. Shadows whispered against the stones, closing in on me like pools of living night.

From the inside, the ink cloak was like stepping into a twilight world, where everything was muted, casting faint ripples across my vision. The world beyond was hazy; the edges of objects blurred as if they had been painted in watercolours. My magic exhilarated and terrified me—as though I had stepped onto the pages of one of the fanciful tales in the bookshop—but I had no idea how to bend it to my will. The black tendrils of my cloak of ink already unravelled. I veered around a corner in glimmering torchlight, my hand skimming the bannister for balance, and slipped on smooth stone.

Skies, I was exhausted.

The ink cloak flickered once before dissolving completely. Panic rising, I stopped short, yanked the dagger from my boot and slashed a slit up my gown to aid movement. Then I dug deep and continued at an unrelenting pace that made me grateful for all the years Father prodded me to train a little harder, a little longer. That made me miss the arrogant tilt of Maren's head when she taunted me into one more jab with the training sword, one more leap on the apparatus. I missed them so much.

Roughly midway, the stairwell narrowed around me like a coiled serpent as though I was trapped within the very carcass of Ebonspire. Instinct and desperation made me stagger forward. The space opened up, and there it was.

A door grander than the others.

Wild hope surged in me. The door jutted out from the wall, seemingly forged directly from the cliff face. I approached it, the shadows an icy breath on the back of my neck. Rusted iron bands crisscrossed its surface, etched with runes that warned of old magic. A small crack of moonlight trickled around the door like a thin ribbon of silver, teasing me with the promise of the open sky just beyond. Through it, I could smell the night air: fresh and cold, with a hint of salt from the sea. The distant boom of wild waves called me, as dangerous as the shadows at my back.

I had to be fast. I had to secure my escape.

I lunged for the door, but there was no handle. I threw

my full body weight against it, but it didn't budge. I kicked the base of the door over and over, the plum fabric of my gown clinging to my damp skin. But the door didn't groan or creak. It gave no indication that my efforts had brought anything at all. My panting filled the hollow silence as I prised my fingers into the cracks around the door and clawed at the edges, uncaring that my nails bent and the tender skin tore.

My intuition flared. The mercenary leader was coming. I could sense his storm-cold eyes. "Please. Please. Open for me."

My fingers traced the strange carvings, searching for a hidden mechanism or some way through. But it was useless. The door's magic was beyond my ability to break. Chest heaving, I pressed my forehead to the cold rock. The fresh air seeping through the cracks tormented me.

Freedom was inches away.

It wasn't fair. It wasn't fair to come this far and be caught in the net of the mercenaries again. My skin prickled as I turned, knowing I wasn't alone. My breath quickened as shadows slithered up from the floor, dark tethers wrapping around my waist, almost like an embrace. Every part of me rebelled against them.

The mercenary leader emerged from the gloom like a phantom, his tall frame cutting an imposing figure against the torchlight. His grey-blue eyes locked onto mine. "It's too late to run, Ysadora."

My heart hammered against my ribs as the shadows tightened around my waist, leaving no doubt they belonged to him. Knuckles white on the hilt of my dagger, I squared my shoulders. "Let me go."

He gave a tight nod, and his shadows retreated to the edges of the room, where they lurked.

With more instinct than thought, I sprinted for him, blood roaring in my ears. I aimed the blade low, aiming for his thigh, wondering wildly if fae could bleed, if I could wound him as I would a mortal. If his blood might unseal the door.

The mercenary leader shifted. He was calm, fluid, his stance unbothered by me, and my anger spiked.

He sidestepped me easily, his hand a blur as he caught my wrist mid-strike, jerking my momentum to a halt. Before I could blink, he twisted my wrist, a sharp pressure that forced my fingers open. I stumbled against the warmth of him, my dagger clattering uselessly to the floor as if he were scolding a child. "Like a fawn challenging a wolf."

I was close enough to feel the heat of him, to smell the honey wine on his breath, and the sandalwood and sage in his freshly washed hair. I had easily bested the village boys, but this male made me feel frustratingly small. The humiliation of it stung deeper than any wound. I yanked my arm back, fury boiling beneath my skin. The loss of contact was jarring.

His gaze flicked to the fallen dagger. "Pick it up. You won't get a second chance."

Magic pulsed in my veins like a live current, faint but there all the same. It would take me the briefest moment to pull the quill from my hair. But the mercenary leader's eyes gleamed like he could tell how hollow my bones felt. As though he was certain that if I tried, I would fail. And where would I go in this forsaken place, where he wouldn't find me and drag me back to the stone room? I would only expose myself more if I tried and failed again.

Eyes narrowed, I scooped up the blade. Following his orders was a bitter pill to swallow.

I would gut him from navel to groin when the time came. For all his arrogance, I would carve out a way to escape him, to hurt him, to make him regret crossing paths with me. But not tonight.

"Good. Now, listen." Zephyr's tone was almost weary. "I can't let you go, Ysadora. But I will. When you're ready. There are things waiting for you outside these walls that will tear you apart. And not all of them are as patient as I am."

I hated the part of me that believed him. Hated the quiet voice in me that questioned whether Father and Maren were alive. The whisper that told me I needed the mercenaries' help. I frowned. "You want me to survive Faerie? What's in it for you?"

Steel flashed in his gaze. "Never mind that. Are you prepared to follow my lead over your own instincts?"

Pride flared up in me like a flame. *No*, I wanted to scream. *No way in hell.* All my life, I thought I'd been in control of my fate, but here was someone else treating me like a puppet on a string, taking away my choices. I rubbed my temple, trying to find a way out. As always, when I needed comfort, Mother's books came back to me. I thought of the warnings and cautionary tales in them, passages underlined in her elegant hand as if she knew one day I'd need them. Passages about fae bargains. Bargains, I remembered, were the heartbeat of faerie deals, more binding than any law in the mortal realm: a promise given for a promise returned, but always at a price.

I shook my head as the mercenary leader watched me. But they were just stories. I couldn't base my decisions on stories. Not when a whole new world had formed around me, where shadows moved independently of light sources, males had wings of eternal night, and my best friend could summon flame in her palms.

Not when ink had responded to my turmoil and risen around me like a veil.

But I couldn't let Zephyr have all the control. I wouldn't allow that.

My goals were as important as his. "A bargain then. A temporary alliance."

His lips curved like a warning cloaked in charm. "You wish to bargain with me?"

I swallowed hard. Father had raised an independent daughter. I had negotiated agreements with sources and courtesans in the book trade. I had to have faith that, though the stakes were higher, I could hold my own. "I do."

"Be careful, Inkheart. Bargains are a tangling of destinies I'm not sure you are ready for."

He wielded the nickname like a claim. A flicker of warmth ignited in my chest, uninvited and unwelcome.

I hated that he made me feel anything at all.

I weighed my words carefully. "I will remain with you for a brief time. Directly afterwards, you will escort me to where my family is held. For all the time I am in your *care*, until the point at which I reunite with my family, you will guarantee my safety."

Zephyr's predatory smile deepened, and a lone dimple studded one cheek. "You must choose one. Your Father and your friend are not together."

I bit my lip, guilt flaring. Maren had said she would find me. "Father. I choose Father."

He opened his mouth to speak.

"Wait. I'm not finished. I will specify the amount of time that is written into the bargain." My mind whirred. The number three appeared in ancient symbols, the oldest stories, and the very laws of the universe. Three questions, three trials, three promises made. Three fairy godmothers. The maiden, mother and crone. The three Fates. Even life was written in threes: birth, growth, and death. Past, present and future. The number had a sense of symmetry that was impossible to ignore. Maybe, in a world of magic, it would be lucky for me. "Three days."

He toyed with the cuff of his sleeve as though he had all the time in the world. His shadows stirred at the walls. "No."

I tried not to flinch. "No?"

His velvet voice was smooth and controlled. "Nine days."

I seesawed between relief that he'd not outright refused me and despair that I would be trapped at Ebonspire with him for that stretch. That I'd be separated from Father and Maren for so long. But they were of Faerie, and I was not. It would have to be enough. I bit my lip. "Fine. But you must never speak to me of my mother ever again." Even now, bile rose in my throat at how he had rummaged around in old wounds.

His storm-cloud eyes frosted as he inclined his head. Wavy hair flopped forward into his eyes, but he made no move to push it back. "As you wish… You'd agree to a bargain without knowing its cost?"

Unease mushroomed in me as the threads of his web

pulled tighter around me. Perhaps it would have been better to be taken by the Thorn King or his beetle. "Name your price."

I could almost see the gears turning in his mind. "You must trust me completely in our nine days together."

My pulse quickened at the mere thought of it. Mercenaries weren't fair. They craved power. I imagined how he might use my trust against me: binding my magic to his will, demanding a personal sacrifice, locking me into a game that was not of my choosing. Or worse. With his slinking shadows and expression of cruel detachment, Zephyr was far more dangerous than any storybook fae. I shook my head. "That's too high."

Sharp teeth glinted as his shadows snaked around me, darker, almost vibrating, as if reacting to his emotions. "You're my captive. I'm in no rush to bargain."

"Why should I trust you? You killed Lunarys."

"Would you believe me if I told you she asked me to?"

"Right after I sprout wings." Slow fury bubbled in me. "If you want me to trust you, tell me all your secrets. Show me proof that what you say is true. Hold nothing back. Convince me that I can trust you."

He stalked forward, hands flexing like he wanted to grasp my arms and shake sense into me. Instead, he stopped short, forcing me to look up into his face, and bit out the words, "Trust doesn't work like that. Besides, I'm not asking for mere trust. I'm asking for unconditional trust."

Defiance poured out of me. "No."

Shadows darted across his face. "Right now, Inkheart, you have no fucking choice."

He thrust his hand into the space between us as if he

were offering me a lifeline and a trap all at once. I studied his palm for a moment, then grasped it. It dwarfed mine, our connection immediate and electric. The shadows around us thickened, and I tried to stay calm, tried not to give into the temptation to jerk away, to flee and bite and mewl like a cornered animal. Heat radiated as our fingers entwined, a pulse of raw magic, as though a binding tied us together in an unseen knot. And it seemed impossible to me that I could be so far from Larkspur, so far from Father and Maren and Ferrith.

That I could be here with him. With a fae male—a killer —who held such power over me.

But maybe now I held it over him, too.

Magic and shadows swirled around us, and I gasped at a burn behind my left ear. Gasped as a mark appeared just beneath the mercenary leader's collarbone that I knew was replicated on my own skin: bold, interlocking triangles with a solid circle where the lines converged, like the eye of a storm.

A mark neither of us could escape until the bargain was done.

Ebonspire came into sharp focus: the cold stone walls, the flickering lanterns, the scent of moss and sea salt and the late hour. Magic buzzed faintly in my veins, and my limbs felt heavy as if every muscle had been stretched to its limit and left to hang like a wet cloth. A dull, fatigued ache pulsed through my body.

"Should I escort you back to your room?" he said stiffly.

I couldn't bear another moment in his company. "That is not necessary. Unless you wish to lock me in."

"No need." Calloused fingers brushed over my gouged

nail beds from my attempt to open the cliff door. "I'll send a healer."

Before I could respond, he backed away, fluid and silent like a shadow retreating into the darkness. When he reached the stairwell, his storm-cloud eyes flicked back to me, focusing on the jagged tear in my sweat-drenched gown, my legs peeking through the hurriedly made opening.

His voice carried an edge of something I couldn't place: perhaps regret or yearning. "That garment belonged to my sister." Then he turned away, his footsteps receding down the stairwell. "We train at sunrise. Be ready."

Trembling, all alone, I wondered if the remaining shadows belonged to him. I traced the tender skin behind my ear with careful fingers. The second mark he'd put on this strange new body of mine. The rune behind my ear was still warm to the touch, my skin too tight. And yet, how hard could it be to trust a stranger for nine days? Maybe I was wise enough—thanks to Mother's books—to survive this. After all, I had wrangled some control back, if not my freedom. The mercenary leader would escort me to Father and guarantee my safety.

Then why did it feel like I was in free fall, like the meteor that Maren and I had found in the forest?

13

KAZIMIR

Heartthorn Briar
A vine with heart-shaped thorns. Often found
where faerie love rituals have taken place.
Properties: thorns are used in love spells, either to
bind two hearts or, in darker uses,
to sever bonds.
—A Compendium of Faerie Flora and Terrain

The world shifted around Kazimir as the portal flared in a burst of swirling indigo and spat him out in Echohold, Thiago's seat in the Court of Silence. He slumped at the faerie king's feet until the spymaster gave a dismissive flick of his wrist, unravelling the bonds over Kazimir's mouth. The faerie king's footsteps stalked away across the flagstone floor without a backward glance. Kazimir lay prone, spewing bile, inhaling hard and trying not to vomit. Compared to dragons, portals were a crude form of travel that his stomach tolerated poorly. He fought to compose himself and heaved himself up, blinking to clear his swimming vision.

That's when he saw Danaë.

The woman who had once pieced his heart back together and then ground it into shards.

She stood with her back to him at the far end of a banquet room framed by the silver light pouring in through an arched window. Her fingers gripped the stone sill as if consumed by worry. For a moment, he remembered the woman he had known: a natural beauty whose windblown mane of honey-blonde hair fell past her shoulders, which was always tied with ribbons, who looked so pretty in modest blouses in shades of rose, and who favoured soft linen skirts in delicate florals that twirled in time to music.

He remembered how Danaë sank her nose into the crisp freshness of sheets from the laundry line, how she over-salted soups and thirst for knowledge about Faerie sometimes scared him. How she gathered tulips with Ysa and sang lullabies to her, and most of all, how her golden hair caught the sun as she sang ballads in the village square, her voice as sweet as the wind through the trees. How her voice held a lightness that eased the most calcified heart. Even his own.

Then she had left, and bitterness had almost cleaved Kazimir in two.

He had pulled himself back together, eventually. For Ysadora.

And the tower of lies he had built had grown taller.

All that passed through his mind in an instant as Thiago crossed the floor and laid a proprietary hand on the small of his wife's back. Then Danaë spun slowly and gave a soft command to two snow leopards he hadn't noticed, curled at either side of the arched window. She moved towards him with the grace of a queen.

Kazimir stared back at her, dumbstruck. The first inkling of her change was that she hadn't aged a day in twenty orbits. He noted no signs of mortal decay: her back was not curled like a question mark, no lines marred her perfect mouth, no grey threaded her hair. His former wife's once brown eyes were now an unearthly gold. She wore a sleek silver-grey dress adorned with delicate filigree reminiscent of frost-covered branches. Her lips, once pink and curved as if always on the edge of song, were a polished crimson. Her thick blonde hair was twisted into an elaborate braid around her head that left the pointed tips of her ears plain to see. Her beauty was as cold and untouchable as a distant planet. She was no longer the woman whose head had rested on the pillow next to his. She was the ghost of someone he used to know.

He felt a sharp tug of longing and loss as she halted before him, and their eyes met.

Stars, the tight fury there. It hit him like a punch to the gut.

Danaë broke their eye contact and whirled to the faerie king. There was no mistaking the sharp edge in her voice when she spoke. "Did you have to treat him so roughly?"

"He's breathing, isn't he?" said Thiago coldly.

Thiago had won her affection and her allegiance, but Kazimir thought that perhaps Danaë still cared for him. She turned her back on her husband with such self-possession that Kazimir realised she had not only survived

Faerie, she had thrived. She was a head shorter than him, even in heels, but the power was hers. "What in all the realms did he do to you?"

Her words cut through the fog in his head. He glanced down at himself: at the torn, dirty tunic, the blood that hadn't yet dried, his fingernails caked with mud and snow. Shame curled in his gut. Speaking was a wrench, as though the mouth bindings had not yet fully dissolved. "I imagine I resisted."

The faerie king snorted. "Hardly. A youngling could have brought him in."

Danaë frowned at the bloodied mess where Kazimir's head had struck the memory stone. She reached out a hand but then stopped herself just short of touching him. "Is this how you keep your promises, Thiago?"

Her husband responded with cool indifference. "You should count yourself lucky that I agreed for him to stay under this roof, even if it is under lock and key. What male would allow his wife's former lover to breathe the same air as her?"

The tension in the room thickened. "Send a healer."

"Fine. But understand this, wife…he's a guest here on my terms. And those terms are far from friendly." The faerie king nodded at four guards at the exit to the banquet room. Only when they took up formation close to Danaë and Kazimir did Thiago twist the ornate door handle with a hand gloved in black leather. "I will see you presently in our chambers, wife." Then he melted into the shadows in the dim corridor beyond.

Kazimir had never completely unravelled the story of their parting. He'd always thought that she could soothe even the fiercest storm with her song, but her voice hadn't quelled the storm the night she had left. It was almost as though she had beckoned it, calling Thiago from across the vast distance from Faerie. When the storm came, she had let it take her, willingly, her hand in the faerie king's. Kazimir had never determined whether theirs was a true love or whether the old spymaster had stumbled upon him by chance, with Danaë a prize he simply happened upon and decided to keep.

A prize to buy the faerie king's silence about his whereabouts.

Kazimir could barely manage a smile through the pain, but he forced it anyway. "Danaë, I—"

"Don't." Her strange gaze snapped back to him. "Don't speak."

His words dried up in his throat. When they were married, her anger had been like fire: something to be endured. This was different. It was cold and sharp.

The healer came in then, a frost dryad with polar skin, icy hair and lips tinged a delicate blue. She bustled past Danaë with a bow and urged Kazimir to sit on a chair before kneeling before him. Faint snowflakes fell from her skin, and she exhaled wintry breath despite the spring. The dryad's hands left a trail of frosty mist as she sealed his cuts and soothed his bruises. She wore no clothes, and he averted his eyes as she healed him, choosing instead to watch Danaë, who stood just out of reach, arms crossed tightly over her chest. Disgust warped her beautiful features as though everything about him screamed of a world she had left behind and had never mourned. When the dryad reached for the wound on his head, Kazimir shrank back from her touch, but she held him like a vice. She formed crystalline structures from her fingertips, pressing icy lattices to his injury that knitted his skin together and siphoned out what remained of the Binder's elixir.

His strength had almost returned by the time she had finished. The human glamour had fused so tightly with him that even with a healer, it would take a few hours for the effects to dissipate. But he didn't want Danaë to see his withered mortal self. He didn't want her to see the ravages of age and the fragility of this frame, more decrepit even than the husband she had abandoned all those orbits ago. He wanted her to see him as a strong fae male for no other reason than his dignity. He tried to stand up, but Danaë shook her head, holding his gaze as the healer retreated from the room with skittish, fawn-like steps.

She sighed. "You always did make the smallest paper cut seem like a battle wound."

Kazimir's eyes roamed her face, her pointed ears, the regal stance of her posture. "How?"

He didn't need to expand. She'd been expecting this question. "Faerie is full of limitless possibilities. Of all the betrayals in our marriage, it was that one that stung. You hid all the biggest secrets of this world from me. You fed me faerie stories. You didn't even feed me your real name. Thiago loves me. *He* made me fae."

Kazimir recoiled from the venom in her voice. How could he explain to her that the spymaster had access to all the information in Faerie? That Kazimir himself was a simple male: someone who loved ink and words and who had operated in silos. That he wouldn't even have fathomed making her fae when she had been utterly perfect as a mortal. That he hadn't meant to hurt her or disappoint her or even to pretend to Ysa that her mother was dead.

Skies above, he was tired. "Why did you bring me here?"

Danaë gave a sad smile. "Because you are the calligrapher, and everything is falling apart."

"Your faerie king is chasing Ysadora. He means to capture her. If you ever loved her—"

"How dare you?" A tempest rose within her, and her snow leopards growled. "Thiago is your king now."

14

YSADORA

Firevein
Fiery-hued petals with glowing orange veins.
Properties: sap creates ink that burns words onto
parchment, stone and other surfaces.
The ink binds itself to the writer's intent, making
it nearly impossible to alter once written.
—A Compendium of Faerie Flora and Terrain

I spent a fretful night in my chambers after Wylda healed my torn fingers. Each day I was separated from Father hit harder. Until the day he was taken, there hadn't been one day we had been apart. What a fool I'd been to pledge my unconditional trust to the mercenary leader for nine whole days when every second under this roof felt like a lifetime. When sunrise came, I was dressed in loose clothing, with my hair in a bun at my nape, ready to battle him.

But when the door opened, Cyprian stood there instead.

Cyprian wore a light shirt designed to wick away sweat and trousers reinforced at the knees. He gripped two swords in one hand and a bread roll filled with meat in the other. "Come on, eat up. I'm supposed to put you through your paces."

I brushed off the slight dip of my heart at the unexpected change. I would have to wait a little longer to put my blade to Zephyr's throat. "Fine." Mother's books had warned against ever thanking the fae, in case of triggering a debt owed, obedience or servitude. So I bit down on my instinct to say thank you and nodded in appreciation instead when he offered me the roll.

His hazel eyes gleamed as he waited for me to eat, lips curving at my obvious pleasure. Then he pulled a pot of vibrant coral ink from his pocket. "We had some in our stores. Zeph thought it would be a good idea for you to try some out. Bring the quill. Let's see what you can do."

I swallowed the last mouthful, my heart jumping to a fierce rhythm at the thought of exploring my magic. "Already ahead of you." I had no intention of letting the quill out of my sight. I pointed at the crimson feather tucked into the coil of my bun and held out my hand for a sword. He gave me the smaller one without hesitation, and I fell into step with him.

I snuck him a glance, wondering whether he commanded shadows like Zephyr or ink like me.

Wondering if I should fear him, though his presence didn't raise my hackles as Zephyr's did.

We walked the twisting, darkened hallways and spiralling steps. I tested the weight of my sword, eager to work out the tight knots of my anxiety during training and to try out the limits of my body, unchained from the effects of Lunarys's elixir. I maintained my bearings while Cyprian made idle conversation. Every archway, every flight of stairs, and every dent in the wall was a piece of a puzzle I mentally mapped to aid a possible escape.

The early morning light spilt through a window, tracing the high ridges of his cheekbones and the smooth planes of his dark skin. "That was quite a display yesterday. We're a tough, weathered bunch, and yet you surprised us."

I let out a soft laugh. "It's always a pleasure to exceed low expectations."

"I'll have to keep my guard up when we spar." He paused. "Have you done that before with the ink?"

The sharp tip of the quill rested against my scalp, daring me to believe. "Not unless you count how many times I've ruined perfectly good parchment." I eyed him with open curiosity. "My turn. How long have you lived here?"

He ran a loving hand along the pocked walls. "Ebonspire was once partially collapsed, but we rebuilt it. It's more than a base for someone like me. It's a home." Something about his uncomplicated, amiable manner reminded me of Ferrith.

I felt a pang of loss for my friends and shook my head to untangle my thoughts. "This isn't a home. A home isn't just walls and stone. A home has warmth. It has books you can lose yourself in, with pages that smell like the past and words that make you feel. It has soft blankets you can wrap yourself in when the world feels harsh. Blankets that smell of home, of safety. It has portraits of loved ones on the walls, familiar food in the cupboard and your favourite shoes in the hallway. A home has keepsakes that remind you of where you've been and who you've known. A trinket. A scarf knitted by a friend. Even if they're just sitting there, gathering dust." I gripped the hilt of the sword tighter, my words becoming more personal, unravelling the essence of what I longed for. "A home gives you the freedom to come and go as you please. And real laughter. Not the kind that echoes through empty halls. The kind that makes the walls feel like they're breathing with you like they're part of the family. A home has neighbours who visit with fresh bread or a jug of mead just because. It has the hum of other people living around you. The clink of dishes as someone next door sets their table for supper, the murmur of voices in the street, the rumble of a cart on cobblestone roads. So that you know you're not alone but included in the rhythm of the world. Ebonspire isn't that."

"It is for me," said Cyprian quietly. "It is for the rest of our group."

My lips curved into a bitter smile. "Well, it's just a stopover for me. In nine days, I'll be gone."

We approached a door hidden in plain sight. It blended with its surroundings, crafted to resemble a smooth stone wall, but when I looked closer, faint etchings of symbols ran along a central seam. Cyprian held his forearm to the stone, pressing a rune depicting a scroll with curled edges against it. The door unfolded outwards like a pair of wings, the seam parting down the middle, and cool air swept over me, crisp against my skin. The first sunrays brushed across the horizon.

I stepped over the threshold, turned my face to the light, and inhaled deep and long.

It had been three days since I had been outside. Since Father and Maren had been taken.

Then I lifted my gaze, and the vast expanse north of Ebonspire unfurled like a canvas. The land stretched out in uneven patches of rugged terrain, sparse vegetation, and the occasional twisted tree clawing at the rosy, blue sky. The wind whispered through long grasses. The outer boundary was shrouded in deep shadows. It felt desolate as if the world itself had chosen to forget this place, these mercenaries.

As I turned, Ebonspire itself recaptured my attention, and I understood its name at last. It loomed in full view, towering over me. A spire rose dramatically at its centre, and moss crept over its walls. Its weathered structure hinted at battles long past. The gatehouse seemed almost an extension of the land itself, blending with the craggy contours of the rocky cliff. Despite the amber glow of the morning sun, Ebonspire shrouded itself in shadows. The growing light revealed every detail: the worn, blackened stone, the unforgiving angles, how half the building was buried beneath the earth.

I wondered, not for the first time, whether anything *other* occupied the spaces I had not explored. If the mercenaries lived simply, content amongst themselves, or if unseen household staff wandered the halls of the gatehouse, if they brought back wenches to satisfy their physical needs, or shady dealmakers to line their pockets with coin.

Cyprian opened the ink pot and set it on a tuft of grass. His eyes were focused yet playful. "Are you ready? Here are the ground rules. We spar, you avoid smashing the pot and touching the blade to my throat, and we both get to put our feet up for the rest of the morning."

I gave the ink pot a wide berth and set my stance. "Sounds easy enough."

He rolled his shoulders, craning his neck with a satisfying pop, then motioned at me to begin.

My heart hammered, not from fear but from the gnawing need to prove that I could survive without my protectors. That I would be worthy of winning my family back.

We circled each other, the ink pot on the ground between us like an anchor, small but impossible to ignore. Cyprian's eyes locked on mine without a hint of malice as if to assure me that this was training, not battle. But my weapon was no training sword: it was forged for war, finer than any blade Maren or I had practised with. Its sharpened, oiled edge gleamed in the dawn light.

I struck first, my pulse elevated, my mind whirring. I danced around the ink pot, accounting for its placement with every step, every swing. My fae body felt like a song. I was faster, but it was more than that. My reflexes were sharper, every muscle was taut with the potential for speed. I could arch my back and stretch my limbs further. I could jump higher and strike harder. My stamina had increased.

But my physical improvements gave me no advantage over Cyprian who was taller than I and stronger still, and who had learned the nuances of his own body for over a century. His posture was fluid, almost casual, feet positioned in a manner that suggested he could move in any direction at a second's notice. I marvelled at how his braid swung behind him with every pivot, how he barely broke a sweat. His body flowed like water, unfurling as he twisted and turned, his sword arm flashing out at opportune moments. Maren and I had trained, yes, but her build was similar to my own, and Cyprian was something else altogether. There was a quiet strength in his build that wasn't ostentatious, the kind that comes from discipline and strategy rather than brute strength. So, I began watching for flaws in his form.

The world narrowed to just the two of us. His strikes were fast, but I could tell he was holding back, even as the rhythm of our sparring quickened and our breathing deepened. I liked him in spite of myself, even though I was an unwilling guest at Ebonspire. He was intuitive, patient, and never condescending.

My brow glistened with perspiration, but I pressed forward, my feet quick and light on the ground. He watched every movement like a hawk, and I reciprocated with interest. His left foot was slightly more turned out than his right, and I thought I could perhaps use his balance against him.

Bending my knees, I dropped low, slid to the side, and sliced my sword through the air in a sweeping arc aimed at his legs. He blocked me and lunged a moment later, slicing a triangle from the bottom of my tunic in retribution, his eyes flashing with mischief.

"You're hesitating. Commit or don't strike at all. Faerie doesn't give second chances."

I ducked, sweat dampening my tunic, redirecting my blade in a sharp arc aimed at his unprotected shoulder. "So I've heard."

He rolled out of my reach with unfathomable agility,

then came in close, his hazel-gold eyes sharp. "You want to know how we survive? We adapt. Quickly."

"That's what this outfit is? Living mission to mission, for coin…" I feinted to the left, then the right, and almost struck him true. "Then why are you helping me? Why not just let me go and make my own way?"

He gave an exasperated sigh. "Because we don't do things like that here."

My blade cut through the air, probing not only for weaknesses but information. I wanted to get a sense of how the mercenaries operated. How they thought. "What's your cause, Cyprian? Tell me what I'm missing."

"You're as tenacious as he is." He dodged my next swing. "We don't have a cause. We have a contract."

I frowned, coming at him with more force this time, testing my strength. "With whom?"

"By the slumbering sky, I think I might turn you out myself." He glared at me. "All you need to know is that we don't take on any mission. We're in the protection game. But at a cost."

"I have no coin." That was what I didn't understand. That's what made me unwilling to trust them despite the bargain I had made with Zephyr. They hadn't told me the full story, and I was sick of lies.

"Who said the cost was to you?" He grazed my arm with a mere whisper of his blade and shrugged in apology at the thin line of blood that bloomed there. "Now focus, dammit."

Our barbed remarks slipped into silence as we both focused on our footwork, our weaponry, on reading each other's flaws. How long did we spar? An hour? More? All was quiet apart from the whip of the wind as it rattled the high stones of the gatehouse, the muted rhythm of our feet on packed dirt, and the clang of steel. Cyprian smirked, always one step ahead, and I began to realise we wouldn't be finishing anytime soon. On we sparred until my muscles ached and white spots entered my vision. Bruises formed on my body from repeated falls, the impact absorbed by the mossy ground.

"Again," said Cyprian. "Again."

It didn't make sense that he was always ahead, however hard I tried. There was a fraction of a second in time when it was as though he almost anticipated what movement I'd attempt before I had envisaged it.

I needed to regroup. "Teach me how to best you."

"You give up? The others are taking bets on how long you'll last." He pointed behind me.

I spun around, attention snapping to the group of figures at a high window. The early sun cast a muted radiance, illuminating the edges of their forms without revealing their faces. The quiet weight of their attention made me feel exposed. My steps faltered for an instant. "No. I'm not giving up. Teach me how to win."

Cyprian lowered his sword. "You play by the rules. Good for you."

I glowered at him. "Wasn't that what you wanted?"

He shrugged. "The rules of Faerie are meant to be broken, more often than not, slyly. Ours isn't a world of moral blacks and whites. You need to use every advantage on the field, every ounce of magic."

"Then let's go again." But I was too daunted to use the quill, too ashamed of failure under their scrutiny.

Our exchange faded once more into a rhythm of breath and motion, the clang of steel ringing through the air, mingling with morning birdsong and, somewhere, the thunder of hooves. Cyprian's braids whipped behind him like they marked the space he occupied. He feinted left, forcing me to adjust, and when I pulled Maren's dagger from my waistband, he whooped with glee, though he avoided my thrust as easily as a child batting away a ball.

"That's more like it, Ysadora. The game is always growing, always changing. Bending the rules is how you stay alive." He stared past me into the distance, stiffening. "That's all for now. Well fought."

Unease stirred in my chest as I followed his gaze.

A lone figure approached on horseback, cutting a stark silhouette against the bleak landscape. The rider sat slumped slightly forward, clearly weary, a sea of shadows stretched out behind him. His cloak billowed, and a gust swept his dark hair into his face. The horse beneath him moved with steady purpose, its flanks glistening with sweat and its hooves kicking up tiny clouds of dirt with each step. As he drew nearer, the details became clearer. His leathers were torn, covered in dirt and ash, and blood trailed across his cheek and neck. Bloodied but unbowed, the brutal evidence of violence clung to him like a second skin.

My heart faltered, suspended in a brief, breathless pause.

The mercenary leader was home.

15

YSADORA

Shadebloom
A small, midnight-black flower that only opens
under the new moon.
Properties: The nectar makes ink that only reveals
itself in starlight or moonlight. Notoriously
difficult to cultivate, thriving only in areas where
fae magic is strong. Can react to strong emotions.
—A Compendium of Faerie Flora and Terrain

The mercenary leader swung his leg over the saddle and slid down from his inky stallion. I longed to retreat inside Ebonspire and sink into a hot bath, but it was unlikely that the gatehouse would allow me to reenter without an escort. So I watched. He ran a gentle hand over the horse's neck and retrieved a waterskin from the saddlebag. The stallion nudged him, and the mercenary leader stroked him again. Only when the horse wandered off to graze did Zephyr glance across the terrain.

The sun caught the crossed blades on his back as his gaze skirted past Cyprian, jogging out to greet him. Our eyes locked, and I stood a little straighter, holding his stare with a boldness I hadn't intended. His lips pressed together before his focus shifted back to Cyprian. I stood, transfixed by the sense of a dark secret unspooling and read their body language as if they were parchment. The wind carried their hushed voices directly to me.

"I told you I should have gone with you."

Zephyr sighed. "I'm okay. The blood's not mine."

"I thought the plan was to bring it back?"

"I tried. They're getting more powerful." A pause. "I had to burn it."

Cyprian breath's hitched. "Skies, I'm sorry. Did you collect its story?"

The mercenary leader didn't answer.

"Let me help. Talk to me."

"Later… How was training?"

"She worked hard. She's no novice. She can fight, but her choices are too mortal."

"I'll take it from here."

"She's tired."

My ears burned. I wasn't sure who he was protecting: me or his friend.

"A few minutes more won't hurt. Or did you forget my uncle is chomping at the bit?"

"You're a brute."

"Not when it counts. Or I would have turfed the lot of you out."

Cyprian laughed. "There is that. One more thing. She's avoiding magic use."

"We'll have to change that."

He squeezed Zephyr's arm. "Out there…it wasn't your fault. Whatever's going on is unnatural. It's bigger than any of us."

The mercenary leader gave a sharp nod, then strode towards me. I studied my blade, feigning disinterest, looking up only when inches separated us. He looked like a male who had just returned from the edges of the world. The rawness of his appearance unnerved me: blood, dishevelled hair, torn clothing, his stubble-lined jaw. They made him more vulnerable. But it was impossible to empathise with a male of such unpredictable moods, who had rescued me and imprisoned me, who had branded me with runes, lied about my dead mother and yet agreed to a bargain that might help me accomplish my goals in Faerie. A male who, even in his current state, posed a coiled danger.

The expression in his shadowed blue eyes was thoughtful. "You're still alive, I see."

"Guess I'm tougher than you thought. You, on the other hand, look like you've been in a fight with the whole damned forest."

"All in a day's work."

I glanced at the waterskin he clutched. He uncorked it with a practised twist, the leather creaking slightly as he pulled the stopper free. There was a quiet challenge in his storm-cloud eyes when he offered it to me as if daring me to drink from a spout his mouth had touched. I drank deeply, the water a sweet relief after my exertions. When I lowered it from my lips, he took it back, his calloused fingers brushing mine. Without a word, he drank from it himself in slow swallows, then decanted the remaining water over his head, scrubbing the blood from his face.

He glanced at the quill in my windblown bun. "Limber up. Training's not over yet."

"You didn't get your fill out there?" I searched his eyes. "What are you involved in?"

His mouth pulled into a tight line. "You agreed to trust me."

"Regardless of the bargain, you can't force trust."

"I get it. So let me prove to you that I'm not just another empty promise."

I sighed. "If I draw first blood, I get to have a bath. And you can only use one of your swords."

One corner of his lips quirked up. "You're better at deal-making already." He laid one sword on the ground with his waterskin and cloak. "That's off-bounds to both of us. But the ink pot is entirely in play, as are my shadows."

My heartbeat accelerated. "Great. Well then, let's get on with it." I adjusted my footing.

The air snapped around him as he sprang towards me, his movements as precise as a drawn bowstring. I almost let out a yelp. Our swords clashed, and the force of his blow rattled through my frame. The impact pushed me back, my feet skidding on the earth. His broad shoulders shifted as we broke apart, and he came at me again. Unlike with Cyprian, there was no coddling here, no room for hesitation. Zephyr pressured me with every step, every clang of steel, leaving no time to breathe, demanding nothing less than complete focus. My sword arm strained, muscles burning as I threw my all into the fight. His eyes flicked over my body with a discerning, almost clinical precision, taking in my centre of balance, the curve of my aching arms, the rhythm of my breath, the nuances of my technique.

I was determined to rise to the challenge and claim a drop of his blood.

I lunged for his lower ribs, but he slipped away from my strike, and his arm came around my waist, securing me in a firm hold against his chest before it dropped to my waistband to remove Maren's dagger. A hot flush rose to my skin, frustration knotting in my belly. His breath was steady compared to my erratic inhales, and it made me madder still.

"You're thinking too much about force and not enough about tactics."

"Let go." I wrenched myself out of his grasp and renewed my attack.

Each of his blocks felt like a rebuke, each parry a reminder of my inadequacy. He was right. Maren and I were fairly matched in size, but to win against Zephyr and Cyprian, I had to be more devious. I had to change the game.

Without pausing to examine my instincts, I let my sword fall to the ground with a soft thud. The release of my blade felt like surrender, and my brain screamed out that I was prey, prey, prey, that humiliation and defeat were seconds away, but it was too soon for regret to play out in my head.

I darted towards the ink pot nestled in the grass, pulling Father's quill from my hair as I ran. Dark strands spilt loose around my face like ink from an open bottle. Zephyr was a millisecond behind me. Tufts of grass whispered against my legs. I leapt, revelling in the strength of my fae body. For a moment, I was airborne, weightless, and then I landed softly beside the open ink pot. The world slowed as I dipped Father's quill into the coral ink like a painter dipping their brush into a perfect pool of colour. The ink sloshed as I withdrew the glistening quill and rose from my crouch into a balanced stance, alert to the mercenary leader.

He had stopped a metre away, sharp-eyed and expectant.

I narrowed my eyes. "Don't you dare hold back."

He smirked, his velvet tone a caress. "I wouldn't dream of it."

I cut a line through the air with my quill. The ink twisted and formed, bending to my will. For a moment, the ink seemed to respond and then cascaded to the ground, seeping into the soil like it had never been there at all.

"The elixir is no longer in your bloodstream. These limitations are your own."

"You try it." I gritted out, more agitated by his calm than my own failure. Agitated at Father, who had never shared his expertise or written a manual even though he was the calligrapher, who had left me and lied to me, instead of guiding me.

"You're focusing on the quill as a tool of wordsmiths. The brothers at the Order of the Glyph had decades of training, but your magic is instinctive. When you conjured your cloak of ink, you were triggered by heightened emotion and sheer will."

With a flick of my hand, I sent ink spiralling towards him. The ink curled mid-air like a living vine, seeking his sword hand. It wrapped around his wrist, coiling tighter, and the weapon tilted in his hand. His shadows swirled in response, crawling up from his feet, rising like smoke around his body to assert control. My ink splattered to the ground.

"Not bad. But not enough." Zephyr's sea-mist eyes hooded. "Think smaller. Emotions. Needs. Desires. Make it simple so that the ink is just an extension of thought. Nothing more. There's no weight attached to it. It's just a flicker of possibility."

I'd never reach my discarded weapons from this position without him catching me. I pulled my hair impatiently over one shoulder and studied the quill in my hands. I'd only dipped it in the ink once, but the ink hadn't dried out. It clung on, thick and viscous, defying logic. It pooled on the nib, inviting me to try again. I cast aside my caution and reached for something primal and dangerous to use against the mercenary leader.

Zephyr circled me, sword aloft, eyes gleaming.

This time, when I lifted my arm, the quill felt heavier than before. Its crimson feather quivered. My will bled into the ink as I thrust my hand out and unleashed it like a torrent. It stretched and twisted into a new form: larger than the tendrils that had grasped the mercenary leader's corded forearm, larger than the cloak that had hidden me from his sight as I climbed the stairwell. The ink congealed into something dark, slowly at first, then surging into a shape that made my eyes widen. A golem emerged, eyes of pitch beneath a black, uneven brow, its body hunched and hulking. It waited for my command.

Zephyr froze in confusion.

The golem lunged towards him, limbs crackling with energy. Its swinging fist aimed for Zephyr's jaw, but he ducked. The golem caught him in a vice-like grip by the shoulders, and the mercenary leader dropped his sword. For a split second, he struggled to push against the golem. Ink seeped into his clothes, a congealed red rather than coral. He cursed in frustration, then his shadows rose. Zephyr dropped his centre of gravity, shadows coiling around the golem's neck, constricting without mercy. The golem began to break apart, its solid body softening at the edges. Zephyr's shadows jerked sharply downwards, and the golem crashed over him. He evaded its fall and whipped around to find his sword, even before the creature collapsed in on itself.

But I was ready. A deep thrill ran through my chest.

His gaze snapped to his weapon in my hand, disbelief flitting across his face.

The blade was cumbersome, its hilt wrapped in worn leather, supple from use. But I didn't need to wield it for long. In a blink, I made a quick light cut along his cheek, the sting of the blade barely touching his skin, a half-smile playing on my lips. His clothing was in a worse state than before. Behind him, the dark remains of the golem dissolved from the ground.

Pride surged through me, jumbled with something darker. I pulled my hair into a bun and reinserted the quill. "I win."

Zephyr exhaled sharply. "Yes, you do. You've earned your rest."

I sputtered. "What? No praise?"

His slate-blue eyes fell to my lips. "You want my praise, Inkheart?"

"Don't bother." I handed him his sword, and lesson

complete, turned my back on him and located his grazing stallion.

The raven-hued horse flared his nostrils, skittering backwards as I approached with careful steps and a sing-song voice. I extended my hand towards his muzzle in invitation. The horse huffed and side-stepped, but when I brushed my fingers against his neck, he watched me with large brown eyes and lowered his head slightly as if I could continue. My fingers traced the warm texture of his coat, grounding myself in the simple act of connection. I didn't want to think about the golem. Not now. The memory of it—how it had taken form so easily from ink, how it had been mine to control—was a tangled knot in my mind. My limbs jittered with power from summoning it and the thought of it enacting my will.

I had surprised Zephyr, and the knowledge of it was delicious.

My heartbeat quickened as I thought of the golem again, but I pushed it to the recesses of my mind. I focused on the stallion. The horse was real. The horse was solid. There were no sudden shifts in reality when I stroked its mane. Everything was ordinary, as it would be in Larkspur. The boundaries of my perception didn't decompose. There was just the steady beat of the animal's pulse beneath my palm and his slow acceptance of me. I'd find Father and Maren, and we would embrace normality together.

My fingers stilled on the horse's mane as a sharp tug, like a thread pulling tight, jolted my attention. My breath hitched, and I looked up, mouth parting slightly as I noticed a flash of rusty hair that could have been the sapling of a copper beech, just beyond the shadowed boundary of Ebonspire, then an unmistakeable flash of violet fire.

The fire sparked out almost as soon as I'd seen it.

Maren. Maren was there. She'd found me, and I was no longer alone.

I squinted into the distance. Her clothes were frayed and streaked with dirt and blood, and her pale skin bore the faint shadows of bruises. Her hair tangled around her face, and her lips were set in a thin line of determination. Whatever it had taken to escape the Thorn King's creature and get back to me hadn't broken her, but it had taken its toll.

The very sight of her made me explode with joy. Made me want to haul her into my arms and wrap her in my care.

Until a cold realisation washed over me and panic flared in my breast. The mercenaries wouldn't let me leave. Not yet. They'd see Maren as a threat. They'd capture her or kill her. I couldn't let that happen.

And so, I drank in the sight of her beloved face, and then I shook my head slowly from one side to another. My lips mouthed the words I hoped she'd catch, silently, pleading. *No. Not now. Wait for me.*

Maren's amber eyes flickered with understanding. Then she tilted her head like she was weighing her options and gave the faintest of nods in return. Slowly, she melted into the treeline, her figure fading like a spectre dissolving into the landscape.

A prickle ran down my spine. I stiffened, turning midstroke in the direction of Ebonspire.

Zephyr stood at the entrance, his gaze fixed on me, brooding and intense. He beckoned me to follow him inside, his shadows defying the noon light to skim the surface of the gatehouse.

I did as commanded, as per the bargain we had struck.

***

ZEPHYR ASKED me if I wanted to dine with the mercenaries. I told him I preferred a tray in my room and to rest. All the while, my heart sang, *Maren, Maren, Maren is here.* By the time I reached my chamber, my body protested with every step. My once-lithe muscles felt like they were made of stone, and my arms tingled from the force of the strikes I had endured and delivered. The bath was already full of steaming, sage-scented water, and the stories painted on the stone walls glimmered in the soft light. I stripped quickly, washing my skin in wide sweeps to melt away the sharp edges of my discomfort, but my mind was full of schemes.

My ink magic bewildered me, but I pushed my trepidations down, concerned only with reuniting with Maren. Heart pounding, I visualised the scroll rune on Cyprian's arm: the key to escaping Ebonspire.

When I emerged from the bath, my skin was pink from heat. I dressed quickly in clean clothing, and when I returned to the main chamber, I found a tray of bread and cheeses had been left for me, together with a fresh pitcher of water, a jar of salve for my muscles, and a stack of books and sheets of plain parchment on the low table near the fireplace.

Curiosity stirred, and I padded over to them, the faint scent of leather and parchment filling the air. I hadn't heard anyone enter, and yet here they were: adventure novels, poetry, and three non-fiction volumes titled *A Tapestry of Courts and Crowns*, *The Dragons and Riders of the Nebula Court* and *A Compendium of Faerie Flora and Terrain*.

It was the kind of thoughtful touch that fitted with Cyprian's character. Like in the mortal realm, the books looked old—though well cared for—as though even in Faerie, writing had slipped from being a skill mastered by those who applied themselves to something foreign and somehow unattainable. Once, I would have eagerly snatched them up, unable to believe my luck or resist their allure. But reuniting with Maren eclipsed anything else.

I took a few bites of the bread and cheese, then dipped my fingers into the ointment and massaged my aching arms with it. Then, I packed the remainder into my satchel for Maren, together with Father's compass and jars of water. Certain that the mercenaries would still be dining, I padded out of my chamber, Father's quill tightly gripped in my hand. The stone stairwell swallowed the sound of my footsteps as I climbed. The thought of seeing Maren again made me giddy with joy. I clung to the last threads of my focus. Faint voices echoed from below, and my pulse quickened as footfalls drew closer. I pressed my back against cold stone, but mercifully, they veered off into the labyrinth of the gatehouse.

It wasn't long before I found the door hidden in plain sight. I visualised the scroll rune once more and traced it on my palm with the remnants of the ink from the quill, praying for it to activate, needing to know I wasn't a prisoner here, needing to have a way out in case it all went wrong, in case I couldn't trust them after all. The rune that marked my bargain with the mercenary leader burned behind my ear, but still, I pressed my palm to the door seam, but it didn't unlock.

A shadow fell over me. My pulse jumped. Even indoors, even scrubbed clean, he smelt of lashing wind and mossy ferns.

"Leaving so soon?" Zephyr's voice was rough. "I didn't take you for stupid."

I turned, ink staining my palm as he stepped into view. *No. No.*

"And here I was thinking we'd come so far."

My stomach plummeted with the thought of not reaching Maren, of not being able to dole out solace and build each other up again. "I needed to test if Ebonspire would let me out."

His sharp jaw was set, and his expression held a dangerous calm. The shadows at his feet rippled. It wasn't just his physicality that unnerved me. It was the sense that, at any moment, the storm within him could break. "You took what I offered. My roof. My food. My protection. You accepted our bargain. You don't get to question it. You don't get to run from it."

I balled my fists, my grief so overwhelming that it almost broke the dam of my chest. I couldn't, wouldn't tell him of Maren. I didn't want to tell him the truth. "The people I trusted most lied to me, and you want me to trust *you*? I'm not going to apologise. No one is honest anymore, so I don't have to be either. Maybe a certain amount of deception is necessary to get what I want."

"It's just about what you want, though, is it?" A bitter laugh escaped from him, and his stormy gaze bored into me. The cut I had given him had already healed from his cheek. "Don't be such a child. In Faerie, a blade can be thrust into your breast without you even seeing it. Who you choose to ally with, who you trust, who you're willing to deceive all determine your fate. You can cling to your resentment, or you can choose to work with those around you."

"Tell me what I'm dealing with then," I cried out. "I can't bear all these secrets."

He watched me for a long moment before releasing a long breath. "Then let's start chipping away at what is still unknown to you." His dark hair fell across his forehead as he pulled the ink pot from his pocket. "For practice. The ink has been in my possession for decades. Wylda will work with you on the seed pouch, but for now, don't use all the ink. There is no more."

My chest fluttered as I closed my hand around it. When Maren and I did reunite, I would be stronger. I would make her proud of me. I would make up for failing her tonight. "What if I need help? What if I endanger myself somehow?"

"My shadows will tell me. I can be there in an instant."

I bit my lip, unsure if I was disconcerted or reassured. "Where's the ink from?"

"The Court of Nebulas, where your Father hails from."

"But that is not your court?"

"No. That is not my court."

"But you have access there? That's how you have the ink."

"It is all different now." He sighed. "Tomorrow, you begin your history lessons with Gabor."

I furrowed my brow. The male with wings the colour of night. "Okay."

"Don't try this again, Inkheart. The shadows belong to me, and they are everywhere. I will always find you."

He hadn't touched me once, but part of me had wanted him to unleash his anger. Part of me craved the raw intensity that could come from clashing with him physically. Part of me wanted to take what release I could get.

It wasn't lost on me that I had broken a promise to him. I looked at the mess of coral ink on my palm. "I'm sorry," I whispered, unsure of whether I was talking to him or Maren.

But Zephyr had already melded into the shadows, and Maren was beyond my reach.

16

ZEPHYR

The Court of Silence embraces secrecy, espionage and stealth. Its members are spies, assassins and shadowmancers, skilled in the arts of subterfuge and deception.
—A Tapestry of Courts and Crowns

It had been seventeen years since Zephyr had taken a leap of faith and let Cyprian—an outcast from the fallen Court of Languish and the first of his mercenary group—into the ruins of the gatehouse. Seventeen years since they'd rebuilt the broken parts one brick at a time, quarrying stone, melting glass, carving wood, mixing mortar, hauling and hammering until sweat drenched their brows. Until he had believed Ebonspire might one day be a home again.

Until he had believed that maybe, just maybe, he and his fellow outcasts could change the fate of Faerie.

He didn't tell anyone about his dream at first. Even

now, only Cyprian knew the full extent of his yearning and his plans.

Zephyr was so very careful.

His shadow magic obscured Ebonspire. He created the illusion that the gatehouse was no more than a crumbling, ghostly ruin, a place once full of love and stories, hollowed out by time. At first, he cloaked it altogether, but masking their home under a façade of decay was easier to hold than constructing an impenetrable shield, especially when he wasn't in residence. His mother's wards still held, their magic bound to those who carried Ashmoor blood or were gifted a drop of it. Still, Zephyr took care to make the area around Ebonspire seem inaccessible to any passing fae. He and Loxley created hoax trails leading away from the gatehouse, and the mercenaries had strict protocols about when they could enter and leave.

Zephyr took other precautions, too. When the mercenaries visited taverns or rival courts or met with dealmakers or intermediaries for new contracts, they spread trickles of misinformation about their activities. Sequoia was especially skilled at it, taking dark satisfaction from the rumours that protected the group.

Most effective was their decoy base: the abandoned inn where he now stood. The inn was situated in a thicket in Ashenvale, on the border of the Court of Silence and the Court of Chaos, with Greystorm Ridge rising in the distance. With his shadow-walking magic and Sequoia and Gabor's flight, it was simple enough to skirt Spellmyst Shore and cross Ashenvale to reach the decoy base.

The inn was rugged and utilitarian, with a training room, a rudimentary kitchen that Gabor wouldn't dream of cooking in, sleeping quarters, equipment storage and a cellar for more unsavoury tasks. Mercenary life was hardly stable. They camped or rode through the night often, but the inn contributed to their myth and drew eyes away from Ebonspire. They came and went, taking it in turns, sleeping there sometimes, making the inn seem like a hive of activity and keeping his uncle's spies at bay.

It was no longer enough.

Zephyr could feel Thiago's noose pulling tighter around him. Around them all.

He had jeopardised the safety of his whole group. For the calligrapher's daughter. He hadn't delivered Ysadora to his uncle as he had promised, and that made Thiago suspicious. Especially when the spymaster and his spiders —his most trusted spies—had scoured both the mortal realm and the fae courts and found no trace of her whereabouts. No one had seen or heard anything about Kazimir's daughter since her run-in with the Thorn King. The longer Ysadora remained hidden, the more the faerie king would pry.

And by the ancients, Ysadora Silberquill fascinated him more and more each day.

He'd never known Mythros to exhibit such warmth to a stranger. It wasn't unusual for the stallion to snap his teeth, deliver a sharp kick when approached by a stranger, or toss his mane with dramatic flair. But he'd pressed his muzzle into Ysadora's hand, responding to her touch like an old friend returning home.

Zephyr had wished her hands had been touching him instead. He envied his horse, her quill, and even Gabor, with whom the calligrapher's daughter shared an easy rapport. He had to get a grip on himself.

And yet, she was a bright spot in his days, even when she scowled at him.

She was a riddle he couldn't solve, who pulled him deeper with every glance. Her fae form suited her. She'd been beautiful with her mortal glamour, but lies always corroded. He didn't like masks, although he wore plenty of them himself. He preferred the openness of lore to the darkness of shadows. Though he was a male who prided himself on his self-control, her true essence left him reeling. She was a blend of vulnerability and strength, just like his beloved sister. The other mercenaries reported that she was agile and determined during sparring sessions. She had a sharp intellect, connecting the threads of history astutely for someone not versed in the ways of Faerie. Her inkweaving transcended the limitations of mere letters and sentences, breaking free from the confines of words on a page or the rigid structures of contracts and grimoires. There was an unpredictability to her magic, a wildness that mirrored his shadows. At night, when he returned from missions, he heard the soft scratch of her quill on parchment and the rustle of turned pages of the tomes he had left for her.

Like Zephyr, she was caught between different worlds and determined to survive.

For the life of him, he wanted to help her. But her history still puzzled him.

He was determined to piece her lineage together. In those dark days, before the fall of the Order of Glyphs, who had the calligrapher bedded to bring his daughter into the world? Zephyr's enquiries revealed that Danaë and Kazimir had met only after the calligrapher's arrival in Larkspur. Danaë was not Ysadora's biological mother.

That much was confirmed, even if the calligrapher's daughter wasn't ready to hear it.

But when Cyprian fed Mythros his carrot and disappeared back inside, the memory of the ink golem slinked into Zephyr's mind. Ysadora had taken him by surprise conjuring it. Not so much because of her skill—he was learning not to underestimate her—but because the golem itself was unsettlingly familiar. But try as Zephyr did to sift through the recesses of his mind, the recollection wouldn't resurface. Perhaps the golem had been taken from a story—Ysadora was the daughter of a bookseller, after all—or he had encountered its like before in another time, another place.

The calligrapher's daughter had given him a triumphant smile at her victory, and the golem had seeped into the soil, taking Zephyr's half-formed remembrance with it. It frustrated him to come up blank. Memories, like history, deserved to stay intact.

Sometimes, they were all that was left.

He was over a century old—young perhaps, for a fae— and sometimes the days melded into each other, and the endless monsters too, so that one beast might as well be another. A slash with his sword, a dance through grotesque limbs, a coiled rope of shadows, the slam of a cell.

He closed his eyes, remembering his mother's embrace and his sister's pleasure when she showed him her art. Was there more to life than shifting shadows, curling dread and the howls of beasts losing the final vestiges of themselves?

He didn't know anymore.

YSADORA

Astral projection is a common practice among the fae of the Nebula Court—dreamers, scholars, and mystics alike slip from their bodies, visiting far-off realms, gathering knowledge and sharing stories of their travels.
—A Tapestry of Courts and Crowns

It hurt to leave Maren out in the cold. Out where monsters like the Thorn King roamed. She'd found me, and it made a bittersweet ache swell in my throat. Ebonspire loomed over the landscape like a forgotten relic, wrapped in Zephyr's shadows, and yet she'd found me. Outside, the howling wind seemed to carry my sorrow.

I told no one she had come.

Instead, I weathered my days. Inside the gatehouse, the air was heavy, almost damp, as though the walls themselves had absorbed centuries of secrets and sorrows.

Stained glass windows, beautifully crafted, barely let in any light. The environment suited my mood. Yet, despite my early impressions of the gatehouse and its inhabitants, despite my yearning for family, the days began to pass more quickly. I caught only glimpses of Zephyr, returning from missions with one or another of the mercenaries in tow, and he didn't interfere in my lessons. However, I noticed his absence, given the intensity of our interactions.

When I raised my perspective above my grief, I found bright spots.

Each dawn began with a simple breakfast in my chamber, followed by a sparring session with Cyprian in the field in front of the gatehouse. I hoped to glimpse Maren, but I never did. As the days progressed, my body grew stronger. I didn't once best Cyprian, not even with my ink magic. Although I didn't wholly trust the mercenaries, I began to trust my fae body and my magic, and Father's quill and the pot of coral ink became familiar companions.

As the days passed, the mercenaries no longer all seemed gruff and dangerous. Their distinct personalities emerged, and I learned it was best to avoid Loxley, who had a cruel wit, and Sequoia, who was sullen with strangers. Cyprian was easy to love, with his easy smiles and steady encouragement, and Wylda's quiet strength and gentle nature made her the calm at the heart of Ebonspire. Their magic surfaced at unexpected moments. I learned that while Zephyr commanded shadows, Gabor had flight and healing, Loxley could temporarily influence the actions of others, and Wylda controlled the growth of bushes and plants. I liked Wylda and Cyprian best of all, though Gabor had a singular charm and brought me delicious morsels from the kitchen.

In the afternoons, with help from *A Compendium of Faerie Flora and Terrain* that appeared in my chamber, Wylda and I cultivated seeds from Father's pouch under the watchful eye of her sister. They led me to a garden, where life flourished in a way that was absent from the rest of Ebonspire as if the garden hoarded sunlight and joy.

Hemmed in on two sides by high, weathered stone walls, the space opened dramatically to a glorious view of the sea, where salt waves crashed against cliffs far below. The walls were made of the same dark stone as the rest of the gatehouse but softened by cascades of clematis, with blossoms spilling over cracks and crevices like nature's lace.

The pathway through the garden was laid with smooth white stones, their edges framed by tufts of emerald moss. Ivory statues of fae figures stood amongst flower beds of irises, marigolds and roses. The tenderness of the garden contrasted sharply with the rest of Ebonspire's gothic severity.

Wylda smiled at my incredulous stare. She wore green leathers, reinforced at the elbows and knees with patches of bark. Her earth-toned clothes merged into the rich hues of the plants, her soft brown curls occasionally catching the light. "You like it."

My stomach fluttered. I couldn't shake the feeling I was trespassing. "It's so at odds with—"

"The rest of the building?" She nodded. "It was Zephyr's mother's pride and joy. We call it the Forgotten Garden, but it's not forgotten, not really. I tend to it whenever I get the chance, and the others all like coming here, except for Loxley, who doesn't quite appreciate beauty in the same way. And Zephyr. He doesn't come here anymore."

My brow furrowed. For a moment, I couldn't fathom why the mercenary leader would avoid such a place. Our cellar in Larkspur had made me feel closer to Mother. But then Zephyr and I were nothing alike. Maybe he didn't appreciate beauty or sentiment or connection. Or maybe he hadn't loved the woman who had brought him into the world, even though my reading of *A Tapestry of Courts and Crowns* made it clear that not every fae couple was blessed with nor wanted offspring. Faerie was often considered too dangerous for younglings. It was a world apart from Larkspur in every way.

"Why doesn't he come here? Was he not close to his mother?"

"Oh, Ysadora, they were inseparable. But Rowena Ashmoor was gone long before his adulthood. When he was a youngling—not old enough to master his magic, but old enough to feel the sharp sting of regret and grief and loss—his mother sent him here while she and Zephyr's sister Veda fought intruders. Zeph's shadows shielded him in this garden." She sucked in a breath. "Back then, he wasn't strong enough to extend them further. His—"

Sequoia's approach was swift, her mouth set in a hard line. "That's enough."

Her sister grew silent, and I imagined the trembling boy and his shadows in this garden. What wrongs had been thrust on his shoulders before he was ready, before he could even fight back? What had happened to his family to make him spurn this beautiful garden his mother had loved? But the male he had become was far more complicated. He had killed Lunarys. He was secretive, dangerous and unapologetic. He had pushed me harder than Father, harder than Maren, harder than Cyprian.

He was someone whose soul was as shadowed as the halls of Ebonspire.

Even so, my presence in the garden felt like an intrusion of the mercenary leader's privacy. It was here, with Wylda, that I learned about glimmerthorns and their luminous sap that fae scribes used for writing secret messages. I learned about shadeblooms that thrived in places of abundant faerie magic and only opened under a new moon. I learned about veilstems with their slender blue stalks, whose ink could disappear at a scribe's command. And firevein, that my clever, courageous Father had chosen to ink his message in the snow because it was nearly impossible to alter once written.

We conducted careful trials with a scattering of dormant seeds from Father's pouch. To Wylda's surprise, her whispers coaxed only a paltry few from the soil. I watched, awe-struck, as stems thickened and deepened in colour, leaves unfurling like the pages of a book. With Wylda's magic, we grew a mistweave fern, harvesting a thimble of powder that, once mixed with water, made letters blur like fog rolling across parchment. It was this, Wylda said, that was used to write many parts of the Grimoire that controlled the magic between the fae and mortal realms. The inkweeds and starbinders wouldn't grow at all, but that didn't stop us from trying while Sequoia sulked in a far corner, her gaze out to sea.

I nodded in Sequoia's direction, admiring the thick braid crowning her head and small black wings that shone like a raven's feathers at dawn. "Your sister doesn't like me."

Wylda shrugged. "It's in her nature to be protective. For a while, we were all each other had."

"I heard it was Sequoia and Gabor who gave me the truth drug."

"That was Zephyr's call. I would have chosen something less harsh than whisperroot. It's ruined your appetite."

"You think that's why I've been picking at my food?"

Wylda pulled her hands from the soil. She had the sweet, strange scent of mushrooms. "That and homesickness."

My voice was quiet. "It's not that. Well, not all of it. We didn't always have enough to eat in Larkspur. I'm accustomed to thin broths and stale bread. I've had to take it slow here. Tiny bites. Careful sips." The foods from Gabor's kitchen were a wonder: roasted meats glazed with honey, spiced vegetables, bread still warm from the oven, berries bursting with flavour. They almost felt too indulgent, not just to my stomach but to my mind. Each forkful tasted like a memory, a story, a temptation. I sensed the subtle magic woven into the food, coaxing me to eat more, to lose myself in the extravagance.

I knew instinctively it could undo me if I went too fast, if I let Faerie submerge me.

In truth, I had forgiven Gabor for the whisperroot, and I enjoyed my lessons with him more than my time with Wylda in the Forgotten Garden. He was kind and attentive as he led me through my history lessons. We pored over books in the kitchen while he tended sporadically to dishes on the stove, coaxing me into tasting spoonfuls of tangy golden sauces or sticky blends of grains mixed with roasted figs. His dark, fathomless eyes lit up with delight each time I agreed to try something new.

Then we returned to history, and Gabor leaned forward on his stool, long hair loose over the honed muscles of his back. A single dagger was strapped to his thigh, and his large hands rested on the edges of an old map of the faerie courts. His storytelling enraptured me. Each thread pulled me deeper into understanding the tangled history of the fae. Sometimes, he absent-mindedly thumbed his twisted silver and sapphire necklace. Gabor had a way of making even the most complicated lessons feel like stories told by the hearth, and I missed Father fiercely. Occasionally, he stood, acting out a battle move or a negotiation between rival faerie courts. He spoke with a clear, deliberate voice, each word chosen as if he could already see the destination before the conversation had begun.

His blended black and silver wings quivered on his back, edges dusted with glittering specks of light, like constellations in flight, as though they had long since carried him away from his people. And they had.

It turned out that Faerie had been in disarray since my birth.

His dark eyes gleamed like twin stars. "Faerie wasn't always as monstrous as it is now."

I studied the worn parchment as he tapped it, pointing out different regions of the map. Thirteen courts in all had existed once, both seelie and unseelie, and yet only seven remained. The Court of Cavernous Dreams, Court of Languish, Court of Starry Flight, Court of Lore, Court of Madness, and Court of Wild Ferns had been utterly lost. Relief flooded me that the Court of Nebulas remained intact. That maybe, one day soon, I could visit the court that was Father's and Maren's, and maybe mine. The names of the fallen courts danced in my imagination, conjuring up terror and magic. How could such established cultures vanish, swallowed by time and conflict?

Pulling myself away from the map, I glanced up at Gabor. "What happened?"

His face was all sharp lines and smooth angles. "Greed. Fear. A hunger for more power than the world could give. Then wars. Decades of blood and bargains, curses and intrigue, until the courts tore themselves apart."

I frowned, thinking of Father's compass. "The orientation of the Court of Nebulas is wrong on this map. It should be farther to the west, surely?"

Gabor snorted. "Hardly. I have flown leagues. I have checked the veracity of these maps myself, I assure you. Although, not even I would be cocksure enough to question the work of the great fae masters. Now, do you want to listen, or do you want to question me?" He spoke of ancient fae who had crossed into the mortal realm from faerie. He spoke of the Grimoire that kept the balance of the faerie and mortal realms in check and mixed personal anecdotes into our lessons: how all the mercenaries originated from the fallen courts and how his home had been the Court of Starry Flight.

For a moment, I wished he'd fly me through the sky and swoop through billowing clouds like I'd dreamed of as a child.

He showed me the different sigils of the courts, telling me which faerie kings and queens ruled with cruelty and which ones had tried to broker peace. His interest was contagious. The faerie queen Tanuhja of the Court of Chaos captured my attention, whose diplomatic skills and alliances transformed enemies into allies. She wielded her power not through weapons but through understanding and negotiation. Tanuhja sacrificed pieces of herself for the common good.

"It's a source of pride for our group of mercenaries that Tanuhja contacted us to kill the monsters who have been roaming ever deeper into Faerie when all other kings and queens turned a blind eye."

My chest tightened. "That's what you've been doing when the wards sound and you leave Ebonspire?"

"Among other things."

"These monsters…what are they exactly?"

"Flesh-eating wyrms that strike from below ground, sickly wolves with crawling skin, harpies that look like our own mothers, serpents the size of mountains, bone goliaths, flesh weavers and blighted dryads. More and more each day. Unnatural creatures never seen before in Faerie that challenge even seasoned warriors. That may never bite us, lest they empty us of our magic."

"Skies!" My heart pounded like a war drum, and I peered out of the narrow window to the dark beyond, where Maren was alone. Maren, who I had seen blaze with magic only once. Whose fae form I wanted to know as well as her mortal glamour.

"So you see why we didn't leave you in the Shrouded Forest."

I locked eyes with Gabor, seeking any hint of cooperation. "This is my eighth day here. The others have been placing bets on me. Where do you judge my capability? Have I learned enough to survive Faerie?"

"You're growing stronger each day, and though I've lost coin on your bouts against Cyprian, it's only a matter of *time*—" His emphasis wasn't lost on me. "—before you outwit him."

My eyes widened. "Cyprian has time magic… That's why I can never best him."

He folded his arms across his chest, dark eyes twinkling. "Ysadora, please don't tell him I spilt the beans."

"That rascal." I laughed in spite of myself, then grew sober. "My friends call me Ysa."

Gabor gave me a radiant smile like he was pleased to have broken down the barnacles of my reluctance to trust.

I couldn't trust him completely, but perhaps he could be my ally. He'd been less guarded than all the others put together. "If Zephyr doesn't fulfil his end of the bargain, can I trust you to help me?"

He took a deep inhale and rose from his stool. The afternoon light cast a warm glow over his long, straight nose and lips that rarely smiled. His neck scar glinted grey. There was a nobleness, a gravity to him. "Helping you would not be without consequences. Zephyr Ashmoor is not a male to break a bargain, and I owe him my allegiance. However, broken bargains create chaos in Faerie. They have unforeseen consequences. I have had enough of rifts and discord. If Zephyr breaks your bargain, I will help you."

I sprang up and embraced him. "That means more than you could know."

Strong arms, then his wings, folded protectively around me for a heartbeat. His feathers brushed my skin, and I found temporary sanctuary: there were no looming threats, no haunting shadows.

A blush crept up my cheeks as I pulled back and met Gabor's surprised gaze.

Wincing, I fled to the window. I caught sight of Zephyr backlit by the afternoon sun, a swell of shadows behind him, Loxley at the rear. The mercenary leader's shoulders were tight, his chin low. I leaned into the pane, wondering what horrors he had encountered out there. Gabor's grotesque tales echoed in my mind. I wondered if Zephyr knew loss as well as I did, if doubt or despair eroded him as much as exhaustion. I wondered whether I had done him a disservice by considering him a villain when perhaps he was Tanuhja's knight.

I flinched when he glanced up, and our eyes met, acutely aware of my need to bridge the distance between us.

Then I turned back to Gabor and the history books.

18

ZEPHYR

*Perhaps Orin would have been someone else had
he not lived his life in Thiago's shadow. I made
my decision based on whom he was, bitterly
aware of whom he could have chosen to be.
—Rowena Ashmoor's letter to her son Zephyr*

As twilight deepened, Zephyr took up vigil outside
the abandoned inn, where Cyprian and Loxley
played cards. The scent of damp pine filled his
nostrils. Only the soft blows of Mythros, the hoot of an owl
and his friends' laughter punctured the silence. He hadn't
wanted his friends to accompany him tonight, but they
had insisted. It was safer for them all for him to meet the
spymaster alone, but they were under no qualms that
Zephyr's blood ties to Thiago would spare him from
wrath.

The faerie king was getting closer and closer to
Ebonspire.

Zephyr exhaled deeply. Though the inn was well warded, he scanned the landscape in a full circle, ending with his gaze towards Greystorm Ridge. His uncle revelled in grand entrances. He might slip from the silent shadows, arrive amongst a cluster of veiled spies, or with the fury of a storm at his back or emerge from the churning vortex of a shadow portal.

Faerie itself crowned the rulers of the various courts, determined not by birthright, ambition or armies, but by whose magic outshone all others of their kind. The courts that fell did so because their rulers, despite their innate skills and ancient blessings, did not sacrifice enough or exert enough cunning to control the shifting currents of magic when the Grimoire frayed. It was a bitter pill for Zephyr to swallow that his uncle had succeeded where his mother had not.

And now Ebonspire was at risk again.

This moment had been inevitable from the instant Zephyr swept Ysadora into his arms in the Shrouded Forest.

The faerie king's summons meant one thing: his focus had shifted squarely onto Zephyr. He had seen firsthand the cold precision with which Thiago could dismantle a person's defences and uncover their most guarded secrets. He clenched his fists at memories of all he had witnessed at Thiago's side. The grim fates of those mutilated or silenced forever by his uncle would haunt him until the end of his immortal lifespan. But the spymaster wasn't always so crude. He wielded information like a weapon, using it to dismantle allies and build fear. He planned strategy like a master chess player, calculating every potential outcome. He was patient enough to wait years for his plans to unfold and decisive enough to strike swiftly, even against his own kin.

Cyprian came out into the thicket with a carrot for Mythros and a goblet of mead in his hand, swirling the amber liquid as if the motion would make time go faster. They all hated being out here. "Come and play a round while you wait. It'll take your mind off whatever is consuming you."

Zephyr shook his head. "I don't need Loxley getting his grubby hands on my coin tonight."

Cyprian sighed, too familiar with Zephyr's demons to be taken in by such a flimsy attempt at humour.

Zephyr knew the telltale signs of tension in his friend: the lines bracketing his mouth, the blades tucked so close to his body that even the spymaster would overlook them. "Spit it out."

"You're my brother, and I'd go to the ends of the earth for you. I like Ysadora as much as you do. You know, sometimes I think she could fit into our family. But I have to ask, is she worth all of our lives?"

"I'll keep you all safe." The words already felt like a lie on Zephyr's tongue, but he wanted them desperately to be true.

When Cyprian disappeared back inside, Zephyr couldn't help thinking that Thiago was the reason behind the increasing number of monsters near Ebonspire. The timing was too perfect, the surge of creatures too unnatural. For weeks, mercenaries returning from patrols had spoken about escalating danger, beasts unlike anything they'd encountered before. He had experienced it himself, such that he was loathe to allow any pairings to venture out without him. The frequency and proximity of the monsters made him suspicious that the creatures weren't drawn to the vicinity of Ebonspire by chance. They were being led.

His uncle's talent for strategy and eagerness to trap Ysadora made him the most likely suspect. What better way to smoke out Zephyr's deception than to send waves of chaos toward Ebonspire, forcing him to react, to slip up, to reveal whatever he was hiding? But still, hadn't Thiago been good to him after his mother had died? Hadn't he, having discovered Zephyr's skill for shadows, absorbed him into the Court of Silence against the wishes of Zephyr's father?

His father had never wanted him.

He had made that abundantly clear the moment Zephyr's shadows manifested. His sister Veda had been a painter and storyteller. How Orin had marvelled over her. For his son, there had been neither love nor protection, not even the protection of Orin wedding Rowena. Orin had shown his bastard son only disdain, as if Zephyr's very existence was a curse. Then his mother and sister had died, leaving father and son behind and a deepening chasm that could never be breached.

Thiago hadn't been capable of the warmth Zephyr craved as a grief-stricken youngling, but he had seen something worthwhile in him, nonetheless. While Orin left him adrift in a court where he was barely tolerated, his older brother had nurtured Zephyr's talents. It was Thiago who taught him to harness his shadows. Zephyr had learned the art of shadows, how to summon them and wield them and carry out great and terrible feats, all the while yearning to rewind the clock to protect his mother and sister. All the while burning with anger that his father withheld any training that might have saved their family.

For a time, Zephyr had become not Thiago's favoured nephew but something closer to an apprentice, at least until the faerie king had wed his then-mortal mistress and sired younglings of his own.

Zephyr's shadows stirred at his feet, mirroring his inner turmoil. Despite Thiago's cruelty, he owed him a great deal. Withholding secrets from the spymaster stirred dread and pain in him. How long could he hide Ebonspire and Ysadora before his uncle saw through his carefully crafted lies? The idea of being exposed felt like a blade poised at his back.

Still, for all their fragile bond—a bond that had once been Zephyr's lifeline—the two males differed in their outlook. It wasn't just their sense of family, how Thiago ruled even his intimate spaces with an iron fist, while Zephyr's assorted friends became his found family, knitted together by affection, laughter and common experiences. It was more than that.

Thiago was a male willing to tear apart Faerie for his own gain; Zephyr was not.

Mythros whinnied as, at last, the faerie king's portal of darkness opened amidst the twisted trunks of Ashenvale with a slow, deliberate tear in the air. Shadows spilt forth, thick and tangible, like black smoke, curling and twisting at the edges. The darkness bled out, consuming what little remained of the evening's glow, tugging at the space around it.

An eerie stillness followed before Thiago stepped out. Blue veins bulged like frozen rivers beneath his porcelain skin, giving him the appearance of a spectre risen from the depths of winter.

The faerie king nodded in greeting. "Nephew."

They had never embraced, not even after his mother and sister's death. "Uncle."

Thiago's anger was palpable by the aura of despair that leeched towards him, snatching at Zephyr's emotions, destabilising him. Turning Zephyr into just another mole of the spymaster, just another potential traitor rather than family. He'd forgotten how it felt to be at the receiving end of the faerie king's wrath, and by the gleam in his uncle's pale eyes, he had intended for this encounter to be a reminder. A warning.

Zephyr had never once raised a hand to this male, never once tested his strength against the faerie king's, though he'd taken a fair few beatings at the hands of Thiago's spiders when the spymaster deemed his nephew had withheld the truth. Thiago didn't like secrets that he couldn't control, even childish exploits like when Zephyr —desperate to escape the quiet after the vibrancy of the Court of Lore—had taken his uncle's steed out for a gallop across the icy expanses of the Court of Silence.

Zephyr braced himself for the inevitable confrontation and adopted an air of nonchalance. His hands, loosely resting at his sides, betrayed none of the tension tightening his chest. Every controlled movement was a deliberate act of restraint.

The spymaster's gaze was as sharp as a serrated blade. "You're hiding something, nephew." He probed for cracks in Zephyr's calm, searching for any telltale signs of deceit: a slight change in breathing, a bead of sweat, a clenching of fists, a facial tick. As if the faerie king could peel back his very skin to find secrets buried beneath. "I am close to finding out what."

Zephyr's heart thudded, and he hated himself for it. Hated that his heartbeat remained calm whatever beast he faced, and yet, with his uncle and father, it betrayed him. "You're mistaken, uncle."

His uncle's pale grey eyes narrowed. "Where is the calligrapher's daughter? Or am I to believe you failed when your mercenaries track and hunt more efficiently than any spy? When I trained you myself?"

Zephyr kept his expression carefully neutral, adding a touch of callousness to his voice that his uncle admired, that aped how Thiago himself walked through the world. "These things take time, uncle. She's in hiding, and we are drawing her out. I could move faster, but if we spook her, she'll vanish for good. Better to let her squirm a little longer, make her feel comfortable before we take her." He studied his uncle's reaction, knowing the spymaster would never be satisfied with anything less than results.

The faerie king's voice softened to a purr. "You see, there are things that just don't fit. The girl. The monsters. This inn. It all smacks of…manipulation. My spiders have looked for the bodies of the monsters you slew. They have found nothing."

Zephyr's storm-blue eyes hooded. "I won't leave unnatural creatures to rot in Faerie's soil."

"They have found only a handful of cremation sites. Why would a mercenary take the time to cremate those he is contracted to kill?"

"Sometimes fire is the only way to ensure they stay dead."

"Then there's your visit to Elwyck for new armour for

a female." Shadows swirled menacingly at the faerie king's feet, and Zephyr clamped down on his instinctive need to reciprocate and smother the threat.

"Come now, uncle. I trust females amongst my mercenaries. There are many gifted with a dagger amongst your kitchen maids. Perhaps you should do the same for your guard. "

"Yet you provided new measurements." Thiago's lip curled. The trees around them seemed to lean in closer, their branches twisting like gnarled fingers. "I am practised at sniffing out deception, and you reek of it."

Zephyr allowed a note of scorn to slip into his tone. "You'll get your prize when the time is right."

Thiago leaned closer, his voice menacing, like a growl rumbling in the belly of a beast. "You mistake my generosity for weakness, nephew. I won't wait forever. We must find out if the girl is capable of manipulating the Grimoire. Careful how long you string this along. There are consequences for letting a quarry slip away." He moved with an unsettling speed towards the horse. "You once rode my steed without permission."

"I remember, uncle." Zephyr's heart jolted as Mythros snorted nervously, sensing Thiago's malevolence, sensing it would be death to move through the pooling shadows. He turned his head towards Zephyr, eyes wide and ears pricked forward. "Easy, boy."

A cold smile lifted the faerie king's thin lips. "I can't abide entitlement. A male's possessions are his own. And I have marked the girl and her father as mine. Just as you are mine, nephew. After all, I allowed you to stay at court. I gave you a sense of family." He reached out, a hand poised to touch Mythros's flank. When the stallion shifted away, muscles taut with apprehension, Thiago's shadows shackled his legs.

Cyprian and Loxley ran outside, and Zephyr felt the air charge with the threat of violence from all sides. They didn't hesitate one instant about putting themselves on the line for Mythros, but they didn't know Thiago as he did. His uncle would read their action as weakness.

A chill snaked down Zephyr's spine. He'd almost forgotten they were there, not grasped that his uncle had smothered all sounds of happiness with his arrival. But if his friends interfered, the faerie king would gut them like fish right after he'd done the same to Mythros.

Zephyr's hands flexed reflexively at his side. Darkness wove around his fingers, alive and responsive, rich with potential. It pulsated like a heartbeat, eager to be commanded. He wondered if they could take Thiago together. If he could bring himself to take that step, despite familial ties.

Mythros would die. And it was likely his friends would, too.

He signalled for Cyprian and Loxley to stay where they were. "He is *mine*. Don't touch him." He knew it was a mistake as soon as the words left his lips.

Thiago's knuckles flashed in the dark. "There's no correlation between the magnificence of a creature and how well it dies. Death is always messy. It's one of life's little jokes."

White-hot anger ignited in Zephyr. "You aren't the only one capable of violence, uncle."

Thiago stepped back, his smile widening. The shadows around them shifted, and Zephyr wondered how much uncle and nephew mirrored one another. If his command of shadows meant that he was borne of the darkness and would always belong to it, no matter how hard he tried to escape it.

"You have your mother's softness," said the faerie king. "That's why my brother can't bear to be near you. Oh, he hates the shadows, of course. But his real problem is that you remind him of Rowena."

Zephyr growled. "Take my mother's name out of your mouth."

Thiago flashed a smile. "Finally, something you and your father agree on."

"My father would rather I were dead in a ditch."

"Perhaps he'll get his wish if you keep up your many deceptions." The faerie king retracted his knuckle blades and stroked the quivering horse. "It would be a shame to break our alliance, nephew. I have so enjoyed it. It would be much more satisfactory all around were the calligrapher's daughter to be found. I would very much like to make my wife happy, and your cooperation would —" his eyes flicked to Cyprian, Loxley and Mythros, "— save the hides of those you are fond of."

Zephyr held his uncle's gaze. "Understood."

"Good." The faerie king stepped into the yawning portal. The air rippled and hissed as the void embraced him, its tendrils lapping at his heels. Then, with a final flicker, Thiago vanished into the void. The portal closed behind him, leaving a sense of unease that lingered like a bruise.

Only then did Zephyr resume breathing.

Cyprian came to his side. "Sweet repose, the male's a bastard. This isn't just about surviving anymore. It's about who we choose to be when it's all over."

Loxley—reckless, unpredictable, always willing to escalate matters—lounged against a twisted tree, idly twirling a dagger between his fingers. "He thrives on order. We can break him."

Zephyr stroked Mythros rhythmically, reverently. His forehead brushed the horse's neck in silent apology for the dangers that neither of them could escape. "You're right. We won't win by playing it safe." He had to outthink Thiago, not outmatch him in cruelty.

More importantly, he had to protect the people he cared about.

That night, after the long journey back to Ebonspire, Zephyr spent extra time tending to Mythros in the stables and checked the locks on the dungeons. When he returned to his chamber, it was Ysadora's smile he saw, her rosebud lips on the spout of his waterskin, her dark hair loose as she wielded her quill.

Her tentative trust in a world where trust was in short supply.

19

YSADORA

*The king is eager to challenge the dark power
hiding in the shadows. After my bravery at
Bloomtide, he has made me his lieutenant and I
am to enter the forest. Despite his trust, I am
gripped by thoughts of Vixora.
—Ferrith's diary*

By the ninth day of the bargain, I was accustomed to the rhythm of life at Ebonspire. I trained with Cyprian, and sometimes, the others joined us in the yard, sparring against each other. The mercenaries moved with precision and aggression, muscles taut and glistening with effort, jibes and laughter mingling with the clang of metal. Zephyr stood out amongst them, his movements mesmerising and clever. His sword skill was poetry in motion, his shadows fluid and ever ready to exploit an advantage.

When physical training depleted me, I endured seed

mishaps in the Forgotten Garden, practised ink weaving, read my history books or snuck into the stables to see Zephyr's stallion. I learned the horse's name was Mythros. I found I liked the name. It was one I might have given my own horse. His gleaming coat and polished hooves revealed a depth of responsibility and even kindness buried beneath the mercenary leader's sharp edges.

The once-jarring silent halls and camaraderie between the group became the backdrop to my days, oddly comforting despite my need to be reunited with Father and Maren. Sometimes, new books appeared in my room as if by magic: romance and mystery novels, and a non-fiction tome titled *A Short History of the Order of the Glyph* that made me cry when I recognised a likeness of Father in a bookmarked page.

At supper that evening, I bypassed a brooding Zephyr to sit with Cyprian when Sequoia called out for my attention.

"Ysadora." She looked beautiful tonight in a sleek thigh-length tunic with cutouts for her feathered wings and her hair interwoven with leaves from trees she could summon with a mere thought. She pointed at three elements around the remnants of our meal: a candelabra, a flowerpot and a wine jug. "I have yet to face you during training. How about some target practice in here? Your quill against… I wouldn't want you to feel overwhelmed… I'll use my sister's bow."

Wylda frowned. "Isn't it a little uncivilised having target practice at dinner?"

Cyprian leaned back. "That wine is far too precious to be spilt by the likes of you, Sequoia."

I lifted my chin. "Why not."

Zephyr's expression was dark. I thought he'd been miles away. "She doesn't need to prove anything to you, Sese."

"Spoilsport." Sequoia pouted and stashed her sister's bow under the table again.

The tension eased, and I leaned over to resume my conversation with Cyprian. "Shame. I might have beaten her with a little fair play. As for you, you utter swindler. Time magic? No wonder you were always one step ahead."

He chuckled and had the grace to look shamefaced. "I wondered how long it would take you to figure out."

"How does it work?" I reached for a piece of bread, the warm crust breaking easily in my hands.

"Pretty simple, really. I can turn back the clock for a few seconds. So, say you land a good strike… I can make it so you start your action again and I anticipate it better or adjust myself so that I have the upper hand."

My eyes widened. "Skies, you've been busy. I *knew* there was a reason I was always one step behind." My mind whirled. "Have you ever used it on me in any other situation?"

He bit into a cinnamon-crusted roll. "Once. I made a stasis field at Bloomtide when you met Zephyr, so no one else would notice him. When you made eyes at him over toffee."

"Oh." I put down my fork and dropped my voice. "You mean I made demon eyes at him."

Cyprian's eyes twinkled. "If you say so." He hesitated. "You're not sore about it?"

"A little. But the books you've been providing make up for it."

He opened his mouth to respond but shut it as the blare of a compromised ward sounded. The wards had shrilled with increasing frequency as my days at Ebonspire progressed. It was the norm for two or three of the mercenaries to venture out to face the threat and to return dirty and ravenous a few hours later.

Sequoia stood abruptly. "It's the Wraithwoods."

"Gear up. We'll need everyone." Zephyr's eyes hooded as he looked at me. "You're coming with us, Inkheart. Wylda, you know what to do." And then he disappeared with the others into the armoury, bringing back armoury–sharpened swords, obsidian daggers, sleek bows and heavy axes that could cleave through bone to the dining table.

Wylda pulled a handheld mirror from the kitchen drawer and came to sit beside me. "If you're going to come with us tonight, we need to take precautions. A glamour." I shook my head, and she rushed on. "I'd be hesitant, too, but this isn't like the elixir. It will fall away as soon as we return to Ebonspire. There are factions looking for you, Ysa, and you won't be safe otherwise."

I sighed, unwilling to lose myself completely again. "At least leave enough of a trace so that I can recognise myself."

She pressed the mirror into my grasp. "Done."

Her glamour enveloped me like a silken veil. I caught the sweet, strange scent of mushrooms again, and I wondered if her gift for conjuring glamours was linked to hallucinogenic magic or whether they could all do these tricks, whether Father and Maren could, and what fun we could have had in Larkspur had I known. And then the frivolous thought was drowned out beneath the strangeness of the glamour as I held the mirror up. My long dark hair became glassy blonde strands that fell to my chin. My curvy build slimmed into boyish lines, and my cheekbones shifted lower. My lips thinned, and my proud nose tapered into a more delicate line. The fae blue-violet of my eyes remained the same shape but became the soft brown they had been in Larkspur. The dissonance between my outer and inner self didn't throw me off guard as it had when I broke free of the elixir. Faerie had chipped away at my sense of self, dissolving my expectations of the familiar, even in myself. Here, identity was fluid, and I found that sometimes, sometimes it suited me better than the rigidity of Larkspur.

Wylda gave a satisfied nod. "There. That will do."

Cyprian returned, blinked once, then handed me a sword, its hilt cool against my palm. "You've used this one before. It's perfectly balanced. You'll do just fine with it and your quill." He hesitated. "You should know, the Wraithwoods are disconcerting. It's an ever-shifting maze of trees that constantly change their arrangement. Worse, the wraiths are remnants of mortals who have lost their way in Faerie. They'll try to lure you deeper into the maze. You can't help them, so please don't try. And remember, we always work as a team."

My blood froze at his words, but I masked my apprehension, not wanting to seem weak. The rest of the group buzzed around us like a hive of hornets, lacing their boots and slipping on leather bracers, thick vests and enchanted chainmail shirts. For me, they brought a supple, boiled leather dyed in a midnight blue, with small plates of faerie-forged metal stitched along the ribs and shoulders and a thin mesh of chainmail beneath.

Wylda slipped it over my head and adjusted the clasps. "Zephyr had it made for you in Elwyck at great risk to himself."

I frowned; according to Gabor's maps, Elwyck was hundreds of miles away in the Court of Embers. It would have taken days for the mercenary leader to travel back and forth, but he had been at supper each evening, sullen and watchful. Mythros had only left the stables on short missions. "But he's been at Ebonspire each night since I arrived."

"He travels well. As you'll find out." Wylda's tight braid swayed like a pendulum as she moved. "Come on."

Less than a quarter hour had passed since the wail of the wards. Heart pounding, I cast one last glance at my reflection before trudging after them into the stairwell and out into the night. The thrill of adventure and the chance to see more of Faerie after all I had learned was intoxicating. I smothered the flicker of kinship I felt. I didn't belong with them; they were not my family. This was a means to an end.

Outside, the moon hung low over the ancient spires, and only the soft rustle of our reinforced clothing broke the stillness of the night. Around me, the mercenaries stood poised in a circle, their chatter fading into a focused silence. The thrill of the impending hunt lit their eyes as they awaited the signal for departure.

Zephyr grunted in approval at the gleaming weaponry. "Loxley flies with Gabor. Wylda with Sequoia." Gabor and Sequoia were already looking at the cloudless sky. "Cyprian, have you enough recollection of Wraithwoods to create a pathway?"

Cyprian hefted an axe over his shoulder as if already anticipating the other side. "Yes."

"Good. Stay alert, everyone. I don't want any frights tonight. We meet by the silver birch."

A grin split Loxley's face beneath his tangled beard as he looked at me. "Try not to vomit."

Then Zephyr approached me, his twin swords crossed at his back. He examined me with a slight frown as if he was learning the planes of my new face, snagging on my eyes, and then he put out a hand. "Unconditional trust, remember?"

I gazed up at him and, with a deep inhale, put my hand in his. As I did, Gabor and Sequoia unfurled their wings and sprang into the air, entwined with their passengers. Gabor flew harder, faster than Sequoia, closer to the stars while she skirted the tree canopies. Then I only had eyes for Zephyr as he tugged me closer, releasing my hand and curving his arm around my waist, tucking me against him so his hard thigh pressed against mine.

"Stay with me," he murmured into my hair.

Then he propelled us through the fabric of night, and his words became a distant bell. My heart jolted as we surged through the shadows. We were weightless, as gravity had no meaning. The landscape flickered in and out of view, shifting from murky water to jagged mountains and sprawling forests. The darkness around us was alive, swirling and pulsing. I glimpsed ancient trees, their silhouettes twisting like dancers against the moonlight. Shadows stretched and morphed, revealing hidden paths and groves. Through the rushing night, I saw distant cities, their lights twinkling like stars fallen to earth and a domed castle with minarets. We shot through canyons and over mountains, each mile unveiling new wonders: glowing caves, fields of phosphorescent flowers, and ancient ruins draped in vines. Zephyr's shadows cradled me, and his warmth radiated, countering the cold rush of night air. Then he turned me into him, his steady heartbeat at my ear. His scent, like damp moss after rain, filled my senses, and for a moment, I melted into him and turned off my thoughts and my fears, grateful for a steady anchor amidst our wild flight. Each twist and turn brought us closer together, our bodies perfect jigsaws in the spaces between shadows.

We crossed miles in mere moments, and then, he tightened his grip around me, and it ended.

Cyprian was already standing on a carpet of ferns at the foot of a silver birch, scanning the otherwise dark terrain. The others landed in the clearing seconds after our arrival. First Gabor and a grimacing Loxley, then the two sisters, their movements synchronised as though they had spent a lifetime soaring together.

Zephyr's chest rose and fell rapidly as he regained his composure. "These woods play tricks and hold terrors of their own beyond what we face tonight. Stay close, Inkheart." Then he sent his shadows forth. They broke away from him and darted into the underbrush, gliding over the damp earth and slipping between the trees like phantoms. Moments later, they returned, swirling around him in a jubilant embrace. He sprinted forward. "This way. Same rules as always. We don't kill it unless we have to."

I frowned. Why didn't they kill the beast? Were they collecting coin simply to incapacitate the monsters?

There was no time to question, no time to say anything at all, as Loxley, Cyprian, and Sequoia lit torches and followed Zephyr. Flickering flames illuminated their determined faces as we stepped beyond the safety of the silver birch into the dark woods beyond. Wisps of fog curled around the underbrush, muffling our footfalls. We ran as a cohesive unit through trees that shifted and swayed, rearranging themselves, disorientating me even when I matched footstep for footstep so that Wylda snaked a vine around my waist to ensure I didn't stray from our path. I kept pace with the mercenaries, my senses heightened, trying not to give into gnawing fear as ghostly hands grasped me and snatches of children's voices floated to my ears. Faces loomed before me, with hollow eyes and mournful mouths, and I wanted to go back into the safety of Zephyr's shadows.

"Don't listen. Don't look," said Gabor grimly. "Keep going." Then he cursed.

The hair on my nape stood up. My gaze swept upwards, and I saw it: a towering flesh-less feline, its skeletal frame a grotesque mockery of life. Its bone claws glinted in the torchlight, designed not just for climbing but for battle. Its maw was filled with jagged teeth, and spines lined its back. Its hollowed eyes glowed with unnatural light. Zephyr stood closest to the monster.

"Quench your torches. We can't risk fire," he said quietly.

A scream built in my throat as the bony feline stalked towards him, and shadows swirled around him like a living storm. But there was nothing for the shadows to grasp. They simply slipped through the empty spaces where muscle and sinew should have been. As though the creature was a half-formed thing, part ghost, part nightmare and his magic had no purchase.

"Dammit," he muttered as the monster snarled, and he drew his swords from his back.

Behind him, we were already moving. A chorus of battle cries mingled with the growl of the beast. I was right beside them, pulse skittering with the rhythm of the chaos. It used the labyrinth of trees to mask its approach, leaping from canopy to canopy, attacking with blinding speed before retreating amongst the maze and the wail of wraiths.

Wylda's vines exploded from the ground, winding together in a net to capture it, but the bone feline was impossibly agile. Her vines surged forward again, only for the beast to tear through them with its jagged claws. Wylda pulled an arrow from her quiver, its tip glistening with a strange, sticky sap. She nocked and fired it, aiming arrow after arrow at the feline's path, driving it towards Gabor and Loxley, whose axes were at the ready. With a flash of bone-white claws against the murky backdrop of the trees, it was upon them, sending both males tumbling to the ground. Gabor scrambled to avoid its snapping maw and shattered a rib with his axe. The creature let out a bone-chilling screech as it swung towards me. Its elongated limbs gave it an unnatural reach. Instinct took over as I dodged to the side, glimpsing the tightness in Zephyr's lips before he masked it with his usual cool demeanour.

It came for me again, and I scrambled to find secure footing. I swung my sword with renewed vigour, working in tandem with Zephyr, who was at my side in an instant. Our blades connected with a dull thud against its bony hind legs, but the creature barely flinched. The sound of metal scraping against bone echoed through the woods, and the bone feline's unnatural eyes narrowed as it calculated its next move.

"Watch and learn, big sis." Sequoia spread her palms wide and the maze of Wraithwood shifted under her command, with trees groaning and bending as they moved to trap the beast. She was the key to navigating this unholy place, the only one who could stabilise the ever-shifting labyrinth, but the trees were too strong, and she could only hold them for so long before they snapped back into place, releasing the bone feline once more.

We fanned out, creating a perimeter.

Even Cyprian's time magic couldn't hold it.

The monster paused mid-lunge, its ivory bones frozen in time, but only for a moment before Cyprian's temporal magic unravelled. The bone feline let out a deafening roar, its rage intensifying. Loxley darted in, and for a brief moment, the creature faltered, its movement slowing as his magic took hold, but it quickly regained control. Gabor surged upwards, his blended silver-black wings blurring as he circled, looking for an opening to dive with his axe. The wailing of the wraiths increased to a spine-tingling crescendo, as if mourning the bone feline even before its impending death, and the trees of the Wraithwoods trembled.

Zephyr's voice was sharp against the eerie wails of the wraiths. "Stay your hand."

Loxley tried to find an opening but the beast was too clever, too powerful. "We have to kill it."

Why were they hesitating? Why were their blows landing with care rather than sheer power? I knew they could fight harder than this. I had seen them toil in mere training sessions, and their magic left me slack-jawed, yet still, the mercenary leader clamoured for restraint. The questions burned in my mind as the bone feline lashed out its tail, knocking Sequoia off her feet.

She hit the ground hard, her breath forced from her lungs in a rush.

The bone feline pounced, its skeletal maw snapping open. The beast's fangs glistened under the eerie light of the Wraithwoods, aiming for Sequoia's throat. But hadn't someone told me that the bite from these monsters negated faerie magic? Sequoia was too magnificent with her wild wings and command of trees to meet that fate. I was closest.

In the blink of an eye, I threw myself between Sequoia and the creature. Its fangs grazed my arm but didn't pierce the mesh of chainmail beneath the midnight blue leather. I jammed my sword between its snapping jaws. Sequoia's eyes flashed with resentment as she pushed herself up, and the beast spat out the blade and slunk into the thicket, her eyes flickering like dying stars. It was cunning, so cunning, and I almost thought it smiled as the trees shifted once more.

Failing our mission was unthinkable.

With a burst of speed, I charged after the beast, even as warm shadows surged for my waist.

KAZIMIR

In the silent spaces I call home,
your voice blooms like the first light
through a darkened grove.
—Thiago's love poem to his wife Danaë

Kazimir's chamber was like a tomb. He slept poorly despite the healing and the heavy drapery that hung like shrouds at the window. A day passed, each minute an hour. Thick, stagnant air made his throat close as though this court required its guests to swallow their very words. Dust motes floated in the dull light as though frozen midflight. The weighted air pressed against his skin with an eerie calm, at odds with his internal panic. As if time itself slowed to a crawl within these walls when he so desperately needed to know whether Ysadora and Maren had enacted their escape deeper into the mortal realm.

He didn't demand to be let out of the tomb-like chamber, knowing well the spymaster's tricks.

Better to wait it out. Still, Kazimir missed his quill bitterly. Not that it would be any use to him. He had neither ink nor seeds. No means of tapping into the power that surged in his veins.

If only he hadn't lingered at home in Larkspur. If only he had salvaged his precious plants instead of surrendering them to Thiago's butchery. If only he hadn't foolishly indulged in memories instead of forging ahead to the tavern and reuniting with Ysa and Maren. He would be with them right now, counting his lucky stars. It was a relief when Danaë appeared at his door.

Her eyes examined every line of his face, accusation in her tone. "You are feeling more like yourself, I see."

In the mirror that morning, he had noticed his features had acquired the predatory lines that had been smoothed out by his human guise. He wondered if it made her desire him more. "I am."

"Is the clothing satisfactory?"

"Yes." They were servant's clothes, simple and clean. Nothing that her faerie king would deign to wear, but he did not mention it. Nor did he mention how they had been laid out on the bed like she had laid out his clothes when she was his wife, with the tunic positioned atop the trousers and socks tucked into clean shoes with the laces in a neat bow.

"Would you like to join me for a walk?"

"Yes," he said, craven for freedom.

Kazimir followed her through the cavernous castle, the floor cold and uneven. He was unsure whether to treat

Danaë as friend or foe, and so he busied himself with taking in his surroundings. No paintings or tapestries broke the cold, grey expanse. No colour brought relief. Echohold remained a shell rather than a home. He had visited it before with a delegation of his brothers as part of his duties with the Order of the Glyph: sealing forbidden rifts, renewing wards and siphoning unspoken histories into the Grimoire. Even then, Echohold had been a place of secrets.

It was, after all, the spymaster's home.

The layout was deliberate, with narrow winding passageways leading to rooms of strategy and quiet dealings. He knew what happened behind the thick walls and sealed doors here. Cloaked figures bent over ancient maps and coded parchments. Spies exchanged fragments of information like ghostly traders in the dark. Alchemists worked in isolation, blending potions that granted invisibility. Blacksmiths hammered shadowsteel, their work muffled by spells. Back then, it was the hidden chambers that Kazimir and his brothers had whispered about. Chambers accessible only through concealed passages that housed informants or those who had fallen foul of this court. Males and females, whose names were never spoken out loud and whose screams were never heard.

The Faerie King of the Court of Silence was not above torture.

Today, it was the castle servants who caught his attention: child-like creatures in size with pearlescent grey skin, hollow eyes that shuttered oddly in bright light and mouths stitched shut. They moved with practised silence, passing unnoticed through walls, their eyes keen, their ears sharper still as they carried pitchers of water, brooms, or trays of corked vials. Rigid guards were stationed at intervals, attuned to the needs of Echohold and its ever-watchful faerie king. They understood the rhythms of this place: when to vanish and when to reappear, when to take care of a task and when to fade into the background. Kazimir did not bother them in the slightest—they did not acknowledge his passing—even though he accompanied the mistress of the house.

Almost as though Danaë did not need their protection.

They left the castle itself, Echohold piercing the sky like a black arrow, and crossed a moonlit expanse to where her snow leopards waited.

"My snow leopards will accompany us," said Danaë. "They will not harm you unless you are foolish."

He wondered what *foolish* meant. If her parameters included a simple stumble or a sharp look in her direction or a brazen kiss of the mouth he had once claimed as his. He decided not to find out. She said nothing of her husband, which meant only one thing: Thiago would lurk in the shadows, unseen.

Of the thirteen fae courts, this was the one Kazimir loathed, with its unnerving absence of everyday sounds. He walked with Danaë and her snow leopards past scarce groves of still trees, their bark as pale as bone. The silk of Danaë's cloak did not whisper as it brushed the ground. There was no crunch on the gravel path; silence magic absorbed their footsteps. There was no distant call of birds returning to their nests, no chirp of crickets or the creak of swaying trees. The wind did not groan, water trickling in the nearby stream did not splash, and grotesque creatures did not howl. The Court of Silence stifled even nature's voice.

In comparison, the Court of Nebulas was filled with the intoxicating hum of the universe. Kazimir's heart gladdened at the memory of Celestiva, where the skies never truly darkened and the air crackled with latent magic. Harmonies soared from the heavens, their melodies shifting like constellations. Scholars tangled in vibrant debates. Shooting stars ignited behind ancient spires. Dancers whirled in the astral amphitheatre. Roaring dragons carved through the clouds.

Even with Thiago's gift of immortality, it was hard to accept that Danaë chose to live her days in a place like this. Hard to believe that his former wife would leave the simple joys of Larkspur for the cold, harsh landscape of the Court of Silence. Though Kazimir was an educated man who knew the pitfalls of ego, her choices added insult to injury because he couldn't understand them. Most of all, he couldn't understand how, for all their bond, she had chosen to leave Ysadora.

After all this time, he could still hear the youngling's desolate cries for her mother in the days that followed the storm. The heart can hear what the ears cannot.

He walked beside her, unsettled by how faerie she had become, trying not to cower from the prowling snow leopards that licked their lips as if awaiting a meal. Danaë, quiet as death, stole glances at him from beneath the sweep of her lashes. He supposed he looked different this evening: straighter-backed, limbs more muscled, hair fuller, and eyes sharper than his bespectacled human form. Every unsaid thought hung between them, through air thick with the scent of night-blooming flowers. He could feel the prickle of her ego, the way she enjoyed having this power over him. After all the absence stretching between them, any emotion was acceptable to him, any chance to untangle what had been and to find something new.

Eventually, she spoke, a wistful smile on her crimson lips. "When Thiago first brought me to Faerie, it filled me with wonder. We travelled for months, visiting the thirteen courts. Sometimes, I was his wife. Sometimes, he cloaked me in shadow. It was a time of great joy. Our relationship, the discoveries we made together…" Her hand drifted over her belly. "Our adventures across Faerie. For all the stories I devoured in Larkspur, for all my research and learning, this was so much more. Trees stretching so high they touched the very stars. Rivers singing melodies of their own. The sky shifting like liquid gold. A world where magic breathes. It was in the boulders, in the leaves, in the very blood of the creatures that live here." Her words slid past him like water over smooth stones until her lips twisted into something between nostalgia and pain. "I was satisfied for the first time in my life."

Kazimir frowned. "What changed? Was it Thiago? Is he treating you unkindly?"

She raised an elegant eyebrow. "Thiago is twice the male you ever were. All your books and learning, and still you stumble on the wrong answers. You are the last remaining calligrapher. What do you think happened to the Grimoire when you left Faerie?"

He smarted at her callous handling of what they had shared. "You can't put all of that on one male's shoulders. The Order of the Glyph had safeguards in place. The blame for whatever is happening in Faerie lies at someone else's feet."

A bitter laugh bubbled up the elegant column of her throat. "You old fool. What do you think happened since your brothers from the Order died?"

The old pain stabbed at Kazimir's heart. "They burned. What else is there to know?"

"Know this, Cairn." She didn't even realise she had used his old name, the lie, such was the force of her conviction. "Know the painful truths that the Binder tried to tell you but you were too stubborn to heed. The *days of plenty* didn't simply end. They ended because of you. It didn't happen overnight. It was a creeping corruption that even the faerie kings and queens didn't notice at first. A trickle of dark magic. The light that once flowed freely in Faerie became fractured. A sinister power had taken hold while you were playing daddy."

I listened to her descriptions, uncomprehending. "No, that cannot be."

"Believe it," snapped Danaë. "Magic has always been volatile in Faerie, but now its chaos can't even be channelled by those who understand it. Parts of this land crackle with an intensity that make your skin burn just to be near it. There are places where the trees themselves move with a dark hunger. There are ruins, places that used to be thriving villages and cities, now abandoned, swallowed by the earth. Of the thirteen courts, only seven remain."

A cold sweat broke out along Kazimir's neck. His words tasted like ash. "Lies. Lies. They must be." But fae couldn't lie, and she was speaking so plainly.

His mind filled with splintered thoughts, each sharper than the last. They spiralled to the ancient courts—his own and others—wondering which had fallen. How could it be possible for the very underpinnings of Faerie to collapse? Where had that power gone? What had it devoured? Who had suffered? What damage had been left in the void? Seven courts left, if Danaë were to be believed, of which the Court of Silence was one. No, no, it wasn't his fault. It couldn't be his fault. He prayed to the stars that the Court of Nebulas had survived.

Danaë's voice was flat, as though she had emoted over this time and again, and there was nothing left. "The boundary between Faerie and the mortal realm is getting thinner and, worst of all…"

He swayed and gripped her arm, hastily letting go when the snow leopards bared their teeth. "Tell me."

"You want to know the hard truth? Do you, Cairn?"

"I do." Kazimir didn't. He could barely breathe.

Danaë's golden eyes mirrored the intensity of her snow leopards' gazes. They peeled him open, a merciless stripping of his ego and of the principled, honourable male he had believed himself to be. "Monsters roam this land. Half-remembered nightmares that hunt. They feast on souls. They slip through walls. Some blend into groves like this one. They nullify magic. There is no place in Faerie that is safe anymore. All that remains is a broken dream."

He saw the truth in her eyes, and it flayed him. He wanted to escape it then, to prove her wrong. "Let me see for myself. Let me explore Faerie and put it right, if I can."

Danaë's voice was brittle. "That's not a good idea."

His heart drummed. What truths existed beyond these strange gardens? "Please. I'll take an escort. One of Thiago's spiders."

"You'll venture beyond the Court of Silence only when my husband decides the time is right. Not before."

Though they were outside under the stars that he loved, the walls closed in on Kazimir. He couldn't fathom a route to redemption if he remained at Echohold. If he couldn't act, then it was better to fade away. He felt a visceral urge to retreat from the world or disappear altogether. Ysa would be better off without him.

Maybe Danaë sensed his despair and pitied him because something softened in her eyes, and there was a quiet intensity in her gaze. "Ysa was not yet four orbits when I left. Tell me, Cairn, what is she like, the daughter we shared?"

How could he describe Ysa in a way that captured all of her complexity when Danaë had missed the entire journey, all the tiny revelations of personhood? He knew he shouldn't tell her in case he gave Thiago ammunition for his hunt, but he was so proud, and she had loved their daughter once. A mother's love for her child was pure. How could that change overnight?

Kazimir smiled, healed by the thought of his daughter. His voice was almost reverent, and it was as though the very stars listened. "She loves books. She has an inner light and has a sharp mind, like you. Quick to learn, quick to challenge anyone who thinks they can outwit her. She's beautiful and strong. She makes friends easily but only needs a few. There's an innocence about her, a hope that doesn't belong in Faerie." He looked down at a lone flower pushing through the gravel path. "She hates lies. I haven't always been…what she deserved."

"You were not a good husband, but you were not a bad father. You stayed, at least. That counts for something," she said, not unkindly. She stooped to pluck the flower from the path and tossed it aside. "You are all that she had."

Kazimir locked the secret of Maren deep inside him. "Yes."

"Does she have your magic?" Danaë waited for the answer with bated breath.

That's how Kazimir knew that all their eerie wandering through the Court of Silence, all their poignant conversation, had led to this point. That's how he knew to lie.

He didn't tell her about Ysa's innate ability for writing in a mortal world where writing had become a lost art. Where children could barely read despite sustained effort, let alone write. He didn't tell her that at five orbits old, Ysa's handwriting practice sometimes transformed on the page despite the elixir. That the ink would bleed into the parchment, and the letters she had struggled to form would straighten, lengthen, grow rounder, perfecting themselves under her touch as though the ink obeyed her will. That the letters had rearranged themselves into neat lines as if guided by an invisible hand.

Neither did he tell her about finding Ysa asleep at her desk five orbits ago, her dark head resting on a notebook she'd been annotating. The ink on the page had swirled in slow patterns beneath her slumbering fingers in a way that made his blood congeal in fear. He'd stood, frozen, as the ink took on a dreamlike quality, rising in images in the air, as she wove the ink into an otherworldly design even in her sleep. Or the nightmares that manifested as inky fog above the inkwell on her bedside table and left dark smudges on her pillow and the soft cheeks of her skin.

His daughter certainly had magic. Sometimes, he imagined it could be stronger than even his own.

Without the yoke of the elixir, he feared she would be unable to control it.

Kazimir met Danaë's gold eyes. "She does not. Not even an ounce of it."

"You were always a poor liar. With your words. With your deeds. With your body. Even between the sheets."

"You don't mean that. What we had meant something."

Her strange eyes flashed. "I was a *survivor*. Did you think I wouldn't find out about the heartthorn briar? That you could bind our hearts and trap me in your small life?"

Kazimir flinched. It was true their story had started with the heartthorn briar, but how else would he have given Ysadora what she needed most of all: a mother? He had loved and cared for Danaë, with or without the coercion of the heart-binding.

Pure ambition glinted in Danaë's eyes. "You were right, I think, to suggest that more than one calligrapher is needed to reimagine the Grimoire and right the wrongs of Faerie. That is why Thiago and I need Ysadora."

A desolate wave crashed over him. "No."

She was right to be angry with him, he realised. But perhaps he had chosen Ysa's mother poorly. Kazimir realised at last that in the years since their parting, he had reimagined Danaë's character, embellishing her virtues and minimising her flaws. He had taken all the good in her and magnified it—for himself, for Ysa, for her myth in Larkspur—and let it eclipse the complexity of the individual she truly was. He hadn't wanted to taint the memory of what they had shared, not when that was all he had left of the family they had built. In truth, Danaë had always been a hard woman to know, full of sour moods and secrets.

Danaë's voice cut through the silence, and Kazimir wondered if she had ever been gentle. "Where is she?"

They didn't have her, and it made his heart so glad that a choir of angels might have appeared. "I won't tell you."

Danaë gave a sad smile as her sneering husband emerged from the shadows. "You will."

Kazimir's bladder loosened. He wondered how Thiago would torture him, whether it would be a thousand cuts of a silent blade—immortals could endure more pain than their human counterparts—or whether he would be smothered by an aura of dread and despair that the faerie king would only lift if he gave away Ysa's whereabouts in the mortal realm.

The corners of his lips lifted. They did not know that the depths of his despair were already at their lowest. The Faerie King of Silence could do whatever he desired, and Kazimir would not break. He would hold fast for Ysa.

Danaë lifted the hood of her black cloak over the golden warmth of her tresses. Thiago caressed his wife's back. Then the woman who had once been Danaë Everreed and who was now Danaë Hendrick, consort to the Faerie King of the Court of Silence, sang.

Her voice shattered the silence, and such was Thiago's bliss that Kazimir understood at once why Thiago had coveted his wife. Why the faerie king had fallen in love with a mortal woman and made her fae. In his court of muted sound, where even his own voice was a thing of rare use, her song was a revelation. When unleashed, her voice defied the quiet that dominated her existence and stirred parts of him that were long dead. Kazimir knew it because Danaë had stirred the same feelings in him once he had left the magic of Faerie behind.

The song began softly, like a ripple across still water, and Kazimir was entranced. Her voice was more beautiful than ever before, as though she had been trained by fae bards. It was smoky with vulnerability, delicate and warm, an echo of life. It was the kind of melody that stirred the soul before the mind could catch up. Each note brought sweetness and colour that he didn't deserve, that soothed his very soul and made him forget his troubles. He closed his eyes and remembered his wife on the village square, Ysa twirling to her mother's song.

But then, the song grew darker, and Kazimir's eyes flashed open.

Danaë stepped towards him, her lungs at full capacity, her melody shifting. The sweetness of her song took on a darker hue, like the slow deepening of day into night. The notes twisted, pulling away from their original harmony, dipping lower, becoming more sinister. Kazimir's chest tightened, and his heart faltered as each note pushed down on him. Each inhalation was a battle. He believed with cruel certainty that her songs could command even breath, even blood, to still. That she could wield her voice with such force that could stir hearts or bend minds, a blessing remade into a curse. His legs weakened, and his knees buckled, sending him to the cold ground. Blood trickled from his ears, but he didn't avert his gaze from Danaë, from the intense gleam of her gold eyes, from her predatory focus. His mouth formed pleading sounds as Danaë's notes seeped into his bones, hollowing them out, twisting sharply as each note bled into the next, every fibre of his being at her mercy. His face was slick with blood, his newly healed body at odd angles. Her voice climbed to its crescendo.

He was just a calligrapher, just a father, trying to do his best.

Darkness claimed him.

The memory of her song accompanied Kazimir, lingering like a brand on his soul.

Somewhere, her snow leopards chuffed.

YSADORA

Mistweave
A delicate fern with silver-grey fronds that curl
upward. Used by fae to write
shifting tales or elusive contracts.
—A Compendium of Faerie Flora and Terrain

My sword had been instrumental in saving Sequoia from the bite, but it was the wrong tool. I left it behind. A wild rhythm drummed through me, my heartbeat erratic, quickening as the maze shifted behind me. I was all alone. Without Father, without Maren and Ferrith, without even the mercenaries.

The bone feline slipped away, and I didn't know if it was on the ground or in the canopies. I pressed deeper into the Wraithwoods, and the air grew colder with every step. My nape tingled with the instinctive knowledge that I was being watched. The wraiths were a breath away. I wondered whether it would be worse to fall prey to the siren call of the wraiths or the bone feline. I wondered how Father and Maren fared.

This was how you died. This was how Lunarys had died, and Mother and Ferrith's little sister Vixora.

It didn't matter how powerful you were. One wrong step, one wrong decision, one moment of doubt was all that it took. Maren and Cyprian had drilled it into me time and again that doubt was a surefire way to breathe your last. And I loved life, I realised. I loved it in its complex beauty, with all its pain and loss, friendship and discoveries.

Dragging in a breath, I pushed everything out of my mind except the bone feline. I knew it was near, knew by its cunning look that it wanted to pick me off from the others, that it wouldn't flee until the matter was settled. It wanted me vulnerable and defenceless. It wanted to snap my bones and devour me in the dark.

When I caught up to it in a small clearing, it turned its feline skull—partially obscured by mist—towards me. Its pale ivory ribcage, elongated limbs and swaying bony barbed tail dominated the clearing. There was a strange intelligence in its gaze as if it weighed up on how to finish our battle. Steady, torchlight eyes dared me to come nearer.

I didn't allow fear to cloud my mind. I drew the quill from my pocket. A channel of ink gleamed in its central channel: mistweave ink that had once been used for the Grimoire, according to Wylda. I only needed a small amount. Belief and innate magic were more important than anything else in Faerie. More important than weapons, emotions, or even destiny. And the well of my magic was deep.

I learned that in my training. I had learned that even the elixir hadn't suppressed the memory of that power within me. I held the quill aloft, and warmth spread through my veins. First, it was a warmth building under my skin, like the stirring of a long-forgotten rhythm. This was when I believed it, this was when I believed I had become something more than mortal. When I sensed that my control was the only thing that stood between order and chaos. My breath became sharper, and a pathway between me and the bone feline vibrated with anticipation as though my intention had already connected us.

As if I would assert my will regardless of its next move.

I let myself believe it.

Lifting Father's quill, I inhaled deeply, filling my lungs with the intoxicating essence of Faerie itself, and harnessed my intentions, sending the silver-grey ink through the foggy clearing. The ink diverged into thin streams, mingling with the innate mists of the Wraithwoods, flowing, clumping, and then forming glyphs. Some I had seen in Mother's annotations or the texts in my chamber, others were entirely unfamiliar. Some were circles, others angular. They pulsed with energy, expanding and contracting as if breathing. Then they spiralled out towards the bone feline, latched onto the bone feline's limbs one by one and sank to ground level.

Anchors heavy, so heavy, that the creature yowled.

Every time it yanked its paws forward, the ink shifted and separated, only to reform with stronger, brighter glyphs that secured it in place. That pulled wider until the bone feline collapsed with a heavy thud, splayed against a carpet of moss. The fog swirled thicker around us as though the Wraithwoods themselves were furious, but the mistweave ink held fast. The glyphs solidified. All that was left was for the bone feline to writhe and snarl, its maw scraping uselessly against the ground.

When it was done, I sat in the clearing with Father's quill clutched in my hands, my mind a whiteout, my body chill. I wrapped my arms around my legs as the bone feline howled and the wraiths wailed. The wraiths came for me, rushing at me, brushing my skin, coiling my hair. I shut my eyes and ignored their pleading. I blanked their hollowed eyes and gaping mouths from my mind. The mercenaries would come. I was sure of it. I just had to hold on.

But when they came, it wasn't Sequoia, who I had saved. Or Cyprian, Wylda and Gabor, who had been kind to me.

It was the mercenary leader. His shadows cascaded into the clearing like a dark tide, cocooning me before pulling the wraiths into a suffocating embrace. The wraiths' ghostly features dissipated as his shadows absorbed their essence, drawing out their sorrow. As each wraith was consumed, the chilling aura in the clearing dwindled, and their anguished whispers faded into silence.

Zephyr emerged from the shadows. His storm-blue eyes widened at the sight of the subdued bone feline. Then he knelt beside me, silver light woven through his dark hair. His shadows receded, absorbed into him.

He cupped my cheek. Wild terror reigned in his eyes. "Are you okay?"

"I think so… You found me."

"I told you I always would."

I nodded. "Are the wraiths at peace?"

"They experienced too much pain in life for that. But they are gone for now." He gazed at the bone feline, confusion marring his brow. The fierceness had drained from it, and there was a pathos to it now. The solidified glyphs were now pearlescent grey and pulsated like the beating of a heart. "How did you know what to do?"

I shrugged. "I've been reading *A Short History of the Order of the Glyph* that Cyprian brought me. I just took what I understood and my intentions and willed it."

He sucked in a breath. "You didn't kill it."

"No. Why didn't you want me to?"

"I will show you." He helped me to my feet, and I folded my hands over Father's quill.

Then he approached the monster and laid a gentle hand against its shoulder bone. I frowned, more confused than ever by his kindness to a creature he had fought. His shadows swirled around the bone feline's skeletal frame, almost as if they tried to comfort it. Independent of the shadows, a soft glow emanated from the mercenary leader's fingertips as he channelled a new magic I hadn't seen before. Almost as though he drew upon the creature's essence. Then the glow subsided, and the shadows retreated once more. The bone feline's gaze was no longer wary.

I stared at them, transfixed. "What did you do?"

"I gave it access to its memories. Its deeper truths. And I collected its story. It deserves a chance to understand, and we should honour its story." He bowed his head to the bone feline and then came towards me. "It was driven by instinct, just like us. But it's not our enemy."

"I don't understand."

"You will." He paused. "Tell me, Inkheart. Why did you save Sequoia? Why didn't you leave?"

"I don't know." I frowned, realising that the chaos of battle had swept me up and escaping hadn't once crossed my mind. Even when the bone feline lured me in and the wraiths surrounded me. Instead, I felt an unexpected sense of belonging with the mercenaries.

The rune behind my ear tingled with a gentle warmth. As Zephyr touched the mirror image of it on his collarbone, I searched his dusky eyes and understood that even though I had acted in ways he hadn't anticipated, this mission had been more than about confronting a beast.

It had been about me: a test of trust.

Zephyr smiled, and it was like moonlight reflecting off a calm, endless sea. My breath hitched as his gaze lingered on my lips, and I thought he might kiss me, there in the clearing of the Wraithwoods, with the subdued bone feline at our feet. My heart hammered in my chest. I wanted his kiss. Maybe I had wanted it since our meeting at Bloomtide. And maybe, just like the bone feline, he wasn't all monster. The warmth of his nearness pulled me in like the quiet promise of something more. But just as the kiss seemed inevitable, his eyes darkened, and the spell between us shattered. He pulled back sharply, the warmth evaporating as if it had never been. Regret flashed across his face.

He held out his hand, carefully. "Let's go home."

Home. Home to Ebonspire for one last night before he took me to Father. "Okay."

The shadows swallowed us.

YSADORA

*Maren is not only my friend. She is my constant,
a sister in every way but blood.
—Ysadora's dream writing,
as seen by Cairn Everreed*

The return journey was a blend of disorienting sensations and closeness. Zephyr and I moved through veils of cool darkness that brushed my skin. The sounds from the world beyond were muffled and distorted. It created a dreamlike quiet, a balm after the deathly silence and howling pockets of the Wraithwoods. Mostly, I was aware of Zephyr, whose warmth countered the chill of the shadowed paths. I caught glimpses of his face, focused and serious. Occasionally, he cast a concerned glance down at me.

We didn't speak. I was glad to process my confusion alone.

When we reached Ebonspire, Zephyr's tawny skin was

wan as if the journey had tired him out, but the rest of the group were too full of the glories of victory to sleep. We returned our weapons to the armoury, scrubbed the grime and sweat from our skin and met in the dining hall for a nightcap of spiced rum and sharp cheese.

"We were worried for you when the maze closed around you," said Wylda.

Gabor slurped his rum, dark eyes keen. "Tell us everything. How did you succeed?"

So I told the tale, and they congratulated themselves for how well they'd trained me when my daily bouts with Maren in Larkspur had given me my fire, and my survival had been sheer luck and the need to prove myself.

Then the conversation moved on as though such occurrences were everyday fare. Gabor slapped Loxley heartily on the back, recounting how his colour had drained to a sickly green with each gust of wind on the flight home. The sisters whispered in the corner about the night's perils. Judging by Sequoia's expression, the rescue hadn't improved my standing with her. Even Zephyr relaxed, his usual watchful gaze softening as he leaned against the hearth, absorbing the general mood of elation and relief.

For the first time in days, I felt like an outsider. Flashes of the bone feline and the wraiths buzzed under my skin. Within hours, I would be leaving Ebonspire and traversing Faerie again—unknowable and wild. Each time I glimpsed my reflection in the window, a stranger looked back. The mismatch between my sense of self and my glamour fuelled my unease.

I slipped into the shadowy stairwell without a goodbye, intending to go to my chamber.

A hand closed around my elbow. "You did well out there. What you learned will help you fight the next one."

I gave Cyprian a small smile. "Thanks." His words did nothing to quell the storm inside me.

"Come on. If you don't get some air, you'll not sleep a wink. We'll go and see Mythros." He grinned. "Oh, I know you've been chipping away at that old boy's stubbornness. Zephyr's noticed, too."

Warmth bloomed in my chest. I shrugged. "Animals see past the masks we wear."

We headed outside, and our boots crunched on the short gravel path to the stables. The tightness in my chest eased with every step into the gentle night, and the cool air was a balm against the heat of my thoughts. It was hard to believe that the canvas of the night sky encompassed both Ebonspire and Wraithwoods, both Larkspur and the Shrouded Forest. That Father, Maren and I were all in Faerie under the starry sky.

Cyprian spoke first. "The others like you. Some more than others, granted."

A laugh escaped me. "By that, I take it you mean Sequoia. The overprotective sister?"

Cyprian picked a twig out of his braid. "*That's* what Wylda told you? Sure, she's protective of Wylda. They didn't exactly have an easy time when the Court of Wild Ferns fell. That's not why she bristles around you. For a long time, Sequoia and Zephyr were together. She doesn't like the thought of someone else treading that ground."

I stiffened. "I'm not sure why that would cause her to dislike me. Their past relationship is none of my business."

"If you say so." He searched my face and then regrouped. "My friends have forgotten how hard our first battles were. You mustn't hold their thoughtlessness against them. Faerie lives are long. They've buried the sharpness of those early encounters under other battles, other causes. They've forgotten what a blade felt like when it weighed the world."

"Your memory is clearer?"

"My time magic means I remember more than most, whether I want to or not."

"I'm sorry. That must be hard." Some things were best forgotten or faded. Like the short-lived love of a mother, gone too soon. Or when people didn't come back from battle. Grief burrowed deep enough without the curse of a razor-sharp memory.

A bittersweet smile tugged at the corner of his mouth. "I've seen countless skirmishes over my century of living. Each one carves a piece out of you that you never get back. Even the ones I've come away unscathed from. Something you sacrifice. Something you see. You end up leaving fragments of yourself on every battlefield, whether you notice or not."

I shuddered. "Thank you for accompanying me out here."

"I'm sorry."

"For what?"

"That your life got upended. Sometimes, I think Faerie is the loss of innocence."

I gave a slight shrug. "I'd rather live a life of authenticity than spend my days hiding in false comfort."

"You are angry at your Father."

"I hope there is time to forgive him." Did the secrets Father kept from me press against his ribs, like my lies about taking Lunarys's elixir the day she visited the bookshop? I could never hold a secret without great difficulty. They weighed me down like stones in my pockets.

We arrived at the stables, greeted by soft whinnies and the scent of hay and leather. The stables were crafted from timber that mirrored the darkness of Ebonspire, with an arched roof and an old swinging sign that depicted gallant horses mid-gallop. Tack and saddles hung on the walls in neat lines, and flickering lanterns suspended from the beams were a bulwark against the grey of the new day. There were four horses in residence; with their wings, Gabor and Sequoia had no need to ride, and I was uncertain how far Zephyr and Cyprian could travel with their magic. Each stall was spacious and well-kept, with large troughs of fresh water, sturdy wooden dividers and plaques bearing the names of the steeds. My heart lifted at the sight of Mythros munching hay.

My voice was a caress. "Hello, you." I ran a hand through my short, blonde locks, the unfamiliar texture under my fingertips, trying to shake off the oddness that clung to me.

I worried he wouldn't recognise me, but the black stallion lifted his head with a soft whicker. Large, brown eyes focused on me, and for a moment, I imagined he could see into my soul. The fine muscles beneath his coat rippled as he shifted to nuzzle against my hand, and the tension faded from my shoulders.

Cyprian leant against the entrance to the stall, one knee bowed against a post. "He would have recognised you by your voice and scent anyway, but for the record, the glamour's fading. Your eyes are turning violet-blue again."

"My whole life, I thought they were brown." My hand went to my cheek, sensing my face tingling and my curves filling out. And for a moment, I wanted to leap on Mythros and ride, ride back to Larkspur, back to the home I knew and the people I loved. But they weren't there, and I had changed, too. Tears clogged my throat. "Every step here feels like walking into another question. I'm always on guard, waiting for the next impossible thing, the next piece of context that Father never taught me."

Cyprian heaved a breath. "It's okay to feel disconcerted. That's why Zeph wanted to take it slow. It might not look like it, but he's been going out of his way to make the transition easier for you. He knows what it's like to be pulled between two places. He knows he can be intense, that you might be frightened by his shadows. So he asked Gabor to teach you history when Zeph has a natural affinity for it. Believe it or not, he's better at letting people in than he used to be. We were interrupted earlier when the wards went off. The books in your chamber weren't from me. They're from Zephyr."

A thrill ran through me, unbidden, as I mulled over his words. "Cyprian? Why did he collect the bone feline's story? Is that what the faerie queen of the Court of Chaos is paying coin for?"

He snorted in disdain. "Tanuhja isn't interested in their stories. She was only paying us to rid the land of the ones that venture close to overwhelming the wards at the border with the mortal realm. She doesn't care about the rest. But Zephyr does."

"*Was* paying?"

Cyprian's mouth flattened to a hard line. "She's stopped. A while ago now. Something changed to make her no longer care about the border with the mortal realm. Not that it's changed our stubborn leader's mind."

"Zephyr is still rounding them up…"

He nodded. "He insists on it. He refuses to abandon those creatures. Tanuhja's coin was generous while it lasted. We've built up enough of a stash to survive, but it won't last forever. There is another who would pay handsomely if we were to reroute the monsters to him. He wants to repurpose them into an army, but Zephyr isn't interested."

I traced the silken waterfall of Mythros's mane. The hayloft above was stacked high with bales, and faint scrabbling sounds suggested mice found shelter there. "I've been worried that the bone feline is still in the Wraithwoods, bound with my magic, unable to move or feast. It would have been better off dead. But that can't be right. Because Zephyr *cared* for it."

"I was hoping a bookseller's daughter is the sort of female who can see past the outer cover to what lies beneath." He stood up tall and dusted wood shavings from his breeches from a recent repair to the stables. "Don't you see? He's not perfect. But he cares. About you, about all of us, about this land. That's why he insisted we bring you here from the Shrouded Forest, despite knowing it would bring him into conflict with others. Zephyr is an ocean of mercy because, after his mother, no one showed him any. And like the ocean, he has both darkness and light."

My pulse quickened as the dark surged. I dropped my hands from Mythros and whispered. "And the creatures?"

Zephyr's growl startled us as he stepped out of a

pocket of darkness. "This isn't your story to tell, Cyprian. It's mine."

"I didn't mean to… I was comforting her."

Stormy eyes fell on me as his stallion pawed at the ground with one powerful hoof, mirroring Zephyr's agitation. "Hide in the hay loft, Ysadora. My uncle approaches."

"What?" I stuttered.

Cyprian's eyes widened in alarm. "He's found Ebonspire?"

A curt nod. "Rewind the clock to give Ysadora time, then get Mythros and yourself out of here."

Cyprian gripped his friend's arm. "Let me stay. Let me protect our home. Let me protect you."

Shadows swarmed into the stable, joining with Zephyr. They retained their potency despite the dawning day. "He won't breach Ebonspire itself. Not today. Not alone. Do as I say, Cyprian. He's almost upon us." Zephyr brushed a strand of hair from my face. "Don't use the quill, Inkheart. He doesn't know of your magic."

The glamour was gone, I realised. My hair was dark, and my eyes were violet, and my body was my own. I wondered why—if his uncle was such a threat—he didn't shadow walk me away from Ebonspire or cloak the stable. I wondered what secret he kept in the vault of his heart about the creatures. Most of all, I wondered why I worried about him and Cyprian and who his uncle could be to command such a response in males as powerful as them.

All the while, my heart was a hummingbird in my chest.

Then Cyprian's eyes went from hazel to gold, and the air shifted around me, stilling like a suspended breath. A gentle distortion rippled. Colours deepened, and edges softened around me as Cyprian stretched time's fabric. The familiar warmth of the stables turned cold and strange, and the flicker of torchlight froze. This time, unlike during our training sessions when he pulled the wool over my eyes, Cyprian allowed me to keep my awareness. Words retracted, Zephyr vanished into the shadows in reverse, and my body seemed caught in a quiet, controlled whirl as I counted to fifteen: each second, an entire orbit.

When the flow of time trickled back, Cyprian was there, urging me up to the hayloft, telling me to hurry, even as my feet slipped on the rungs. I watched from above, heart clamouring, as Cyprian turned out all but one of the lanterns above Mythros's stall. The stallion lowered his proud head, and Cyprian led him into a fold of time. In a blink, they were gone, and someone was tugging me between hay bales, wooden slats at our backs, as familiar shadows extended like a dark veil to envelop us.

The shadows thickened as a stranger's footsteps sounded beneath us.

I didn't flinch at the body beside mine. A rush of gratitude and relief flowed over me despite the impending danger. I recognised the scent of her rusty hair, the shape of her messy bun and the feel of her arms around me. I knew suddenly, why Zephyr had sent me up here and not away. It hadn't been scuttling mice I'd heard in the hay loft but her.

My friend. My heart-sister.

"Maren," I breathed.

I buried my face in her shoulder, inhaling the familiar scent of autumn bonfires. Our foreheads pressed together, a gentle collision that felt like a celebration. Against all odds, we were together again. We had shared so many embraces, but this one was different. We were no longer young girls whispering our dreams under the stars. Those innocent nights felt far away, like echoes from another lifetime. We had faced darkness, loss and truth, and all artifice had been stripped back between us. I loved her more fiercely in the wake of our enforced separation. Enveloped in our shadow cocoon, my own emotions were mirrored in her face. Flecks of green danced in her amber eyes, but she held a finger up to her lips.

We huddled together, hearts pounding in synchronicity as clipped male voices pierced the shadow veil. I found myself clutching Father's quill regardless of Zephyr's warning. His uncle's chilling voice veered between notes of sadness and menace. It had an unsettling familiarity, like an old nightmare resurfacing in the light of the new day.

"How disappointing, nephew, that after all my efforts to lessen your mother's influence on you, we find ourselves here. "

Zephyr sounded almost bored. "It started as a little wager with myself. How long could I keep Ebonspire a secret from the spymaster himself? I thought you liked games, uncle. Especially games that stretch out for decades. Or maybe you lose your taste for them when you're the one facing the risk."

There was a sigh of fabric, a cloak perhaps, then the click of a lock as a stall opened beneath us: Mythros's stall, I thought, by the placement of footfalls. "I've lived long enough to know that the stakes change, and so do the players."

A dull thud of steps sounded as Zephyr followed him

into the stall, his voice calm, uninvested. "How long has it been since you've been to Ebonspire, uncle?"

"I was here the day your mother and sister died, as you well know."

"Too late," said Zephyr softly.

"Yes, too late to save her. But not you." His voice dripped with scorn. "Look at Ebonspire now…an overgrown relic, hidden away like a shameful secret. Your mother's grand vision twisted into a crumbling husk of what it once was. Did you think your shadows would shield it forever? From me?"

"Forever is a long time in Faerie."

"I taught you better. Power is the only currency here, and yet you waste your skill on collecting Tanuhja's coin. On sentimentality. Pathetic, really. To see you grasping at the straws of Rowena's legacy."

"Mercenaries are hardly in the game for prestige. Coin feeds my group. Besides, I like to work undisturbed."

"I gave you the keys to my court. I nurtured you like a son. Tell me why you did this, and perhaps I will spare you."

His uncle released a swarm of shadows, more violent in their energy than Zephyr's. A scream built in my throat as I realised his uncle was more powerful or equal in power to Zephyr. That Maren and I were in mortal danger, even as the rune behind my ear pulsed, exacting its demand for my unconditional trust. His uncle's shadows slithered across the hay loft, rushing up to the vaulted beams, then sliding down with unnerving intelligence, pulsing and probing the protective cocoon around us. The moment they made contact, Zephyr's shadows converged closer around us.

I gripped Maren's hand tighter as my muscles tensed and the fight or flight instinct kicked in.

"You never cared for lore," said Zephyr. "And I needed something of my own."

"In your mother's day, Ebonspire was a sanctuary. But for you, it's an attempt to have *something of your own*?"

"You have a wife and children, uncle. What is yours is not mine."

"Indeed." His uncle's tone was dangerous. "And yet, I cannot let this deception stand."

Zephyr sounded so bleak, so despairing, that I no longer could unravel what was an act and what was real. Whether he was being coerced or whether he played the game as well as his uncle. "I have your prize. I will surrender the calligrapher's daughter to you in exchange for continued privacy at Ebonspire."

My stomach hardened at his betrayal of me, and Maren balled her fists, even as his uncle's shadows explored the contours and textures of Zephyr's veil, searching for weaknesses and inconsistencies, winding around us like a suffocating mist.

"Surrender is such a beautiful word. Why not give the girl to me now?"

"That would make me look weak. I will not look weak in the eyes of your court. Make no mistake. You need me, uncle. Your own children do not serve you as well as I have. Why not let Ebonspire be our secret? Unless you wish to look like the foolish spymaster who missed its reemergence for decades? Far better that I present the girl at court."

His uncle's shadows swelled like dark waves against Zephyr's veil before ebbing back. His voice was as cold as the breath of a northern wind, and yet beneath it, there was perhaps a grudging respect. "Well played, nephew. Our bargain is struck. I expect you and the girl at court at twilight. Do not be late."

Zephyr groaned. The cocoon around us thinned, and whispers crescendoed, making the wooden slats of the stable walls quake. Then, the oppressive stillness in the stables melted away as if the entire space had been released from a silent chokehold. Zephyr's shadows receded from us, and ambient noises filtered back in: the rustling of straw, the gentle creak of wood, the horse's soft, snorting breaths and the slop of water in the troughs.

I waited, straining to catch any lingering signs of his uncle, but there was nothing: no slinking shadows probing the hay loft, no chilling presence lurking at the edges. Only the shaky breath of someone in distress. I turned to Maren, deliberating how we should proceed. The mercenary leader would not separate us again. He wouldn't harm her. I would make sure of it.

His velvet tones were strained as if he were holding back a groan between the words. "You can come down. Both of you."

I climbed down the ladder into the new day. Maren descended next, a bundle of rage and resolve.

We found him on his knees in Mythros's empty stall, his jaw clenched. A shimmer of a bold blue rectangle marked his forearm. He dragged himself to his feet, and our eyes locked. "What you heard…I can explain."

Maren's pent-up fury burst forth like a comet. She charged at him, her fists flaring with fire, ripples of indigo and silver that made the horses shriek. "You took Ysa. You want to give her to the faerie king. I will end you."

Zephyr sidestepped her lunge. His shadows quenched her starfire as though he were extinguishing a candle, and he caught her by the wrists. She struggled, muscles taut as she tried to twist free.

A vein throbbed in his jaw. "You must be Maren, Ysadora's friend. Truce? Or do I have to keep hold of you?"

Maren bristled. "Rowena Ashmoor was a titan. She gave sanctuary to the vulnerable. You—"

His eyes hooded as he released her. "Guard your words, fire wielder, and you can share Ysadora's chambers until we leave."

Confusion clouded Maren's face. She stumbled back a step to my side, chest rising and falling. "Oh."

"But first, Ysadora and I must talk." A kaleidoscope of emotions flickered across his face: determination, exhaustion and pain.

I sucked in a breath. "Who is your uncle?"

Maren folded her arms. "His uncle is Thiago Hendrick, the Faerie King of the Court of Silence. The spymaster."

I swallowed hard. "Does he have my Father?"

Zephyr held my gaze. "Yes."

My stomach clenched. "So you will be meeting the terms of our bargain."

"Don't believe him, Ysa," said Maren. "He's a mercenary. Brutal. Ruthless. He's just delivering his bounty."

I laid a hand on her arm. "You don't know him like I do."

The shadows that sometimes wove around Zephyr stilled, allowing me to see him more clearly than ever before, and his eyes were a storm of need and hope. "Do you trust me, Inkheart?"

It was the hope that made me succumb. Nine days and nights, he had prepared me.

Maren stared at me, aghast, her body rigid.

Maybe being reunited with her imbued me with additional courage. Or maybe it was because Cyprian had hinted that once you belonged to the mercenary leader, he protected you always. I had experienced it, witnessed it. Maybe it was because Faerie was complex, and so was I. But I found that, during the course of the nine days, an unexpected answer had formed on my tongue.

"Tell me you trust me."

"Yes, unconditionally."

KAZIMIR

*The dragon riders of the Nebula Court atop their
mounts are a sight to behold. They serve as
protectors of the court, emissaries across the
realm, and upholders of the Grimoire
governing the balance of magic
between Faerie and the mortal realm.
—A Tapestry of Courts and Crowns*

Kazimir hated Danaë's snow leopards. Their presence was as silent as it was intimidating, sleek and shadowed as they slipped through the halls or watched from high, concealed ledges. Though utterly loyal to her, the slightest misstep or raised voice from others triggered their ire, flashes of teeth and claws and golden eyes a reminder of their wildness.

Beasts not even the faerie king could tame.

His ex-wife had always liked cats, he supposed. She put out milk for them in case a stray was lurking nearby.

She let them come and go, leaving windows open just wide enough for them to slink inside as if they were as welcome as any guest. They slept in a cosy spot by the hearth or curled around her ankles in the village square. She had melted at their purring and traced idle paths along their sleek coats. He had craved her touch himself, but their marriage hadn't delivered much in the way of spousal affection, try as he did.

Cats were unknowable creatures, prickly and single-minded, much like her.

He didn't know how Danaë had come to have snow leopards as her shadows. Whether they had been a gift from the spymaster or creatures she had attracted due to her own cold nature. His blinders had been removed these past days about her true nature. About the black heart beneath her elegant blonde hair and silken voice.

Kazimir shuddered. He couldn't help but think that perhaps he hadn't been the one to choose her after all, all those orbits ago, when he had arrived in Larkspur and needed a mother for Ysa. Perhaps Danaë had chosen him because she had *already* known of Faerie. Perhaps she had set her sights on him because she imagined he might take her there. He had never been able to resist her pleading. He had gifted her more and more books about Faerie. It hadn't been enough; it had only whetted her appetite. It had made her more unhappy. Then Thiago had come along to steal his wife and complete the deal instead.

Not that Danaë explained herself to him. She didn't seem to think he deserved an explanation.

She seemed to think broken hearts were nothing. She was perfectly happy to break him even more.

Once a day, she asked a simple question. "Where is Ysadora?"

Kazimir held firm at first: his beloved daughter's whereabouts would go with him to the grave. But as the days passed and the torture became too much, his courage gave out. He pleaded for Danaë to stop for the sake of what they had shared. When that didn't work, he bought momentary reprieves by providing answers that could be true. Bookshops he had visited in the mortal realm once upon a time that he knew no longer existed. Churches where fae would never venture. The abodes of long-dead mortal acquaintances. Any attempts to follow these leads were as futile as chasing shadows. But the faerie king and his spiders made quick work of such falsehoods.

Danaë's fury grew with each subsequent misdirection.

Each time she tortured him, she began with a soothingly beautiful melody, usually one he recognised, that would pull him back to the time they were husband and wife. Her soft notes floated through the air like petals, and he was almost lulled by it, almost willing to believe that they were not enemies.

Then his whole body tightened as she pulled up her dark hood over golden tresses. The lifting of her hood signalled the descent from beauty to cruelty. Danaë revelled in theatrics. The hood masked her eyes, leaving her twisted lips in stark relief. Then her voice twisted around him like a blade sheathed in velvet, starting as a ballad and ending as a requiem. The warped melody rang through his mind until it scraped at old scars and left fresh wounds. Her song raked against his skull like claws on bone. Songs weren't supposed to be punishing; they were meant to uplift and bring comfort. But each note his former wife conjured was an arrow sent to unmake him. There was no mercy. There was no resisting, not with her chuffing snow leopards circling. Kazimir's ears ached, then burned. Blood trickled, then gushed. Danaë looked beautiful and terrible, hands relaxed at her sides. She was detached, almost exacting through his pain. Even when he clutched his head. Even when her song inhabited him, leaving nothing else. Not even the memory of Ysa's face. Even when he blacked out.

He felt so lonely without the kindness of loved ones.

The faerie king suspected that Kazimir's dragon would come for him. Dragons sensed when their riders were in pain. Thiago had a strategic mind. If torturing Kazimir led to Ysadora's whereabouts, as well as the capture of a dragon, the amplification of his power and influence would be vast. But no one had spotted Caldoron in decades; at least, that's what the guards whispered. Not since Kazimir had fled with Ysa to the mortal realm.

Even so, the faerie king took precautions. Kazimir heard the stomp of battalion boots as they filed out of Echohold on Thiago's orders to hunt for Caldoron. But Kazimir wasn't worried. The Greystorm Ridge that bordered the Court of Silence was a good hiding place. His dragon was so intelligent that Kazimir's bonding process had lasted longer than any other rider's in history. His dragon knew well how to hide from shadows, and he wouldn't be bested.

After all, Caldoron had waited for an age to see Kazimir again.

To fly through the skies with Kazimir on his scaly back.

It helped Kazimir to believe the dragon might come, however futile. It helped to believe that the dragon hadn't perished in the intervening years, although without the Order of the Glyph, the dragons would have to fend for themselves. He didn't let himself think otherwise in those long, cold, painful days at Echohold. Ysa and Caldoron both lived. It had to be so.

The only glimpse of kindness he saw was from the frost dryad. She came time and again to heal him, her delicate blue lips drooping in sorrow as she wove crystalline bonds and ice lattices over his wounds. Each visit left him colder, like fragments of his spirit froze beneath her touch despite her intent to heal. How many times could a soul be stitched back together? How often could a heart be thawed only to break again? He began to wonder if one day the frost would settle so deeply that only silence remained where he once was whole.

Occasionally, he supped with Thiago and Danaë. They enjoyed making him feel the fool as they paraded their love; at least, that is how it seemed to Kazimir as they passed each other morsels and spoke of matters relating to the court like the tithe or some minor kerfuffle that they didn't mind him knowing.

On the ninth day, guards collected him from his chamber for supper. He had been relieved that a whole day had passed without a visit from Danaë. There had been a hustle and bustle at Echohold that had punctured the thick silence as if the faerie king and his consort were expecting visitors. Usually, they were careful to lock him away from the prying eyes of guests. This time, he was surprised to see not three place settings at the needle-thin supper table but five, his own set apart at some distance from the rest. Plates of fine black ceramic were set with stark precision, together with silver cutlery, burnished to a dull sheen as if too much gleam might disturb the hushed atmosphere.

Kazimir waited alone at the table while servants brought in dishes of slender game, dark roots and thin slivers of smoked mushroom. Rich rugs absorbed the footfalls of servants clad in grey attire that made them nearly indistinguishable from the shadows. Then the door to the hall opened, and in came the faerie lord and Danaë, flanked by her snow leopards, and behind them, a young male and female.

Kazimir met Danaë's now golden eyes, and she preened, tucking her hand deeper into the crook of Thiago's elbow. All at once, it occurred to him that these were Thiago and Danaë's children—twins perhaps—and Kazimir's heart squeezed in his chest. Their son had inherited his father's gaunt build and black wavy hair, though he wore it longer, together with Danaë's once-brown eyes. Their daughter's soft blonde hair was almost silver by the candlelight, her features more refined and ethereal than her mother's, who had begun life as a mortal. Her mouth—unlike her brother's—was bound shut.

"Cairn." Pride glimmered in Danaë's eyes. "I'd like you to meet Xaire and Elowen, our children."

He hated that she chose to use the name he had used in their domestic life together, with its soft vowels and sweet brevity. He would have preferred her to give him the respect of his true name. Of course, she didn't. Of course, his eyes lingered on her belly as he wondered what she had looked like when swollen with child. If her pregnant form had resembled the other woman he had loved—the woman he couldn't and wouldn't name—Ysa's biological mother.

"My wife is too tired to sing today," said the Faerie King of the Court of Silence. "It is a shame."

Danaë patted his arm. "Be seated, children."

"How old are they, Your Grace?" intoned Kazimir.

Thiago's grey eyes gleamed. "Nineteen years."

He nodded bleakly. The faerie king had not only made Danaë fae, he had given her children from her own womb. A gift that had been impossible for Kazimir to bestow. After all, the Binder's protection had come at the cost of his future seed: she had insisted her diligence was only worthwhile if Kazimir focused on Ysa and Ysa alone.

Little good it did any of them now.

Their mother's snow leopards prowled around the table as the family took their seats. Their son, Xaire, moved with languid grace, the shadows stretching and bending around him as if reluctant to let him go. Elowen, who was shadowless, at least at that moment, wore dark, draping fabrics that nonetheless hinted at the court's shadows. She held herself with dignified poise despite the binding across her mouth: a silent statement of control, perhaps, or a reminder of the secrets she was forced to keep. When the bond dissolved long enough for her to eat, she didn't speak. The absence of her voice left a palpable void in the air.

They ate, but they didn't seem to be a family at all. There was no hum of conversation or sly ribbing between the siblings, no glances full of meaning that spoke of intimacy or stories passed over plates. No laughter to soften the sharp edges of the room. There was none of the closeness between father and son or mother and daughter that he might expect. They were like strangers forced into proximity, each a cold, self-contained figure moving with careful precision. Every bite was taken with mechanical calm as the faerie king watched over his family with proprietary interest as if they were yet more pieces on a board he controlled.

He didn't control the snow leopards. That task belonged to his wife alone. To those Danaë disliked, the snow leopards were silent stalkers, slipping through shadows or lounging just close enough to unnerve, their golden eyes unblinking and watchful. Tonight, they prowled close to his chair or weaved in and out of sight, an ever-present reminder of her silent command. There was a ruthless elegance to how she channelled the snow leopards: their muscular forms slipped soundlessly across the edges of the room. She summoned them with a single flick of her eyes, turning her creatures into tools of intimidation and aggression far better than any weapon, all without her lifting a finger. Kazimir himself was unable to eat. Every bite he attempted lodged in his throat. The textures were too slimy, the scent too pungent.

When she had finished, Danaë pressed a serviette to her mouth. "The children are currently learning about the Order of the Glyph for their schooling, and I decided to present you as a piece of living history, Cairn. Or should I say, Kazimir Silberquill?"

Xaire's hair fell over his forehead, partially obscuring his eyes. "So you were the calligrapher."

Her son's calm, dispassionate tone peeled away the last shreds of Kazimir's pride. He was being paraded to her children as an artefact, relegating him to the past and therefore dismissing any agency over his future. "Some call me that, yes."

Elowen twisted a ring on his finger, watching it turn and catch the light, only occasionally glancing up.

Her brother continued. "But you possess none of the power you once had. Not the dragon, or the brotherhood, or the level of ink magic that once made you a legend. You are, some would say, a fae shell with a smattering of magic that some mortals might possess if they didn't dismiss the signs of their power. I find it hard to believe that my parents would be able to keep you here otherwise."

The faerie king leaned forward as though savouring the exchange. Kazimir wanted to recoil from the insult, but he forced himself to remain still. Kazimir loved the mortal realm, but the comparison to humankind felt like a degradation when once he had commanded power so effortlessly. The traces of magic lingering beneath his skin were fractured by his absence from Faerie, his dragon, his brotherhood, and now, by Danaë's torture.

Kazimir refused to be reduced entirely to the image her son painted. "Even a shell remembers what it once was."

His thoughts turned inward. Even if he did escape, this loveless family of high walls and cold ambition would continue their relentless pursuit of Ysa. She was their obsession, and his meagre magic left Ysa vulnerable to their scheming. He couldn't let them take her. He wouldn't. He needed to regain his lost magic to fortify himself for the battles to come.

The Binder flashed into his mind. Lunarys might be gone, but his mind flickered to the meteor that had fallen at Bloomtide when she had set Ysa's fate free. Its descent had been spectacular, a blaze of light cutting across the sky, drawing the eyes of many. Few understood its true significance, but Kazimir had belonged to the upper echelons of the Court of Nebulas. He had convened with the Binder often. That is how he had known to go to her in the first place. The meteor, in all rights, belonged to Ysa now that the Binder had perished. It contained rare, potent magic, remnants of the cosmos mixed with Ysa's possible fates. If she held it, it would amplify her ability. As her ancestor, it would do the same for him.

If he could find it. If it hadn't already been taken.

Glee throbbed in his chest: a dangerous thrill mixed with the weight of desperation. What if he could carry out the duties of the brotherhood as Thiago and Danaë demanded and reset the balance of Faerie and the mortal realm? Would that be enough for the Court of Silence to leave him and Ysa alone? What if he could tap into the essence of the universe itself? What if, as well as protecting his daughter, he could reset Faerie and turn the tides of fate to bring back the Order of the Glyph?

Kazimir would need cunning, stealth and speed. He needed his dragon.

Xaire's voice cut through the haze of his thoughts, his expression carefully neutral. "Did you love my mother, calligrapher?"

Kazimir's voice was hard. "What does it matter now? She's made her choice."

Danaë glanced at her son. "Cairn was just a part of my story. A chapter now closed."

Her son locked eyes with his sister, and it was as though they shared silent communication despite her bound mouth, as though Xaire was her translator. Kazimir's blood ran cold at the sight of it. Here was a life stripped of voice and agency, and for a male who valued words and life in all their forms, it was hard to fathom.

Xaire addressed his mother. "Elowen wants to know why you asked Father to bring the calligrapher here?"

Danaë smiled at her daughter. The tension in the room coiled tighter. "To teach you both about choices and consequences, dearest."

A pang of sorrow filled Kazimir as he looked at Elowen, although he understood by the stiffness of her gait that she didn't want his pity. The intensity with which she assessed him made his skin prickle. "Your children deserve more than this spectacle."

Irritation passed over her otherwise controlled expression. She set her goblet down with utmost care, and it seemed to Kazimir that the temperature in the room had dropped. Her voice was a silken whisper. "My children have everything. Wealth beyond measure. Protection. Privilege. Influence. Can your child say the same? Or did you teach her to look for meaning in bonds that break? To grasp fleeting joy at the expense of her power? This spectacle, as you call it, teaches my children that power is not in frivolity or fleeting warmth. It is in control, over oneself and others."

Her children looked down, eating in their clockwork fashion.

"Well said, wife." The faerie king drained his goblet. "I think tonight has had the requisite impact. I must leave now to convene with my nephew. Tonight has the promise of being very fruitful indeed."

They wanted to break his mind, as well as his body. He might have escaped physical torture today, but this had been psychological warfare, showing him their intact family when his own family was realms apart. The faerie king and his consort wanted Kazimir to know that they thrived while he suffered.

But it hadn't worked. Finally, Kazimir had realised he didn't envy this world that Danaë had built for herself. He didn't want silent halls and bleak landscapes. For all the children she and Thiago had, it was enough for Kazimir to have Ysa. He couldn't envy a barren existence devoid of connection. Every carefully crafted smile, calculated gesture and hollow grasp of power revolted him. Real life was messy and loving, vibrant and vulnerable, or it meant nothing at all.

They had waged war on his mind, but it had forced him into action.

It had forced him to remember the meteor.

Later that night, when the guards returned Kazimir to his chamber, he knelt by the bed and begged the stars that Ysa and Maren were safe, like he did every night. Then he crawled, shivering under the covers.

When he felt his dragon's scalding heat at the snow-covered ledge, Kazimir didn't cover his face. He smiled, a tear trailing down his face. He wondered if Caldoron had sensed his resolve at supper. He was such a clever beast.

Then he reunited with the noble creature he had missed ever since he had fled Faerie.

He wasn't cold anymore.

2 4

———

ZEPHYR

Do not rush to love, darling. True affection grows
like a slow, patient bloom, not like the quick,
bright flame that soon burns out.
—Rowena Ashmoor's letter to her son Zephyr

Ysadora trusted him, and it healed his damn heart that she could look past his darkness and make that choice, even with all he had done. All she had heard. He had grown so accustomed to wearing his armour—both literal and emotional—that he had forgotten what it felt like to let someone new in.

Still, he didn't give any credence to Veda's painting: what his sister had told him so long ago.

He had barely held it together when Thiago had been there. All Zephyr had worked for, all he had dreamed of, all that his mother had instilled in him: it had all been on the line. The tight knot of dread in his stomach had made it almost impossible to think or speak to his uncle. He'd thrown a fervent prayer to his maternal ancestors that the wards around Ebonspire itself would hold. That they would keep its inhabitants safe against the faerie king's spiders attempting to breach the walls. That he could put on a convincing enough performance for the faerie king for him to consider Ebonspire worthless.

But it was the thought of the calligrapher's daughter being caught in the crossfire of faerie dealings—of his uncle's wrath—that had almost killed him. He didn't understand how it had happened.

He was consumed by thoughts of Ysadora Silberquill every waking moment.

After a century, training was like breathing to him, like stepping into the current of a familiar river: an effortless dance of muscle and instinct. He knew every angle, every calculated shift in balance, every silent footfall that granted him an edge. But the calligrapher's daughter disrupted that flow. Every glance she cast his way rippled through his concentration, causing his movements to hitch. As though they were performed for her pleasure. He replayed their interactions in the solitude of his chamber. He became riddled with jealousy if she smiled too generously at Gabor or Loxley. He'd even envied Cyprian for the intimate conversation he had shared with her tonight because Cyprian had provided Ysadora with the comfort that Zephyr himself wanted to give.

He gave a snort of derision. His emotions were usually under lock and key.

He was a grown male, not a youngling in short breeches.

Cyprian told him he was a fool for keeping secrets. About her mother. About the monsters. He said that

Ysadora had been the victim of such subterfuge that holding back essential truths would poison any affection she had developed for the mercenaries. He said that they needed Ysadora's help and that he remembered Veda's painting. Zephyr ended their training with a ruthless surge of power he usually reserved for the battlefield.

He had wanted to shout himself hoarse after her recklessness against the bone feline. Wanted to howl in frustration that she could be so stupid. She knew too little about the dangers of Faerie, despite all his group had endeavoured to teach her. Hadn't he told her to stay by his side? Didn't she know he had lost his mother and sister? How it haunted him that he hadn't been able to protect them.

Then his shadows had found her in the clearing, the bone feline utterly helpless against her magic, and Zephyr had felt almost light-headed with relief. She'd been sitting there, legs folded against her chest, and his heart had quickened, even as his shadows drove away the wraiths. He'd been intoxicated by her. He wanted to kiss her in that starsforsaken place, in front of that starsforsaken creature. The strength of the feeling had surprised even him. He had drawn back only because of the blasted glamour. Because Ysadora wasn't herself, and it was her lips he wanted, her actual body pressed against his. Not Wylda's imitation of whichever passing stranger she had drawn her inspiration from.

So he had pulled himself together. He'd held her during the shadow walk home, inhaling the scent of sunlit herbs that reminded him of the Forgotten Garden before it had become a place of misery for him. Her scent was the only thing unchanged by the artifice of the glamour: that

blood was spilt in Faerie. Wouldn't understand why he hadn't intervened to rescue Kazimir. He knew the patterns of the Court of Silence. Torture, heal, torture, heal on repeat, at least while his uncle still had use for his victim. Kazimir would survive. Playing the long game was how to thwart his uncle. He had learned that lesson early. Zephyr had to choose his interventions with emotionless clarity, lest the whole game unravel too soon.

As much as he hated himself for it, Kazimir wasn't Zephyr's priority.

His priority was Faerie itself. His friends and his home, certainly. And inexplicably, Ysadora.

Surely her Father would forgive him for his slowness to act if it meant Ysadora was stronger for it?

She followed him into the dim, cool interior, and he led her down the spiral staircase, deeper and deeper, feeling his shoulders coil with strain, his skin prickling like it always did each time he visited the cellar. He wanted to warn her of what awaited them in the darkness, but it would be better to show her. She would never believe him otherwise. He wanted so much to keep her trust. Wanted so much to earn it, craved it like a lifeline in a turbulent sea. Bitter experience had taught him that the truth often met with more resistance than elaborate webs of lies. He worried she would recoil in disgust.

He led the way over worn steps, polished by time. An earthy scent rose from below, mingling with the cool bite of damp, underground air. Now and then, he checked over his shoulder to see if the calligrapher's daughter was all right, though he could barely make out her expression in the dim light. She followed close behind, never hesitating, her hand brushing the rough stone wall for balance.

At the bottom of the stairs, Zephyr took a moment to collect himself. His shadows pooled thickly around the cellar. They were alive with whispers, eager for his company, tired of his demand for impenetrable shielding and constant vigilance of this part of the building. At his approach, they shifted just enough to reveal the outline of an old iron door.

Ysadora tensed, but she said only, "I'm not afraid of your shadows, and I've never been afraid of cellars."

He remembered that the cellar in Kazimir's house in Larkspur had been her haven. That it might still be her haven had Thiago not kidnapped her father and cleared the cellar of the fae books so that Danaë might read them once more. Ysadora's dark hair curled at her nape with a slight sheen of sweat. He cursed himself for not knowing whether it was from fear or whether he'd taken the steps too fast. They both needed rest after that damn mission, her more than him.

He steeled himself. "Are you ready?"

Their eyes met. He noted in her silent agreement that she still trusted him. That was all Zephyr needed. He commanded his shadows to ebb and pushed the door open.

A hinge creaked and echoed in the silence. Then, the monsters began to howl.

25

YSADORA

Ironjaw Bear
Metallic teeth, fur like rusted metal, thunderous
roar. Once, Jarek Ironroot of the Court of Wild
Ferns, brother of Ivor, gifted in binding metal
to the forest to fortify it against threats.
—The Secrets of Faerie's Veiled Beasts
by Zephyr Ashmoor

Our eyes locked, and it didn't feel wrong to follow the mercenary leader into the bowels of Ebonspire. Clearly, there was something to be feared here. This cellar didn't house wine barrels, dusty shelves, winter stores or old tools. I understood by the gravity of Zephyr's demeanour that something down here would shift the axis of my understanding.

I could sense it: a darkness that had nothing to do with the absence of light. It wasn't precisely evil. No, that wasn't it. This darkness thrummed like a string instrument tuned too low. In the stories Father had told me at bedtime, all the stories I had read growing up, this was the point when a vine closed around the heroine's ankle, and she realised there was no escape.

I reminded myself that I wasn't afraid of cellars. I wasn't afraid of dim light, chill stone or quiet solitude. Poring over Mother's books in our cellar in Larkspur had held a forbidden sweetness. While others might shrink back, fearful of what lay beyond the reach of light, the quiet shadows calmed me. Darkness softened the world and removed the harsh edges. It allowed me space to be, my fears and flaws softened and submerged. I could find the true contours of myself without the world's noise or scrutiny. Cellars had taught me to crave knowledge, not to fear what it might cost. I felt an almost painful desire to delve under Zephyr's layers and find out what lay beneath.

If Zephyr had a secret in his cellar, it only mattered that he was prepared to show it to me.

If he had a secret in his cellar, it meant only that we were alike.

Maren's fierce warnings rang in my ears, but I stepped through the door after the mercenary leader, nonetheless. Mere inches separated me from his broad back.

The stench hit me first. It made me retch: rotting meat and unwashed fur, pungent sweat and excrement, an astringent medicinal scent and fresh hay. A wild musk prickled my senses, which I recognised as the tang of magical energies. Then Zephyr lifted his shadow hold. The darkness breathed, and a cacophony of sounds assaulted me: wolf-like howls, whimpers and guttural growls, long hisses and eerie rattling, screeches and the scratch of claws against stone.

It took all my strength not to turn around and run.

My hand closed around Father's quill in my pocket. "By the moons, you brought them here."

Zephyr's brow furrowed with concern. "We won't stay long, but you need to see."

Maybe I was a fool to stay. A fool to trust him over the erratic rat-a-tat of my heart, clamouring at me to choose safety over curiosity. Father had told me to run, but I wasn't a little girl. I understood that the world was comprised of darkness and light. I braced myself and faced the dark. His shadows peeled back, and my hand flew to my mouth as I held back a scream.

A vast subterranean room stretched before us, such that the ceiling disappeared from view. Faint light leaked through grimy glass lanterns. Deep alcoves ran along the walls, each closed off by heavy bars. Within the alcoves, monsters writhed.

I stood frozen for a moment, then I inched into the cavernous cellar at Zephyr's side. I needed to understand, even though it seemed like I'd stumbled into a twisted dream. Monsters shifted in the half-light. I could almost taste their foulness on my tongue. They watched and howled and scuttled as we passed them. A humanoid creature curled enormous, bat-like wings around itself. A wolf with skin like a tarnished mirror licked its paw. Another with decaying flesh twanged muscles like wire. A dark serpent raised its head, as big as my own. Two harpies perched high shrieked our doom. A snarling bear with mottled skin pressed against the bars. A creature crouched low, its tail like a twisted root. There were fusions of rock and shadow with fiery eyes. Monsters so unnatural, so forlorn, that pity swelled in my chest. The cells were littered with bones, scraps of food, and lumps of excrement. Dark tunnels branched off the main chamber as if there were more monsters still.

Zephyr watched for my reaction, gauging the line between shock and judgment.

For a heartbeat, I didn't dare look at him because I was afraid I might not like the answers to the questions that plagued me. I wanted to close my eyes and plug my ears against the horror of it. To return to the maypole and Bloomtide, to the simple joys of toffee, and lake swimming with Maren and Ferrith. But how could I turn away from the truth when I had asked to receive it? The monster's moans and growls settled deep inside me, like the fading notes of a funeral march, as I turned at last to Zephyr. His slate-blue eyes seemed to absorb all the light around us.

I didn't want him to be a cold-hearted warden, a mad scientist, or a male purely interested in coin. I had seen glimpses of his humanity, I was sure of it: flickers of vulnerability in his eyes only when he thought I wasn't watching. I wanted to believe that the monsters in the depths of Ebonspire were here not because the mercenary was heartless but for something reasonable. I didn't need him to be perfect. I was well past expecting that of anyone. I needed to know that his intentions were not stained with cruelty or indifference.

Hope was a fragile bird, and I willed him not to disappoint me. "Why? Why keep them here?"

He signalled a large alcove further along. "There's one more I'd like you to see."

I edged forward, my footsteps tentative against the

rough floor, scalp prickling. The bone feline sat in the centre of the cell, freed from my ink magic. One rib, partially shattered by Gabor's axe, hung at an odd angle from the shining lattice of its bones. It emitted a low, mournful growl, recognition glimmering in its eyes.

"It remembers you," said Zephyr softly.

My heart lurched. I reached out a tentative hand despite the gnawing fear in my gut. The bone feline shifted closer to the bars that separated us. "You brought it to Ebonspire."

"Not too close. Never too close." The rich timbre of his voice wrapped around me. "Yes, we did."

"Why?" My breath came in thin wisps.

The corners of his lips tugged, but his voice was steady when he spoke. "This creature was once Grayson Cygnus of the Court of Starry Flight, gifted in healing." The name hung in the air between us.

I shook my head, my mind racing to dismiss the idea as madness. "You can't possibly know that."

"I wish I didn't. But the pieces are all there, scattered like broken glass. I only put them together."

Was it really a stretch to believe him? I'd witnessed wonders and horrors beyond my comprehension since stepping into Faerie. I'd seen sentient shadows and heard the wails of the tormented. The evidence of magic and its consequences had been in front of my nose since my foray into the Shrouded Forest.

I peered at the bone feline. "Grayson?"

The creature trembled, blinking as if to acknowledge its name.

I sucked in a breath. "This is why you held back your full strength in the Wraithwoods. Why you didn't want to kill them and why you were distraught when you did."

He nodded, and his mouth drew into a grim line. "When the Grimoire's magic unravelled, six courts fell. It wasn't just the loss of history and traditions, Ysadora. A faerie court falling means the loss of protection for all its members. Those fae faced bleak futures. Their magic diminished. Old alliances disintegrated. Some tried to reestablish the fallen courts and perished during their attempts. Others wandered, vulnerable to hostile territories and creatures that preyed on the isolated. A few were absorbed into the lower ranks of other courts, far below their former stations: chamber assistants, cooks, stablehands, envoys, playmates for princes and princesses…" The monsters quietened because it was their story he told. "Those who were captured but refused fealty were corrupted into the creatures you see here. Like nightmares made flesh."

His words settled over me like a layer of ice, chilling me from the inside out. I searched his face. After Father and Maren's betrayal, I wasn't sure I could tell when someone lied. Even in the hell hole that was this cellar, his account rang true. Mere days ago, I had thought him cruel and cold. But the quiet resignation in his stance as he looked over the alcoves showed me that this responsibility was as much a cage for him as it was for the monsters. "Who did this to them?"

A vein throbbed in his jaw. "I don't know. That part of their stories is lost to me. I've tried to help them remember who they are, to sift through the fragments of their pasts and glue them back together. But some pieces never slot into place, however much I expend my lore magic. Even with my help, the creatures can't hold onto the threads of who they were. Who they still are. That's why they're here. They're dangerous."

A lump formed in my throat. His actions weren't driven by greed but by honour. He carried out this dark and unforgiving task to protect others, even at the cost of his own peace. "Can't they be changed back?"

Hope flared in those sea mist eyes. "Maybe. One day. Until then, I'll protect them, ensure they can't cause harm and collect their stories."

His mission struck me as both noble and profoundly sad. "Why are you trusting me with this?"

"Because you deserve to know. Because I have been asking the question of how to right the wrongs of Faerie for decades, and I think you might be the answer." He drew in a shuddering breath and looked down at the rectangular mark of his uncle's bargain on his forearm. "I need you to know that whichever masks I wear at the Court of Silence, it is my mother's court, the Court of Lore, that holds real sway over me. I need you to know that you are welcome at Ebonspire because you are my friend, and my group will protect you. I need you to know this cellar is my deepest secret so that when we are tested, you'll know that there is good in me."

It didn't feel like he was my friend. The word felt so small against the backdrop of everything that hung between us. We weren't just companions who could walk away unscathed. Each look, each accidental touch, each unpicking of a secret felt like more than that. When he looked at me, it was as if he saw me completely, like he was piecing together every detail he noticed. Not just looking but knowing me, claiming me. My own heart tightened each time he entered the room. Each time he offered that slight, reluctant smile. I prayed that he didn't know my pulse raced each time he was near.

"What do you mean when you say I might be the answer?"

"If you choose to, Inkheart, I think you have it in you to restore the balance of Faerie."

My heart dipped. "Do you still consider me your prisoner?"

"You were never that. Not to me. Help us and I will see to it that not a hair on your head is harmed. I will see to it your loved ones remain safe. Help us put things right."

A jolt of exhilaration came over me. But helping him wasn't the plan; the plan was to reunite with Father and Maren and return to the mortal realm. Then why did my heart ache with something akin to loyalty? Loyalty that I couldn't afford in Faerie when, in mere hours, Zephyr Ashmoor would be handing me over to the Court of Silence.

"And if I say no?" I held my breath.

He sighed and coaxed Father's quill from my hand with a small smile that softened the tension between us before slipping it through the fastening of my ponytail. "I will guarantee your safety regardless of your choice. I don't want to leave you with this impression of Ebonspire. My home is so much more than the monsters."

"I know that."

"Even so, will you let me show you another corner of it?"

I nodded. The monsters' sorrowful laments faded as he led me out of the cellar. We climbed the spiral staircase and, close to the top, veered off into a hallway where faded tapestries hung like ghosts in the dim light, their once-vibrant colours muted. There were moss-covered statues, engraved doorways, and alcoves of books with indecipherable spines that I longed to research. Books that evoked a deep longing for Father's wisdom and passion, for his hand on my shoulder after some little discovery.

I caught a glimpse of the skeletal remains of what was once a vibrant space as we rounded a corner. A dilapidated stage sagged under the weight of age, its splintered wood barely holding its form. Tattered curtains hung limply, their hue dulled to a murky shade. A crumbling backdrop bore remnants of faded paint.

Zephyr's stormy gaze met mine. "Believe it or not, it used to be a place of joy. It could be again."

We lingered a while so that I could browse the books. My life in Larkspur had been full of limitations. Zephyr's words lingered in my mind, like embers catching in the dark: a promise of adventure and purpose greater than I had ever dared to imagine.

26

YSADORA

The sun glinted off my blade as I sharpened my
sword on the training field today. It reminded
me of village races with Maren and Ysadora.
I wonder where they are.
I wonder if they think of me.
—Ferrith's diary

I found Maren in my chamber, scrubbed clean and in a sleeveless oversized shirt that fell to her knees as if she had shunned the more feminine offerings in the wardrobe. My exhausting vigilance of the past nine days dissolved as I drank in the sight of her face.

In that moment, I didn't need to be strong. I didn't need to map new personalities, track agendas or look out for traps. There was security in old friends, regardless of the occasional storm. The façade I had constructed for the mercenaries crumbled.

I pulled her into a tight embrace. "I'm so glad you're here."

"I kept worrying I'd let you down. That you would struggle without me, but look at you."

The dam broke and we cried until we were both snivelling wrecks, until Maren—ever the more practical of the two of us—wiped her face and thrust her shirt towards my nose.

"It's not my shirt. I'm accepting their hospitality. It doesn't mean I'm going to behave."

I laughed. We exchanged a glance, tears still streaking our cheeks, as a knock sounded at the door.

Gabor's voice called out. "Open up before I drop these."

Playful defiance lit up Maren's amber eyes. "No, my lord. We're having a private moment."

Gabor's tone shifted to confusion. "Shall I come back later?"

The heady aroma of cacao drifted to my nose. "That's a mistake. He's a great cook."

"In that case…" Maren opened the door. The veins and edges of Gabor's silver-black wings shimmered as though he aimed to dazzle us. She ogled his offering. "My, what a fine specimen."

I giggled, unsure if she was talking about him or the food. The platter was stacked with layers of glossy chocolate: the first dusted with gold powder, the second with edible flowers or mint sprigs, and the third with flecks of sea salt or crushed hazelnuts.

Gabor lifted one muscled leg to step into the room. But Maren swiped the platter clean from his hands and shut him out with a playful thud of the door. I could almost picture his bewildered expression on the other side. I'd have to make up for it later.

My voice was laced with laughter. It felt so good to be with her again. "Now you've done it."

"I'm not going to be polite when we've got so much to discuss." Her voice sobered as she put the platter on the bed. "Cyprian says there are mere hours before you leave for the Court of Silence. I won't go back on my word. We'll find Kazimir, but we have to play this cleverly. If you change your mind—"

I jutted out my chin. "Father needs me. I have to go through with it."

She huffed in frustration. "Tell me everything. Have the mercenaries treated you well? Can you really trust them? What in the stars were you thinking getting mixed up with Rowena Ashmoor's son? I've never known the apple to fall so far from the tree."

I shook my head. Her thin frame had already shown me that she hadn't fared as well as I had at Ebonspire. "You first. Start at the beginning. The beetle wounded you. How did you escape it? Where have you been these past days? How did you get into the hayloft?"

We climbed into bed together, drawing the platter of chocolate-encased berries nearer as though Gabor had known that a reunion between female friends required indulgence as well as conversation. We settled into the comfortable pattern of our friendship: Maren's animated scattered storytelling versus my thoughtful reflection; her instinctive assumptions versus my analytical ones; her nostalgia for the past versus my eagerness to discover the truth, warts and all. We munched on the berries or crossed our legs at the same time, unconsciously mimicking each other's movements.

"The beetle was a rotten, clever thing. Too fast-moving and gifted at burrowing and climbing to evade, even when my fire made it drop me. It hummed and clicked like it could track my movements through sound vibrations." Maren popped a chocolate berry into her mouth. Her eyes misted as though she were remembering the sweet treats Anja prepared for the bakery. "Eventually, I realised it wasn't bringing me to its young. So I went limp and tried to get the measure of Faerie. It took me back to where it determined I belonged. To the Court of Nebulas."

"You looked for Father there. You didn't find him."

"Mother always described the Nebula Court as luminous. Full of constellations, creativity and knowledge. She told stories of music and mystics, travellers and scholars, dragons and dreamers. She said council meetings were not held in stuffy chambers but beneath open skies. Alliances weren't forged through bloodlines but intellectual collaboration. Can you imagine? Treaties weren't sealed with signatures but the exchange of creative works. Star maps were painted across the ceilings of homes. Every fae, from the youngest to the oldest, was encouraged to create, explore and discover. She and Father were incredibly happy, she said, until the tides of fortune turned against them." Maren gave a sad smile. "Do you know what I found when the beetle brought me there?"

My breath caught. That part of my life had been stolen from me. I wanted to experience my heritage so very much. "Please say it hasn't fallen."

Maren's flame-coloured hair spilt over her freckled shoulders as she leaned closer. "It's still there, Ysa, but I don't know for how long. The Order of the Glyph is gone. The once-sacred space where my father died still lies hollow and cold and littered with ashes. But it's worse than that. The court's magic has grown corrupted. There are no open skies. No dragons. The scholars, the dreamers, and the mystics have been driven mad by the corrupted energies around them. The seelie fae who remain are in a cavern system, hiding from spectral creatures that roam unchecked."

"Stars, no." Despair welled in me. I'd wanted to walk Father's path, but it had turned to smoke before I had even learned of it.

"There are rumours of a sisterhood of dragon riders, but no one has seen them. How can you hide dragons? All stories to keep hope alive in hopeless times." She squeezed my hand. "I managed to find a healer to help with my wounds. Then I waited for the beetle to leave before I attached myself to a group of fae who abandoned the court and came in this direction." Maren drew in a shaky breath. "I had to use my star fire more than once just to survive the journey. There are spies and informants of the remaining courts everywhere. Faerie is unravelling."

I hung onto her words, realising the extent to which Zephyr had cast a protective sphere around Ebonspire.

"There were sudden heavy rains without the presence of clouds. Gales uprooting trees. Rivers freezing in spring, confusing flora and fauna. Perpetual fog that refuses to lift in once-lively places. Pockets of Faerie experiencing constant daylight." Her eyes clouded as though reliving her encounters. "Frostbears are awake during their usual dormant periods. Small creatures like sprite frogs release uncontrolled bursts of magic. Lone animals, such as the shadow elk, now travel in large, erratic herds, trampling through meadows. Forest-bound creatures have moved into marshlands."

"Gabor would have been better teaching me about the present than history lessons."

"I tried so hard to get into this damn place. Only last night, when you all left, did the shadows draw away from the stables enough for me to sneak into the hay loft. Yet, you were having *history* lessons."

I swatted her. When she put it like that, it didn't seem fair. "How did you find me?"

"The creatures in the forest told me you were with Rowena's son, the one who tracked the monsters. I only had to come across a monster and wait to find the mercenaries. I followed a red-headed male close to Ebonspire. After that, it was just a question of waiting. Now and then, the mists opened until I finally caught a glimpse of you."

"I had my own run-in with the beetle after it was done with you. When they brought me here, I was in a bad state. The mercenaries healed me and protected me. They've been teaching me about Faerie."

She harrumphed, clearly unimpressed.

I pointed to the well-thumbed tomes on my side table and reached over for Father's compass, pursing my lips. "Gabor has been showing me maps of Faerie. I've tried getting my bearings with the compass, and I don't think it's pointing to the Court of Nebulas at all. According to the maps, that is in a north-easterly direction from Ebonspire, but the compass is showing true north, where Father is at the Court of Silence. I think he tinkered with it to show his own location."

"Show me." She turned it over in her hands with a soft whistle. "Remarkable work. Attuned to a drop of his blood perhaps?"

I nodded. "So you see, there's nothing to stop us from finding him."

"Don't tell them. Don't tell the mercenaries what it does. Promise me."

I frowned. "I promise. But I trust them. I've been training with them, eating with them. We're not friends, exactly, but I feel safe here."

"More fool you." She gave a heavy sigh. "We're like a pair of lambs surrounded by a pack of wolves."

"They've been teaching me how to use Father's quill."

Maren's gaze sharpened. "You can do ink magic?"

"I'm powerful, Maren…and there's more beneath my skin, just pushing to get out. I can feel it."

"I don't like it. I don't like any of this. There are those in Faerie who will use you, Ysa, who will break you. It's what Kazimir was always afraid of."

"But I'm not broken, Maren." As the words left my mouth, I realised it was true. "I'm strong. There are creatures in Faerie who are more broken than I will ever be."

I told her about the fae in the bowels of Ebonspire, whose very flesh had been corrupted and reshaped into something monstrous. Fae who were once noble or kind, or even beloved, now bound by nightmares etched into sinew and bone. How there were claws where fingers had been, scales crawling over what was once skin, gentle voices had been lost to snarling rage. I told her about the tangled ruins of their minds and my kindling desire to help. About how if I helped, Zephyr would guarantee not only my safety, but hers and Father's.

When I was finished, she remained quiet for a long while, chewing her inside cheek like she had done since childhood when she was thinking over a particularly knotty problem.

"I've never seen you like this. You like him," she said, eventually. "The mercenary leader."

Heat crept into my cheeks. "What makes you say that?"

"You're scared of how he makes you feel. I know the signs. Because that's how I am with Ferrith."

My heart ached for her. "Ferrith will be in Larkspur waiting for us when this is all over."

Affection and worry danced in her eyes. "Nonsense. He'll be swinging his sword for the King's Guard by now. I've thought about him in a constant loop since we left Larkspur. What I wouldn't give to know what he is doing. Whether he is thinking about me. But he and I could never be. He hates the fae after what happened to Vixora. I can never tell him what I really am."

I realised then that maybe Maren hated herself for being fae. She might know more about it than I, but she had been equally a victim of forces beyond her control. "You're doing him a disservice. Ferrith is kind and compassionate, and he would go to the ends of the earth for his friends, especially you."

Frustrated tears brimmed in her eyes. "This isn't about me. I knew this was Rowena Ashmoor's stronghold as soon as I saw it. Did your history lessons teach you about her? The Faerie Queen of the Court of Lore."

I swallowed hard. Ebonspire was a dilapidated

gatehouse. Nothing more. Zephyr had none of the airs and graces of a faerie prince. He preferred practical to elegant clothing. There was no regal detachment or polish to his movements. He used simple, unadorned words rather than the flowery language of courts that came to life in Gabor's history lessons. "Zephyr is a… prince?"

"Not anymore. That future faded the day the Court of Lore fell." She met my eyes. "You didn't know his ranking or his origins, not until his hand was forced or someone else fed you the truth. What else is he keeping from you?"

"Just tell the story, Maren, please."

"When Rowena became queen, she didn't revel in the power or luxury that came with her position. She made it a point to walk amongst her people. And what a people they were. They were creative. Not musically, like at our court. But in storytelling. Stages and campfires and vast libraries in which they collected the knowledge and wisdom of past generations. They had the ability to alter, erase or enhance memories. Some of them could see and interact with past events, gaining information about even the smallest details in history. Queen Rowena cherished unvarnished truth over the advice of courtiers who flattered her. Some say it was their enmity that led to her fall. When Faerie began to change, she took to the frontlines to protect the great libraries of lore, but such a people do not have great attacking powers."

Bitterness flared at all she had known and never shared with me, but I said only, "You admire her. At least the legend of her."

Maren shrugged. "She and Mother were friends once. Perhaps Zephyr would have been a different male if she had lived longer. But he was just a pup when she was killed. You can't trust him, Ysa."

Memories of my own mother's lullabies seeped into my mind. He had more of his mother in him than he even realised. I found that instead of wariness, a profound sympathy bloomed inside me. "He's been truthful, unlike you and Father."

She rolled out of the covers so she could face me. "I said I was sorry. And I am. I just want you to make your decision with your eyes open. Shadows writhe around Zephyr Ashmoor, literally and figuratively. He was so small when the Court of Lore fell. All his adult life, he's been influenced by the Court of Silence. He's a mercenary; doesn't that tell you all you need to know? His uncle holds sway over him. Trained him. Uses his services still. I don't want you to find he isn't who you think he is."

My heartbeat thudded against my chest. "He's done things to help me. To help the monsters. He's taking me to Father."

"Fae are tricksters, Ysa. What Kazimir and I did only underlines that. We're known for our cunning. Maybe Zephyr is playing a game with you. Bending the truth. You don't even know what magic he truly has. Maybe he warped your memories. How do you know that what you saw in the cellar is true? How do you know he's not trying to become the faerie king of a resurrected Court of Lore at your expense?"

Fear snaked up my spine. Was he manipulating me? Was power more important to him than I realised? "He said that my mother was still alive."

Maren inhaled sharply. "That's ridiculous. She would never have left you."

"He hasn't mentioned it again. I included it in our bargain. I think he was testing my limits after I arrived, trying to get a rise." I rubbed at the mark behind my ear. "You want to dismiss him just because he's fae. So are we. You want to dismiss him because he has suffered. Well, so have I. So have you, Maren."

She threw up her hands, and her amber eyes flared. "By the embers, you're so set on this path. Don't do this. Don't let yourself be ensnared by his charm. By his darkness."

My voice was quiet. I didn't want to argue. Not with her. Not now, when there was so much at stake. "Is it enough for us to rescue Father? Don't you want to save the Court of Nebulas?"

"That battle was lost long ago. The line between ally and adversary is razor-thin in Faerie. Think of my Father. Someone must have smiled, even as they turned a dagger in his back."

I scrambled for something to soothe her anxiety. "Gabor promised he would help me if Zephyr broke his bargain."

She frowned as if it didn't count for much at all. As if only the smallest circle deserved my trust: Father, Ferrith, she and her mother. "That's something at least. I want you to find happiness, but I don't want it to come at a price. Please, promise me that you'll be careful. Question everything. Your heart is worth protecting."

"Maren?" Discomfort swirled in my stomach. "Why does it sound like you're not coming with me to the Court of Silence?"

"I don't agree with your decision, but I won't abandon you. Kazimir taught me enough about Faerie to know we have to have a backup plan. Zephyr's shadows did one thing. They protected us from the spymaster's sight. He doesn't know I exist. I'll be staying on the outside in case you need me to get you out."

"You'd do that for me?"

"Of course." Her eyes shone. "Now show me your ink magic, Ysadora Silberquill."

A frisson ran up my spine. I uncurled myself from the bed and withdrew Father's quill from my hair. The nib gleamed with shadebloom that Wylda and I had cultivated. Then, with a focused breath, I summoned my ink magic. Maren laughed with delight as a fluid strand whipped through the air. I crafted glowing glyphs that formed a protective—though still meagre—barrier around us. I called forth a creature that skittered around up the covers before evaporating, that Maren swore had been taken from her fitful dreams while we had been apart. I showed her the ink cloak.

I wondered if Father would be proud. Today would be the day I saw him again.

I hoped that I wouldn't need my magic.

I hoped Zephyr wouldn't break my heart.

27

ZEPHYR

Starvine
A winding, star-shaped vine that climbs
the highest trees in faerie.
Blooms at night, casting faint light.
Properties: petals used in navigation spells.
—A Compendium of Faerie Flora and Terrain

Zephyr repeated the words over and over again until Ysadora was sick of hearing them.

"It's an unseelie court. Do you know what that means?"

"I've been reading faerie books my whole life. I live in a bookshop."

"Do not reveal your magic. That is the most important part of my plan."

"You've said it a thousand times. Even the trees have it memorised by now."

He tried not to smile at her aggravation. "Good. In a

few days, they will accept that you are a mortal, and then I can bargain for the release of your father—who I hope has had the good sense to appear a diminished version of himself—and go about our business repairing the Grimoire with my uncle none the wiser. That is if you still wish to help."

He didn't press her for an answer, though he thought he saw a glimpse of one in her eyes. She still insisted on taking her quill and a trio of ink pots, although he would have preferred her to leave them behind. It was no bother for him to cloak them in shadow, he supposed, and it pleased him that she seemed less anxious as a result.

Five of them travelled from Ebonspire to the Soulforge and Murkthorn mountains before crossing into the Court of Silence. Zephyr shadow-walked with Ysadora and Maren, while Gabor took to the skies with an unwilling Loxley once again.

He could tell the females hadn't had much rest, and he had to bite his tongue not to chide Ysadora. He needed her to be alert and strong. But she didn't belong to him, so he kept his reproach to himself. It was almost painful not holding Ysadora closer during the shadow walk, but Zephyr behaved like the perfect gentleman. More fool him. The females didn't say much while he transported them, as though after talking all morning, their words were spent. He knew, like him, they noticed the strange, vibrant rainbows appearing and fading without warning en route, lingering in places untouched by rain.

Cyprian stayed at Ebonspire with Wylda and Sequoia to guard their home, tend to the monsters and in case of foul play. He had seen the hurt in Cyprian's expression that he hadn't been chosen for the trip to Echohold, but

Zephyr didn't put anything past his uncle and consort. It was hard to believe Danaë Hendrick hadn't been born fae.

There was plenty of hurt to go around these days. He'd watched Ysadora's goodbye to Maren at the border of the Court of Silence. It wasn't just a goodbye; it was a surrender to the unknown. The parting from Maren stripped away the brave mask Ysadora usually wore, and he wished he could take back all his demands, all of Faerie's demands on them both. Even Maren, whose vitriolic glance left him under no qualms about what she thought of him, despite the fact she had raided the larder at Ebonspire as well as the armoury. Without an iota of permission or gratitude. It made him like her, in spite of himself.

"Take this." They hugged fiercely, and when they pulled apart, their hands were still entwined.

"Don't make me come into that starsforsaken place after you." Maren wiped her snot away with the back of her hand. "It's too grey and bleak for a redhead."

Ysadora squeezed her hand. "I'm worried you'll be cold and alone."

"Stop fussing. I have fire, remember? It keeps me warm. It gives me light. It protects me. If I tire, I'll sit beneath some starvine for respite." Then Maren jabbed a finger in Zephyr's chest—though by the looks of it, the shadow walk had played havoc with her balance—and winked at Gabor. "You take care of Ysa. Or I'll set fire to your nether regions."

Zephyr raised his hands in mock surrender. "No need for drastic measures. I value those regions too much to risk them."

He didn't need reminding of the serious stakes at hand.

Zephyr had planned the visit meticulously, building in safeguards to quiet his unease. Gabor, with his healing, was a good choice to accompany them in case the calligrapher was in poor health, or, perish the thought, if Ysadora was injured. Loxley, with his short control of other people's actions, was the perfect failsafe. His friend's chaotic nature, courtesy of the fallen Court of Madness, was an in-built antidote to the suffocation of the Court of Silence that plagued Zephyr, even after all these orbits.

They were met by an entourage of his uncle's most trusted spiders: two male and two female fae, who had been in Thiago's employ for longer than Zephyr had been alive. They merged with the grey, clad in dark, indistinct garb, their faces obscured by hoods, more phantoms than guides. The Court of Silence had crafted itself to be an enigma. He hated that he couldn't assemble a complete image of them. They were like puzzles he couldn't solve. He'd only ever caught glimpses: a hooded eye beneath a fold of fabric, a cruel mouth whispering a jibe, a bony ringed hand emerging briefly to gesture or beckon. Each fragment haunted him, vivid yet complete. He'd rather fight an arena of known devils than one of these masked monsters. Underneath, the spiders had real faces, real expressions, and perhaps even weaknesses. He vowed to find them one day. To make the spiders pay for the thousand harms they had done under the auspices of the Court of Silence. Still, he wondered what this court might be if his father had been firstborn or if his cousins Xaire and Elowen claimed the throne.

But such daydreaming was foolish.

By the time Xaire and Elowen came to the throne, they would be as underhanded as Thiago.

They trudged through the desolate landscape in a sorry procession—a show of power so beloved of his uncle— when they could have travelled through the shadows in an instant. Their path wound through groves of skeletal trees that he had hidden in as a youngling when he had missed his mother and sister. Their branches strained towards the sky in silent agony. Small, shrivelled creatures darted in and out of sight. A distant sound echoed: a faint, strangled cry that was quickly swallowed by silence. Gabor and Loxley wore grim expressions, and a chill burrowed into Zephyr's bones. Ysa shivered beside him, hugging her arms to her chest against the creeping cold despite her cloak. They were offered no shelter, warmth or even a single word from the spies who herded them forward. He wanted to shout out that Ysadora was cold. That the laws of hospitality had been breached.

But he didn't. To show he cared about her would be the worst mistake he could make.

So, instead, he threw her his cloak as if her shivers irritated him. As if he expected more from her.

Finally, Echohold loomed in the distance, a monolithic shadow against lifting fog. Zephyr rarely returned by choice. He could still remember the cold halls, the feeling of being swallowed by its quiet, empty spaces. His shadows had thrived in that stillness, and he had feared that the part of him that his mother had nurtured would be snuffed out. He remembered the endless corridors at sharp angles, flickering torchlight casting distorted images, silent servants slipping through walls, and how other people's shadows had watched him, even in sleep. To survive, he'd retreated to the few warm spots he could find. Small nooks where a finger of sunlight filtered through the window or the corner of a courtyard where the wind was blocked. But the warmth always felt transient, and soon enough, his uncle noticed his weakness and forbade him to seek comfort when strong males despised it.

He didn't let Ysadora glean his fear. Her shivering was almost uncontrollable, her skin pale.

But her violet-blue eyes, when they met his, were determined. "My father is in there."

Zephyr's chest tightened. "Yes."

"You completed your side of the bargain."

"I don't take bargains lightly."

She gave him a luminous smile from within the folds of his cloak.

He hoped she would smile at him the same way when she discovered the mother she believed was dead was alive and well within these walls. When he donned his mask of pretence was the only way to survive here. When she discovered that the Faerie King and his consort would do anything to discover her magic, and the fragile trust between the two of them was the only thing that would allow them all to keep their skin. He hoped it with all his shadowed heart.

28

YSADORA

*Kazimir Silberquill, The Order of the Glyph
Dragon: Caldoron (Cometfiend)
Skills: aerial combat, close-formation flying
Known Alliances: The Binder
Whereabouts: presumed dead
—The Dragons and Riders of the Nebula Court*

As I stood quivering before Echohold, the need to see Father again was almost overwhelming. I felt it in every breath, every step. I'd envisaged our reunion over and over as the faerie king's spiders shepherded us through the Court of Silence. I'd pictured Father stepping into a room where I waited, only for me to rush towards him, my feet barely touching the ground. I'd imagined looping my arms around his neck, clinging fiercely, as if holding him could erase all the pain of the lies and stitch us back together again. I'd smell the familiar scent of his favourite cardigan. He'd reassure me that everything would be all right.

I had no doubt it would be once we were together again. Father had always protected me, regardless of his mistakes.

There was no one I trusted more.

I wished I hadn't accused him of lying to me at Bloomtide. *What are you hiding, Kazimir?* I wished I hadn't stiffened under the kiss he had pressed to my forehead. Now, those words felt hollow, like a cheap shot. I could have asked him respectfully for the truth somewhere private, away from prying eyes where he might have given it to me. I would do anything to go back, to smooth over every misunderstanding, and certainly, my reaction, to assure him I understood and that I loved him beyond all else.

If the past nine days had taught me anything, it was that Faerie was complex, and the decisions that seemed foolproof in the mortal realm could not always be replicated here. I would tell Father I was sorry for parting from him on difficult terms. I would tell him that I had lied, too, about taking the elixir, but it was okay because it had worked out all right.

Zephyr would bring us home, eventually. We would get Father's spectacles fixed and tidy the bookshop, and maybe, after fixing Faerie, *the days of plenty* would return. The villagers would enjoy reading again, and we would have more coin and bread than before. At night, I would no longer creep down to the cellar—I dismissed the sting of Mother's stolen books—but beg Father to share stories of his life. That would be enough. To hear of Faerie through his eyes, with him safe, and Maren safely back with Anja. Both of us where we belonged.

The Thorn King's beetle had thought we belonged elsewhere, but I didn't dwell on the discrepancy. Father and I would be reunited soon, and all else was secondary. Zephyr looked subdued as the gates of Echohold opened, but I knew. No force in any court, no danger lurking in the shadows, could keep Father from me now.

The spies led us through a run of endless corridors, every footstep swallowed eerily by the stone floor. Zephyr was sullen, forward-facing, but Gabor and Loxley scanned every nook and cranny with keen eyes. At the end of one hallway, the doors swung open to reveal an austere hall draped in muted shades of silver and deep slate. Two occupied thrones loomed at the far end, carved from slick stone. One was large and imposing, the other diminutive, though no less striking given the snow leopards which lay on either side, breathing slow and steady, narrowed eyes fixed on us.

A male sat stiff-backed on the larger throne, half-concealed by shadows. Gaunt and severe, he wore darkness like a mantle, and his eyes contained a strange, knowing light. I recognised his latent energy. He was the male from the stable, whose shadows had pulsed against Zephyr's: the Faerie King of the Court of Silence.

A figure rose from the smaller throne. She was beautiful, blonde hair spilling in waves over her shoulders, catching the dim light like spun gold. She was somehow familiar, a memory I couldn't quite place but felt in my bones. The female's gaze was piercing, holding mine as if she could see past the orbits, past my bravado, to my hidden hurts.

There was satisfaction in the spymaster's voice as if he had pulled a gossamer thread into place. Each syllable stretched through the silence like a spell. "Welcome. I have waited so long to meet you, Ysadora." He assessed me with predatory curiosity. Then his eyes slid to Zephyr, savouring the moment, though he disregarded Gabor and Loxley entirely. "And nephew, there is honour amongst mercenaries after all."

A nerve ticked in Zephyr's jaw. "Indeed, Uncle. We don't turn on our own."

A shadow crossed the faerie king's cold eyes. "Our bargain is met. Let it not be said that I do not deal fairly."

There was a sizzle of flesh as the rectangular mark disappeared from the forearms of both males.

The female—his wife?—spoke. "I have waited so long to see you again, daughter." As she moved closer, the snow leopards chuffed a low, affectionate rumble that belied their watchful stares.

My heart ricocheted in my chest as the rune on my wrist—the one Zephyr had given me at Bloomtide—heated. I flicked him a glance, but he gave nothing away.

Gabor stepped forward, the planes of his face sharp with suspicion. "Take care, Ysa."

Even Loxley raised an eyebrow. "She gave up the right to call you that when she set up home here."

The faerie king's shadows swooped, along with his spiders. "Do not intervene at my court, outcasts."

His wife neared, and her face came into sharper focus, the pieces of a familiar outline slotting painfully into place. The woman's sing-song voice, the love in her eyes, her open arms—all of it left me rooted to the spot, torn between disbelief and yearning. For so long, Mother had been a figure of the past, an absence filled with questions, that I didn't believe the evidence of my own eyes. This had to be some trick. Some heinous magic to destabilise me.

Zephyr had warned me Mother lived, and I had forbidden him from mentioning it again.

Her eyes travelled over me as if searching for the child she once knew in the wild curls of my windswept ponytail, the olive pallor of my skin, my pointed ears and my twilight eyes. In her face, I discerned a myriad of emotions: joy, sorrow, and something else, something ravenous, like a shadow creeping over moonlit ground. "How beautiful you are. It breaks my heart that I wasn't there to see you grow, to see you change."

I shifted under her scrutiny, my legs weakening. "You died in a storm. Father mourned you."

A touch of sadness creased the female's brow, and I realised her thin arms were open still. "I never forgot you, Ysadora. Not for a single day. You were such a sweet child."

Warmth blossomed in my chest. I leaned into her arms, doubt warring with my need to believe in happy endings. The female folded her arms around me with a sigh of happiness and began to hum a lullaby: one Mother had sung night after night until her voice was hoarse. Or so Father had told me. Her voice threaded through the chill air of the throne room, nourishing me. I didn't remember the exact words of the childhood lullaby, but it didn't matter. The melody swam inside my psyche, tender and reaching. It was woven of a few simple notes and evoked a deep, joyous ache. She used to sing this to anchor me through restless nights and nightmares when the shadows seemed too dark and the world too vast. Fragments of memory snapped into place with dizzying clarity: the gentle sway of those nights, the sense of safety, her flowery perfume, her gentle touch as she swept my hair from my face, the quiet moments before sleep when nothing existed but the two of us. Not even Father.

Something inside me cracked open. I had clung to her lullabies and her faerie books even when I could barely remember her face. No disguise, no shadow could hide the truth of that melody, the voice that had cradled me with love so long ago.

I drew back, inhaling sharply at her pointed ears. "How? You were mortal."

Mother stroked back my hair. "I will explain everything."

A disquieting smile tugged at the corners of the faerie king's mouth as he turned his gaze from us to Zephyr. "Let the females speak, nephew. My guards will show your fellow mercenaries to their chambers." He beckoned him forward with an elegant, sweeping motion. "I have missed you in these halls. There is much to discuss now that you have returned to us at last."

His words carried a dark promise: an invitation that left no room for refusal.

Zephyr gave me a long look, his stormy eyes unreadable, before he stalked to his uncle's side.

29

YSADORA

Does Faerie ever let go of those who belong to it?
Or do they become something else entirely?
—Danaë Everreed's annotations
in her Faerie books

Mother remained mostly by my side, but the faerie king's summons were relentless. I caught glimpses of him in shadowed hallways, a glint of his icy eyes or a flash of his cloak, and I knew she would soon be called back. Each time, she murmured soft reassurances to me, brushing a hand over my cheek or tucking my hair behind my ear, promising to return quickly.

While she was away, with my cloak of ink wrapped around me, I slipped out of Mother's private drawing room, where an image hung of me as a child. Father's compass sat heavy in my palm: a lifeline, a reminder of my purpose. I was never gone long, always finding my way back before her return. I took care to leave and return by unguarded doors in her suite of rooms. Mother didn't seem to question whether I would stay put until she returned.

Not when we both felt such immense joy at finding our way to each other again.

But the needle of Father's compass acted with frustrating imprecision, leading only to dead ends or veering away from Echohold entirely. Like somehow, despite my care, the compass had broken during the shadow walk to the Court of Silence. My frustration grew heavier with every misstep. I clenched the compass until its edges bit into my palm, desperate for it to show me anything but these maddening loops. I'd been convinced I had it right. That Father had wanted me to find him, despite his note in the snow. But why wasn't it working? My frustration pulsed into a deep, hollow ache at the thought he was beyond my reach. I willed the needle to steady, to point somewhere—anywhere—that held a trace of him, that showed me that Echohold hadn't swallowed him whole.

I couldn't explain why I held back from asking her about Father. Somehow, it felt wrong—almost ungrateful—to see her again after all this time and still be caught up thinking of him. Like she deserved me to concentrate fully on her story.

That night, Mother showed me to the chamber she had prepared for me, heavy with the scent of lavender and incense. The walls were draped in deep blue silks adorned with silver threads because she remembered that even as a small child, I had loved the stars. A canopy bed dressed in layers of cool linen beckoned me to rest. On a nearby table, delicate glass figurines of a family of three were grouped alongside a leather-bound journal and a feather quill.

"I wanted to make it a place you can call your own. You will always have a home here, Ysadora. Here, you can be free to dream, to be whoever you wish," said my mother. "I want to show you the world I've built, to share everything with you."

"I want that, too." It felt so good to surrender to the pull of hope.

Her kindness erased endless orbits of loneliness and longing. It felt miraculous to be with her, to create new memories to bridge all we had lost. Her sincerity poured over the scars of grief, building me anew. Silent servants glided through the walls of the chamber, bringing teapots of chamomile and honey tea and slivers of vanilla and poppyseed cake. We walked in her private gardens as afternoon stretched into evening and talked on a secluded bench beneath the sole flowering tree. It showered us with soft petals like confetti from a celebration as her snow leopards dozed a few metres away. She spoke of the seasons turning, of how she had nurtured the garden during her darkest moments. How Thiago had stolen her away from Father, and it had broken her heart, but how, as a mortal, she had no defence, and had made the best of it.

"Thiago's arrival shattered my world. One moment, I was with my husband and child, living my dreams of being a songstress. The next, I was thrust into a nightmare, stripped of my identity and my family. I was forced to adapt to survive in hostile Faerie."

Her confession struck a chord in me, and I was glad that her Faerie books had given her some warning of what she might face. "Thank the stars you survived. It must have taken incredible strength."

Mother gave a serene smile. "Thiago isn't a bad man. He is resolute and strong, and I command great respect as his consort. I've learned to love him and Faerie. Do you think you could be happy here?"

My stomach twisted despite my gratitude to have found her. "Perhaps."

"I lost you once. I'll never let it happen again." Her eyes shone with tears. "When I think of what might be possible together. Just think, you might have faerie gifts you never imagined. Have you, Ysadora? Have you noticed any special talents?"

A strange wave of panic washed over me, and even as it did, Zephyr's shadows thickened around the quill in my pocket. Before I could even think, words spilt out of my mouth. "I wish."

A flicker of disappointment crossed her unlined face. "There is time yet."

My intuition had told me it was too soon to ask her about Father when she herself mentioned him only by necessity. Maybe that was why I didn't trust her enough to be honest: to tell her about my ink magic, Father's quill, and Maren, who waited for me at the border of the Court of Silence. My thoughts tangled like the vines climbing the garden walls. Part of me wanted to spill everything, to share my fears and the complicated web of truths. But another part clung to prudence, whispering that some truths were too dangerous to reveal to a female I hadn't seen in twenty orbits, even though she was my mother.

So I kept those secrets vaulted in my heart like the mercenary leader had cautioned.

Then, at last, I gathered the courage to ask the question that had plagued me since stepping foot in Echohold. My mask of calm belied the tempest within. "Mother, why did you and Thiago take Father?"

"We wanted him to repair Faerie."

"You caused us pain by taking him like shadows in the night. You could have simply asked."

"But Ysadora, we tried that. He wouldn't have come. He no longer cares what happens here."

Her words rang false against the image of the father who had always tried his best. By me, by our neighbours in Larkspur, by Maren and Anja, even by her. "Can I see him?"

Mother's expression wavered. It was as though the world around us came to a standstill. The wind eased. The petals stopped falling. Hurt seeped into her mother's voice. "He is gone. We tried to help him, but he slipped through our fingers."

Numbness spread through my limbs, and a ringing silence filled my ears as I processed the words. "Gone? Gone where?"

Her lips curled in distaste. "Thiago's spiders have been despatched. We found only molten glass in his chamber."

"He wouldn't just leave. Not if he knew I was coming. Your husband, the faerie king, made a bargain for me." That's why the compass hadn't worked. Father wasn't here. He was no longer at Echohold.

"I wanted so much for this to be the reunion you deserved. But your father couldn't bear to see my happiness."

He is gone. A shudder rippled through me, followed by despair. "Stop it."

Bitterness crept into her mother's voice. "Cairn deceived you, Ysadora. He kept all the marvels and power of your birthright hidden from you. He stole all knowledge of Faerie from you, all knowledge of the courts and their peoples. He deprived you of the world to which you belong. I would never have denied you that."

Red hot fury stole through my veins. "Don't. Don't talk about him like you have any claim to him."

"I was forced to learn about Faerie of my own accord. I did it for you. I can show you Faerie in all its shadows and splendour. I want you to see all of it, to experience every part of who you are meant to be. You are fae, Ysadora. You were meant for so much more than a mundane life."

Amber eyes brushed over the rune of interlocked keys at my wrist that Zephyr had given me, as though she knew he had somehow nudged me along the journey. I pulled my sleeve down over it, feeling like a pawn, feeling like every faction in damn Faerie had a stake in my future but that nobody centred me. I wanted to find Father so badly it hurt.

Mother took a deep breath and patted my hand. A dull silver ring gleamed on her finger. "I'll see you at tomorrow's ball. Preparations have been underway for some time. We wanted the court to see that my daughter was home. I will be singing in your honour." She rose from the bench, and her leopards prowled over to accompany her. "The guards will escort you back to your chamber. There is an assortment of gowns in your wardrobe for you to choose from. My handmaidens will help you dress."

A pair of guards stepped from the garden walls, emerging from darkened crevices where ancient stones met dense foliage. They flickered like candle flames before their forms solidified to reveal dark uniforms as snug as a second skin, hats low over shadowed faces and long curved blades.

"I do love you, Ysadora. A lot may have changed, but not that." Her words sounded like a melody played too sweetly, masking dissonant chords underneath.

"Mother, was he in good health at least, while he was here?"

She smiled brightly. "Oh yes. We took very good care of him."

I watched her leave, my initial joy tainted by confusion. What kind of daughter was I to doubt my mother? To put my love for Father above all else? Guilt settled like stones in my chest. This was the mother I had envisioned countless times through her absence. The universe had given me such a blessing. After wanting to curl up beside her, to hear her laugh and her song, to have the chance to really know her, the dissonance was almost unbearable. My doubts felt like an unforgivable betrayal.

Yet, try as I did, I couldn't banish them. Mother had been both familiar and foreign, her kindness edged with something darker. We had talked for hours. Why hadn't she been upfront about Father no longer being here? How could she seem so loving and eager one moment and an enigma the next? I wanted so much to believe that Mother had returned to fill the empty spaces in my life, but not at the expense of Father. Was it her I doubted or my own intuition?

Desperation bloomed in my chest, making it difficult to find the strength to rise above it and forge a new path. My plan had hinged on convincing the mercenaries to bring me to Father. There was no other endpoint. I intended us to navigate treacherous Faerie together. I had utterly failed. Zephyr was beholden to the spymaster. Their bargain had succeeded, with me as the collateral. My own bargain with the mercenary leader had failed. He, too, was unworthy of my trust.

As I thought it, the rune behind my ear flashed with heat.

Fists clenched, I asked the guards to escort me back to my chamber.

I had never felt so alone.

30

YSADORA

*This world will ask you to give your trust freely,
but remember, not all hearts are pure.
Guard yours until you've seen the truth in theirs.
—Rowena Ashmoor's letter to her son Zephyr*

The halls of the Court of Silence were just another cage. Every carefully placed item in my chamber whispered promises of my mother's love. Yet I couldn't rid myself of the persistent nagging sensation underneath the surface. How long had it been since I had properly rested? The hours rolled into each other since the Wraithwoods. The spymaster in the stables. Reuniting with Maren. The monster cellars beneath Ebonspire. Finding Mother at Echohold. Finding Father had gone.

I craved the oblivion of sleep if only to wipe the residue from my mind and allow me to think clearly.

I drew the curtains as if closing them might shield me from the chaos in my mind. Then I kicked off my shoes, tucked Father's quill underneath my pillow and crawled beneath the cool linens. The room was draped in shadows, the only light seeping from the glinting stars stitched to the blue silk wallpaper. In the dark, they seemed like eyes watching me. I focussed on their soft gleam, hoping the pattern would lull me to sleep.

Sleep didn't come gently, and when it did, it was like sinking into murky water. The stars on the walls blurred, melting together until they stretched into dark streaks. I fell into a void, where my limbs moved sluggishly as if coated in thick goo. Shadows closed in from all sides, pressing against me, whispering words I couldn't quite understand but that rang familiar, terrifying, bewildering words. In the distance, I could almost make out a figure: Father in his cardigan, a book in his hands, the glimmer of a smile on his lips. I tried to call him, but no sound escaped my lips.

Then, Mother's voice slithered through my mind, warping and reshaping until it was my own voice, repeating the words back to myself, locking me in place. "He's gone. He's gone. You'll never find him."

The nightmare shifted, its oppressive landscape cracking and peeling back to reveal a pale, wintry light. I was in my garden in Larkspur, near the stone Father loved so much. Snow blanketed the ground in soft drifts, and Father's spectacles lay in a patch of sludge, the glass fogged, and the frame warped. There was Father and Thiago, and I realised that this was just before Father was taken. The night of Bloomtide. I tried to warn him, to shout out. The wind carried away fragments of my voice, but Father didn't turn. He was focused, utterly focused on staying alive. Focused on the faerie king.

"Odd to think my wife once loved you. Even with the heartthorn binding. A male so flawed, so weak."

Father went slack, the fight draining from him. "I wondered if you'd ever come back again."

"Yours was a lukewarm kind of love, of course. Nothing like the all-encompassing bond a male and female can enjoy."

Father winced, but he lifted his chin. "She slept in our marital bed. She brought up my child."

"Another woman's child. Not her own. She always wanted her own." Thiago's eyes gleamed. "She didn't touch you, did she? Not as a woman touches her lover. She instinctively knew your deception. That's why she came with me so willingly. She sensed what was real between us and that what you shared was a sham."

Father deflated, his back curving over. "I'm no threat to you."

Thiago nodded as if he agreed they were not romantic rivals. That ship had sailed.

"Of that, we can be certain," said Thiago. "But it is yet to be determined whether you and your daughter are threats to Faerie. My wife believes you are its saviours. But I deal in cold hard facts."

I reached out for Father, wanting, needing to close the distance between us—inch by inch. I dragged my feet forward. I could almost touch his shoulder when the scene shifted, twisting. The snowdrift turned dark, sinking into shadows. Our garden blurred and stretched until it was nothing but an echoing emptiness. My pulse thundered. *Father. Please. Wait.* The spectres of Father and Thiago faded, their forms bleeding into the dark.

A rough shake dragged me out of the dark currents of

my dream. I jolted awake, breathless and drenched in a cold sweat. Zephyr leaned over me, his expression tense, his hand still on my shoulder.

"Ysadora. You were calling out. I couldn't just leave you."

I blinked, adjusting to the warm, lantern-lit glow of my chamber and three figures gathered there. My voice was hoarse. "What are you doing here? *How* did you get in here?"

Loxley's gaze darted between me and the door as if on watch. "Don't be mad. We were doing our gentlemanly duty by looking out for you in this hellhole. I managed to snag a key to your room from some poor fellow who'll be wondering why he dropped his guard. My magic's not as flash as his—" He cocked his head at Zephyr. "But it's useful in a bind."

Father had known Mother—*no, Danaë*, I corrected myself bitterly—hadn't been taken from us. The village searches and vigils had all been in vain. His spiralling grief had been—what—a ruse? All those possibilities that had been recounted to me over the years had been nothing but a mirage. Mother might have fallen down a well, they said. She had been taken in the storm, they said. She had become lost in the Shrouded Forest, they said. She had met some misfortune that left her confused, they said. She had been killed by a wild beast or ravaged by a traveller, they said. On and on. Lie after lie. I gulped in a breath as the foundations of my identity unravelled further with every passing moment. Mother herself had told me tonight that Thiago had taken her. But she had left of her own volition. All these orbits, Father had covered it up. He had let her go and concocted another narrative.

A mother didn't leave her child of her own accord.

I fixed the mercenaries in my gaze, ignoring the whiteout in my mind.

Gabor grunted. "We're here to keep you safe, Ysa. It's not just your dreams that seem restless tonight. Shadows thick as tar are converging on this chamber. Zephyr's working overtime to keep them away."

I pushed myself up, willing my pulse to slow. Zephyr's hand fell from my shoulder. He had failed me beyond all doubt.

Zephyr gestured towards the mercenaries with a tilt of his head.

Loxley waggled his eyebrows. "We'll be off then."

Embarrassment and prickling irritation heated my skin at his lewdness. I was pretty certain that he liked his bedfellows as well hung as I did.

"We should stay," said Gabor.

"Nah, boss-man doesn't like his orders questioned."

Zephyr flashed his canines. "Wait for me in our quarters. Stay together. Try not to get lost."

Loxley gave a curt nod. After a beat—in which Gabor's eyes met mine—Gabor did the same. Their footsteps were soft and practised as they slipped out of the room, and the door closed with a soft click.

Zephyr knelt beside me, his slate-blue eyes steady. "Are you okay?"

I clenched the covers, trying to bury the vulnerability that clawed its way to the surface. "Father isn't here."

"I came to the same conclusion a short while ago." His voice grew rough, and he looked away as if shamed by his failure. "My shadows searched every corner of Echohold. All the dark alcoves, every narrow passageway, and dozens of chambers no one dares to enter."

I wanted so much to be able to hate him, to blame him for the emptiness in my chest where hope had been. But his regret gave me pause, softening the harshness I wanted to throw at him. I felt his betrayal keenly, but it had only been a business transaction. Nothing more. "You broke your promise."

"No. Our bargain wasn't time-limited. I will find your father. I swear it. Is your trust in me broken?"

He was so solid before me. So real, even though he looked like he'd stepped from the pages of one of Mother's leather-bound Faerie books. *Danaë*'s books. "I don't know."

Zephyr gave a bitter smile as he stood. "At least that's not a *no*."

My chest constricted. "It's not a *yes*, either."

"What did you dream to make you thrash and shout out, Inkheart?" he said quietly.

"You have no business knowing what goes on in my mind."

He towered over me, his expression unreadable. "Dreams in the mortal realm are usually fleeting. A wisp of a waking thought that looms large. In faerie, dreams have meaning. Dreams have masters and victims. They are memories that linger or spells that lie in wait. Here, dreams don't just live in sleep. They wander, waiting. They hover at the edges of thought, even in waking hours. Some tempt you with places you once loved. Others may pull you into depths you may not escape. Tell me about your dream, Ysadora."

"I dreamt of my father and your uncle."

Darkness flickered in his gaze. "Go on."

Grief sat in my chest like a stone. How unfair to find and lose her all over again. "Danaë is not my biological mother. She chose to leave us. You knew, didn't you? That's why my rune heated." I looked down at my wrist. One key glimmered with a radiant filigree akin to golden stardust. The other key was a shadowy silver that absorbed the light, featuring subtle engravings of ancient scripts. "What does it do, Zephyr? You owe me that much."

His eyes hooded. "The Rune of Unveiling is a gift from the Court of Lore. All of my people carried variations of it." He tugged down the waistband of his trousers just enough to reveal a tattoo on his hip that stood out sharply against his tawny skin. The shaft of the key was etched in clean black lines, with delicate white filigree woven through it like ivy. The head was a mandala in monochrome. Silver flecks glimmered within the white portions. He thumbed his waistband back into place. "They encourage fae from my court to confront the secrets others hold from us and the truths buried inside ourselves. The dual colours represent the balance of light and shadow in understanding. The importance of contrasting perspectives. The connection of past and present."

"I see." I swallowed hard, wondering if the rune had driven me to uncover things I wasn't ready to face. It felt like an invasion and an invitation all at once. "Did you? Did you know about my mother—about Danaë?"

Time stretched between us before he inclined his head. "I had no proof, but I suspected."

"And I am the fool all over again," I said bitterly.

He sighed. "No. You're not a fool. She raised you in your infancy. You felt her love. That is real."

No pretty words could soothe me this time. The shell of my heart cracked open. Nothing I'd held sacred was true. "Nothing is real. Not Father. Not Mother. Not even you, with your broken dreams and your damn monsters in the cellar."

He blanched at that, tight lines forming around his mouth. "I'm trying to help."

Something broke in me. "I don't want your kind of help."

"Inkheart—"

My voice was a fierce, quiet howl. "Go. Leave the tangled web of my life."

The hurt in his eyes flared and disappeared so quickly I must have imagined it. He gave a mocking bow. "As you wish. My shadows will make sure you are safe in your chamber tonight. Regardless of how you feel about me, you will always be welcome at Ebonspire. My home is protected by ancient wards cast by my ancestors, with access only granted to those an Ashmoor willingly shares a drop of blood with. If you come, you don't have to see me." He unsheathed a dagger at his thigh and pricked his thumb. A pearl of faerie blood bloomed there. "May I?"

I nodded, my throat tight, and I wanted to take back the hurt between us.

I had no safe havens in Faerie. It was a safety net, that's all.

His touch was featherlight as he murmured an incantation—faerie words both foreign and familiar—and guided the drop of blood along the skin of my wrist above the rune of interlocked keys. He marked me. A scroll with curled edges appeared there, like the one I had tried in vain to copy from Cyprian. As his blood seeped into my skin, his expression blazed with an intensity that made my breath hitch. There was surprise there, vulnerability and longing. His touch felt electric, and I shivered as though I was on the precipice of something new.

Confusion battled with want inside me. "I don't know what to say."

His expression shuttered, resettling into his enigmatic mask of neutrality. "You don't have to say anything at all."

The scroll rune shimmered once, bright blue lines against my skin, before vanishing beneath my skin.

"It's better this way. There are too many adversaries circling to make allegiances obvious." He flipped his hand without warning and gripped my forearm for an instant. "I release you from our bargain."

I sensed the mark of our bargain lifting from behind my ear, the magic unravelling with a faint metallic scent. I touched the tender skin, feeling a soft pulse as the last traces of the binding disappeared. Hurt and indignation surged within me as the matching mark faded from his collarbone. We had both agreed to the bargain. What gave him the right to dissolve it without my consent?

Zephyr walked to the door, throwing a remark over his shoulder so casually that it cut all the deeper. "You'd be wise to consider who your biological mother is now that it is clear that it is not Danaë. In Faerie, every scrap of knowledge, especially self-knowledge, marks the difference between life and death."

Then he slipped into a pocket of shadows.

His blood smear still caked my skin. He had given me the keys to truth and the key to Ebonspire. But what if it was all just another manipulation? I hated myself for wanting him to come back. Hated myself for wanting to believe the lies for a little longer so that he could be someone I could count on.

As I waited for sleep to claim me once more, a new scheme formed in my mind: one that didn't rely on the mercenary leader at all.

31

KAZIMIR

Species: Cometfiend
Appearance: bronze scales, strong jaw,
sharp spines along their backs
Characteristics: grumpy, discerning,
strategic battle sense
Abilities: fire-breathing, rapid acceleration, a
unique ability to speak with other
flying creatures of the nebula
—The Dragons and Riders of the Nebula Court

Kazimir stepped through the melted frame of the window. He was met first by the scent of sulphur and brimstone. Beneath it was the scent of mountain peaks, cosmic air and burnt amber. He almost sank to his knees and wept. His boots crunched softly on a floor dusted with ash, but he barely noticed. His focus was entirely on the massive, coiled form before him, bronze scales glinting in the evening light like treasure.

Caldoron. The dragon's deep-set golden eyes narrowed on him with sharp intelligence.

Kazimir had longed for this moment, dreamt of it, and lamented the impossibility of it. Sadness engulfed him for the separation they had endured. He hesitated, the enormity of the reunion stealing his words. But then the dragon's slitted pupils narrowed on him, and the faintest rumble, like distant thunder, filled the air. His breath stirred the debris around them.

"Caldoron," he breathed, his voice cracking. Nothing, not even time itself, could erode the bond they shared. He bowed reverentially, like he had all those orbits ago when he pledged himself to Caldoron, and the dragon had bound himself to him in return. *I missed you, old friend.*

The dragon's low, guttural growl reverberated through Kazimir's chest. The sheer size of the beast was staggering. His bronze scales had dulled with time—or perhaps grief. The edges of the scales, sharp and proud, had softened with age, and a few patches of deep rust had appeared where once there had been a flawless sheen. It was as if the fire that once blazed in him had smouldered into something quieter.

Calligrapher, his tone was weary, almost as weary as their last strained goodbye. *I sensed your return.*

Kazimir's emotions nearly choked him as he stared up into his dragon's eyes. He took a step forward, then another, his legs almost buckling until he stood just a breath away. He knew they had to be fast in case the faerie king discovered them. *I'm sorry. I should have come sooner. I thought…*

Caldoron lowered his head until his warm, leathery breath washed over his rider. *You protected your kin. Your flesh and blood. It is forgiven.* The words weren't accusatory; they carried a gruff understanding.

Kazimir's hand trembled as he reached out to touch the dragon's scaled jaw. *After everything, you waited.*

Two centuries old, and he had ridden with Caldoron since he was forty-two. He was more than a dragon. He was part of Kazimir's soul.

The dragon huffed softly. *Do not mistake my patience for softness. We have work to do.*

A choked laugh escaped Kazimir, tears blurring his vision. *Still grumpy, I see.*

The dragon's chest rumbled. *You smell of blood and sweat. I have carried rotting cargo with a more fragrant scent.*

Kazimir wiped his eyes. *You're as tactful as ever.*

They treated you poorly. I will raze the Court of Silence to the ground. It will be a fitting pyre to make my return to fae company. A plume of embers escaped his yawning nostrils.

Kazimir shook his head. *We won't make another pyre of our past. There's a future to rebuild.*

You have become boring, calligrapher. The dragon released a plume of smoke that almost singed his eyebrow. *Are you ready to fly again? Or do you wish to refuse me in that also?*

A tender weight pressed against his chest, equal parts anguish and affection. Twenty-four orbits since they had set eyes on one another. A lifetime in many ways. Ysa's lifetime, but also encompassing utter change for both rider and dragon. Yet, seeing Caldoron now, it was as though time had folded in on itself. Every memory came rushing back—the soaring heights, the synchronised breath, the trust that had defined them. Kazimir's throat tightened. *I've been ready since the moment I left.*

About time, rider. You've been neglectful. I should leave you stranded next time.

Kazimir's lips twitched. *Leaving me stranded is hardly a winning move. We've always been unbeatable together.* For a moment, he almost imagined they were young again. That the Order of the Glyph still existed and that he could fly in formation with his brothers. *I miss my brothers. They are all gone.*

Caldoron's talons kneaded the earth, leaving furrows in the ash. *Your brothers may be gone, calligrapher, but there are others who have risen in their place and others still of my kind who survived what was done that night. Let us go to them after we scour the realms for your kin. What is your intention?*

Kazimir met the dragon's unblinking eyes. *No, old friend. I seek the fallen star.*

Caldoron snorted. *The Binder is up to her old tricks.*

Let's hope it plays out in our favour. Without another word, Kazimir leapt gracefully onto the dragon's back, the movement instinctive despite the weariness of his bones and the time that had passed. He settled into place between the spikes along Caldoron's spine, the rough texture of the dragon's scales bringing joy to touch.

Claws scraped against the ground. Then, with a powerful flex of his legs, Caldoron launched into the open sky, wings snapping wide as he caught the air. The motion sent a gust through the barren land, scattering ash and loose debris into the maelstrom. Below them, the Court of Silence shrank into insignificance. *Your form is somewhat wanting, Kazimir. You are out of practice. Perhaps you need a harness.*

Kazimir smiled. *As much as you need a muzzle.* He leaned into the wind, pulse quickening as they climbed higher, the ground spinning away in a blur. Nothing mattered but this. Not the torture. Not the state of his broken body. Not the burden of his station. Not even his worries for his darling Ysa.

Everything evaporated in the exhilaration of taking to the skies together.

Higher and higher they climbed, the air growing cleaner as they soared, Caldoron's tail flowing behind them. The bond between dragon and rider strengthened with every passing second, a rhythm as ancient as the constellations themselves. Kazimir closed his eyes for a moment, allowing the rush of wind to sweep away the lingering tension in his chest. The freedom of the skies swept over him like a tide. A familiar hum rose in his chest, an echo of the connection between him and the stars, now bright and close.

This was where he belonged. Not on the ground, chained by the mistakes of his past, but here, soaring towards the heavens with Caldoron. Kazimir tilted his face to the stars. Beneath him, Caldoron exhaled a low rumble as if he, too, felt the energy of the cosmos enveloping them.

For the first time in decades, both rider and dragon felt whole again.

Kazimir pressed closer to Caldoron's bronze-scaled neck as the stars blurred around them. *Keep flying.*

The dragon swung his neck around. *With you as my rider? Always.*

32

ZEPHYR

Ysadora Silberquill was his fated mate. The realisation hit him like shattering glass, scattering his thoughts into a thousand directions. It hit him like a crumbling mask, fragments falling away on stage.

Zephyr had considered whether Ysadora could be the one when he first laid eyes on her. The similarities to his sister's painting were undeniable, even for someone like him, who ran from matters of the heart. The Binder herself had unearthed his long-buried memories of that tender conversation with his sister when she had spoken Veda's name.

Directly before Zephyr killed her.

He released a pent-up breath. He was in the grand ballroom shortly before the appointed start time. Heavy velvet curtains were drawn back from towering windows to reveal the maze, where he had cowered as a youngling and kissed both wenches and illustrious daughters of the court as an adult. But where the evening sun should have streamed in, only a pale blue tint filtered through. Attendants moved like wraiths adjusting candelabras that burned with cold flames. They didn't make a sound, of course, but tension lined their faces.

How the Binder would laugh at how fate was balanced on a knife's edge.

Zephyr hated this part of a plan: the moment when it could all unravel.

He leaned against the pillar and closed his eyes, spooling his mind back, back to when Veda still lived. Eighty-eight long orbits had passed since her death. Eighty-nine orbits since she had painted the walls of a bath chamber at Ebonspire with images from the past and future. Since she had painted a dark-haired violet-eyed faerie queen, her skyward gaze reflected in stars as she stretched out her hands.

Veda had a beautiful mind. A beautiful soul.

Veda had been a seer capable of revealing the past and illuminating the future. For many at the Court of Lore, it would have been a curse. A shortcut to madness. But Veda wore the mantle of seer lightly, and painting helped her crystallise what she saw and discard the rest, like chaff from wheat.

"Is she in my history books?" he had asked of the faerie queen his sister had painted.

"No, Zephyr. She is not yet of this world. You will have to wait a long time to meet her."

He stared at the painting. "Who is she?"

Veda poked him with her paintbrush, her eyes full of dreams for him. "She is your mate."

His heart jittered. "Mother says love for our people is more important than romantic love."

Veda ruffled his hair. "Mother's heart is broken. Promise me, you'll remember this moment when you meet her? Promise me that you'll help her piece together what was taken from her. Promise me you'll help her walk the road that leads her home." Her face filled with gentle sorrow. He saw that same sorrow one orbit later when, in the Forgotten Garden, Mother and Veda told him to hide.

He glared at the dark-haired faerie queen. Waiting a long time didn't sound like fun, and the idea of fated mates was too distant and abstract for him to grasp. "What if I don't want to wait for her?"

She dipped her paintbrush in a gloop of yellow. "Oh, my Zeph. You'll have no choice. Your destinies are intertwined. And you'll find such happiness, even though you might suffer."

Zephyr opened his eyes in the present, allowing his memories to mist away. He dragged in a breath, disconcerted by the comings and goings around him. Troubled even more by how he had left matters with Ysadora. How strange for the revelation about her origins to come to her in a dream. And now this... He had known the truth of Veda's prophecy the moment his blood had seeped into Ysadora's skin. Had wanted to pull his Inkheart into his arms and kiss the worry and hurt from her eyes until she trusted him and him alone. Stupid, stupid of him to demand unconditional trust as the price of their bargain to win more time with her, to increase the odds of her favouring him. When all along he should have come clean about it all. About what he had suspected she could be, to Faerie and to him. About what he knew about her origins and what he was still figuring out.

Cyprian had warned him it would come to this.

Not even his oldest friend would be sanguine about how royally Zephyr had cocked up.

Now, he had to tread carefully. Their mate bond was exhilarating yet terrifying: a double-edged sword that left him reeling. How could she forgive him for failing to bring her to her father, let alone want him? Telling her about their mate bond now would only deepen the chasm between them. Dread churned in his stomach. She had expressed in no uncertain terms that she needed space from him.

He would give it to her. They needed only to survive this ball without her revealing her magic, and he would find a way to extricate her from the Court of Silence. He would find her father, and he would tell her the truth: she was his mate, and he would die for her. He would have died for her, even before he had known the full truth of it.

Zephyr sighed, scanning the ballroom for her. The garments he had borrowed from his cousin Xaire were a disaster. Every movement pulled the jacket a little too tightly across his back, and his trousers clung uncomfortably close, making him conscious of every step he took. Xaire's little joke, no doubt. The seamstresses at the Court of Silence could have tailored an elegant offering in mere hours, but his fuckwit cousin had always fallen prey to the petty rivalries Thiago stoked. At least he was wearing black and a simple shirt. Loxley, in a ruffled shirt that kept snagging his beard, and Gabor, in a garish fuchsia shirt and trouser combination, had fared less well.

He nodded at his friends as they sauntered over to him. They looked as tired as Zephyr felt, with dark crescents under their eyes and their foul moods painted on their faces. He cast a shadow veil around them in case of snitches and snoops. "Cheer up. It'll be home time soon."

Loxley pulled at his shirt collar. "Blasted thing… I'm impressed you've avoided all your uncle's ploys to ensnare you into his schemes. Has he added any more to the list?"

Zephyr picked up a wine goblet from a passing maidservant. "He's pushing hard for me to turn over the monsters to him for a dark army. He wants me to marry cousin Elowen to secure this court's future. And he tried to convince me to steal an enchanted shell from the Court of Silver Seas."

Loxley swiped the wine and took a deep slug. "The last one doesn't sound like a bad idea. For a weighty pouch of coin, of course. Might refill our dwindling reserves since Tanuhja's coin dried up."

Zephyr glowered at him and took his goblet back. "The whisper rings are safely stashed?"

Gabor smirked. "On the highest branch I could find, just north of here."

The smirk struck Zephyr as odd, but he suppressed his prickling doubt. He was tightly wound—on tenterhooks because of Ysadora. Tonight's gathering was crucial, and he wanted everything to go smoothly: no surprises, no complications. But still, the way Gabor hovered near her, too ready with a laugh or a quick, approving glance, unsettled him. He brushed it off as paranoia, a byproduct of his need to protect Inkheart.

"Good." Zephyr slapped his shoulder and scanned the room again for his Inkheart or any sign of trouble. His plan was coming together nicely. It was a shame about his heart. "A few more hours then. You know what to watch for."

After he had left Ysadora's chamber last night, his shadows had searched Echohold once more. Not for her father this time, but for something much smaller. Something inanimate. In Faerie, where loyalty shifted like mist and secrets multiplied faster than mushrooms, relying on a single scheme was as dangerous as walking unarmed into battle. Each backup plan, each twist in Zephyr's strategy, was armour against the scrutiny of the spymaster and his spiders.

Just like Zephyr, Thiago was a collector of artefacts.

Zephyr glimpsed the very artefact he coveted on the hands of the spiders who marched them into Ebonspire: whisper rings that amplified meagre Silence Court magic into something far more fearsome. The rings muffled the wearer's footsteps, breath, and even their heartbeat, enabling them to move undetected. So Thiago's chosen few could slice throats unchallenged, eavesdrop in the shadows for days on end and slip poisons into the goblets of enemy kings and queens. Only those who knew precisely where to look could see the wearers of the whisper rings. Taking a whisper ring from Thiago's highest-ranked spiders risked outing Zephyr's shifting allegiances too soon.

Better to steal directly from the faerie king's vaults.

Zephyr had located the target vault deep beneath the eastern wing, one of the many scattered around the Court of Silence, each guarded by enchantments or curses or shadow beasts. He, Loxley and Gabor approached behind a shield of Zephyr's shadows, every choice risking discovery.

As they approached the vault, an old protection spell juddered to life. Claws flexed, and a faint shimmer of magic rippled over a hulking stone gargoyle with unblinking eyes. For a moment, Zephyr doubted their chances of success, not that he showed it. A general never showed his soldiers his own fear. Loxley had never tested his magic against a creature that spent most of its life as stone. When Loxley placed his hands on the gargoyle's cold temples, a pulse of resistance surged back at him. But then Loxley closed his eyes, letting his own will seep into the gargoyle's mind. With a creaking shudder, the gargoyle stepped aside, bowing deeply as the door swung open, because Loxley willed it so.

The vault was disappointingly bare, save for the two whisper rings glinting dully in the half light. The silver bands were marred by age. Zephyr plucked them from the vault and turned the cool metal over in his palm. Fifteen of the whisper rings had been made by an ancient fae smith. Six of Thiago's spiders were current recipients. Danaë and Elowen wore one each. A few had been lost to time and greed. He had hoped to find more, enough to arm his group. With his uncle in the know, Ebonspire was a more dangerous place. Still, two rings satisfied his primary objective.

They would keep Ysadora and her father safe from their enemies.

Whether she remained in Faerie or not.

Zephyr gave his friends a tight smile. "Go and be merry. We'll be gone soon enough."

He'd long resolved to be Ysadora's ally, even if it meant bending the rules of the court. Finally, they had the whisper rings. Loxley and Gabor would spirit her away. He had already laid the groundwork to ensure his friends' departure followed the schedule that he had already informed his uncle of. Ysadora would simply lie in wait, shielded by the whisper ring until Loxley and Gabor reconvened with her.

Zephyr would stay behind—however long it took—to convince the faerie king that he had no part in the matter. It had to work. The alternative didn't bear thinking about.

He let his shadows fall and watched as Loxley and Gabor chose different paths through the grand ballroom under frost-touched chandeliers. The ballroom floor had been polished to a gleam, each step taken appearing like a shadow against a mirror. Members of the court slipped in from hidden hallways and grand arches, wearing robes in muted colours and speaking in hushed tones. Masks were a common adornment, resembling beasts from faerie tales, because the Court of Silence valued discretion and brutality above all else.

But Loxley wasn't one for restraint, solemnity or decorum. Even tradition held little sway over him. He was an agent of chaos. He thrived by unravelling rigid structures and careful order. His steps were sharp, almost defiant, sashaying between quiet conversations as though daring court members to remark on his ruffles. Gabor moved with languid ease, blended wings folding elegantly behind him, dark eyes skimming the room with detached curiosity.

Zephyr blew out a breath and circled the outskirts of the room to avoid small talk with courtiers eager to learn what brought Orin's son back to court. Tables laden with delicacies lined the walls. Jewels embedded in the plates held the light like a snare, glittering against the backdrop of polished blackwood. There were thimbles of bone broth, slivers of salted venison, mushrooms soaked in brine, ash-infused bread, silverleaf salad from the court's gardens, thin rounds of pressed fennel, ice-cured fish…and glazed anise toffee that made the corners of his mouth tilt up. He'd stolen a piece of that from the kitchens for her before the faerie king's spell casters had worked their enchantments. Thiago wouldn't be leaving an evening such as this to chance.

His shadows told him Ysadora had arrived a fraction of a second before she entered the ballroom. The soft forewarning brushed against his ear like a gust, giving him just enough time to gather himself. Her presence filled the room like a slow inhale, a tremor that pulled his attention with quiet insistence. The world dulled around her as though she alone held all the colour, all the light. His frail heart could only sing *my mate, my mate, my mate.*

He wanted to kiss her so badly. He had barely restrained himself since finding her in the clearing with the bone feline, when he'd been so afraid she would be harmed that his magic had failed him for a second. But he couldn't kiss her then. He wouldn't. Not when the glamour made her look like a stranger.

Ysadora's twilight gaze found his from across the ballroom, and Zephyr smothered every flicker of feeling, masking the longing that threatened to surface. It was too dangerous to reveal their bond here amongst the vultures of the Court of Silence, too much of a burden for Ysadora to know now, in any case. His expression regained composure: a perfect mask forged from years of practice. He acknowledged her with a subtle nod, noting from her demeanour that she had decided to continue the ruse that Danaë was her mother.

Now that Ysadora was here, they just needed an opportune moment to make a clean escape. That was if she trusted him enough to be persuaded of his plan.

Beneath his calm exterior, his heart hammered.

His uncle's grey robes swept the floor, resembling a storm cloud in fabric, with his dark hair slicked back. Danaë had chosen a floor-length gown of dark green, reminiscent of deep winter forests. Her hair was swept into a chignon with frosted combs. Silver circlets set with moonstone crowned the faerie king and his consort's heads, marking their unity, although Danaë was not a faerie queen, and Thiago would have baulked at the suggestion that she should be. The twins wore dark plum and matching earcuffs. Xaire's dark hair was tousled, giving him a rebellious look that his father disapproved of. Elowen's silver-blonde hair was poker-straight and tied at her nape with a black ribbon. Her mouth was not bound, but she would not speak. She rarely spoke out loud anymore, and her telepathy worked only with her twin. All four wore slippers in varying shades of black, grey, and deep blue, silent as shadows.

But the family that had been his bane all Zephyr's life didn't matter.

Not when he only had eyes for Ysadora. Nor was he the only one looking at her. Some held goblets frozen halfway to their lips, others exchanged sidelong glances. They took her in from head to toe, eyes tracing her face, her bearing, scrutinising her for signs of magic. The whole court was attuned to her presence like a thousand strings tightened to one chord.

She wore a gown of midnight velvet, cut with hints of purple undertones that shifted as she moved, like the petals of a black tulip. The bodice was adorned with dark lace, and her loose hair spilt in waves across her bare shoulders, a thick lock rolled on one side around her Father's quill as if she had wanted to hide it in plain sight. Her amethyst eyes darted to the twins often, and he understood how jarring it must be to maintain her mask through it all: Danaë's parade, sibling introductions that were a fantasy and the strange nature of the court. Her expression revealed cautious curiosity, a queenly presence touched by fragility.

His mate stole the air from his lungs, and she was blissfully unaware of the effect she had on him.

He was terrified of letting his mask slip.

The group proceeded forward, looking straight ahead: Thiago and Danaë, Xaire and Elowen, followed by Ysadora, with the snow leopards prowling at her rear, faintly dusted with frost. Every step fell in synchronicity, attesting to unity and control. The procession had clearly been rehearsed, often enough to cause sore feet, judging by Elowen's limp. They'd accepted Ysadora into the fold, but he knew the price of their acceptance was steep: stripping her of agency, the freedom to question and to act apart. They'd want to mould her into their own creature.

The faerie king and his consort led the way onto the dais. Once seated on their thrones, Ysadora, Xaire, and Elowen fanned out beside them, with a snow leopard at either side. Danaë's expression was meticulously crafted: a regal smile, a gleam of warmth for Ysadora, a hint of malice. Beside her, Thiago held himself in a commanding silence, his gaze sweeping over the court as if he could see every ambition and raise the stakes with his own.

Danaë raised her hand to command attention, and her whisper ring gleamed. "My daughter Ysadora has returned to me at last. This ball is in her honour." She reached for Ysadora, pulling her forward with a possessive pride that made Zephyr stiffen. "We are grateful, Ysadora. The court stands stronger with you here in these troubled times."

Ysadora inclined her head slightly as if to suggest an intimate, unbreakable bond. Zephyr gritted his teeth. This was no simple homecoming: it was a stage, a show of allegiance, a lie spun for the court's approval, and his mate was the centrepiece. Eyes sprang between mother and daughter, hunting for resemblance, cracks in the performance, and signs of how this reunion might serve their own interests.

The faerie king leaned forward. "The Court of Silence is a place of legacy, strength, and resilience. Ysadora's return is not only a joy to her mother and me but a sign that our court, our bloodline, and our future remain unshaken. For she is the calligrapher's daughter, and she alone can reshape Faerie."

A thickset male in a wolf's mask stepped forward with a single ruby dangling from one ear. "Forgive me, Your Grace," he addressed Danaë and Thiago with a bow. "I am but one interloper to this court. Like many others, I had to endure a trial to be accepted here. If your daughter is to stand amongst us, if she is going to save us, she should prove herself. After all, there are rumours that her origins are in the mortal world. Mortal influence could have… softened her. Her fae beauty could be a glamour. However, ink magic is not something that can be denied."

A ripple of agreement spread through the room as though the court relished the doubt. As though they demanded a trial. What was legacy without proof of the strength to uphold it?

Zephyr's gaze narrowed. By his guess, the male hailed from the fallen Court of Cavernous Dreams. He wore a tailored suit of deep purple, with intricate black threading that resembled the labyrinthine tunnels of his former court. Beneath his mask, his neck bore delicate lines that spoke to the dreams that kept him up at night. His earring and belt of jewels suggested he was a merchant who had worked his way to the upper echelons of the Court of Silence.

Danaë's smile faltered only for a second. "A reasonable request."

Zephyr bit back his instinct to intervene. It would only make the stakes of a trial higher if the courtiers smelled his fear.

The faerie king studied Ysadora with cold judgement, and his children's eyes lit with glee. "It is true we cannot afford weakness. Not in these times. Even the daughters of this court are tested. Ysadora will find a place amongst us only if her magic is deemed worthy. I trust this decision satisfies the court."

The court buzzed with excitement, fuelled by a palpable hunger to see her falter or triumph.

"Indeed, My Grace," replied the bejewelled man.

Though his mate shielded her eyes with the sweep of her lashes, Zephyr noticed her curled fists.

A wave of protectiveness washed over him. He wanted to rush to her side, but the formality of the court forbade it. He had to get her out of there. What if the court saw her as nothing more than a lost mortal? No, he wouldn't let her face a trial. She didn't need to show the court she had magic. She would be far safer if that remained a secret.

Her twilight eyes met his. Conflicting emotions danced across her face—anger, doubt and a spark of defiance— then she looked away.

Giving her space didn't mean he couldn't protect her.

Danaë stood, and her snow leopards accompanied her. "It is right that my eldest daughter shows you she is one of us. But first, I will sing in her honour, and you will dance."

Her pearlescent lips parted, and her voice propelled forth, casting a spell across the ballroom as she sang a lilting melody that wrapped around the court, summoning each member to the dance floor. Couples turned to one another, their eyes softly glazed, bodies moving in unison like enchanted marionettes to Danaë's melody. The majority wore their masks, still. Some meshed their bodies together with fervour, others kept a prim distance as if the task were more duty than pleasure. Her song rose and fell with a hypnotic quality that kept the dancers in a trance as the faerie king watched from his throne. Shadows stretched across the walls, moving with them. The room was filled with the whispers of silk brushing against velvet, the rustle of layered fabrics shifting with each turn and the occasional chiming of jewellery.

Zephyr had despised this ritual since Danaë had arrived at court. Her song tugged at his body, and each note required effort to resist. Some struggled for a moment, resisting the spell's pull, but the magic was relentless, and eventually, their feet found the rhythm and locked into the beat. Most succumbed to it easily, swept into the rhythm without a second thought, but Zephyr had learned to sense the strings and pushed back against them. It didn't make him beloved in Danaë's eyes.

It was dangerous to thwart the faerie king's consort.

But Zephyr had always courted danger one way or another.

He needed to confer with Loxley and Gabor about getting Ysadora out of there sooner, even if it meant creating a diversion rather than waiting for a natural opportunity. His lips twitched as he found Lox, who danced like he was mocking the entire court. He didn't flow with the music so much as disrupt it, inserting spins and flourishes, and stomping his boots. He spun with swagger, leaning too close to his partner, a strapping male who grew stiffer with each step, his disdain clear.

A flash of fuchsia and elegant wings made it easy to spot Gabor. Zephyr frowned. He was moving towards the dais, his gaze locked on Ysadora. Gabor extended a hand, and Ysadora stepped down onto the floor with him. Jealousy simmered in Zephyr's chest, intensifying as he watched his mate fall into dance. Gabor's hand settled against the small of Ysadora's back, guiding her with ease across the dance floor. There was a quiet authority to his movements, a mastery of rhythm and control. He spoke softly in her ear, just out of earshot. The answering smile on his mate's face stirred something hot and uneasy within Zephyr, and he felt his uncle's gaze linger on him.

He held it together for a beat or three, too long. When he could bear it no longer, Zephyr cut through the crowd and tapped Gabor's shoulder. "I believe this dance is mine."

The winged fae shifted aside with an apologetic glance. "Sorry, boss. I thought she could do with a friendly face."

Zephyr gave a curt nod. Then he turned his attention to Ysadora, who hovered with a look of confusion on her face as if Danaë's song still had her in its thrall. He held out his hand, fingers steady despite the slight tension in his stance. His voice was soft, almost hesitant. "Will you dance with me, Inkheart?"

Ysadora glanced from his outstretched hand to his face. "Yes."

She took his hand and let him lead her into the dance again. The music swelled around them as he rested his hand on the lacy folds of her hip. For the love of lore, she was beautiful.

They drew so many eyes that he wanted to encase them in his shadows, but he didn't give in to the temptation. This was a performance, and her life depended on it. Except to Zephyr, it didn't feel like a performance. It felt like everything he had always wanted. A love of his own. A love that nobody could take away. He wanted to tell her, but he held his tongue.

Once, he'd found the forced pomp, rigid rules and

graceful bows of dancing suffocating. With Ysadora, every step felt natural, as if they had danced together a thousand times before. They moved in slow, sweeping circles, his touch light but sure. He wanted to anchor her through this storm. Danaë's song drew them deeper into the spellbound embrace of the night, and he didn't want it to end. For a moment, as the music rose, the glittering ballroom disappeared, leaving only the two of them. *His mate.* His heart thundered under her palm.

He hoped, somewhere in the universe, Veda was smiling.

YSADORA

*One step closer, one breath near,
In the night's embrace, I lose all fear.
—Danaë's song lyrics*

The female who had been my Mother sang, and my skin prickled with unease. Then Gabor came to lead me in the beautiful compulsion. The music's spell wove through me, bending my body to its will. I relinquished my control to the guiding pressure of Gabor's hands, only half-present as if caught between worlds. When I tried to stop, the strange song swept me back into its smooth, seamless rhythm.

In Larkspur, dancing had been freedom. There, my body had moved with unrestrained joy. Each step and twirl had a release, carrying me beyond worries. Maren had spun me in circles until we both collapsed into a giggling heap. Ferrith had led me through dramatic waltzes while Maren hooted with laughter on the sidelines. I'd danced alone under the stars, my bare feet skimming across wild grass and soft earth, every cell alive. There was no need to consider form or elegance. In Larkspur, I danced for myself, not others.

At the Court of Silence, dancing meant giving up a piece of myself.

Gabor rescued me from the company of my false family, and I was grateful for that and more.

But when Zephyr clasped my hand, the court around us faded to a blur as we danced over the polished floor. He held me almost tenderly as though the trust between us hadn't fractured. As if I hadn't driven him away. His strength and quiet confidence brought me a strange, stolen comfort. Comfort that I desperately needed amidst the scrutiny of the court and palpable danger. Serpentine smiles. Cold eyes. Sheathed claws. Coiling shadows. They all retreated in Zephyr's arms.

We moved as if nothing had come between us, letting our bodies speak when we could not. He was striking in the dim, ethereal light of the ballroom, dark hair falling loosely around the sharp angles of his face. He had the look of someone who had spent a lifetime holding secrets close. But the way he enveloped me in his solid frame made my heart catch. His sea mist eyes, usually so steely, held an undercurrent of vulnerability tonight, and his touch was reverent as he guided me across the floor. When his calloused hand cupped my hip, my chest tightened with something akin to longing.

I leaned into our fragile truce, knowing it wouldn't last.

My heart rebelled despite the strange clawing of Danaë's song, wishing that we could be suspended in the dance together just a little longer.

He slowed our pace just enough for us to catch our breath, drawing me into a gentle turn before presenting me with a toffee. A boyish grin lit up his otherwise solemn face. "In case the night drags on."

My laugh was soft and disbelieving as our bodies swayed. "You remembered I like toffee."

"There's nothing I'd forget about you." His voice carried an almost hypnotic quality in the midst of Danaë's magic. He unwrapped the toffee, pocketed the wrapper, and offered it to me with his thumb and forefinger. The gesture was thoughtful, given my harsh words last night.

I hesitated for a beat of the music. In honesty, he had given me more than I had ever anticipated: protection when we had been enemies and when we had been friends, the Rune of Unveiling, mentors, books about Faerie, the key to Ebonspire. He had given me his secrets: some of them, at least. And yet, I was surprised that he had brought me toffee. Zephyr was full of surprises.

I parted my lips wide enough for him to place it in my mouth, and his eyes darkened. The spark of intimacy between us felt rare within the cold beauty of the ballroom. The caramel richness melted on my tongue, with a sharper edge reminiscent of liquorice. I caught myself before I moaned.

Zephyr's cheek dimpled. "I'm glad you approve." He beckoned me into the hypnotic, flowing motion of the dance again, pulling me close and dipping his head so that his mouth was at my ear and mine at his as the music soared close to its closing notes. His voice vibrated in my ear, a caress. "I'm getting you out before the trial begins." I stiffened in his arms, and he must have noticed because his tone roughened. "Please. You don't have to stay with me or help me. You don't have to do anything at all. Meet Loxley by the western arch after this song ends, and we'll make sure you get to safety."

His *please* almost made me tell him the truth. But being given orders only ever fuelled my urge to defy them. I settled for absolving him of his guilt like I should have done last night instead of taking out my fear on someone who had shown me kindness. Someone whose proximity my body shamelessly responded to. "It isn't your fault Father isn't here. I know you tried."

Danaë's song curled around us, her final note lingering in the air like the last breath of a storm. Zephyr dipped me. My head tilted back, my throat exposed, and he paused, his lips just inches from mine. In that moment, even sound fell away. For a heartbeat, there was only him.

"Careless to wear Kazimir's quill in your hair."

"Or brave," I replied softly.

His eyes, fixed on my lips and clouded like sapphire, held a question. An invitation: silent but clear.

Electricity pulsed between us that was nothing like the fumbles in Larkspur. Nothing like the boys and men I had known in the past, whose hesitant touches left me cold. His proximity thrummed in my chest. He would unravel me if I gave him the chance. I wanted to give him a chance.

I didn't want to leave unfinished business between us.

Yes, I thought. *Yes, yes.* I'd never needed a kiss as much as his. I could allow myself that.

Zephyr read the flicker of consent in my eyes, the soft tilt of my head, the dart of my tongue that told the story of how ready I was to taste him. Then he leaned in slowly. His hand cradled my neck, and his lips brushed against mine—testing the waters—as if waiting for me to change my mind.

My thoughts blurred as I returned the pressure of his lips. The kiss ignited every nerve in my body. A surge of recognition stirred within me, though I didn't understand it, and a soft ache bloomed inside my chest as though I'd finally come home after a long journey. The press of his lips grew more fervent. His warm hands against my back pulled me closer. My hands found their way to his chest, fingers curling into the fabric as if to anchor myself. Time slowed, and my heartbeat thundered in my chest. There was only him: his touch, his warmth, the scent of the wilds on his tawny skin. The feelings that swirled between us were as intense and wild as a forest fire through dry woods. The kiss was everything unspoken between us: a promise, an awakening and a release all in one.

Then he eased me up and pulled away, leaving me breathless and reeling. The world rushed back in, courtiers exhaling and drawing to a halt as the music faded into silence.

"Remember. The west arch," Zephyr murmured. His thumb brushed the back of my hand, a fleeting gesture that felt like the beginning of something new when, for me, it was a goodbye.

The court came into clearer focus, and I glanced at the dais where Danaë stood.

Her hard gaze flicked from me to Zephyr as if she didn't want anyone to have influence over me other than her. The court's attention sharpened to a point as she spoke.

"Mother," I called out across the silent ballroom, her word a bitter lie on my lips, my cutting tone making it clear I knew she had woven a web of lies, just like everyone else. She bent the truth into smooth stones, but turning them over revealed sharp edges. "I'm ready for my trial."

The court's atmosphere shifted and darkened. My heart pounded, and despite everything, I looked to Danaë for a sign of reassurance. But her face remained calm as she petted her snow leopards, and her twin children watched on with smiles that did not reach their eyes.

I glanced over my shoulder at Zephyr. His face had tightened in surprise, but he gave a solemn nod as though accepting my decision. My lips still tingled from his kiss, and for a moment, my foolish heart wanted to choose him over what lay ahead. The mercenary leader didn't accept people easily, but when he did, the acceptance was without caveats. It made me sorry for what I was about to do.

The room closed in on me, hundreds of eyes boring into me as if I were nothing more than a spectacle. As if I was just meat, not someone's daughter, or friend, or their salvation. Their masks made it worse. There wasn't time to second guess my decision before Danaë whispered in Thiago's ear.

The faerie king's lips twisted into a skeletal smile that didn't reach his shadowed eyes. "We begin."

His thin fingers splayed wide, and a strange light pulsed from his palm, casting ghostly shadows over his hollowed face. With a flick of his wrist, the ballroom floor groaned, then cracked, splintering outward in jagged lines. Each fissure spread like the web of a spider, fracturing the polished surface into shards that hovered.

At the first tremor, masked court members skittered to

the edges of the room, clutching the folds of their robes and gowns as the prism storm cast fractured rainbows across their shadowed faces. Hurried footsteps sounded as attendants abandoned their wraithlike manoeuvrings in favour of speed, saving tilting tables and teetering goblets, collecting half-finished platters and a pitcher of amber liquid that toppled to the ground.

My foolish heart tugged my gaze towards Zephyr. To the untrained eye, he was unaffected by the chaos that had erupted around us: his stance impassive, sea mist eyes hooded beneath dark brows, face neutral as he observed the unfolding storm. But for nine days, I had watched him as closely as he had watched me. I was attuned to the subtle shifts of his body, the slight flex of his shoulders, the tightening of his jaw—the quiet signs that revealed what others could not see. His hands were subtly clenched as if he might act at any moment. His gaze watched every fractured shard that spun through the air, every wraith-like servant scrambling to maintain order. His body was coiled.

Zephyr wasn't indifferent to the chaos; he was waiting, anticipating.

Then, as the faerie king sent his prisms rocketing towards me, I pushed Zephyr to the periphery of my mind. Each one refracted light in dazzling bursts that painted the sombre court in hues of brilliant colour, an explosion of life in a place that usually knew only silence and shadows. The spectacle elicited applause from the courtiers and a surge of fear from me.

But I had no need to be afraid. Not when I had made the choice to shine.

Not when I had decided to ignore Zephyr's advice to

hide my magic and be myself. I wouldn't make myself small for them. I wouldn't cower. I wasn't just another broken piece in the Court of Silence. I wasn't here to play the quiet, obedient pawn that the faerie king and the woman who had been my mother thought I would be. I had grown more dangerous by the hour since I had set foot in Faerie.

My belief, my rage, and my power were mine to wield, not theirs.

I wanted to show I was not beholden to them. I wanted *them* to be afraid.

My hair cascaded around my shoulders as I slipped Father's quill from my hair. Thiago's shards pulsed with blinding hues, blues, purples and golds, refracting in a furious whirl of light. I had no ink, but it didn't matter. Not when my instinctive magic told me to use my blood. With a deliberate, steadying breath, I used the nib's sharp edge to cut a thin line of crimson in my palm. The quill's feather was the same colour as my makeshift ink. I soaked the nib in my pooling blood, then raised my quill, using its tip like a conductor's baton, just in time to meet the faerie king's assault.

A trail of blood arced through the air, responding to my will and weaving into the storm. Each slash and sweep channelled my magic, steadying the prisms. I took care over the crater at my feet as I pulled on the spinning shards, drawing each one closer to balance and order. The jagged edges of the shards smoothed, their wild spin calming. My blood danced through the air. I bent the storm's rage into something controlled and beautiful.

The court's attention was rapt. I didn't dare look, but I sensed their scrutiny.

I sensed Zephyr's heavy gaze most of all.

The court buzzed with approval, their awe increasing with every heartbeat. Such a display was rare here, where muted colours and restrained magic reigned. They accepted me—the calligrapher's daughter—into their sorry court.

The faerie king preened, and the woman who had been my mother shone with pride.

And the mercenary leader watched on with a solemn face, his relief palpable, at least to me.

The moment I felt the court's acceptance—an acceptance I didn't want or need—I twisted my magic until the prismatic whirlwind opened a narrow passage. With one swift movement, I edged through the corridor of twirling prisms, feeling the edges of the ballroom fade behind me as I approached the doors. The maze awaited, cool and dark beyond the threshold. The ballroom doors loomed ahead, just a few steps away. With one last pull of my power, I twisted the storm's fragments, nudging the path open and sprinted through. My dress caught on my leg, the fabric restrictive, but I willed myself onwards.

I ran into the maze. I ran towards Gabor.

ZEPHYR

Guard your heart as you would a treasure, for it is the only thing that can remain truly yours in a realm full of shadows.
—Rowena Ashmoor's letter to her son Zephyr

The court gasped as his mate made her daring escape, leaving the glimmer of ballroom shards in her wake. Her trial had been a triumph and a rebellion that Zephyr sorely wished he'd had the courage for when he first arrived at the Court of Silence. Some courtiers made to follow Ysadora, but Zephyr moved to block the exit to the maze with a coy wag of his finger.

His voice was a soft, warning purr. "She's earned a moment to herself, don't you think?" The amusement in his storm-cloud eyes suggested he'd take pleasure from making their pursuit of the calligrapher's daughter more trouble than it was worth.

He was proud of his Inkheart and so fucking angry at her for putting her life at risk.

He had almost lost his wits watching her.

It should have been impossible for her to do that. She shouldn't have been able to defend herself against a faerie king's magic. Zephyr had known it by the tightening around his uncle's eyes, the glint of disbelief beneath Thiago's smooth mask of composure. Faerie's spymaster wielded his magic with absolute authority. He wasn't accustomed to it being answered, let alone challenged.

Yet, somehow, his mate had not only risen to the challenge, but she had been a marvel.

He wanted to crow with pride, but not as much as he wanted to follow her into the maze. However, that was not his designated role. Clearly, his mate had decided meeting Loxley in the maze after outmanoeuvring the faerie king was a better plan than meeting by the western arch. He signalled to his fellow mercenaries with a dart of his shadows: they should wait to avoid suspicion, then follow Ysadora into the maze at an opportune moment. But his mind was already racing, anticipating her path through the maze, the pitfalls she'd need to avoid, and the quickest way to intercept her. If she wanted to play this dangerous game, they'd play it together. Even so, he would give her a stern talking to once she was safely in his arms again.

Zephyr's pulse quickened, his thrill mingling with worry. Ysadora's magic was a joy to behold from the moment she had unleashed her cloak of ink at Ebonspire. It was powerful. Instinctive. Untamed. But seeing her bend the very nature of the court to her will was beyond even his expectations. It painted a target on her back. She was now both the maker and unmaker of any number of possible faerie futures. He had to pull himself together and pivot. A stealth escape was a pipe dream now that Ysadora had tired of being a pawn. After all, wasn't that what the gleam in her twilight eyes had meant?

She hadn't been running from him. He had to believe that.

No female poured herself into a kiss so fiercely, so unreservedly, without needing every stolen breath and touch. Kissing her for the first time had shattered every restraint Zephyr had carefully fixed in place, flooding him with longing he could barely contain. Her lips against his felt like a wildfire, spreading warmth and hunger through him in equal measure. In that one kiss, Zephyr knew he was lost to her, bound in a way that went deeper than magic, deeper than fate itself—as though he'd finally come home. Their kiss was a promise: she was his, as much as he was hers, in every way that mattered.

He was utterly terrified Ysadora would vanish. Utterly terrified that his uncle would attempt to crush or control her.

Zephyr tensed. Over his dead body. Or Thiago's.

He returned his attention to the court, stalking towards the dais, slipping back into the role he had mastered since his mother's passing: the dutiful yet dangerous nephew, sharp as a blade sheathed at his uncle's side. His expression fell into practised neutrality, the kind that invited confidences without revealing his own mind, the face of a male who played his part to perfection. But inwardly, he kept one ear tuned to any mention of Ysadora's absence, one eye to any movement on the dais, his mind calculating his next steps.

He thanked the ancients that the court members sensed

weakness like bloodhounds on a fresh scent. They watched with glee as their faerie king of three centuries—who had ruled with an iron fist and fed their hunger for cruel entertainment—faltered. They smiled behind masks at the thought their king might actually be breakable. Fresh sport and a shift in loyalties or alliances was a thrill greater than any spectacle they'd witnessed under Thiago Hendrick's reign.

The faerie king's hands hovered as he forced the prismatic storm back down into the cratered floor. His jaw was set in concentration, but the shattered floor resisted his command. Its cracks refused to heal, even as the faerie king renewed his attempts. A curse of frustration escaped him, but no matter how he struggled, the pieces refused to align. Eventually, he regained some control, and the surface clicked into place with a series of unnerving, jangling noises, although some pieces still protruded. Instead of the polished, seamless floor, Ysadora's magic was etched into the floor like a scar. Around Zephyr, clusters of courtiers noted blips, not only in form but also in colour. There were small pulses of light and veins of colour coursing through the cracks in the floor's dark polish. Though the ballroom floor mostly returned to its former stillness, mocking flickers suggested something had shifted in the foundation of the court itself.

Zephyr hid a smile. Ysadora's defiance lingered in the room: her imprint was neither erased nor entirely subdued.

It was a reminder of the storm she had brought with her and the storm yet to come. For a moment, the mercenary leader wondered if Veda had known this moment would come, as well as the fact that Ysadora Silberquill would steal his heart.

On the dais, Danaë's face was schooled into perfect serenity. She held her head high, shoulders squared, lips set in a dignified smile, as though the disturbance had all unfolded by design, a masterstroke of the faerie king's own making.

She allowed a brief, measured silence to stretch before addressing the room. Her voice, low and musical, rang out. "See what power a child of this court wields? Consider it a testament to our court's strength that we welcome one so fierce and capable into our fold. Consider it a prelude…a small taste of what our court nurtures and protects. We shall be the envy of Faerie."

The faerie king stood beside her, lips pulled into a taut smile, his displeasure clear beneath the veneer of his approval.

"Let us return to revelry." With a languid sweep of her arm, Danaë summoned attendants from the shadowed edges of the room. They floated forward, smoothing any disarray and filling wine goblets. Their mistress's unearthly gold eyes drifted over the court, offering each member a pointed, composed nod that made clear her expectation: the evening would continue.

She beckoned a lute player forward, and he struck up a low melody that seeped through the ballroom like fog. Hushed conversation resumed, and most fell once more under the sway of the music and the rhythm of the Court of Silence.

Danaë had been born mortal, but she was as adept as any faerie king or queen's consort at intricate power games. The calm way she held the court in her thrall—

masking the tension, tempering the unrest—was masterful. There was no hesitation in her voice, no sign of the woman who'd once been outside this world. She'd never quite let him get close enough to read her history. Still, if Zephyr hadn't known better, he'd think this court's grace and cruelty had always been her own.

The faerie king and his consort descended from the dais arm in arm, chins lifted regally. Zephyr's stomach tightened as they despatched their children and the snow leopards towards the maze exit. Xaire's eyes were sharp as they traced the path Ysadora had taken, and the sleek leopards tensed in anticipation of the hunt.

But Loxley—loud, brash and chaos incarnate—was already running interference.

He glided in front of Xaire, feigning a thoughtful expression. "I'd be careful if I were you. Perhaps the leopards are more interested in your scent than your leadership. You wouldn't want them to get any ideas out there in the dark."

"Out of my way, you bearded imp," snapped Xaire.

The snow leopards bristled at Loxley's nearness. Neither his foreign scent nor his manner endeared him to them. He watched the leopards intently, a mischievous grin creeping onto his face.

"I'm not finished." Loxley raised his silver goblet in a mock toast. His free hand gestured theatrically. "To the faerie king's generosity. May we each live further centuries to witness such delights. To the Court of Silence, where every hush is filled with secrets, and every ruckus has its purpose. To the brilliant minds that keep this court in motion, whether in silence or storm." The goblet in his hand fell with a musical crash as he pretended to stumble, his hands brushing the temples of the leopards.

Loxley mocked the rituals and gravitas that the court prided itself on. His presence was too unpolished and absurd to win favour here. The more exaggerated his antics, the more he drew attention from Ysadora.

Zephyr loved his friend for it.

The leopards snarled, and the larger one bared its teeth, but Loxley was unfazed. His magic whispered through his touch, not enough to harm the leopards but more like a tug on the leash of their instincts. Their feral instincts faltered for a fraction of a second, and then the larger leopard blinked, confusion clouding its predatory gaze. In that moment, Loxley's magic took hold, coaxing the creature onto his hind legs and into a twirl. The second leopard followed, stance shifting, its hostility melting away as it fell into step beside the first, the two of them moving in tandem.

The lute player's fingers stumbled in his surprise, briefly losing their place on the strings before he continued the melody. The courtiers—ever watchful, ever hungry for spectacle—joined in, gawping and murmuring as the leopards were sucked into the rhythm of the ballroom, their sleek, muscular bodies twisting in an elegant, unexpected dance.

Xaire's gaze darkened, his lips drawn into an angry line. "What a farce."

A wide smile creased Loxley's face. It was a beautiful distraction. He bowed low, brushed the front of his ruffled shirt, and, with a final sly glance at his handiwork, melted into the throng of courtiers.

Zephyr glimpsed Danaë, a few dozen feet away with

the jewel merchant who had stirred such trouble earlier. Her jaw tightened so sharply that it could crack as she observed her precious snow leopards swaying in a forced rhythm, and though their compulsion lasted a mere moment or two, the elegant length of her nails pressed into her palms, a movement so contained that it was nearly invisible. She was quick to anger, slow to forgive.

Like mother, like son, thought Zephyr as his cousin slipped into the maze, his plum cloak billowing behind him.

At least Loxley had seen to it that Ysadora didn't have to worry about Danaë's leopards. For a moment, it bothered Zephyr that his shadows hadn't located Gabor. Shadows didn't like chaos, but still, it was unusual for them to fail him. A flicker of worry coiled in his chest as he glanced around the ballroom, his practised calm starting to falter.

But Zephyr didn't have long to dwell on the thought.

The faerie king appeared at his shoulder. "I like the ginger mercenary."

Zephyr's eyebrows jackknifed. His uncle had always found Loxley's antics troublesome, though not entirely without merit.

Thiago let out a soft chuckle, dark and rich. "My wife pays too much attention to her leopards. They were useful gifts, of course, especially when I first brought her to Faerie before she became fae. Who would dare to think my mortal wife was weak or vulnerable with fierce beasts prowling at her side?" He followed the passage of one of the beasts weaving through the crowd towards Danaë. "Now, I can never quite approach her without one of them watching me. So yes, I did enjoy the fool's antics."

"I shall be sure to tell Loxley of your pleasure, uncle."

The faerie king tilted his head, considering the uneven floor. "The girl's stronger than I anticipated," he murmured, almost to himself. "Clever, too, to turn my storm against me and with such elegance."

A roiling mix of anger and fear twisted in Zephyr's chest. "Indeed. I think the last trial discharged with such aplomb was close to two orbits ago. That minor lord you ended up feeding to the leopards."

Dark humour tilted Thiago's thin mouth up. "Yes, they have their uses. I was pleased they took his face first. He had an arrogance about him. And he did insult me. There are rules of civility to uphold."

Zephyr repeated a refrain Thiago had drilled into him during a beating many decades ago. "Without rules, chaos reigns."

"I am pleased you remember." A mocking lilt entered the faerie king's voice. "I was surprised to see your enthusiasm for our new guest, nephew. That kiss was bold, even for you. A little indulgent. So that's what you were doing when you had the girl at Ebonspire… My wife would prefer you not to lay your hands on the girl. But I am not so hasty… Rut if you must. Males have needs. Naturally, you will put this court above any distractions." His words had a steely undertone that brooked no rebellion.

Zephyr forced himself to meet his uncle's cold gaze without a flicker of reaction. "I take my responsibilities seriously. Wasn't it I who brought her to you?" All the while, his heart sang *my mate, my mate, my mate*.

"We were right to hunt her. She'll be useful in time." The faerie king's dark eyes gleamed. "It won't be long before Xaire retrieves her. The boy enjoys opportunities to prove his worth. It doesn't pay to fail me."

Zephyr maintained his mask of obedience though his mind spiralled like a hawk hunting. As his uncle doled out the poison he had injected into Zephyr since childhood about how he had been a superior father figure to his brother, Zephyr dissociated. His thoughts struck out in every direction for any rational explanation that would ease the growing tension in his chest.

For as long as he remembered, Zephyr had hated this court, where dreams festered in silence. He had longed for the fallen Court of Lore, where fae had dreamed out loud. He missed living joyously. He missed colour and warmth and the touch of loved ones rather than the icy formality of what constituted family at his uncle's stronghold. Yet, in that moment, Zephyr would have given anything for the silence of peace. The peace of knowing Ebonspire was safe. The peace of holding his mate in his arms. The peace of trusting his friends and allies. That peace felt further away than ever.

Zephyr was starting to wonder where the hell Gabor was and why he hadn't checked in.

Doubts crawled like insects, burrowing into his trust for a friend he had known for close to nine orbits.

Had Gabor's attentiveness to Ysadora signified more than kindness or attraction? Every lingering look, every offer to help her learn the ways of Faerie, had seemed benign on the surface. Zephyr himself had been so captivated by Ysadora that it had been easy to imagine another male felt the same way. But with the sting of betrayal in the air, he considered whether Gabor's motives were darker. Gabor seldom invested time and charm without cause.

Zephyr's gut told him that he had been blind to something dangerously obvious.

The challenge in weaving a family from a tangle of outsiders was that each of them brought the histories and loyalties of fallen courts. Customs clashed more often than they aligned. It had been a delicate task to forge a stable unit from disparate pieces, but Zephyr was forgiving. He had been burned before and had learned to make careful choices about who he accepted into his inner circle. In the main, he was tolerant of differences and disagreements as long as they didn't harm what he was trying to build. Not this time. Not if Gabor had broken his trust at such a crucial moment.

The nagging sense of betrayal simmered in him, and he could no longer ignore it. Every shared morsel of food, every quiet word of counsel, every misstep on past missions now took on a sinister edge. It wasn't unusual for fae cast adrift from fallen courts to agree to unsavoury roles to gain acceptance at a new one.

Could it be that Gabor was no mere wanderer, struggling to find his place in a changed Faerie?

Was it possible that he knew more about Ysadora than he let on?

Zephyr's heart pounded as the faerie king talked on and as the court whirled around him. The way Ysadora had controlled and moved through the prismatic storm had been a paradox of control within destruction. She had controlled the chaos so effortlessly, so instinctively. Could Kazimir's daughter stem from two courts, just like he did?

The golem she had conjured when they had trained at Ebonspire had bothered him more than once. All at once, he remembered where he had seen a similar creature: it had been a favourite pet of Tanuhja's at the Court of Chaos.

No, no. He had to be mistaken.

He was allowing paranoia to take root where there was only uncertainty. Ysadora's biological mother couldn't be from the Court of Chaos. Zephyr had almost been relieved when Tanuhja's coin had dried up. The Court of Chaos was wild, untamed and untrustworthy. But every possibility brought him back to the same chilling truth: Ysadora's magic was too unpredictable, too powerful for anything else to make sense. He shook his head to clear the thick fog of suspicion, but it was no use. The icy grip on his heart refused to loosen. His lore magic had always been like that for Zephyr, as it had been for his mother. They didn't see the truth like Veda did, but once they gleaned it, the truth stuck fast.

It was a stubborn thing, really, like a burr that clung to Zephyr, even when he tried to shake it free. Even when he would have preferred the comfort of a lie. It was like a stone lodged in the heart of a river, enduring currents and time. It didn't yield to wishful thinking or bend for convenience. If he was right about Ysadora's origins, would the Court of Chaos seek to claim her?

His mate was in the maze, possibly scared or under attack.

And Gabor, whom they both trusted, could be her undoing.

YSADORA

*Eleven orbits old, and you ran into the Shrouded
Forest today, my Ysa, to rescue that terrified deer
from the fire even as smoke choked the air.
Sometimes, I think you are too brave for your
own good. You make an old male's
heart crack with pride.
—Kazimir's entry to the memory stone*

I stepped into the maze, and silence settled once more. The prismatic storm's fury was finally locked away behind me, and only the echo of its fierce beauty remained in my head. I hugged my sliced palm to my chest as I forged ahead, my quill still entwined in my fingers in case I was followed. The night air felt both heavy and liberating, as if I had left a part of myself behind in the ballroom. I couldn't help but think of Zephyr.

His kiss. His kiss had felt so damn good.

I'd wanted to stay with him. To never leave his side and all he offered: protection, challenge, kindness. Flaming heat.

I wondered if I had hurt him. I had no choice but to claim my fate rather than be Danaë's puppet. I'd allow nobody—neither Father, nor Danaë, nor Zephyr, nor a cohort of damned faerie kings and queens—to control me.

My future was my own. Thank the stars that I had persuaded Gabor to be my ally.

It felt wrong to borrow the whisper ring from Zephyr, but Gabor had said he wouldn't mind. After all, this was a mere adaptation to the mercenary leader's plan. By his own admission, he had wanted to spirit me away from the Court of Silence tonight anyway. By surprising him, I had provided him with plausible deniability when he faced his uncle. Perhaps one day, he would even thank me. I ignored the tightening in my belly and concentrated on my footing.

The maze was a glittering, lantern-lit cage built from towering crystal walls etched with fae runes. The maze distorted sound, turning my breaths into eerie whispers and my footsteps into a dull hum. My form was reflected a hundred times over in glassy surfaces, some appearing to reach back at me, others melting into shadow. Danaë's handmaidens—their eyes as colourless as winter fog and fingers like phantom pianists—had meticulously prepared me. Now, I was a vision in disarray. The lush folds of my gown were now creased and torn, dusted with flecks from the prisms, and the shimmering powder they had applied to my face was streaked with blood and dirt. My heart soared. I'd broken free from their carefully curated image of me.

More importantly, I had a plan to find Father: one that hinged on the compass I'd tucked away in a pocket—the only request I'd made of the handmaidens. Its needle spun with every turn I took. Not much further now. Not much longer until Maren, Father and I were together again.

Gabor had already scoped out the maze from the sky, memorising every twist and turn and translating it to me with painstaking care so I would have no difficulty in finding him. Our meeting point was the bloodheart tree. By all accounts, it was a tree of haunting beauty that stood at the centre of the maze, protected by curved walls. Its bark was dark crimson, like the skin of an old wound. Long, thin branches stretched upwards, each ending in blade-like green leaves edged in red. The air around it smelt of iron, and it was said the tree's roots connected to the very core of the Court of Silence, leading to long-forgotten secrets. He would have accompanied me, but he had to collect the whisper rings from their hiding place to enable our escape. Then we would collect Maren from the verges of the court and find Father at last.

I rounded a corner, panting now, and there it was, stark against the moonless sky like an ancient monument, casting a long shadow on the ground beneath. At first, I thought I was alone, and Gabor had yet to arrive. Then my eyes adjusted, and I noticed a figure leaning against the trunk of the bloodheart. But rather than Gabor's long black hair, it was long silver hair I saw. It wasn't Gabor's winged, masculine form waiting for me. No, it was a female: slim and, for once, smiling.

My heart drummed as I slipped the compass into my pocket. "Elowen?"

I could hardly look at her—the daughter Danaë had

after she arrived in Faerie—without questions coiling in my mind. Had the woman who had been my mother held this child close and crooned lullabies in her ears the way she had with me? Had she traced her fingertips over this daughter's cheek and teased her hair into ringlets? Had they picked wildflowers together, as we had? How could someone love fiercely and then simply abandon me without a backward glance? How could she reshape her love so casually, overwrite me with these new children?

Elowen had a voice until puberty when the faerie king —in a fit of anger that his daughter didn't possess magic but had many opinions—had bound her mouth for the first time. In time, Elowen did develop magic: telepathy with her brother Xaire, and him alone. At least, that was what her mother had explained to me, with a slight droop in the mouth that conveyed her sorrow that Elowen had not followed in her songstress footsteps. But Danaë could be wrong about many things.

Elowen's voice unfolded in my mind, cold and startlingly clear, *Surprise, sister.*

I stifled a gasp, scanning the skies for Gabor, willing him to hurry. "How are you doing that? I thought—"

Each word was direct, almost surgical, in its delivery. Hers wasn't a voice that sought to coddle or comfort. It cut through the noise of the world like a blade through silk. Though low in volume, it lacked softness or empathy. The effect—without a moving mouth to accompany her words —was jarring. *You thought that I was the talentless one of the family.*

"I thought you could only communicate with Xaire."

I choose who I communicate with… I know why you are here.

My pulse accelerated. She was going to ruin everything. I was tempted, so tempted, to destroy her with my quill. Gabor's history lessons had introduced me to the grim notion that killing was a sport in Faerie. There were no laws forbidding it, and all was game unless one displeased the faerie king or queen. Life was a commodity, something to be wagered, toyed with and ended on a whim. Unlike in the mortal realm, there were no laws to protect the fae, no decrees outlawing murder, no laws condemning cruelty, and nothing but the faerie king or queen's personal preferences as a shield.

There was a compelling, magnetic quality to her voice. *It is true, sister. Life is less precious in Faerie. Perhaps my parents would not avenge me, but my twin would.*

My instincts—to fight or flee—clashed like swords on a battlefield. "You can read my thoughts."

Elowen nodded. There was a quiet urgency in her tone. *Will you not listen to what I have to say?*

I shifted uneasily. I had no choice but to await Gabor anyway. "This better be worth it."

I overheard you speaking with the winged male. I know he is coming. I know you wish for him to help you find Kazimir. He has a whisper ring stolen from my father's vault for you. Elowen twisted a dull ring on her finger. *It's like this one. It will help you go unnoticed. Help you disappear. I don't have shadows of my own, but with this ring, I'm a good eavesdropper. I listen. I notice things that other people don't.*

"What do you want?" I gritted out.

All these orbits, I hated you. Mother talked about you. Xaire didn't mind, but it made me feel small to hear of you. It made me wish you were dead or that you had never been born.

Resentment and pity swirled in my belly. I knew how

nourishing sisterhood could be and instead, we had been left with this. "I didn't ask for any of this, you know. I don't know how to fix it. But there's room enough for us both to matter, Elowen. Hating each other won't make it better. I don't want to be your enemy."

Her brown eyes locked on mine. *Good. Because I think we can be useful to each other.*

I thought, looking at her against the silhouette of the bloodheart tree, that perhaps I wanted to help her after all. Perhaps I didn't want to leave everything a broken mess behind me. "How?"

I want to leave.

"Isn't this court your legacy?"

My brother's, perhaps. It's different for him.

I shook my head, perplexed. "You want to leave your family?"

As soon as the words left my mouth, it dawned on me. The faerie king had bound her mouth, stolen her voice, and kept her in the shadow of her brother and cousin, granting them opportunities he'd denied her. My father was the opposite of hers, yet we were alike. Maybe even two sides of the same coin. Just like me, Elowen wanted more than what was allowed, more than what was scripted by others. Just like me, she yearned to carve out a future of her own making. I could read the tension around her eyes now, the defiance beneath her calm. Like a flame hidden in the hollow of a hand, she was determined to survive the silence.

Help me, or I will tell them where you are.

Did I trust or pity her enough to risk it? My plans were little more than a sketch, a wing and a prayer.

I'm not asking you to take me now. I will be of more use to you here. How else are we to make our escape permanent?

Odd to hear her talking about a *we* when I had blocked her from my mind. She smiled wryly at my thought. I felt the tug of the morally grey world that she navigated so well. "You want us to help each other."

But I cannot rely on your word that you will come back for me. And I will not let you go without surety.

My brows knitted, and I realised that, in some way, I was committing to a future in Faerie, even beyond rescuing Father. That maybe my kiss with Zephyr had been a promise to find him again when I had met my goals, rather than a goodbye. "A bargain then."

You'd do that? You'd really come back for me?

I heard the wonder in her voice at such an act of revolution in her world, where males had most of the agency. "Of course. You're my sister. Not by blood. But my sister all the same. Danaë treated us both poorly."

Elowen hesitated, and in that stillness, the five years between us stretched like a gulf. Her youth showed in the tremble of her lips, the fragile hope in her gaze. She looked like someone just on the edge of becoming. *I will keep my silence about this conversation and your plans if you come back for me within twelve moons. Do you agree?*

I stepped towards her so that both of us were shaded by the bloodheart tree. "I do."

Her smile would have melted icebergs. *Then, the bargain is set.* She gripped my forearm, and her voice was a storm in my mind. *Hold on.* Then came words in a lost language I didn't understand. Words carved into brain and bone and essence. Cold and needy.

I gasped as her mark needled across my ankle and her own as if it were being sewn. As if we were bound in a strange type of sisterhood, not one born of blood or community, but one of circumstance. The mark looked like three silver threads woven in an ouroboros, stark and burning against my olive skin. Then the sensation softened as if Elowen had sheathed the dark tools of magic, leaving only the quiet weight of a new bond behind. I looked up into her still eyes.

My tutor told me that even mediocre calligraphers can send messages over distances. If you write, I won't feel alone.

I ignored the implied insult. Rivalry between women wasn't insurmountable but took time to fade. "I will."

You have feelings for my cousin. He has always been kind to me. I will help him.

I bit my lip before meeting Elowen's eyes with a steady gaze. "Good. We need all the allies we can get."

She stiffened as the soft murmur of wings came our way and something else: a flurry of footsteps.

Xaire burst into the clearing, fury and disbelief etched across his face, his groomed hair now a dishevelled mop. His eyes darted from me to Elowen, lingering on his twin as though seeing her for the first time. Tension radiated through every line of his body. "What have you done?" His shadows stretched towards us.

Elowen gave a sad smile. *I'll deal with this.* She paused. *Maybe I could learn to love you.* Then, though her mouth remained closed, I heard the beginning of a rush of sound, as if a faucet had been opened, taking a trickle to a river. Elowen's voice boomed, and then she retreated from my mind, and Xaire clutched his temples and fell to his knees in agony. His twin went towards him and cupped his shoulder as if she didn't want to hurt him, but she didn't have a choice.

Gabor landed behind me with a low, muffled thud, the impact reverberating through the ground. His blended wings caught glints of light like scattered stars. He straightened, his expression both amused and exasperated. "Will you stop getting into trouble when I'm not looking? Come on, we'd better go." He glanced at the siblings. "You can explain this little adventure later."

A flash of autumn bonfire hair and a string of expletives marked Loxley's arrival at the bloodtree.

Before I could explain, Gabor slipped a whisper ring onto his finger and another onto mine. A tingling rush of magic swept over us as he twisted them anticlockwise. The world blurred around the edges as we faded into invisibility. Gabor's arm wrapped firmly around my waist, and in one seamless motion, he lifted me from the ground. With powerful beats of his wings, he launched us into the air over the Court of Silence.

Beneath the bloodtree, Elowen had released her hold and crouched over an inconsolably angry Xaire.

The cold wind pressed against us. I clung to Gabor, heart racing as we cut through the darkness, unseen.

Somewhere, far below, Loxley shouted my name.

36

YSADORA

Greytooth Owl
Splintered feathers, killing screech, a mouthful of
teeth. Once, Sayed Briarflight of the Court of
Madness, mate of Everly, gifted in translating
nightmares into words.
—The Secrets of Faerie's Veiled Beasts
by Zephyr Ashmoor

We touched down in Ashenvale on the borders of the Court of Silence and the Court of Chaos. The ground beneath us was a mottled grey as if the soil had been drained of life. Tall trees rose on either side of the path, their bark ashen and stripped to a pale white, with dark ivy clinging on. Mist drifted in low-hanging sheets between the trunks, and errant patches of bioluminescent fungi glowed at our feet, casting a sickly light. Howls and hoots set my teeth on edge.

Ashenvale was neither quiet nor empty in the way the Court of Silence was. Here, Faerie held her breath, waiting for something to break.

Gabor was in a glum mood as we searched for Maren. I didn't blame him. Faerie's imbalance was in full display here. Birds darted from branches, abandoning their nests in a flurry of feathers. Squirrels scurried unnaturally close to the ground, vanishing into burrows or cracks. Strange stale scents hung in the air, a blend of predator and decay. We found the prints of a massive beast in the soil and piles of scattered bones and feathers lying haphazardly on the ground. We combed the area without finding a trace of Maren.

Neither supplies from Ebonspire, or clothing, or singed areas that would have given me hope.

Gabor muttered under his breath about my inability to follow orders, and his eyes narrowed at every patch of shadow that moved strangely. "She's obviously not here."

My unease grew with every passing minute. The landscape felt less like a place of transition and more like a trap. We'd only been gone for two days. Could Maren have fallen prey to rogue fae or the monsters in that time? Gabor's earlier confidence had waned, and with it, my own. It seemed impossible that Maren, so fiercely loyal and quick-witted, would break her promise to wait for me. But the longer we searched, the more it felt as though Maren had never been here at all.

A prickling sensation crawled up my spine. Where was she? Wouldn't I have known in my heart if she had been hurt? "She can't be far. Let's check that starvine up ahead."

"If she's still alive. These woods are full of monsters, more so than anywhere else in Faerie."

I scowled at him. "Don't say that. She's my friend."

Gabor's wings twitched restlessly against his back, his usual calm cracking at the edges. It was odd he hadn't mentioned Zephyr or Loxley or worried about their safety. He must have heard Loxley's shouts just as I had. Yet, he said nothing.

My own mind was full of the mercenary leader. The pull he had on me was both maddening and magnetic. He had a way of making me question everything I thought I knew about myself, and it unsettled me. My thoughts tangled when he was near, spinning in directions I didn't want to go. I wondered what it would be like to stand beside him, to plot with him.

Gabor's necklace of twisted silver and sapphire shimmered with unnatural life here in Ashenvale, rather than its prior soft glow, as though it was tethered to something old and powerful. I couldn't take my eyes off it. It was as though it wasn't just ornamental; it had been forged for a purpose.

He noticed my gaze and held it for a beat. "It reacts to the land."

"Oh." I frowned. "I'm grateful you helped me, Gabor, but aren't you worried Zephyr will be angry about…not clueing him in? He's your leader. Your friend."

He shrugged nonchalantly. "Zephyr has his rules, sure, but he's also pragmatic. He'll understand. Stepping on a few toes is worth it to keep you safe. The rest can be worked out later. As for friendship, Faerie lives are so long that minor hurts are nothing at all. We've got centuries to work things out."

My pulse quickened as the branches overhead stirred. It was faint at first, almost like a whisper of wind, but then the sound grew sharper: a low creaking of wood as though something large moved through the trees.

Gabor glanced upwards. "That doesn't sound good. We can take refuge with Tanuhja at Gloomhaven. She's always looking for a reason to entertain lost souls, and frankly, I'd rather not face whatever that thing is." His hand shot out to grab mine and he began to move, pulling me along at a brisk pace away from the sound.

Something didn't add up. It wasn't just my unease at Maren's whereabouts niggling at me.

In our history lessons, Gabor had adopted an almost fawning tone over the Faerie Queen of the Court of Chaos. He had told tales of her diplomatic skills and alliances. How she wielded power through understanding, not weapons. How she sacrificed pieces of herself for the common good and that it was a source of pride for the mercenaries to work with Tanuhja when all the other kings and queens turned a blind eye to the monsters.

But why wasn't he as irked as Cyprian that she no longer paid coin for the monster extractions? For that matter, why would she let monsters roam her land? It was hardly the decision of a good-natured queen. Not only that, but in the stables, I was almost certain that Cyprian had not been a fan of Tanuhja, as if she was self-serving, somehow, and no longer cared about the mortal realm. He didn't trust her in the slightest.

We ran, him dragging me away from the bounding above our heads, and all the while, my thoughts reeled. How could the mercenaries have such wildly different perceptions of her? Their loyalties were supposed to be clear, aligned with the cause, and yet their opinions diverged like fractured glass. I was so tired of smoke and mirrors. So tired of second-guessing who was on my side. Doubts prickled my mind like thorns. Surely, I wasn't so blind as to have missed a betrayal hidden in plain sight?

Enough. I was sick of lies.

Sick of false friends. Sick of those who cared nothing for me and only for their own ends.

Father's quill was too precious for such games, but the compass—the compass was sturdy and gleamed even in the poor light. I dug for it in my pocket as Gabor dragged me along and dropped it with a cry.

I jerked him to a halt, and we both stooped in the mulch for it, our hands brushing. The smallest hint of irritation pulled at Gabor's mouth before he masked it again. Not worry, but irritation. It struck me like a slap. I thought he'd been my friend. He had cooked for me, taught me about Faerie, made me laugh, told me secrets and helped me out of a bind. But he didn't care about my safety or Father's plight, not as I'd thought he had.

I'd made a terrible mistake in trusting him.

But I was no longer the naïve woman who had needed rescuing in the Shrouded Forest. I had changed, transformed into someone other than the village girl from Larkspur.

Gabor handed me the compass and urged me onwards. I stood my ground, fingers curling around my prize. He hadn't noticed the sleight of hand with which I'd taken his whisper ring and slipped it on my own finger: the sort of tactic I'd perfected with Cyprian on the training field that tipped the odds against a stronger foe.

My eyes flicked up to the creaking canopy. "I'd give you an apology, but I don't think you deserve one."

Gabor stilled, and his eyes narrowed, the earlier hint of

irritation deepening into something sharper, more dangerous. "Excuse me?"

I tightened my grip on the compass, drawing reassurance from its weight in my hand. My voice sounded steady—stronger than I'd expected. "You heard me." Then I twisted the whisper ring and faded from view.

Gabor's outstretched hand closed on empty air as the creaking above us turned into a snap. His expression was almost comical as he reached for his own whisper ring to find it gone. Whatever his game was, I'd just thrown it into disarray.

"Don't do this. You'll be all alone here." He wasn't even facing me. He had no idea where I was.

That gave me the confidence to speak before I moved once more. "Better alone than with a knife at my back."

His curse was barely audible. He fixed his eyes on the spot where I had vanished but where I no longer stood. His voice was just above a whisper, a tone meant to coax me out. "Ysa? I'm your friend."

Shining stars, I knew what real friendship felt like. Friendship wasn't a battleground.

There was no way I would expose myself to him. Not when my instincts screamed to stay clear of the chaos he thrived in.

I remained hidden, crouched in the shelter of an old ash tree. My breathing was calm and measured. Even without the whisper ring, the dappled darkness would have concealed me well enough. But Gabor himself had crowed with pride when he told me about the qualities of the whisper rings. Unlike my cloak of ink, they muffled the wearer's footfalls, breathing and their heartbeat. They were so effective that the faerie king had chosen them to be worn by his wife, his daughter and his spiders.

I had nothing to fear from Gabor.

He wanted me to be helpless, but I wasn't.

He wanted me to say I trusted him, but I wouldn't.

I was a quick learner when it came to the games of Faerie. It turned out that everyone had something to teach me if I listened and studied them closely enough. Even those who withheld information from me.

I watched Gabor, cloaked in silence, taking in his restlessness and the tension in his stance. Each emotion he conveyed confirmed my suspicions.

His dark eyes swept the tree line, alert to danger. "I know you're here. It's not in your nature to leave your friend. I want you to know, I like you, Ysa. I value our friendship. I bitterly wish my own court hadn't fallen, that I hadn't been forced to make these choices."

I listened carefully as he paced, gut churning.

Somewhere, the owl screeched.

Gabor cursed. "I told her it was a mistake to let the monsters roam. But after suppressing it for so long, the chaos consumes her. You see, losing her daughter drove her mad. Not immediately. But bit by bit."

A chill slipped down my spine. I pressed myself deeper into the shadows. *Her daughter.* He couldn't mean…

"Where was I? Oh, yes. Tanuhja gave me no choice when she ensnared me within her borders." He indicated the deep scar on his neck, and his voice took on a bitter edge. "This was her doing. I had to pledge allegiance to her, or she'd turn me into one of the monsters. Sometimes, making common cause with unlikely allies is the only path forward. It was your fault I was put in that position."

My pulse drummed with an uneasy tempo that echoed through my limbs. So the Faerie Queen of the Court of Chaos had unleashed the monsters into this realm herself. That was the missing puzzle piece that Zephyr had been looking for. Gabor was more of a monster than any of the poor creatures in the belly of Ebonspire, I thought darkly.

"The queen was good, once, though she reigned over a volatile court. She managed the precariousness of the throne well. Then she met Kazimir, just before the burning of the Order of the Glyph, and everything changed. You were a ray of light that came unexpectedly into a bleak world. Yes, that's right. Tanuhja is your mother." He was stalking backwards and forwards in the clearing now, poking at bushes, trying to unearth my hiding place. "Who else has dared to tell you the hard truths? Come out, Ysa. We are friends."

My ribs constricted around the erratic beat of my heart. The word *mother* was a sharp hook in my chest, pulsing through me like a warning drumbeat. I wanted to laugh at the audacity of Gabor being the one to tell me. I knew why he was doing it. I knew he was trying to shock me. I knew he was trying to draw me out into the open. I had imagined a dozen different versions of my mother since finding out about Danaë. Since Zephyr had warned me to uncover my origins. But never this.

Never a queen driven mad by loss, who ruled in the seat of chaos.

My nails dug into my palms as I fought off the tremor that gripped me.

"Let me continue the story then to prove I have your best intentions at heart. After your birth, Kazimir and Tanuhja realised there were dark factions who would have controlled you, had they captured you. So the queen put out word that you did not survive the birth and sent you away, hoping your magic would never awaken. She stayed behind to play her role to keep you safe." He shook another bush, a snarl of frustration on his lips. "But in time, without the Grimoire being maintained, Faerie spiralled into disarray. Tanuhja tried to warn the other faerie kings and queens. She pleaded with them to take control. But they were too busy protecting their own borders. Remember our lessons? Betrayals were rampant. Trust was in short supply."

Even now, he was a good history teacher. Though he had spun the truth of it.

"The fae factions suspected you could be alive, and Tanuhja wanted your safety above all else. And so she chose anarchy. She began to corrupt wandering fae into monsters to keep Faerie's attention turned inwards. The only thing she cared about was not letting the monsters get close to the mortal realm, because that's where you were. That was until you made the decision to enter Faerie. That turned the game on its head."

Branches shivered in the dark canopy above, splintered feathers brushing the branches with a grating sound. I held my breath, although the whisper ring protected me. We were being hunted, still.

"But there is something about your mother. She always thinks three steps ahead. She had seen you and Zephyr in her dreams many orbits ago, and that allowed her to prepare. That is why she embedded me at Ebonspire. So I could be in place to steer events in the right direction if you ever appeared. In some ways, I forgot I was a piece on the chessboard. I enjoyed being with my fellow mercenaries. The camaraderie. The safety. The missions. The cooking. It reminded me of simpler times at the Court of Starry Flight. I was upset when you arrived. When that particular future came to pass. I might have stayed at Ebonspire otherwise." His voice was wistful. "I might have remained one of that group. Those bridges are burned now."

Dread gnawed at me. My every step, perhaps even my destiny, had been quietly orchestrated for years.

"The irony is that of all the threats in Faerie, it is the power struggle between Tanuhja and Danaë, chaos and silence, that threatens to tear it apart. One who made the monsters. And the other who would make a dark army of them." He sighed. "Your real mother has waited so long to meet you, Ysa. Come with me. We'll show her the whisper rings and you will get a welcome befitting a child of destiny. She's so close to fulfilling the dream of holding you in her arms again. Together, you can bring order back to Faerie."

My heart hammered wildly, caught between disbelief and resentment. He'd not uttered one word of Father. Not one word about what an alliance with Tanuhja would mean for him. Or for Maren. Family meant nothing to them. What did it mean to be the daughter of the Queen of the Court of Chaos? A swell of anger rose in my chest, too. If Tanuhja loved me, then surely a simpler way to protect me would be for me to own my power. And now I was supposed to feel what—gratitude? The Court of Chaos could, quite frankly, go to hell.

I was done. Done with anything other than the family I chose for myself.

A deadly scrape moved through the branches.

Something deadly drew closer. Gabor stilled as if he sensed that the slightest shift, a crackle of twigs underfoot, would land him in a heap of trouble. Possibly, both of us.

He lowered his voice, and it had the edge of pure, cold calculation as he pulled the dagger strapped to his thigh. "If you choose to turn away from Tanuhja, you will lose the game, Ysadora. We all will."

From the canopy, an enormous bird—the owl— plummeted from above in a whoosh of splintered wings and rancid breath. Its feathers were a dark, mottled grey, and its eyes were yellow slits. But it wasn't the eyes that terrified me most: it was the screech, a sound so discordant that it cut through the air like a blade. Directed towards a stray sound in the branches, the owl's screech sent a sparrow plummeting dead to the ground.

But the owl had only eyes for Gabor.

He turned his attention to the monster. Its beak snapped open to reveal gleaming, inch-long teeth. Its hunger seeped through the air, a gnawing force that made me shudder. He faced the bird, and I could see him calculate whether his wings would be outmatched by the monstrosity. Its eyes flickered with a sharp glint of calculation before it launched its attack, and I clamped my mouth shut so as not to scream.

Gabor launched himself skywards with stomach-churning speed—dropping his dagger in the process—and zig-zagged through the air to avoid the owl's screech. His wings beat with the power of a storm, propelling him upward with an urgency that matched the danger of the pursuit. The owl unfurled its splintered wings, the sound like the tearing of cloth. It followed Gabor through the canopy into the moonless night, but its wings were slow and cumbersome, its flight laboured as broken feathers caught the wind. Almost as if the creature had been broken and reassembled by cruel hands. Its beating wings made a sickening sound, nothing like the serene murmur of Gabor's, but more like dry leaves scraping against stone. Its body writhed in the air, talons outstretched as it struggled to close the gap.

I pitied it more than I pitied him.

He led the monstrous owl far beyond the treetops, a blur of black and silver against the night. Then he banked sharply, twisting in a wide arc, leaving the monster searching in the dark. My memory of the map of Faerie told me he'd angled himself towards the dark lines of Gloomhaven, Tanuhja's stronghold, in the distance. The owl let out another enraged screech, but Gabor was already hurtling forward, unwilling to lose his chance of escape.

He was a survivor. He hadn't lied about that. My gut told me he hadn't lied about any of it. The tarnished truth was always better than a lie, however much it hurt.

As the owl circled back to me, determined to have a meal, I dusted myself off. I twisted back the whisper ring to unveil myself and took a deliberate step into the clearing, my quill at the ready. My gown was tattered, my hair stuck in limp tendrils to my face, but my confidence was a steady thrum in my veins.

The bird angled downward, spotting me easily with its binocular vision. Its talons were primed for the strike, its hunger sharpened by its second failure to claim Gabor as its prey. I drew a steadying breath. My palm had clotted, but the cut I had made in the ballroom was so fresh that this time when I dipped the nib in, there was no resistance, only a familiar sting. Then I waited for the bird to hit the ground.

It considered itself the predator, but on the ground our chances were even.

At least, that's what I told myself.

The owl landed just paces from me, its talons gouging the earth. It tilted its head, clever eyes scanning my face, darting to the quill. I wondered what court it hailed from. I wondered who it had been and what its story was. Whether it had ever nursed a broken heart or picked flowers with a child.

It had saved me from Gabor; I wanted to save it.

Then its beak snapped open. I rolled to the side to avoid its killing screech and as I sprang up, I raised Father's quill, there in the darkness. Crimson lines flowed, unfurling the same glyphs that I had used to bind the bone feline. They expanded outward, crackling with bright magic. A second screech was cut short as the glyphs wrapped around the owl's beak like a tightening noose. The glyphs twined and solidified, and I sent more and more, to grip it just above its talons. They rooted into the earth like dark vines. The owl thrashed in fury as my magic held it fast to the floor, leaving it unable to advance.

Pity filled me as I watched it, blood dripping from my palm. "Zephyr will come for you," I told it softly. "He said his shadows would always find me, which means he'll find my magic, and he'll find you, too."

I wondered if he was already looking for me. I couldn't cross the leagues that Gabor had in flight or Zephyr could with his shadow-walking. It would take me days rather than the minutes it had taken them. In any case, I wouldn't abandon Maren. Did Zephyr know there had been a viper in his den? I begged the stars that I lived long enough to warn him.

With a sigh, I retrieved Gabor's fallen dagger, pulled out Father's compass and checked its bearing. Then, casting one last look at the owl, I turned my back on it and twisted one of the whisper rings anticlockwise. It warmed my finger, cloaking me as I forged ahead through the underbrush.

My senses were alert to any signs of Maren, any signs of pursuit. The rustling branches above and the snap of twigs underfoot seemed like threats in my heightened state, but I clamped down on my thoughts.

With so many shaping the future of Faerie, one thing was clear: there was a place for me in it.

37

KAZIMIR

*In addition to maintaining the Grimoire itself,
the calligraphers from the brotherhood embed
glyphs in nature—on trees, stones, and rivers—
to ensure that magic flows
harmoniously between realms.
—A Short History of the Order of the Glyph*

The chill of the high altitude clawed at Kazimir's exposed skin. Dragon-riding demanded protective clothing. He thought wistfully of his old riding gear: thick, fur-lined leathers, insulated gloves, a scarf looped twice around his neck, goggles to protect his eyes and sturdy boots designed for long hours in the air.

Even so, he would have accepted this ride even if it flayed him.

Kazimir leaned forward, his hands steady against the ridged curve of Caldoron's spine, trying to shield himself from the rush of air. The Court of Silence had drained more from him than he cared to admit.

Next time, I'll bring gloves. The meteor was the key to dealing with the threats to Ysadora, and he wouldn't risk failure again—not because of something as mundane as frostbitten fingers. Next time, he'd be better prepared. He might even consider a charm to buffer against the elements.

Caldoron rumbled beneath him, tilting his head just enough to glance back. *A rider so fragile, a puff of air could break you. I'm perfectly capable of delivering you to your destination without paraphernalia.* His wings beat a steady rhythm, carving through the endless night. The faint trail of the meteor still glimmered on the horizon to the dragon's eyes—though Kazimir was blind to it—mapping a path to the Shrouded Forest.

Below them, to the right, the dark expanse of Ashenvale stretched out. A burst of light splitting the darkness like a crack in reality: starfire—fleeting but unmistakable—a searing violet radiance that flared against the twisted treetops before vanishing. Then twice more in quick succession.

Kazimir's heart tightened. *Did you see that?*

Caldoron rumbled. *Starfire. There are few remaining from the Court of Nebula capable of it.*

Kazimir gritted his teeth, bracing himself for a rush of icy wind. *Go.*

Hold fast. The dragon's massive wings shifted like sails in the wind. He banked hard to the right, bronze scales flashing in the moonlight and angled downwards. The familiar pull of their bond tightened as they descended. Caldoron soared lower, weaving between trees.

Steady. Kazimir scanned the area. He caught the telltale signs of disruption: starborn residue lingered in the air, and the forest writhed with unnatural energy, its creatures scattering in frenzied patterns. Kazimir's stomach lurched more than it had in flight. Despite the horrors she had inflicted on him, Danaë had been telling the truth about the impact of the unravelling Grimoire.

It was an easy thing to locate someone from the back of a dragon, especially if that someone had fire. Another flash of starfire erupted, this time closer, illuminating a scene of chaos: a wild flutter of wasps, each one as large as a fist, pulsed through the trees. The creatures, their wings glinting like shards of broken glass, circled around her in an unnerving cloud. At their centre was a lone female moving with desperation. Her hands shone with starfire as she lashed out at the swarm, taking care not to light the trees. But despite her power, the wasps kept coming, relentless and numerous. They stung her, rallied again, multiplied.

Maren. Panic gripped him. If she was in Faerie, Ysa had disobeyed him. Ysa had not run.

The wasps were overwhelming her now, stinging her skin. Her face contorted in confusion as she pushed another blast of starfire into the swarm. Its glow cast faint reflections off the dew-slicked leaves.

Kazimir's eyes darted, but he couldn't see his daughter, and Maren needed him. *We must help. Quietly, in case Thiago hears. His borders are too close for comfort.*

Do you take me for a fool? Fire sped from the dragon's throat, a cascade of molten gold that tore through the wasps, scattering them like chaff in a storm.

Then, there was nothing left in the air: no fierce buzzing, no frantic flashes of fire. Only smoke from the burnt remnants of the swarm drifted lazily upward, curling through the fractured moonlight, and a girl on her knees, her shoulders rising and falling with ragged breaths.

She looked up at him and the bronze dragon with incredulous eyes. It was strange to see her this way without her mortal glamour. The intensity of her fae eyes and sharpened contours, her freckles like a map of the stars. Her trembling hands still held the faintest trace of starlight, flickering like embers that refused to go out. "Am I hallucinating?"

Kazimir slipped from Caldoron's back before the dragon's claws fully touched the ground. "Maren."

She blinked once, twice, confusion still swirling in her gaze as she peered at the dragon. Then she reached towards Kazimir with tentative hands. Swelling dotted her hands and cheek. He cursed under his breath. He'd put so much on her young shoulders.

Steeling himself, he clasped her hands in his own. "It's me. I'm here, Maren."

The starfire finally dimmed in her palms, leaving only the fragile warmth of her touch. Amber eyes flecked with green cleared, and for the first time, she truly saw him. "Kazimir."

Kazimir folded his daughter's best friend and protector into his arms. A fox peeked out of its den. A hare darted in the safety of the shadows. Birds that had been startled into the night sky settled back into their nests, their calls subdued. Then Maren Varun of the Court of Nebulas—

whose father had been a dear friend and given his life for
the brotherhood—gave a deep exhale and wept.

They clung to each other as the dragon kept watch.

38

YSADORA

I walked through Ashenvale, holding the compass in front of my nose. One moment, the woods loomed around me. The next, the landscape flattened and stretched. I stopped in my tracks, searching for the familiar. But everything had changed in the span of a single breath.

Instead of firm earth, I found myself standing on cracked stone. The night held an unnatural stillness as though the winds had forgotten how to stir. Monoliths jutted from the ground, sharp edges piercing the sky. Above me, the heavens were not distant but close.

How had I crossed from one realm into another without noticing?

The shadows were deep here, stretching impossibly far across the ground, and the light of the stars cast a silvery glow on the desolation. It was as if reality itself was slowly eroding at the edges, unmoored from the solid world I had known. Yet, the air seemed to cleanse me from the inside out, as if the atmosphere of this place was infused with a purifying energy, soothing the clutter in my mind. And the stillness felt strangely comforting, like an old friend I had stumbled upon by accident, someone who had waited for me in this forsaken place.

A female voice sent a shiver up my spine. "I've been waiting for the right moment for you to join me."

I glanced at the whisper ring on my finger, wondering if its power had limits I didn't yet understand.

"Oh, that silly trinket doesn't stop me from seeing you, Ysadora. Just give me a moment to hang this star. This is the trickiest part of the process…apart from setting destinies free. I have only done that a handful of times. It can go very wrong." She was hanging a brilliant star that pulsed as though it had a heartbeat of its own. It was suspended from the sky by a thread, with a silver clasp binding it in place.

Tiny moons were tattooed onto elegant fingers that adjusted the glowing star. The hands they adorned now moved with renewed strength. My eyes travelled upward to find her cerulean gaze, vivid as the blue ribbons of the maypole in Larkspur. She looked rested, her skin luminous and no longer marked by the grooves of time. Her thin silver hair was lustrous once more and shimmered like polished metal. Her robes, though plain, exuded the scent of forest glades and hearth fires.

A jolt of recognition coursed through me. "Lunarys? You died."

"I find roles are more important than names. I'm the Binder. Now let me concentrate, child."

She adjusted the star's angle, and it cast a soft radiance over her. Her focus was absolute, her cerulean eyes narrowing as if calculating an equation only she could see. When the star clicked into place, it sent out a ripple of light that danced across the cracked landscape, momentarily softening its harshness.

The Binder stepped back, tilting her head to admire her work. "There. That looks about right." She sighed and came towards me. Her cerulean gaze met mine, sharp yet kind, like a teacher preparing for a reluctant pupil. The scent of moss and woodsmoke enveloped me. "Come now, child. I don't bite."

I hesitated, my feet rooted to the ground. The newly hung star glimmered in the air above us, casting fractured light across the strange terrain. "I saw Zephyr kill you."

"Ah…" A ripple of pleasure chased over her face. "The mercenary leader is a male who lives outside the usual rules of Faerie. He has already severed some of his own threads. His choices, his life on the fringes, make him a fate-breaker, someone not entirely bound by destiny. That's why the two of you crossing paths was essential."

"He told me you asked him to kill you," I said quietly.

The Binder grimaced. "I told him that if he *didn't* kill me, his friends would die. And possibly his mate. Not my proudest moment. Too risky, my sisters thought. But manipulation is inevitable in a world with clashing interests."

My breath hitched. "Why would you do that?"

"His unique abilities—his connection to silence and lore—mean he can hide even the most powerful beings from sight. His shadows cloaked my death for long enough for me to hide my whereabouts from those who would wrestle control of Faerie and beyond."

Her words sent a shiver through me. "I saw your body dust."

The Binder's silver hair caught the glow of the stars pinned to the fabric of the universe. They were captured and chained like prisoners in the sky. "My sisters and I are primordial beings. The Fates cannot die." She sighed as though, despite her renewed vigour, life had been very long indeed. "When a child is born, its fate is bound to a star. Those fates are locked, and the soul's path is sealed, not easily altered. My role is to guide the stars and set them in place. Freeing a star is a dangerous act."

"The meteor." I'd been so drawn to its crash site in the Shrouded Forest.

"Yes, Ysadora. The meteor." The tiny moons etched into her knuckles seemed to glint like little windows to ancient, celestial knowledge. "Tanuhja and Kazimir, in their own ways, wanted to control your fate. When I flung down your star, it was because I decided the only hope of balancing the magic between Faerie and the mortal realm was for you to control your own path. Your parents were both driven by love for you, but parents should never control their children. They are guardians of potential, not sculptors of destiny. Love can corrupt, but true love allows freedom. By felling your star, I left you free to follow your path."

My chest ached, and I stepped closer, searching the Binder's face. "Where is he?"

Her cerulean eyes glittered, and her lips curved. "Where is who?"

She had called him the fate-breaker, but he was so much more. "Where's Zephyr?"

The Binder's smile widened. "Finally, you're asking the right questions. He is where he has decided to be. But there was a painter once…not particularly famous—she preferred to paint walls, not canvas, homes, not galleries— who understood that you two would always find your way to each other."

Tears clogged my throat. "I trusted Gabor."

The Binder nodded. "So you did. It's easy to trust the wrong person, especially when they wear a face that promises safety. He made his choice long ago. And you made yours." She was different now, more relaxed than she had been in the bookshop as if she had more confidence in the path ahead. Her demeanour was like an old friend whom one might meet by accident but feel strangely at ease with. "It gets lonely here. I've been enjoying your escapades. I hoped you'd choose to ignore your Father's warning in the snow. I hoped the quill would call to you. Oh, and I very much enjoyed your run-in with the bone feline in the Wraithwoods and how you taught that old fool Thiago a lesson in his court. Very clever to use your blood as ink. An act of kindness to bargain with Elowen, though she teeters on a knife's edge. That might be your cleverest choice yet." Her gaze dropped to my hand, and her laughter rang out like a bell. "Of course, taking both whisper rings was just joyous."

I looked down at the compass in my hand. "Will I see Father and Maren again?"

"Oh, yes." The Binder's cerulean eyes softened. "Almost certainly, sooner or later. When you see Kazimir, tell him that I felt him mourning me, and he nourished a primordial being's spirit by doing so. Such true feeling is precious, and it ripples outwards in ways few understand. It makes up for his deficiencies. He helped rebuild something ancient and enduring within me."

Around me, the surfaces of the obsidian monoliths pulsated with streaks of silvery light as though power was building. The air carried a faint hum, like the resonance of a distant cosmic melody, and the cracked mosaic of stone glinted in hues of indigo and violet as if dusted with stardust.

"Should I stay in Faerie?" I asked her.

She harrumphed like I had uttered a stupid question after all. "You could." She screwed up her face like she was thinking back. "Wishes for newborns are a minefield. There's not much to go on, you see. You're all the same with your scrunched-up faces and chubby fists. But perhaps this will help. My wish for you was about courage and discernment and love. But really, it boils down to one thing. Choose carefully who belongs in your inner circle, Ysadora, then build trust like your life depends on it. Because it does."

I exhaled. Her advice made perfect sense. In this place, attuned to every flicker of starlight in the sky. As if the cosmos itself was in perfect harmony with me. In this place, I was not lost. I had been found.

The Binder stepped closer, and the air between us thickened with magic. She cupped my face, her hand gentle and her eyes sad. A wave of warmth flooded through me to my core. "Your true self is a revelation. I knew it would be. You've begun to understand your place in this world, but there is more for you to learn." Light poured from her fingertips in a silver-blue stream, snaking across the air like a ribbon of liquid moonlight. The Binder's voice came again, but it was softer now, echoing as though coming from far away. "Now hold tight to the calligrapher's quill, Ysadora Silberquill. You'll need that before the night is done."

"Where are you sending me?"

"To where destiny collides with the best possible future for Faerie. To him. To the fate-breaker."

A fierce rhythm echoed in my chest as the light pulsed once, twice—bright and slow—before it burst outward with a rush of soundless power.

For a fleeting moment, endless possibilities rolled out before me: paths untold, futures just beyond my reach, each thread more brilliant than the last. The stars blurred first, then the monoliths, curling like the edges of a dream —shifting, reconfiguring, shifting again—as the Binder wove her magic.

I looked for her, but I couldn't find her. "Lunarys?" The ground beneath my feet trembled as if the land itself was preparing to move with me. Then, without warning, the light burst open in a dazzling wave.

The soft hum of the Binder's voice rang out, low and soothing, like an incantation passed through the aeons. "This is your path, Ysadora. Follow it, and the fallen star will light the way."

The world seemed to bend as if the very fabric of reality was warping. I took a step forward, and the light swallowed me in its luminous embrace. Then, just as quickly, it faded, leaving me in darkness with just the faintest whisper of stardust in the air.

Up ahead, achingly familiar shadows skimmed the silhouette of Ebonspire.

Though it wasn't technically my home, my heart sang a different song.

39

ZEPHYR

Do not be sad that you crossed words with Veda.
Sibling love is not perfect, but it's a love that
survives mistakes and grows through
each of life's trials.
—Rowena Ashmoor's letter to her son Zephyr

L oxley leaned in close as the ballroom emptied, his lips barely moving, his tone sharp and quiet. "Cloak our sound. And keep that charming smile on your face."

Zephyr didn't so much as flinch. The corners of his mouth lifted into an easy grin as if Loxley had whispered something amusing while a faint ripple stirred around his feet. The shadows crept upwards around them, visible only to those who looked closely, a crude noise barrier but one all the same. His gaze brushed over scurrying attendants clearing platters and courtiers milling towards the exits. Guards lined the edges of the hall, watchful but unaware of their whispered exchange. "Speak."

Loxley chuckled as though they were sharing a joke and delivered a clipped report. "Gabor took Ysa."

Zephyr's grin faltered for a fraction of a second. The words reeled through his mind, cutting him open. "Are you certain? Tell me everything."

"I witnessed it myself. Your cousins saw it, too. They argued—fiercely, by the looks of it."

"That's nothing new." Dread tightened Zephyr's chest. He'd hoped there was a logical explanation for why he hadn't been able to locate Gabor since the dance with Ysadora. Fuck, he'd been distracted. A cold, seething anger wrapped around his insides, but beneath it, there was a dull ache. He yearned to protect Ysadora, to shield her from the chaos, and now he'd put her in danger. "Did Gabor betray us?"

Bitterness laced Loxley's voice. "Why else wasn't he happy with me as Ysa's point person? Why else choose the maze as a meeting point if not to avoid clashing with us? He flew south as soon as he saw me. Damn traitor. When I get my hands on him…"

Before Loxley even finished speaking, Zephyr despatched his shadows into the maze, then southwards, seeking Inkheart. He'd considered Gabor a brother. Not like Cyprian and Loxley, perhaps, but he would gladly have taken the bite of a monster for him, laid down his life or ridden into hell at his side. How could a male he trusted betray him? How had he missed the signs of deception?

His gut twisted. "Are they in love? Is that what this is?"

Loxley snorted. "Gabor is only in love with himself.

This is business, not love… He's got both rings. Maybe he's got a bidder? Zeph, we needed them to give us an edge. We're fucked."

Zephyr didn't give a damn about the rings. Not when Gabor had his mate.

"Did it look like Ysadora was under duress?"

Lox scratched his beard. "No, not distressed. She looked purposeful."

Zephyr's shoulders eased a fraction, relief cooling the tension in his chest. His mate was laser-focused on her Father's return, as she had been from the very beginning. Whatever Gabor was playing at, he wasn't hurting her. Even so, restless energy coiled under his skin, urging him to act. "I have to help her."

"Fine, but let's not forget the revenge."

Zephyr's shadows writhed. He wanted to command the court to bow to his will, to bring his mate back to him, and him alone. He wanted to chase after her, to race through the shadows and demand answers.

Loxley smiled at a courtier and slung an arm around Zeph. "Calm your horses, or it's over. We wait until the courtiers are gone, then seek an audience with Thiago. We cover our tracks, *then* fix this."

He was right. If he didn't set out a plausible narrative, the spymaster would see straight through him, and their carefully laid plans would crumble, taking his mate—and everything Zephyr had fought for—with them. Precious seconds ticked by as they waited for the faerie king and Danaë.

Loxley's furious words—if not his face—mirrored the poisonous grip of Zephyr's own emotions. "For the record, I knew Gabor was an arsehole from the way he taunted me when he carted me through the skies. I tried to tell you."

Zephyr's thoughts spiralled. Perhaps he had the same flaw as his mother. She'd believed the best of people even when they didn't deserve it, and it had been her downfall. The few who stood by Zephyr were in peril because of his misplaced trust. He had put everything at risk: his friends, his home, his mate.

He stared at the upended ballroom floor. "Lox…you saw what she did in here. I think Ysadora's a child of two courts, just like me. A child of the nebulas and a child of chaos."

Loxley swore. "You've got to be kidding."

Zephyr's face looked anything but casual. "It's the only thing that makes sense."

A long pause stretched between them. "So Gabor could be one of Tanuhja's?"

"Yes," he gritted out.

"What if Ysadora wants to join with chaos?"

He fought to steady his voice. "That's her choice to make. But I won't have anyone deciding it for her."

Zephyr thought back to when he had invited Gabor into the group. How Gabor had always appeared by happy coincidence when the mercenaries were in a tough spot. His skills—flight and healing, together with his formidable strength—had saved Zephyr and the others countless times.

Then there was the food. Breaking bread together fostered kinship, especially when words fell short after a gruelling day. Gabor's cooking was a way of offering his time and care to the group. It was a reminder that they weren't just survivors. They were a family in unforgiving

Faerie. A savoury stew in the wilderness. Charred meat around a fire. Pastries when supplies were scarce. It had been a subtle seduction. It looked like Gabor had been pulling strings from the shadows all along.

Now, the memory of those meals felt like ashes on Zephyr's tongue.

By the lore, he had even trusted Gabor to give Ysadora history lessons about Faerie. The ancients only knew what he might have planted in her head. But his mate was clever and curious. Zephyr's lips quirked upwards for a fraction of a second. She'd managed to pull the wool over this entire court's eyes, and if that were anything to go by, she'd stay alive until he could make it to her.

He pushed down the sinking feeling that the situation was already beyond repair, forcing his thoughts into a tight, controlled focus. His mind jumped from one calculation to another, determining the moves ahead, the possible outcomes, the perfect deceptions he had to weave.

"We have to make my uncle believe Ysadora struck out alone. That Gabor is still one of ours."

"Agreed. We keep him guessing until we control more pieces on the board."

Until Ysadora was back in his arms. Fuck, he needed her back in his arms.

"You think the creepy twins will make life difficult?"

Zephyr's gaze flicked to Elowen. The rest of them had always underestimated her. But he knew well how the tortures of this court could mould its victims in unexpected ways. "Depends which one wins out."

She and Xaire had returned from the maze worse for wear. They stood in the corner of the ballroom, locked in what appeared to be a one-sided confrontation, but

Zephyr knew that Elowen's voice was in her brother's head. Her posture was detached, as though unfazed by Xaire's heated whispers. Her calmness added to his agitation. Xaire's shadows swirled as if he might erupt at any second.

He and Elowen rarely interacted these days, but Zephyr remembered when she'd been a sweet youngling and had sung like a nightingale and chattered like she would never stop. He had asked her once, long ago, if she wanted something other than the life she had been given. She hadn't replied, but he thought he'd read the answer in her eyes. He would have found a way to get her out if she had said yes.

The twins had always been this way—arguments were second nature, sharp words flying between them like blades, full of passion and sharp edges as they tried to outwit or outmanoeuvre each other. Elowen was the cleverer one, but Xaire had all the natural advantages of being a male in this court. Despite the bickering, when the shadows settled, they were each other's fiercest protectors. No one would dare subject one of them to the hurts they inflicted on each other. Not while the other twin stood nearby.

Zephyr wasn't envious of their bond. It was Veda's gentle sibling love that he missed.

Even if the twins undid his plan, Zephyr couldn't, wouldn't hurt them. Xaire's arrogance and unrelenting rivalry drove him up the wall, yet when it came down to it, they were bound by blood, by history. No matter how close they came to blows, there were some lines Zephyr simply wouldn't cross.

He glanced towards Loxley, catching the tension in his

friend's stance. If things went awry, they would have to fight their way out. He braced himself for it, running through the potential clashing magic in his mind, considering which allies or bargains they might need to rely on.

By the ancients, over a century of life, this gnawing anxiety he felt for his mate was new.

"Come on," he growled through gritted teeth. "We're saying our damn goodbyes."

Loxley's lips curved into a grim, determined smile. "Then we'll pull our friend's spine out?"

A shadow of fury passed over Zephyr's face. "With any luck."

"If you don't mind, I might avoid the murderous songstress after what I did to her leopards."

"Fine, but stay close." He let the sound barrier dissipate and cut a path to Thiago and Danaë. His bow was deeper than usual, almost lingering. He used the motion to steady himself, his jaw tight to keep any tremor from reaching his face. "You must not worry," Zephyr said to his uncle's consort, although his own worries stole his breath. "Your daughter will be found."

Danaë gave him a cool look. "It's clear from your transgressions whilst dancing that you've taken a liking to her."

Zephyr lifted his chin. He couldn't afford to lose his composure. "She is but sport. It's in a mercenary's nature to enjoy hunting of all kinds."

The faerie king inclined his head, a cold smile touching his lips. "Finding her is a certainty, wife. She lacks allies and knowledge. She is impressive for one so uninitiated, but neither she nor Kazimir can hide from my spiders.

Ysadora is but a mere girl who will soon learn her place. And the calligrapher is a broken husk."

Danaë looked off into the shadows, her gaze distant. "Perhaps I should join your spiders, Thiago. There is too much at stake to leave this to chance."

A rush of blood pulsed through Zephyr like a drumbeat. He needed to get to Ysadora first. "You're the heart of this court, my lady. You don't need to leave the safety you've built to protect it."

"Indeed," said the faerie king with his typical directness. "Leave the dangerous work to those who are more expendable, wife."

Her eyelashes swooped to hide her ire, and not for the first time, Zephyr considered that she was as gifted a puppeteer as her husband. "Will you be joining Thiago and me for a nightcap while we await news?"

Zephyr shook his head. He had learned long ago that flattery and a sprinkle of truth were key to deceiving Thiago. "Loxley and I must be on our way presently. It is a shame to leave so soon. It has been delightful to be back within the walls of this court. I had hoped to linger a few days. Sadly, our latest commission has been more fraught for Gabor than expected. He needs our help."

The faerie king raised an eyebrow. "At this late hour?"

Zephyr shrugged. "The monsters do not sleep."

Danaë's eyes darkened. "The children are fighting, Thiago."

The faerie king beckoned an attendant with irritation. "Ask our offspring to come here."

As the attendant hurried off, Zephyr mentally rehearsed any excuse he might need to deploy to cover up what they had seen in the maze. Moments later, Xaire and

Elowen joined them. Xaire's body language was tight with indignation, in contrast to the marble stillness of his sister.

Their mother fixed them with a stare. "You disappoint me, children. Our family is always united. Why such unseemly conduct at such an hour? Speak, Xaire."

After an agonising pause, Xaire cleared his throat. "It was nothing, Mother," he said smoothly, although a flicker of resentment danced in his voice. "We were merely arguing over who looked more attractive in purple tonight. We've already resolved it." He darted his sister a poisonous glance. "It is me."

Danaë frowned and pressed a single question. "Is there nothing else you wish to tell me?"

Zephyr braced himself. Elowen gave the faintest shake of her head.

Danaë turned her unearthly gold eyes on her husband. "I have a migraine, Thiago. I won't have a nightcap after all. I'll be in our chambers." To Zephyr, she said. "Ysadora is not sport. If you treat her that way again, I will sing a melody so high that your bones shatter."

An easy smirk crossed Zephyr's lips as he shrugged. "Understood."

The faerie king offered Danaë his elbow. "Let me escort you, wife. It seems you are not quite yourself."

They walked away arm in arm over the cracked ballroom floor, the snow leopards prowling beside them. The guards exchanged sharp nods with Thiago as they swung open the great doors. A cold draft from outside swept in, ruffling the edge of tapestries that lined the walls, and then Zephyr was alone with Loxley, his cousins and a flurry of servants.

Zephyr stooped to press a light kiss to Elowen's cheek. "I will not forget this."

She stiffened for a split second, her body tensing at the unexpected gesture. Then, a reluctant smile tugged at the corner of her mouth. But as Zephyr's gaze shifted to Xaire, the warmth of gratitude evaporated instantly. If looks could kill, he might have already been a corpse.

"You clearly have something on your mind, cousin," said Zephyr softly.

Xaire took a step closer—he was shorter by half a head—his voice low and dangerous. "Don't forget I also kept quiet about what your fool and the winged one did tonight. Don't mistake my silence for ignorance. You're playing with shadows, and when they swallow you whole, I will crow with glee."

Slate-blue eyes glinted. "We're all playing with shadows in this cursed land. You're no different."

Loxley snorted. "You've the patience of a sleeping dragon for dealing with this pup, Zeph. I would have sent him to the pixies before he grew hair around his manhood."

Xaire's gaze never moved from Zephyr. "I helped you because it's important to Elowen."

"That may be, cousin. But it suits you that Ysadora isn't here. You remain the golden child."

"You're quick to assume the worst of me. I would do anything for family. I thought we had that in common, at least." Xaire indicated to Elowen that they were leaving. His footsteps echoed with a finality that left no room for further discussion. "Enjoy your little games, *cousin*. I can't wait for Father to find out."

A knot twisted in Zephyr's gut as he watched them go.

"Come, Loxley. We change into our leathers, grab weapons and end this."

Loxley's lips twisted into a sinister smile. "I can't wait."

Zephyr stilled, a cold chill running through him.

"Zeph? What is it?"

"My shadows found traces of Ysa's magic in Ashenvale, but there's no sign of her. And Lox, the wards are sounding at home. Gabor is our enemy, and he has the keys to Ebonspire."

"What are we going to do?"

The mercenary leader bared his canines. "We're going to haul whatever beast is just south of here that Ysadora seems to have left tied up for us and surprise him."

40

YSADORA

In the hush of night, when dreams take flight,
The fae walk softly in veils of light.
—Danaë's song lyrics

The Binder had sent me to Ebonspire. To lore and shadows.

To Zephyr, whom she called the fate-breaker.

I yearned to see the mercenary leader to warn him about the snakes in his camp. If I was honest with myself, I wanted more than that. I wanted to tell him that he had helped me discover my true self, painful truths, as well as dormant talents. I wanted to tell him that his version of Faerie was proof that beauty could rise from ruin, that something new could exist without erasing what had come before. Ebonspire was where the broken edges of the world could find refuge and shape something whole. It was a version of Faerie that didn't demand submission but offered a choice. A Faerie that felt more like home than the glittering Court of Silence ever would. Stars, it was more than that again.

I yearned to shelter within his strength and melt at his touch. His kiss still burned in my memory. No amount of distance, no stretch of days, could dull the vivid clarity of that moment. The press of his mouth carried not only desire but something deeper, something I couldn't name but burrowed into my bones.

But Zephyr was hundreds of miles away at the Court of Silence, locked in the schemes and intrigues that kept him far beyond my reach.

I had been depending on him since the moment he stole my toffee at Bloomtide, although I only now realised it. The Binder's revelation that he wasn't a killer—at least, not in the true sense of the word—was like unveiling a truth I had already known: I could count on him without caveats.

Rubbing my rune-inked wrist, I wondered if he was angry at me for trusting Gabor instead of him. Maybe I had burned his desire for me by making that choice. What if I'd fractured something that couldn't be repaired? Trust was about instinct as much as loyalty, about knowing who to believe when the world turned on its head. I had failed that test.

But Zephyr had told me that I'd always be welcome at Ebonspire and had given me a drop of his blood to form the rune key to his ancestral home. That meant something, didn't it? A drop of his blood wasn't just a token. Blood wasn't given lightly, not in Faerie, where a single drop forged ties stronger than any vow. I brushed my fingertips over the Rune of Unveiling—my cheeks heating as I recalled the similar one he'd shown me on his tawny hipbone—and the scroll rune that he'd hidden beneath my skin. It had to mean something that he had dissolved our first bargain, the one that demanded trust, and instead given me one key to myself and the other to his home.

He had freed me of chains and given me choice.

It meant that I was welcome at Ebonspire, even if I wasn't sure of his heart.

The Binder had said that our paths would always be entwined. I had forged a separate path from him during Thiago's trial out of necessity, but it had been like walking against the flow while the tide pulled me back towards him. No matter where I went in Faerie, the current led to him—sometimes gently, sometimes like a riptide that left me gasping for air.

Even though he wasn't at Ebonspire, I knew how important his home and his friends were to him. I knew that he cared for the monsters and their stories. Despite my own goal to find Father, I owed it to Zephyr to warn his friends about Gabor's treachery, how they shouldn't trust him, how he was in league—my stomach lurched— with my mother, the Faerie Queen of the Court of Chaos. That she had made the monsters and had plans that stretched into the past—embedding Gabor with the mercenaries—and also into the future, though I didn't quite know her intentions or her strength.

Or whether, for all her sins, she was redeemable.

Whether she was capable of loving me without coercing me.

Taking a deep breath, I eyed the moonlit gatehouse with its dramatic spire rising against the star-strewn sky and its shroud of familiar shadows. The air here was thick with memories of Zephyr and the life I'd begun to build in the shadows of this fortress. Cyprian, Wylda and Sequoia were inside. The weight of the night pressed against me as I passed the stables, where Mythros's agitated whinny made me frown. The midnight-hued steed was rarely spooked, his fiery temperament tempered by his almost unshakable confidence. Tonight, though, when I peeked inside, his distress was palpable. He hoofed at the ground, his ears pinned back and his eyes wide.

"Easy," I murmured, my quill in hand. "I'll go check what's happening and be right back."

The rustle of the trees in the training ground and the low whistle of the wind carried a strange, almost sour tang. Mythros snorted and shook his head, the sound echoing like a warning.

A chill whispered down my spine.

Skirting the stable, I pressed myself against the weathered outer walls, careful to avoid loose gravel that could betray my movement. The hum of a ward rippled through the air as I neared Ebonspire itself. I made a beeline for the entry door, hidden in plain sight among the mossy, craggy stone. With a steady exhale, I pressed the glow of the scroll rune against the seam of the door just as the ward's hum crescendoed into a shrill alarm. I winced at the noise as bright blue lines flared to life, illuminating the night.

Then the doors folded out, recognising the bloodline encoded in the rune, as though Ebonspire recognised me—not as an outsider—but as family. It was a snatch of hurried movement that left me only a moment to slip inside before they closed again.

But the interior of Ebonspire wasn't the dark, quiet refuge I had come to expect. Torches burned in sconces along the stone walls, their flickering flames casting shifting patterns. The faint hum of enchantments—wards, shields, or something else entirely—pulsed through the corridors like a heartbeat. The clash of steel echoed through the halls, mingling with the sharp cries of combat. My breath caught as I edged towards the sounds of the fight, down the spiral stairs, into the belly of the gatehouse, where the monsters dwelled.

Blistering stars, if they got out.

If they were hurt before Zephyr had a chance to save them.

The armoury was not far. I raced there, a brief detour to arm myself, hoping against all hope that this wasn't what I thought it was. That it wasn't Thiago. That my leaving hadn't undone the bargain that Zephyr had made for Ebonspire to be left in peace.

It was my fault. It was my fault.

The mercenaries dealt with the monsters one at a time. That was how they managed to contain them rather than kill them. That was how Zephyr upheld his dream of perhaps saving them one day. But releasing the monsters—with their twisted natures and bites that not only killed but nullified fae magic—would result in chaos that engulfed not only Ebonspire but all the realms.

I seized a sword in my free hand, an ink pot too—no time to check which ink or remind me of its qualities, no time to do any thinking—running hard now, taking the steps so fast I risked tumbling. Rounding a corner, the scene burst into view: Cyprian and Wylda, one floor up from the cellar, trading blows with a group of fae I had never seen before.

But they weren't fighting with shadow magic. This was something else.

The corridor crackled with spells and clashing blades. Cyprian moved like liquid time itself, his blade a streak of silver against their enemies—six crammed into that tight space. He twisted to avoid a flare of fire and slashed at an exposed female's arm. With a sharp, whispered word, the air around him seemed to slow, trapping one fae in mid-transformation. Thick roots erupted from the walls at Wylda's command, lashing around a shapeshifting fae whose sturdy body melted into a slim one to escape her snare. He slumped as she embedded a dagger in his chest. One fae dissolved into a dense haze of moths, swarming towards Cyprian. Sweat beaded his brow as he slashed through them, muttering another incantation that caused time to ripple and pull them apart.

There was something wrong with the shadows that Zephyr always left behind to guard Ebonspire and the monsters. Sound was seeping through, though the door was closed, as if the barrier had thinned, as if the mercenary leader had perhaps stretched himself too thin. Guttural growls and muffled howls met my ears, high-pitched yelps and deep snarls, scraping claws and slithering sloshing. The monsters were stirring, anxious to escape or to join the fight.

"We can't hold them much longer!" Claws raked against vines Wylda summoned as a shield.

Three intruders were on the ground, unconscious or dead, their weapons scattered like broken promises. There were four more advancing. I could help. I needed to help. I raised my sword—it was more predictable than my magic —but a hand clamped around my wrist, and I swung around, ready to slice and slash and drive whoever challenged me to the ground.

I spun around, instincts honed by Maren and Cyprian's endless drills. My blade arced through the air, ready to slice and slash and drive my opponent to the ground. My momentum stopped just short of striking when I took in a crown of braids and feathered black wings.

"Don't be stupid," hissed Sequoia as she wrenched me backwards. "It's you he fucking wants."

"Hold the line," Cyprian growled to Wylda with the sharp focus of a soldier who knew the cost of losing ground. He turned, and a look of pure venom filled his hazel-gold eyes. "You will pay for this. If not by my hand, then by Zephyr's."

My blood ran cold as I followed Cyprian's gaze.

It was only then that I noticed Gabor skulking out of the fray, his wings tucked in tightly against his back, their edges glinting faintly in the dim light. His face was a mask of careful neutrality, betraying neither fear nor triumph, as though he was merely an observer of the chaos rather than its orchestrator. But his sharp eyes darted towards the cellar door, betraying his intent.

He was a healer, a teacher, a wonderful cook. He was their friend.

Yet, he was here, hurting those he had lived alongside, having betrayed the secret of their sanctuary.

Wylda's cloud of coils narrowly missed the swipe of a blade. She slammed her elbow into an opponent's face.

My pulse thundered in my ears. "They need help."

Sequoia's mouth pressed into a grim line. "Listen to me. Cyprian will memory walk out of here with my sister if he needs to. He can reset time over and over if that door is opened. We've planned for this. Gabor knows it." Her voice was a furious whisper under the clash of battle and the moan of monsters. "Will you listen? He told me about Veda's prophecy. I saw her painting. I blamed it for us not lasting. Forest fires, I didn't believe it until you turned up. You are Zephyr's *mate*. That male might not love me, but I'll be damned if I let his heart be smashed to smithereens because fucking Gabor stole you from under our noses."

My breath hitched, and I swayed, my heart a chaotic drumbeat in my chest. *Mate?* The Rune of Unveiling pulsed warm and wild on my wrist, acknowledging the truth of it. The Binder had mentioned Veda, too. How many people knew of this? Did Zephyr? Was that the pressure in my chest? The mate bond? I tightened my grip on the sword hilt and my quill to steady myself.

"For the love of the forest, you're like a fucking fawn. Are you coming or not?"

I needed to pull myself together. I pushed back the storm raging inside me with a deep exhale. "If you think they'll survive without us, I'll come with you."

She flicked a worried glance at her sister. "Good. I was a second away from knocking you out."

She shoved me up the stairs ahead of her. Even retreating up the stairwell, the vibrations rang under me as if the fight chased us. I didn't dare look back. The sounds painted a vivid enough picture: a hiss of twisting vines, the cries of chaos and steel, the snap of something heavy falling.

I was his mate. And yet we were fleeing. "Where are we going?"

"We have a decoy home, but I'm not sure if it's safe. I'll figure it out, okay?"

Every footfall felt too loud, every breath too quick.

"Keep moving. Don't slow down." Sequoia hissed under her breath. "If we can't get out like usual, we'll head through Rowena's garden and out over the sea."

But when we reached the doors to the open, the shadows came, surging like a living tide, slipping past us like the deepest night. I gasped as they caressed my skin and then flowed downwards to join the melee.

And then, Zephyr was there, stepping from the shadows like a heathen god. His presence eclipsed everything else. Stars, he was beautiful, with his shadow-swept hair and stormy gaze locked on me. Relief flickered in his eyes, tangled with worry and urgency.

"You came back." His voice was a rasp of emotion that sent shivers down my spine.

"You can't trust Gabor or Tanuhj—" I blurted out.

"I know." He pulled me into the hard planes of his chest with unexpected ferocity, then reluctantly loosened his hold. His hands moved to my shoulders, sweeping over me, then he looked at Sequoia. "Are you hurt? Are any of you hurt?"

I shook my head, ears tuned to the battle that still raged beneath us.

"We're fine, Zeph." Sequoia pulled two daggers from her belt, determination blazing in her eyes. "I'm ready for round two."

"Good. You kept her safe, Sese."

Sequoia's tone was dry, though a hint of fondness crept into her words. "Yeah, well, someone had to. And she did save me from the bone feline's bite." A pause. "We have to get back down there."

"My shadows have cleared the path."

Her almond brown eyes narrowed at him. "You're not coming."

Zephyr's jaw tensed. He glanced at me. "I made you a promise, Ysadora, to give you the space to make your own choices. Do you stand with us? Do you stand with me?"

My answer was the same as it had been before Sequoia had said the word *mate*. Before the Binder had spoken. Before Ebonspire had accepted me as family. Before my parentage had become clear. Before the chaos around us tore the calm to shreds. As his storm-lit gaze held mine, I understood this was about choosing *us*. That maybe our hearts and our goals aligned.

"Yes," I said simply.

Zephyr's expression softened. The shadows around him thickened, readying themselves to move. "We need to take you away from here. It's safer for you and safer for them."

Loxley dashed towards us from the direction of the stables. "The cavalry's here."

"You're with Sequoia. You know what to do with *our friend*?"

Loxley drew his axe. "That I do, boss."

Zephyr clasped his shoulder, hesitating. "Take care of them, Lox."

"I'm practically their fairy godmother."

"Sequoia—have no mercy."

She nodded. They parted without another word. Loxley and Sequoia slipped back into the stairwell, and Zephyr watched them go, his expression tight.

Then he sheathed my sword on his back with his own and urged me into a run. "Let's get you out of here. It drained me to shadow walk here with a heavy haul, so we're taking Mythros."

Not a minute later, we were in the stables, where Mythros was already tacked and skittering with restless energy. A saddlebag of supplies dangled at his sides, and I realised that's why Loxley had been delayed. Zephyr slipped the ink pot into the bag and tightened the reins, swung into the saddle with practised ease and reached down to settle me in front of him. He didn't seem surprised when a piercing screech cut through the night, sharp and jarring enough for me to snap around to look at him.

My stomach dropped. "The heavy haul. The Ashenvale owl?" I breathed, stunned.

Zephyr gave a dark smile. "I thought he might come in handy, and you had wrapped him up so nicely."

"He? Your lore magic. You know his story."

"Sayed Briarflight of the Court of Madness. He's primed to hurt Gabor."

We cantered out of the stables, the thunder of the stallion's hooves muffled by the ground. He moved like a shadow come to life, his coat gleaming obsidian under the faint light of the stars. Zephyr's arm wrapped around my waist, his scent—a blend of steel, storm, and something warmer—as the cold night rushed past us. The owl screeched overhead, a spectral guardian circling above us.

I thought Zephyr might cloak us, and I considered using my cloak of ink or the whisper rings.

His sea mist eyes flashed with wonder, then amusement when I offered them to him. "You took them from Gabor?" But he rumbled a warning. "They won't be necessary. Not tonight."

We watched, silent, as Gabor burst from the gatehouse alone, his quicksilver wings catching the moonlight as he sprinted across the open ground in our direction.

Gabor's dark eyes gleamed, focused not on the owl—but on me. "Come willingly, Ysa. For old times' sake. I don't want to hurt anyone, Zeph. I'm under orders to free the monsters unless she comes with me."

My mate growled as his arm tightened around my waist. "Don't you even consider it."

He darted to the dark cliffs where we waited, spreading his wings to reach us all the quicker.

Above, the owl's screech pierced the night, sharp and accusatory. Its pale, ghostly form circled higher, its movements deliberate and predatory. The sound froze Gabor mid-step, his head jerking up towards the source. Then, with a sudden and chilling silence, it swooped. Gabor turned sharply, a streak of silvery movement against the dark, but the owl reached him before he could take to the air. The pale predator descended from the sky like an arrow loosed from the bow. It struck with a blur of ivory feathers and outstretched talons, driving him backwards. It struck with a force that knocked him to the ground.

Behind me, Zephyr's tension radiated through his frame.

They had been friends. Though perhaps it was better this way than burying his own blade in Gabor.

The owl clamped its gleaming talons around Gabor's shoulders, flapped its splintered wings and lifted him from the ground, its wings spreading wide like an avenging force.

From the deep in the belly of Ebonspire, the monsters

bellowed their joy in bone-rattling roars and yowls that rose in a victorious crescendo as if they knew: a savage celebration, a pact of sorts, in the darkness, calling for Gabor's blood.

Gabor didn't make a sound—or perhaps his yells were swallowed by the chorus of monsters—though he thrashed against the bird's grasp. His limbs flailed, muscles straining as he fought to avoid its snapping beak and direct impact from its killing screech. The bite of the monsters nullified fae magic, and I winced as I imagined him falling wingless to his death.

I wouldn't wish that on my worst enemy.

They climbed higher in a stuttering trajectory. What the owl lost in aerodynamics, it made up for in sheer fury. Gabor's figure shrank as the owl bore him into the night sky. Their forms twisted together, silhouetted against the stars for a moment before they disappeared entirely into the inky expanse.

My heart hammered against my ribs. *It's over,* I told myself, but in my gut, I knew it was far from over.

Zephyr's gaze followed them, his expression carved from stone. "That's one problem we won't see again tonight. Ebonspire is safe for now. And now I have a promise to keep."

I stroked Mythos's mane to calm the tightness in my chest. "A promise?"

"A promise is much more powerful than a bargain, Ysadora. A bargain is a transaction. A coercion. A manipulation. There's always a catch, always a price. But a promise is a commitment. It's a pledge taken thoughtfully. It is your honour, your integrity. This one was made to my sister long ago. I promised my sister Veda I'd help you piece together what was taken from you." His grip tightened on Mythros's reins. "Are you ready?"

There was a painter once, who understood that you two would always find your way to each other, the Binder had said. I sank back against him and said the words he needed to hear and I wanted to be true. "I am."

The horse snorted, his hooves stamping impatiently. We cantered on over patches of gnarled roots and dark rock. Faerie seemed to hold its breath, the usual hum of nocturnal life silenced, save for the steady drumbeat of Mythros's stride.

41

YSADORA

*It is unfair that some find their mate and others
are left searching. But the truth is, I am a
coward. I sullied the loves that entered my life. I
hope if you find true love, my sweet girl,
that you will love fearlessly.
—Kazimir's entry to the memory stone*

Zephyr urged Mythros on towards Serrenor, his grip steady on the reins as the stallion's hooves pounded the rough terrain. He intended to put as much distance between us and the Court of Chaos as possible. One arm wrapped around my waist, his chest a solid wall of warmth against my back. It was a protective, intimate embrace. I was acutely aware of every point of contact: the strength of his thighs bracketing mine, the brush of his breath against my temple, the subtle shifts of his hand as he guided the reins. He surrounded me in a way that made my breath hitch.

I thought maybe I had wanted him even when I thought he had killed Lunarys, and I wondered what that said about me. Whether it meant I lacked morality or whether it meant I was adapting to the rules of this darker world. That I was becoming more fae, though I had been brought up a mortal.

The landscape was desolate, though stars glittered above. Chalk cliffs loomed to one side, streaked with veins of black flint and patches of moss. They cast long shadows over our path that edged the Broken Sea. Far below, shoals of tiny fish moved alongside us, their eyes glowing like lanterns as they watched: a further sign of the imbalance in Faerie, Zephyr murmured in my ear. Sometimes, the tide flowed backwards, defying the natural rhythm of the sea, or surged forward, sending violent sprays of saltwater into the air.

It was the kind of dangerous beauty that whispered of forgotten legends and ancient spirits, the kind that spoke to souls hungry for wonder. Beauty that belonged in books, in the stories that Maren, Ferrith, and I had pored over in Larkspur. Back then, we would have leaned in close, dreaming of paths that led to this kind of magic, of landscapes that took your breath away.

I wasn't that girl anymore.

The girl who had dreamed of otherworldly splendour, who had crept down to the cellar to read faerie tales with an eager heart was gone. In her place stood someone who had walked the paths of those dreams and found them lined with darkness, blood and betrayal. I had touched beauty, but it had burned. Though I could still marvel at it, I couldn't surrender to it, couldn't let it fill me the way I once might have.

The biting wind caused Mythros's mane to ripple like a banner and tugged at my gown. Zephyr had long since wrapped his own cloak around me. The wind didn't seem to bother him. He didn't slow the inky horse and rarely spoke, focused instead on forging ahead. As we rode, I found myself lulled by the steady rhythm of the ride, the crash of the waves and most of all, the warmth of my mate.

Sleep took hold. My mind drifted, weightless, until I dreamt of a beautiful woman with dark hair like my own. On her head rested a crown forged from twisted metal that seemed alive, bending and curling, with a central sapphire stone. The light it cast was shades of black, shifting as I stared. Pain and love and something ancient swirled in her violet eyes. *Come home. I miss you. I need you,* she said, her voice as fragile as spider silk, each word steeped in longing, as though she had been waiting an eternity. As though she had spoken them into the very marrow of my being. As I reached out to her, the dream shattered like glass, her image scattering into the void.

"Ysadora. Inkheart, wake up." My mate's voice pierced the edge of my dreams. "This is as good a place as any to stop and rest."

I blinked, my voice groggy with the remnants of sleep. "Where are we?" The chill night air brushed against my face as he slowed the stallion.

"Far enough from the Court of Chaos to remain unseen." Zephyr slid off Mythros in one graceful motion, a faint clink sounding as his boots hit the ground, and offered me his hand.

The warmth of his palm against mine sent a shiver of pleasure through me. I swayed as my feet met the ground, and his hand came around my hip to steady me. Heat crackled between us.

His lips curved into a faint smile. "The ground's uneven. Watch your step."

I nodded, brushing a loose strand of hair from my face and surveyed the terrain while he tended to Mythros. The rocky outcrop would hide us from view should anyone come looking. The sound of crashing waves mingled with the sigh of the night wind, and it felt like the world had shrunk to just us.

If Zephyr was tired, he didn't show it. He pulled a tent from the saddlebag and set down the swords on his back. Then he got to work under the pale light of the moon, spreading the canvas on the ground, assembling the poles and staking the tent into place. There was no hesitation, no wasted effort, as if he'd set up camp a thousand times before.

I stood a little off to the side, watching him as he worked. The moonlight painted his figure in stark silver and shadow, accentuating the sharp planes of his face. A dark lock of hair across his forehead made him look almost boyish. His brow creased with irritation at a small tear in the tent fabric. Every so often, he glanced my way, his eyes catching mine as if to make sure I was still there. His broad shoulders flexed beneath his leathers as he worked the stakes into the ground until the tent stood ready, a small refuge against the cold night. He moved on to the blankets next, lining the floor of the tent with thick layers to ward off the chill and lit an oil lamp. Then, he rummaged through the saddlebag once more.

"You need to eat." He handed me a waterskin and a napkin filled with bread and cheese, and the starshade plum that Cyprian had brought me when I first arrived at Ebonspire.

"*We* need to eat." But the truth was, I wasn't hungry. Not without knowing if our family was okay.

His eyes met mine for a moment, and I wondered if, like me, he was thinking of our loved ones or thinking that Gabor had baked the bread and made the cheese, and that whatever he had done, it shouldn't have ended like that. That's not how friendships were supposed to end. And I was so cold, even in his cloak, so tired. My body ached from the ride, and I needed comfort. I missed Father, Maren, and Ferrith, and for the first time since I had come to Faerie, I wondered what it was all for.

Zephyr's slate-blue eyes combed every inch of my face. "Don't do that. Don't doubt yourself."

He laid a blanket on the ground under the stars, and we ate side by side, sharing food and water, with Mythros softly snorting nearby. When I couldn't stomach much, Zephyr tore pieces of the bread and cheese, and passed them to me bit by bit, like I was a bird who needed tempting, or someone fragile, too proud to ask for help. Maybe it was true. Maybe I was too far gone to be saved. Maybe the weight of everything I had carried was finally catching up with me.

"You need to get out of that damn gown," he said. "I'll fetch a change of clothing from the saddlebag."

I nodded absently. "Okay."

Standing, I crossed to the tent, ducking inside the entrance and slipped off my shoes. My heart gave a little leap as I looked around, caught between anticipation and trepidation. The tent was too small for privacy—not that I wanted any when Zephyr had become my safe harbour in choppy seas. The tent wasn't even large enough to sleep alongside each other with any semblance of decorum. Every inch of space was intimate. Still, the chill of the world melted away, replaced by the warmth of layered blankets and something else, as if Zephyr had stitched shadows around our shelter to keep out the cold. The oil lamp painted the space in hues of amber and honey.

Suddenly, my gown stifled me as if it were a cage. I didn't want to be wearing the damn clothes from the Court of Silence. I didn't want to be thinking of Danaë or Tanuhja, or Gabor and the monsters, or even Father and Maren. It was all too much.

I wanted to feel weightless. I wanted my mind wiped clear, and my body warmed, and I wanted my mate to provide that comfort. I wanted more than anything to feel the graze of his lips against mine, to feel the hard press of his body, to lose myself in his scent and his touch. I wanted him to crowd out the world. I wanted to surrender to the feeling of being held and protected.

"Inkheart?" called Zephyr at the entrance.

I dropped his cloak on the floor. "I need—"

Worry pulsed through his voice. "What's wrong?" He pushed into the tent, his broad frame filling the small space, so tall he almost brushed the canvas above. There was a bundle of clothing in his hands. Storm-cloud eyes lingered on me, searching for the source of my distress. Then he ceded space to me, trying to be considerate, trying to give me room to breathe. Still, his intensity—his readiness to protect, his need to fix whatever was wrong— stirred the air between us.

"I can't...I need to take this off." I yanked at the

buttons of my gown, a long, intricate line that Danaë's handmaidens had fastened along my back.

Zephyr's eyes flicked from the row of buttons to my face, his expression unreadable. Without a word, he dropped the change of clothing he'd brought and moved towards me with a soft grunt.

"Turn around," he murmured, his voice almost rough.

I obeyed, my pulse quickening as I faced the tent wall. I felt his gaze on my back, the intensity of it like a physical touch, and then the warmth of his hands brushed against my back. His calloused fingers grazed the fabric as he worked at the stubborn buttons. He was slow and careful, as though he was afraid to tug too hard, though by now, I hated the gown. It was a ragged mess of torn seams, shredded skirts and blotches.

It wasn't me. It wasn't me. It was another mask.

The moment his hands touched me, I could feel that falsehood unravelling, thread by thread. With each button that came loose, the sense of suffocation eased. The air between us was charged, the howl of the wind only amplifying the tension. My breath caught as his knuckles skimmed my spine, unintentional but intimate all the same.

"Almost finished," he soothed.

When the last button was undone, he stepped back, and I turned to face him again, clutching the gown to my chest. His stormy gaze dipped to the Court of Lore rune on my wrist before snapping back to my face, and I could have sworn he was holding his breath.

"There. You can change." His tone was suddenly gruff and almost distant. "I'll be right outside."

He waited by the entrance, his gaze flickering towards me before he quickly looked away.

But I couldn't bear the distance between us. I reached out for his hand before I could stop myself. "Zephyr." His name was a soft plea on my lips. The remnants of my gown slid to the floor, pooling at my feet, together with my quill and the compass. My voice was barely more than a breath. "Stay. Kiss me."

He turned to face me, his calloused thumb brushing the back of my hand in a slow circle. Slate-blue eyes darkened as they locked on mine, the air between us as taut as a bowstring. Then his gaze roamed over my translucent undergarments and my body, which had already puckered and softened under his scrutiny. Under his slightest touch.

"Ysadora." His voice was frayed as if my plea had unravelled something tightly bound within him. This wasn't just lust. It was deeper, raw and unguarded. "You're sure?"

I nodded, my vulnerability laid bare in the honeyed light of the tent.

"By the lore, say it. Say yes so I know you want this. I'm not sure I'll be able to stop."

My fingers tightened around his. "Yes, Zephyr."

"Say my name like that again, and I'll…" He pulled me to him in a single, fluid motion.

My body collided with his, the force of it sending a jolt through me. His strong hands cupped my face. This wasn't the tentative, romantic kiss we shared in the Court of Silence. This kiss was wild and urgent. It spoke of longing, need and promises unspoken. It spoke of possession. Stars, I wanted him to possess me. Every thought. Every breath. His lips captured mine with a hunger that made my heart stutter, and the world beyond the tent dissolved into nothing.

My body responded to him, a fire igniting as I matched his fervour, matched him kiss for kiss, meeting the pressure of his lips with my own, welcoming him in, sighing as his tongue delved into my mouth. I poured all my emotions into the kiss: all the attraction I had suppressed, the yearning that I had wished away.

My hands found their way to his shoulders, clinging to the solid strength of him as though he was the only anchor in a sea of chaos. They slid up to tangle in his hair, pulling him tantalisingly close. His breath was hot against my cheek as we lowered to a kneel on the blankets. He shoved his boots off, cursing the interruption, before cupping my buttocks, lifting me closer as he captured my lips again.

Stars, heat exploded at my core. The tent felt both like a sanctuary and a furnace, the air thick with the scent of us and the scent of him. The wilds, the wilds just rolled off him. Fate-breaker, the Binder had called him. *My mate. My mate. My mate,* echoed my heart, and I wondered if Zephyr could hear its call. It had never been like this, this raw wanting. Our bodies fitted together like a jigsaw as if my body had always known him, always been waiting for him. I had never known passion to be so consuming, so magnetic. Was it the mate bond that made my body come alive in ways I'd never imagined? Every sensation was sharper, every touch electric, like it was carved into the very bones of us.

My skin buzzed as his hands roamed over me, kneading, squeezing. My delicate undergarments frustrated me when all I craved was his nearness. I could feel the contours of his body through his supple leathers, but I needed more. I arched, moaning, as Zephyr dipped his dark head to my breasts, lapping my nipple through the fabric, plucking it with his teeth before giving the other one the same attention. He gave a husky laugh against my skin, revelling in my response, and I raked at his leathers, needing them off, needing them gone. It was impossible to think of anything but him.

"I have waited a lifetime for you, Inkheart. You were fucking worth it."

"By the moons, take your clothes off."

A wicked grin lit his chiselled face. "You'll have to wait a little longer for that." He pushed me back onto the blankets and slipped my panties down my legs. I gazed at him from under coy eyelashes as he splayed my legs, inhaling sharply as he looked at me in the honeyed light of the oil lamp, with the crash of the waves and the winds outside. "By the lore, you're beautiful, Ysadora Silberquill."

Then he took two fingers and rubbed the core of my sex as if it were the sweetest instrument in the world until I quivered around him. His shadows caressed my skin, tracing the line of my neck, drifting over my shoulders as if his very darkness yearned to soothe and claim me all at once. They brushed against my skin like soft whispers, fingers of darkness tracing the curves of my body, feeling every tremor of my breath. They were a part of him, an extension of his power and desire. The warmth of his hands mingled with the cool caress of his shadows was an exquisite contrast. He worked my core with his fingers and then his mouth until I was putty and slack with pleasure.

Until I could no longer think of anyone but him.

Until nothing else would do except to be filled by him.

When he had wrecked me, his storm-cloud eyes gleamed with satisfaction.

Only then did he remove the leathers that protected him from the dangers of Faerie. His gaze met mine for a fleeting second as he pulled the leather vest over his head. His face was full of brazen desire and love. I caught my breath as he revealed his taut chest, muscles honed by endless orbits of training. The lines of his torso tapered to a lean waist, his inked hip, and my cheeks heated at the dusting of hair leading downwards. His body was a masterpiece of strength and grace. Every line, contour and scar stole the air from my lungs. Then he pushed his trousers over his rune-inked hips and let himself spring free.

My eyebrows shot up, and heat bloomed in my face.

His cheek dimpled. "Do I pass muster?"

I muttered a *yes* that he swallowed with a kiss, joining me on the blankets. He unfastened and tossed aside my brassiere with the impatience of a male who knew exactly what he wanted. Then he started anew, sucking and tweaking and lapping my rosy peaks as if he could never get enough. His shadows traced the curve of my waist and slid along my back. I returned every gift of attention. His heart pounded against mine. I scraped my nails against his back, trailed light fingers across his sculpted butt and thighs with their faint dusting of hair as he bit back a groan. I rained kisses across his torso, sweeping my hands across his chest and lower. He growled, sucking in his breath, at last allowing me to bring him to the same heights. I revelled in my power over him, in his lusty gaze, his groan as I wrapped my hand around his shaft and learned the shape of him, first with my hands, then shimmying down to take the weight of him in my mouth.

Stars, the velvet feel of him.

With each kiss, each touch, I lost a little piece of myself. That piece became his.

When we were desperate with need, when I had exercised the same power over him as he had over me, I straddled him. His eyes locked on mine. Stars, I was so wet for him. So very ready.

"Are you sure?" he asked again, his hands stilling on my waist. His eyes drank in the sight of me as if I were a goddess.

It couldn't be any other way. Even if fate had decided against us, I would have wanted him. "Yes. Always, yes."

"Good." His teeth pulled at his lip as if it pained him to wait.

I gave him a soft smile and put my hands flat on his taut belly as I slipped onto his hardness. I gasped as he filled me. He entered me so deeply, so wholly, that I thought I'd lose my mind. He called my name, then, but my mind barely grasped it. I needed a moment to adjust, to breathe, to get used to the feeling of our joined bodies. He waited, still, his chiselled face a picture of pure concentration, and when I began to rock, bliss broke out across his face. He slid his palms over my breasts—fuller since leaving Larkspur—cupped them, his thumbs circling my areola, his shadows brushing the hair from my face, caressing my inner thighs until he eased us apart.

I frowned, too close to pleasure for a pause, too needy. "What are you doing?"

His laugh was pure desire and male pride as he sat up. "Taking control."

Shining stars, he was so damn beautiful with his tawny skin, his rippling torso, his rugged thighs where old scars interrupted smooth lines. He knelt, then pulled me towards him and hooked my legs around his waist before entering me hard as his lips took mine. His hands wrapped around me, supporting me with ease, as our eyes locked, something akin to wonder in his before he began to thrust.

Then he drove our rhythm, harder, faster, crushing my chest to his own. "You're mine."

My breath quickened against his lips. "Yes, I am, *mate*."

Zephyr's storm-cloud eyes widened. And together, we travelled to the stars.

YSADORA

Veilstem
Slender, pale blue stalk and leaves that ripple like
fine silk. Grows in clusters.
Properties: creates ink that renders words
intangible, making them appear or disappear at
the writer's command. Favoured by illusionists
and fae crafters of enchanted books.
—A Compendium of Faerie Flora and Terrain

Zephyr noticed the mark of my bargain with Elowen on my ankle during our love-making, but he waited patiently for me to tell him, though he bristled at the sight of it, like he was the only one allowed to mark my body. After we had somewhat recovered—and Zephyr had pulled the blankets over us and tucked me against his side—I found that the rigid ball of my worry and panic had eased enough for me to open my mind to him as well as my body.

I told him that the Binder lived, of our conversation and how she called him *fate-breaker*. I told him what had happened in the maze with Elowen, and then later with Gabor in Ashenvale and how I had duped him into letting me take the whisper rings. I told him that Maren wasn't where she promised she'd stay. I told him about the woman I thought was my mother and the queen who really was. I told him that Tanuhja had created the monsters—he grew dark with anger at that—and that he would find a way to save them. I told him about Larkspur and what it had meant, and how it was easy not to appreciate the simple life until it was taken from you. That Father had created that for me. I told him that I needed to put my family back together again, or I'd never be whole.

Zephyr, in turn, told me about his mother and sister and their dreams for Faerie and for him. He told me about his family of mercenaries, and his guilt for allowing Gabor to put us at risk. He told me about how happiness didn't come easily to anyone at the Court of Silence, least of all him. He told me a little about his estranged father Orin, how loss and rejection had been frequent visitors in his life, and how sometimes he didn't know how to laugh when the world was bleak. But that his mother's optimism still somehow guided him, even though it had failed her. He told me that he thought that saving the monsters—if he could manage it—would heal him.

Then his stormy gaze found mine. "There's a painting in your bath chamber at Ebonspire of a dark-haired queen under a star-filled sky."

My chest tightened. "I remember it."

"The day I first saw it was the day Veda told me about you. What you would mean to me."

"What if I am nothing like she promised?"

"Then I will love you anyway."

I swallowed hard. "It was Sequoia who told me."

He gave me a startled look. "I thought it was Cyprian…that he was the one who put it together before me that you are the female in Veda's painting." He kissed the corner of my mouth. "What does the bond feel like to you? For me, it started as a sort of pull towards you that has got stronger with every passing day. It feels like a stream of dark, silken water flowing through my thoughts, with your emotions rippling across the surface. When you're upset, the current churns. When you're calm, it soothes me. And when you're…" His storm-cloud eyes darkened with hunger and longing. "…receptive to me, let's just say it—"

I swatted him, my body already responding to his teasing. "Don't you dare finish that sentence."

He gave a dark chuckle. "What does the bond feel like to you?"

"I don't know." I chewed my cheek. "I guess it feels like the pulse of a distant star, faint but unwavering. I can almost reach out and touch it. Its hum aligns with my heartbeat."

"Does it scare you?" he asked quietly.

I hesitated, then answered truthfully. "No. Love has never scared me. Not finding my family does."

His brow furrowed, and it was hard to imagine that it had been mere hours since we had left the Court of Silence when so much had changed between us and for us.

He linked his hand with my one, where the whisper

rings gleamed dull in the lamplight. "Inkheart…we stole these so that you and your Father would be safe, so that you could avoid coercion by the courts that are seeking to control you and steer your fate. That hasn't changed. Now, all we need to do is find your Father."

"We can shadow walk with the compass. It will be a start."

"Kazimir didn't even want you in Faerie. I don't think he ever intended for you to have the compass. It is crafted to search for something unfamiliar, something outside of you. I don't know—maybe his original intention was to gift it to Danaë when she went with Thiago to Faerie. Maybe it was supposed to lead her back to Larkspur. Faerie magic is topsy turvy like that. It's been working against you, hasn't it?"

I pursed my lips. "Kazimir had left Echohold by the time we arrived."

"Exactly. Don't you see? The compass is designed to search for something unfamiliar, something outside of you, but you have something innate to find your father. You have your ancestral magic and that is far stronger and more reliable than a trinket. You don't have to find him, Ysa. He will find you. All you need to do is tell him where you are."

I shook my head. "I don't know how. I don't know what you're asking me to do."

He inhaled deeply. "That night, you were angry at me after you'd searched for your Father and not found him at Echohold. I searched, too. There was molten glass in his chamber at the window. Molten glass, Inkheart." He shook his head like it was hard to believe.

I thought of the painting in our bookshop. "He had a dragon."

"They've not been seen for decades."

I bit my lip. "Maren told me the brotherhood were dragon riders."

Zephyr nodded. "Nothing could keep a dragon from its rider after the bonding. They were like twin souls. Like mates, in that way…but that changed when the Order of the Glyph burned."

I lifted my head and palmed his chest so I could read his eyes. "You think his dragon has returned."

He brushed a finger over my spine. "Nothing else makes sense." A pause. "Write to him, Inkheart. There is nothing more powerful than a calligrapher with a quill and intent."

My stomach churned. "I am just the calligrapher's daughter."

He gave a soft laugh. "Haven't you realised by now? You are Kazimir's heir, yes, and his truest love, but you are more, so much more than even he dared to hope. Write, Inkheart, and your father will come."

Then he stood, utterly unbothered by his nakedness, and strode out of the tent. Moments later—during which I was almost certain I heard him talking to Mythros—he returned with the saddlebag and our swords. Retrieving the pot of ink I'd taken from the armoury at Ebonspire, he handed it to me, together with Father's quill. We locked gazes, and his left no room for cowardice.

Inside, I quaked, terrified my magic would falter, that I would disappoint him or fail my loved ones.

Sitting up, I wrapped a blanket around me, my breath uneven. "Here goes nothing."

I uncorked the ink pot and realised from my reading of *A Compendium of Faerie Flora and Terrain* that it was glimmerthorn, a silver ink made from a luminous sap that created a shimmering effect, allowing written words to glow in the dark. The once pristine quill was worn and dishevelled from the journey. I smoothed its barbs, running my fingers along the crimson plume until the delicate lines fell back into place, though it still retained a certain wildness as if it had travelled as far and hard as I had. I dipped the nib into the gloopy silver ink, hesitating. A faint glow seeped from its tip, humming softly like a held breath. "I have no parchment."

"I've seen you magic things from the air," said Zephyr quietly. "Trust your instincts."

I closed my eyes, fumbling past my anxieties and bone-deep exhaustion, and let my memories of Father wash over me: sipping broth at the kitchen table together, the way his hands turned the pages of a book, the comforting scent of his old cardigan, the ache of his absence. It all felt so distant, yet impossibly close, like I could reach out and touch those memories if I tried hard enough. My intentions solidified. Then, I lifted the quill, drawing lines and loops in the air. The magic was delicate, but it was powerful in its simplicity. It thrummed against my skin, a soft, pulsing warmth like the brush of a summer breeze at the edge of a storm. My connection to Father and my own power was undeniable. When I opened my eyes, a simple note and a drawing of the outcropping shimmered in the air before me.

Father
I am in Faerie, west of Serennor.

You'll find us here.

~^~

Ysadora

The message hung suspended, tethered to my magic. We watched as the letters curled and glimmered like they were caught in an invisible current. Then, with a final pulse of light, the letters broke apart into tiny motes that floated out through the tent's opening and vanished into the cool, dark sky. The sketch lingered, then followed with a soft sigh.

A strange certainty filled my chest: the message was gone, but its course was set.

The pride in Zephyr's gaze made my heart skip. "You have no idea how extraordinary you are." His tone was gentle but authoritative. "Now sleep, Inkheart. You need to rest. I'll keep watch."

"Yes, my lord," I said tartly, though his words were music to my ears.

He smiled, his breathing slow and even, a lullaby in the night.

I let out a small sigh, my body melting against his warmth and pressed my face into his shoulder.

When sleep came, it was a soft surrender, tinged with hope.

43

KAZIMIR

Danol Varun, The Order of the Glyph
Dragon: Kalythar (Skybeast)
Skills: master of defensive manoeuvres and
cosmic navigation, took the lead in cosmic storms
or dense nebula clouds
Known alliances: Kazimir Silberquill
Whereabouts: Deceased. Killed during the
burning of the Order of the Glyph
—The Dragons and Riders of the Nebula Court

Kazimir and Maren stood in the Shrouded Forest, a half-hour's trek from Larkspur. It was unfathomable to Kazimir how much life had changed since that fateful Bloomtide.

The dragon had made short work of the journey to the crater. He and Maren peered at the wound in the earth and the meteor nestled within it. Despite the destruction, the clearing teemed with strange vitality. Patches of moss clung to the upturned soil, glowing as though lit from within. Silver-veined vines wove through cracks in the ground. Here and there, clusters of flowers bloomed. Shadows pooled unnaturally towards the centre of the crater-like ink spilt across a tilted page. Flora twisted in impossible geometries. The air closer to the fallen star was warped, and small glassy pebbles at its edges floated lazily into the air, caught in currents that defied the natural pull of gravity. A stray leaf spiralled upward.

The fallen star offered no immediate answers, only more questions.

It was as inscrutable as the heavens it had fallen from.

Its call settled over Kazimir like an unseen fog. Though it didn't pulse, as it had the last time Maren had seen it, a low hum rang out from it. It was a sound that reverberated through the bones more than it was heard by the ears. He could feel the promise of untold magic in his bones, a whisper at the edges of his consciousness, urging him to reach out, to claim it, to understand its mysteries.

Caldoron rumbled a low warning in his head, *That is not yours to touch, calligrapher.*

Kazimir's brow furrowed. This wasn't what he'd expected. He had expected them to applaud him. He had a tangible indication of how the star might bind with him to justify why he'd brought the three of them here instead of heading back to the Court of Silence for Ysa.

Maren paced in a tight circle, her agitation palpable. She stopped to stare at him, keeping a wary eye on Caldoron. Her father might have been a dragon rider, but she herself had never set eyes on one until now. "Are you really saying that Lunarys was the Binder—one of the

Fates—and when she died, Ysa's star fell, and that means she now is free to determine her own fate?"

Kazimir wished Ysa and Maren had seen the former glories of Faerie before it all came crumbling down. That he had taught them history and magic and botany. "I know it's a lot to take in. I didn't want to put you in danger by revealing more."

Maren's starfire-bright eyes burned into him. "That's you all over, isn't it? You put us in danger either way. And now Ysa is trying to pick up the pieces. She's in Echohold with those who *tortured* you. And here we are with a lump of rock. And a dragon who could be burning down the Court of Silence instead of hovering over a pebble."

Caldoron sent a puff of smoky air swirling upwards in muted agreement. *She has a point. I'd rather be hunting. Or burning something.*

Kazimir flinched. "Do you think I don't know that? You think I wouldn't burn it all to ash if it meant getting her back?" Shame curled in his chest like a living thing. He understood Maren's anger and felt the sting of it. Every decision he had made seemed to spiral further into disaster. "We made plans to keep her safe."

Maren bounced on her toes in frustration. "But they didn't account for Ysa following her own heart."

His chest tightened at the thought of Ysa amongst the very people who had broken him, all because she had wanted to rescue him. At how he had taken the easy road and let her believe that Danaë was dead. How she might have discovered the truth of it: that Danaë was not her real mother after all and what her lineage truly meant. That she might know of the heartthorn briar and how he had used it to bind Danaë to him in romantic love because he had been too fearful, too weak to raise Ysa alone.

He swallowed the bitter taste of his guilt. He was a failure for not protecting her, but he could do better. He could be better. "This lump of rock is the only chance I have to set things right."

"Enough, Kazimir. I know you care for her. I know you'd give your life for her. But the only chance you have to set things right is to trust your daughter." She glared at the pitted surface of the meteor. "You say it contains remnants of the cosmos. That it will amplify the magic of your family line. This fallen star—whatever potent magic it contains—belongs to Ysa. Not you."

"Maren—"

"If you dare take that away from her, I swear to the starry heavens, I will…"

"You'll what?" The silence between them stretched thin, broken only by the rhythmic hum of the fallen star. It felt like a heartbeat, something both ancient and new, an echo of possibility.

Maren stared at him for a long moment. Then she looked away towards the twisted trees lining the crater. "I decided the night we followed you into Faerie that I would put her first, even if you won't."

Caldoron, crouched beside the crater, let out a rumbling huff. *You've lost the argument, calligrapher. Let's hope you don't lose your daughter.* The dragon's warning was as clear as the crack in the sky.

Dejection ratcheted through him. Wasn't it a father's job to protect his youngling? To shield Ysa from the world's harshest realities? "Maren, how can you talk like this? We're on the same side."

Maren's stance—arms crossed, shoulders squared—spoke volumes. "By the embers, I hope so. Because if Ysadora is hurt because you want her to remain in your shadow rather than embrace her own choices…mark my words, though you are family to me, I will never forgive you."

44

YSADORA

Your mother and I didn't know each other for long, but I will always be grateful to her for giving me you and for her sacrifices to keep you safe.
—Kazimir's entry to the memory stone

I woke in my mate's arms, his warmth anchoring me to a sense of peace. His chest rose and fell beneath my cheek, and I cherished the intimacy for a moment. But the first light of dawn filtering through the tent and the cries of seabirds brought the world back into focus.

Zephyr stirred, his hand tightening at my waist before his slate-blue eyes flickered open. A sleepy smile crossed his lips. "Morning, Inkheart. Did you sleep well?"

"Well enough." I gave him a shy smile, then reached for the waterskin, sipping before offering him some. "Zephyr, this *thing* between us…"

He wiped his mouth and set the waterskin aside, his expression neutral. "Our mate bond?"

"Does it mean…" I trailed off, unsure how to phrase my thoughts.

His tone was like crushed velvet. "Ysadora?"

The words tumbled out, raw and uncertain. "Does it mean we're bound in every way? Will my choices always circle back to you even if I don't want them to?"

He was silent as he weighed his response. "The mate bond isn't a cage, Ysa. It's not about taking your freedom. It's about offering you a piece of mine."

The tightness in my chest eased. "I'm sorry. It's just… this is all so new."

He brushed a stray lock of hair from my face. "I know. The bond means whatever we want it to mean. There are no hard rules, okay?" He squeezed me, just once. "I'll check on Mythros." Then he stood, collected his belongings and walked out of the tent into the morning.

I gathered myself, then pulled on my leathers and borrowed boots—one size too large—and tied my hair into a rough ponytail. After pocketing the compass, quill and ink, I joined him outside. The sky unfurled in streaks of gold and rose, a stark contrast to the barren cliffs and endless sea. Mythros was impatient for us to leave for new ground, his obsidian coat shining in the early light as he snorted clouds of mist into the crisp air.

Zephyr was dressed, our swords strapped to his back. "We need more supplies."

"Okay." The morning was charged with a strange energy, as though the fabric of the world was stretching, ready to snap into something new.

Zephyr sensed it, too, because he frowned and sent out

a pulse of shadows in all directions, scouting. They spilt out from him like liquid night, stretching across the landscape in all directions, far beyond what my eyes could see. They swept into the cracks of the jagged cliffs and the folds of the sea breeze.

My voice was hushed. "What is it?"

His eyes narrowed as if he could see through the veil of darkness he'd cast. The shadows returned to him, curling back like summoned hounds. "Something's moving. Farther up the cliffs. And below."

I followed his line of sight, my stomach twisting. The water frothed under the rising light as if it was alive and waiting for something. The wind picked up, whistling through the cliffs.

Then he came: the dragon from Father's painting.

He swept across the rosy sky on bronze wings that gleamed like molten metal. Each wingbeat thrummed the air with a low sound that reverberated in my chest. His kind of grace could only come from centuries of existence. I barely registered the breath in my lungs as I watched him approach, caught somewhere between wonder and terror. Two riders sat on a precarious perch. The dragon's silhouette stretched over the cliffs, the sea, and us like an omen.

Could it? Could it be what I had longed for?

Mythros pawed at the ground and tossed his head, but Zephyr's hand on his mane calmed him. The air tasted of salt, burnt amber and smoke. The dragon's massive form blotted out patches of dawn as he descended, and his landing made the ground quake and dust kick into the air. Wicked claws sank into the earth, carving grooves into the rocky path. The dragon curled his long tail for stability, inches from the cliff's edge, slitted gold eyes surveying me. Then he folded his wings and exhaled a plume of smoke into the dawn air as the riders dismounted.

I realised that Zephyr had moved away, away from me.

My gaze flicked back to the riders, and tears blurred my eyes. My Father's strength was measured in patience, not heroics. My core memories were of him carefully stacking shelves in our bookshop, counting coins so he could buy us a treat from Anja's bakery or snoring by the fire at home. How strange to see him through this lens: Father perched on a dragon, determination etched into his face, like a hero pulled from the pages of an old legend.

A sharp, aching sound escaped my throat. He wasn't alone. Beside him was a smaller form: Maren, carrying a bulging blanket, her red hair fluttering in the wind.

My heart twisted. They were so small, so insignificant compared to the dragon, but they were everything to me. I found myself rooted to the spot, unable to take the first step towards them.

I had made my peace with Maren, understood her motivations, but so much had changed between Father and me. He had hidden my parentage, my heritage, and though I was glad he was safe, I was certain that it would take a while for my anger to ebb.

I wasn't certain that I could forgive everything.

But still, every wish, every prayer I'd whispered since arriving in Faerie had been answered. An avalanche of emotions crashed over me—relief, disbelief, hope—and then I was running into his arms, ignoring Zephyr's curse behind me to be wary of the dragon.

It was real. They were real.

Father's voice cracked. "Ysa."

His gaze met mine, and we both noted the changes in each other without our mortal glamours. He looked younger and more strained all at once. I thought of the spectacles he'd left behind that he didn't need after all. A mixture of pride and relief crossed his face as if he, too, couldn't believe we'd made it back to each other.

Then I fell into his arms, and Maren joined us, and somewhere, the dragon rumbled his approval. Father's arms tightened around me as if he feared I might vanish again. I clung to him with the same ferocity, but he didn't smell like ink and old books anymore.

The sharp scent of exertion and a bitter undertone of pain clung to his skin. Beneath that, there was the unmistakable fragrance of Faerie. It was the scent of ancient woods after rain, rich with the earthiness of moss and the tang of pine needles. It was the sweetness of exotic plants that only bloomed in realms untouched by human hands. There was the faint trace of dragon's fire and smoke, burnt embers and weathered scales as if the scent of flight and fire had become a permanent part of him. Or reborn. It was the scent of someone who no longer belonged entirely to me and had crossed worlds.

I lifted my head to look at him. "All this time, you lied to me."

He shuddered. "You look so much like *her*. Like Tanuhja." There was wistfulness in the way he pronounced her name. Like maybe things would not have developed this way if they had been allowed to stay together and raise me. I wondered if he knew who she had become.

The dragon coiled its body and laid his head on his talons. A burst of smoke escaped its nostrils. His unblinking eyes flicked between us as though he understood every word.

I searched Father's still-brown eyes, blocking out his increased muscle tone and his fae ears that made him seem alien to me after a lifetime of knowing his face. I decided that the name Kazimir suited him more than Cairn. "We're both keepers of knowledge. That's what we've always been. But you kept our bloodline, our heritage, *our* magic hidden from me."

His face crumpled in devastation. "I thought if you didn't know, you wouldn't be caught in this."

I choked out the words and Maren was so still, so attentive next to me, that I knew, I knew I was right, that it was okay to be angry, even though I loved him. "You didn't shield me, Father. You isolated me. I had to face everything without you."

A quiet ache pulsed in Father's voice. "I'm sorry."

My throat burned with tears and all I could think of was how everything had changed, down to the smallest details. "I was worried you needed your spectacles."

His voice was a sigh of apology and shame. "I never needed them."

I nodded, thinking of his crimson note in the snow and how terrified I'd been. "You told us to run."

"I wanted to keep you safe from the shadows that follow us."

My mate bond flared in my mind like the pulse of the most divine star in the galaxy. "Not all shadows are the same, and not all of them are as dangerous as you think."

Father looked at me thoughtfully, then at Zephyr, and he didn't try to convince me otherwise. My mate met Father's gaze with a cool stare. He made no move to approach, as though he didn't want to intrude, as if he didn't belong in our inner circle. I loved him for it, even as I craved him next to me.

Father's gaze snagged on the quill in my hair. "My own magic…will take time to replenish. It took the calligraphers of old many decades to achieve what you did last night. I'm proud of you."

With that, I let my hurt wash away. I clung to them both like I'd never let them go.

There was a profound rightness in being together again. It wasn't perfect. There was still too much unsaid, too much broken, but in that moment, it didn't matter.

The Faerie of Danaë's books existed. There were caressing shadows, dragons and ink magic, as well as monsters and dark queens. But my old world existed, too: a father who loved me and friends who cherished and fought for me. That was a world I could learn to love.

For the first time since the Binder walked into our bookshop, I let myself believe that maybe—just maybe—there was hope for all of us.

45

YSADORA

The nights have grown longer in your absence.
Every dawn reminds me that
I am here and she is not.
—Tanuhja's letter to her lover Kazimir

I ran a calming hand along the stallion's sleek, quivering flank. His tail swished like a whip, betraying his agitation. Smoke from Caldoron's nostrils curled in wisps through the crisp air, and I couldn't blame Mythros for thinking he might become the dragon's next snack or for worrying for his master. The ribbon of the path seemed impossibly narrow with Father and Zephyr sharing it.

Maren leaned against a boulder, her expression somewhere between exasperation and amusement. A smirk tugged at her lips. "This should be good."

"Maybe I should smooth the way."

She shot me a sidelong glance. "Nah, let's enjoy the show."

"Do you think Father wants the quill back?" I didn't want to part with it, but it was his.

Her green-flecked eyes met mine. "He was tortured by Danaë. His magic… I think it's buried under the pain, but it's healed him to find you and Caldoron. You know, in the Court of Nebulas, they say a dragon's bond can mend what even time cannot."

I could well believe it. Father and his dragon shared an uncanny bond. "They can speak to each other, can't they?"

She grinned. "You noticed. By all that's scorched and sacred, what I wouldn't give for that. Anyway, you should keep the quill for now. He'll ask if he wants it back." She surveyed the males once more. "So…your mate, huh?"

It had taken her less than ten minutes to ferret out the juicy gossip from me. I squirmed. "Yes."

"He works fast." A laugh bubbled from her. "Not too fast, I hope."

My cheeks heated. "Can we move on to another topic? Like how you rode a dragon? Or whether you are pining for Ferrith?"

"No. Not opening that wormhole." Maren nibbled on the last of the bread she'd extracted from the saddlebag. "It's a shame. Gabor really was a talented cook. Letting him be eaten by a monster owl was a little cold. He deserved a quick death for those delicious chocolate-wrapped berries he made us."

Father and Zephyr's raised voices drew our attention. Thanks to Caldoron, it was Father who had the upper hand. The bronze dragon loomed behind his rider, a hulking mass of muscle and scale, slitted eyes locked on my mate. Zephyr's jaw was tense, but he wasn't foolish enough to provoke the dragon.

"You looked after Ysa. You taught her."

My mate's eyes were hooded. "Yes."

"Why? You are Thiago's nephew. His spy."

Maren called out, "I tried to tell Kazimir that he got the wrong impression of you."

Father grunted. "Let him speak." A sigh. "You knew I was being tortured?"

Zephyr's eyes hooded, and my heart clenched, judging him against mortal rules, when Faerie took more from each of us. "I knew it was a possibility. To escape, we needed a clever scheme. We needed the rings."

Father mulled it over. "How do I know you're on her side?"

"I left your message in the snow, didn't I? I would have let her run."

"The Binder manipulated us all to push your fates together. And now I hear she lives."

Zephyr stood tall, shoulders squared, the calm at the centre of a storm. "I determine my own fate, calligrapher, as does your daughter."

I winced. That wasn't going to go down well.

"Bold words for someone who stands under the gaze of a dragon. You speak of fate as if you hold the quill that writes it, shadowcaster. Fate has a way of humbling even the proudest. I know that better than anyone. Ysa is not a pawn in your games."

"No, she's not. She is my equal." My mate's gaze was respectful yet unwavering. "I only play games in service to the ones I care about. I'll protect Ysa from any who try to control her...even you."

Father's shoulders stiffened. "Perhaps you understand her better than I ever did."

I whispered to Maren, "Males and their power tussles. They remind me of the inn in Larkspur and its constant parade of broken furniture and bruised egos."

"Females are no better. We're no less prone to ambition or pride. Battles between us are just as brutal and unforgiving. We fight for survival, for respect, to be heard in a world that drowns us out. Our war drums might be softer, but the song is the same." She finished chewing her mouthful and planted her hands on her hips as she addressed the males. "Now, if you've both sufficiently proved your worth, Kazimir and I have something to show Ysa."

The dragon's rumbling exhale sounded suspiciously like laughter.

She retrieved the bulging blanket she had been carrying when she arrived and placed it on the ground between the four of us. The edges of the bundle were uneven, its folds haphazardly knotted together. Only then did I notice the faint glow emanating through the fabric.

The urge to touch it was almost primal. "You brought the fallen star here."

She met my eyes. "We retrieved it from the Shrouded Forest."

I frowned, remembering how I'd been drawn to touch it when I first spotted it in the clearing. How the impact had carved a crater in the forest floor with curling trees and fused soil, a lodestone for scuttling creatures. Its pulsing power had matched the thrumming in my own veins: the same thrumming that woke in me now. The dark shell of stone housed surface cracks that still burned hot. I peered closer, certain that I could almost see the stars themselves swirling inside.

Zephyr placed his hand on the small of my back. He sounded worried. "Inkheart?"

"The star's power is unpredictable," warned Father.

Maren glared. "The star's been calling to you since it fell. It only pulses in proximity to you. I think you should claim its power before someone else does."

"Many covet it, and not all of them will ask nicely. Perhaps it's best to throw it into the sea. This kind of power always comes with a cost." Father pressed his lips together. "But the choice is yours."

Instinct warred with logic. I glanced at Zephyr. "What would you do?"

Uncertainty clouded his gaze. "It's not up to me, Inkheart. But your father is right in that we don't know what it will do. It's dangerous out here in the open. The more it calls, the more others will listen."

I bent to look more closely at it.

Zephyr stiffened, his hand slowly withdrawing from my back. The shadows at his feet flickered as if responding to an unseen force. His eyes narrowed in concentration. "We're not alone."

A low rumble vibrated in the dragon's chest, and his head snapped towards the cliffside path. Father moved to Caldoron's side, his hand brushing the dragon's scaled neck, just as a group of ten or eleven dark-cloaked figures became visible a mere twenty feet away. I eased up to my feet. I couldn't see their faces, but I recognized the aura of old power that clung to them even before I saw the leopards.

Zephyr's shadows pooled in response, his voice strained. "Uncle."

The male and female at the head of the group lowered their hoods.

The Faerie King of Silence's voice was as smooth as silk, with an edge like a blade hidden beneath the fabric. "Oh, don't look so disappointed at your failure. I have centuries of practice. You are, and always will be, a boy cowering in the garden while your mother and your sister died."

Pain thrummed down the mate bond, like a faint heartbeat in the back of my mind.

Thiago tilted his head, a cruel smile twisting his features. "You stole from me, nephew. First, the whisper rings, then the girl." His pale eyes flicked to me, lingering like a brand, before returning to my mate. "You schemed with the calligrapher. Hid the return of the dragons. Hid the rebuilding of Ebonspire. What else are you hiding? The secrets and the shadows of this realm belong to *me*. I've made kings and queens kneel for less." He stepped closer, his dark cloak billowing around him, and somewhere, the sea churned and the dawn sun boiled, and Faerie itself considered what power it might accrue if it belonged to the spymaster.

Danaë was so beautiful with her braided blonde hair and her crimson lips. "Come with us, Kazimir and Ysa. We'll mend Faerie, and all will be forgiven. Come with me so I don't have to sing."

My stomach tightened. Zephyr's shadows coiled around him like a second skin and extended to me. Our mate bond glowed bright in my mind, and I thought I heard his whispered thought, *I won't let them take you,*

Inkheart. I met his storm-cloud eyes briefly, and in them, I saw the same blend of fear and determination that roiled in me.

"Take the sword," he said.

My hands found my quill and ink pot. "I don't need it."

But the dragon's slitted gaze was not on the threat in front of us, and neither was Maren's. Their eyes were trained higher, higher, to the sky. Caldoron snarled, wings snapping wide, his golden eyes blazing with fury. I realised that the pulsing of the meteor had called dark things to us and that while it still pulsed in my presence, more dark things would come still.

The ruin in Maren's voice wrecked me. "Ysa. Look."

My blood turned to ice. Above us, a monstrous white form shot towards us in the rosy light. Its skeletal wings stretched wide, the tattered membranes straining as the creature swooped lower. Its decayed body bore the unmistakable shape of a dragon with an orange ridge, held together by what little remained of its ribs and sinew, a grotesque parody of flight. On its back sat two figures. One was a man who bore an unsettling resemblance to Gabor, his sharp features tight with determination, though his wings were withered and blackened as if burned.

Beside him, bound and gagged, was Ferrith. His curly blonde hair was matted with blood and his blue eyes were wild with terror as the beast swooped closer. Ferrith, who floated with us in the creek and made us laugh and who loved Maren. A cold knot formed in my stomach, and Maren cried out as if her heart was breaking. He wasn't supposed to be here. He was supposed to be far away, in the mortal king's army. Now, he was just another pawn in Tanuhja's games.

Anger welled up inside me like a tide, hot and sharp, burning my throat.

"A friend of yours?" Zephyr's eyes dropped to the bundled star. "Your star. It's a beacon."

The faerie king's body coiled as though he realised time was of the essence and that he must act before others converged on us from Faerie's disparate, broken parts.

The white dragon landed with a sickening crunch, coating the dewy ground in goo, its wings folding with the groan of decaying bone. The stench of death hit me, acrid and choking. And Ferrith—poor Ferrith. His terror intensified when he noticed us, his oldest friends, and the inexplicable changes in us. The dragon's gaze was lifeless as if it had not known warmth in aeons.

By Caldoron's roar, I realised this creature was not born of nature.

It had been turned by Tanuhja. By my mother.

The white dragon's hollow eyes locked on the fallen star before Gabor opened his mouth, and I knew we were in trouble on multiple fronts. Gabor's sharp features were taut with tension, but his eyes betrayed something unexpected: a flicker of hesitation, a slight trembling in his posture. Heavens, he was ruined. The owl had clawed and flayed him. His wings, once so full of starlight and majesty, were no longer capable of flight. They were sorry, limp rags on his back, and I realised he hadn't been able to heal himself. That though Gabor had survived, he had been bitten, his magic nullified.

Though he had dug his own grave, sympathy flared in me.

He had been so handsome, once, and kind, despite his manipulation.

"You should be dead," my mate growled. There was no room for sentiment now.

"I'm not here by choice, Zeph. Believe me." Gabor's gaze caught my mate's, then darted away as if he couldn't bear to meet the eyes of the brother he had once fought beside and broken bread with. He was a man cornered, trapped by something far darker than himself, a pale shadow of his once-commanding self. Almost like an animal caught in a trap. He shook Ferrith. "If you don't come with me, Ysadora, your friend dies. If you don't come with me, I've been told to take the meteor. Please. Don't make this harder than it has to be. I won't get another chance."

The tightness around his eyes begged for understanding. All he was doing was trying to survive. He wasn't a villain, not in the truest sense. Not to me. But still, I answered. "I can't. I won't."

The white dragon beneath him shifted its weight, its hollow bones creaking, eager for movement.

And Ferrith—strong, brave, wonderful Ferrith— pushed off the decaying dragon's back with a sudden, desperate burst of strength. His feet found rough purchase on the ground, his wrists and mouth still bound, as he raced towards us, fuelled by instinct and sheer willpower. He stumbled, and I jerked forward to help, but a dark tendril shot out from my mate and coiled around Ferrith's waist. It yanked him towards us with stomach-churning speed, just as the white dragon's claws slashed the air where he had been only moments before.

Zephyr's shadows relinquished their hold, and Ferrith fell in a heap next to Maren.

Father urged us onto the dragon, his voice commanding. "We need to move. Now."

Thiago's mirthless chuckle cut through the chaos, cold and knowing. "Running won't save you. Not from what she awakened." His henchmen blurred once more, their forms obscured by their whisper rings even in the clarity of dawn when all things should stand bare beneath the heavens.

Then it began.

Zephyr fought with both swords drawn and glinting in the dawn light, a storm of instinct, muscle, and shadow. His twin blades sang as they cut through the air, weaving a deadly rhythm that matched his shadows. They shifted and twisted to his will, unmasking enemies, tripping them and swallowing weapons before they could strike. His shadows seemed almost eager, coiling and snapping at the air, a warning to anyone who might think of advancing.

I'd never seen him move like this, like a predator, every choice calculated and lethal. His shadows lashed out, wrapping around a foe's wrist to wrench a weapon free or curling into the shape of claws that raked across flesh. Stars, he was beautiful. I could see the focus etched into his face, his jaw clenched, his gaze flicking between the immediate threats and those drawing near. One of the dark figures lunged, a blade aimed at his chest, but Zephyr was faster. He sidestepped, his shadows pulling the attacker off balance as his blade struck true. It was a brutal, graceful dance.

Our mate bond hummed at the back of my mind, his emotions spilling through: focus, fury, and a cold determination to protect me at any cost. Though he fought with murderous precision, I knew this wasn't just about winning the fight. This was a signal to all who threatened what he held dear: his people, his dreams, his home. He wouldn't cower. He would do what needed to be done. Each step he took drove our enemies further away from me, pushing some into the sea as though he were carving a shield of distance with every swing of his blades.

Focus, Inkheart, came the lash of his voice in my mind.

Then I was yelling at Maren to take the rings, to get Ferrith to safety—who wouldn't understand Faerie's rules or the brutality and had no magic, though he was brave and as gifted with a sword as any of us—hoping that Mythros might be willing to spirit them away, though his stubbornness made it unlikely. Father had mounted Caldoron and was battling the decayed dragon, and I could barely watch as the bronze dragon tried to avoid the bite of his feral opponent.

And Danaë, who had been my mother once, and who with her books had prepared me for the secrets of Faerie that Father had locked away, was coming my way flanked by her prowling leopards, her eyes sorrowful, her lungs drawing breath, her lips parting.

YSADORA

Rotting Scavenger Dragon
Skeletal wings, dripping with decay, orange ridge,
immune to flame. Once, Garrick Mudwalker of
the Court of Cavernous Dreams,
brother of Bryndil, gifted mountain climber
and hearing the wisdom of ancients.
—The Secrets of Faerie's Veiled Beasts
by Zephyr Ashmoor

My heart raced as Danaë opened her crimson mouth to sing. Maren had told me about what she had done to Father in her captivity. That her singing for him hadn't been joyous. She had broken him. She enjoyed breaking things. Her voice had the power to fracture minds, to rend thoughts from their foundations, to make us turn on our kin. Her voice quite possibly had the power to kill.

My mate's concern for me rippled down our bond, but I blocked him out.

The air trembled with the quietest of notes, almost sweet at first. Tapered fingers curled like claws at her sides. Danaë's lips parted, releasing a soft hum, the delicate melody drifting towards me like a whisper. She had weaponised her song, harder to counter than steel. I felt her song in my chest, gentle, coaxing, but so very dangerous, willing me to follow her, like the story of the Pied Piper that she had read to me as a child. I wondered if this sweet woman had changed because Father hadn't loved her the way she deserved to be loved. It was so tempting to let my goals melt under the pull of her voice. So tempting to give up and let her look after me. For so many orbits, that had been my dream.

The leopards moved in near silence alongside her as she came towards me, their padded paws pressing into the earth as if they owned it, their pale, spotted coats groomed to perfection.

Inkheart, came my mate's voice, pushing through the walls in my mind.

But it wasn't my dream anymore, I thought hazily.

I wasn't her puppet. That's not what I wanted.

My mind cleared just as her song twisted in shrillness. A searing ache spread through my skull as I dipped Father's quill in the ink pot and lifted it. The magic was so instinctive, so pure, grounded in sorrow rather than fury. My ribbon of ink unravelled in the early morning light, unfurling towards Danaë, binding her mouth just as she and Thiago had bound Elowen's.

Danaë's eyes widened, but the ribbons wrapped around her mouth in an instant, tightening almost lovingly against her skin, strangling her shrieking song. The sound of it abruptly vanished. Golden eyes wide with rage and surprise locked onto me, but I was already turning to the leopards.

The snow leopards' massive shoulders bunched as they surveyed me. Then, they charged, moving with horrifying speed, muscles rippling as they sprang, their jaws snapping open, aiming for my throat and thigh. I barely had time to react.

Inkheart!

Will you be quiet?

I summoned a wave of ink that washed across the ground, slicking it like oil. The leopards, already in motion, stumbled as their paws slid against the wet surface. Before they could regain their balance, I spun the ink like a whirlpool around them, pushing them back to their mistress. Their bodies flailed, a mass of fur and confusion that rolled towards Danaë before I tangled all three in a net of ink.

It was almost too easy.

My voice was cold. "You're not the only one who can fashion silence."

I took a slow, steadying breath, the residual ink magic humming through my veins, and surveyed the scene. The sharp clang of steel against steel echoed across the cliffside, mingling with the crash of the surf far below and the roar of the dragons. Maren, Ferrith and Mythros were nowhere to be seen, thank the stars.

My breath hitched at the sight of Zephyr, bodies piled at his feet, his blades a blur of silver and shadow as he battled two of the faerie king's most trusted spies. The wind whipped his hair, and blood slicked his blades.

Though his breath came in sharp bursts, his expression remained cold and unreadable in contrast to the chaos surrounding him. One spy lunged low, aiming for Zephyr's legs, but a shadow surged from the ground, knocking her blade off course. The other closed in from his left, his scythe slashing near my mate's ribs. Zephyr twisted sharply, his right blade deflecting the strike while his left plunged forward, sinking deep into the first spy's chest. She fell back with a gurgling cry, blood pooling on the rocky ground. The male roared in defiance, feinting towards my mate's side, but Zeph's shadows coiled around the spy's wrist and yanked him off balance. Zephyr pivoted and drove his sword upward into his throat. The spy crumpled to the ground as another raced at him.

Father leaned low against Caldoron's neck, his body pressed close to the dragon's scales for stability as he directed the fight. They danced through the dawn-lit sky in a deadly synchronised ballet, sending gusts of wind tearing across the cliff edge as they avoided the gaping maw and scorching fire of the white dragon. The decaying beast lunged again and again, its wings beating with a sound like torn canvas. The sea reflected the chaos above, its surface boiling with white foam, churning with the rhythm of the battle. Flames erupted from Caldoron's jaws, brilliant and searing, but the inferno sank into its decayed flesh as though consumed by an abyss. Caldoron spun sharply, his talons raking against the white dragon's ribcage, but the creature lunged forward, snapping at Caldoron's tail. Father urged him upward into a dizzying loop. I wasn't sure how long they could keep it up, and I noticed, with a sinking feeling, that Gabor was no longer riding the monster.

That left two unaccounted for: Gabor and Thiago, who coveted the star and me.

I had scarcely finished forming the thought when a presence loomed behind me. The hairs on the back of my neck rose, and the world around me stilled, the dragon's roars muted, and the crash of the waves muffled as if the Broken Sea held its breath.

The faerie king's voice slid into my ear like an icy blade. "Calligrapher's daughter." His tone carried a terrible finality and my instincts urged me to move, but a heavy despair blanketed me that I couldn't shake, although my quill was still in my hands. "You don't truly think that will save you?"

His arm circled my waist and drew me back against him in an almost intimate fashion that made my skin crawl. I wondered how long it took to die. In my head, my mate's voice echoed, urgent and trembling at the edges. *Hold on. Please, Inkheart. I'm coming.* There was a rawness in his tone that made my heart ache. It wasn't the commanding certainty of a warrior; it was vulnerable.

The depth of his fear, for my sake, made me long to reach for him. Zephyr had taught me how to fight shadows. I had beaten Thiago once before. But there was a whole universe of difference between victory in a trail of his making where I had the benefit of allies and besting him solo in close combat.

I was glad Maren and Ferrith had the whisper rings.

Glad my friends were safe and that I had seen Father again.

Ysadora, fight! It was a plea and an order all at once, laced with fear and fury.

Misdirection and surprise, the mercenaries had told me, were the key to winning against someone stronger. I mustered the courage to send a burst of ink into the air, transforming it into a flurry of sharp needles that darted towards Thiago. I used the moment to pivot to face him, already thinking of my next move, but the faerie king's shadows flicked away the needles as if they were child's play. He clenched my leathers, bringing his face to mine as he sank his blade between my ribs.

"I like this part," he murmured as I gasped.

The blade's touch was cold as ice, a line of agony that radiated outwards, spreading like the inexorable creep of winter, stealing warmth from my skin and turning my blood to slush.

I shuddered, and the mate bond quaked, such a well of pain tunnelling down it that I almost said his name out loud. *I could have loved you,* I said to him. The pain stole my focus. I blinked, wanting to see something other than the faerie king's hateful, ashen white face with his frozen river veins and eyes like shards of grey ice.

Thiago was speaking. "My wife will think I had no choice. We're not part of your ancestral line, but with your demise, I suspect the magic from the star will flow to the next nearest powerful vessel: me or the dragon. A dragon can't control this realm, so that is moot. If I gain the power, I will bring back balance to Faerie. That will soften any marital grumbling." He twisted the dagger deeper.

Such a small thing to cause such pain.

My mate came as I closed my eyes, calling my name like a prayer. *Ysa, Ysa, Ysa.* I felt his shadows despite the cold and blood loss. They erupted from him in a tidal wave, surging past me, swallowing the light that filtered through my eyelids. A small number siphoned off to cradle me while the rest rushed past, and I sank into them, comforted. His shadows brushed against my wound, almost as if they wanted to glue me back together, and I opened my eyes one last time.

One last time, as the faerie king's own shadows rose in defence against Zephyr's, like storm fronts colliding. For a moment, the faerie king held his ground, his eyes alight with a manic determination, but my mate's eyes narrowed with a ruthless glint as he sent a roiling mass of darkness towards Danaë, caught with her snow leopards in my ink net that dwindled with my weakening breaths.

"Do you think this ends here?" spat the faerie king.

"My mate or your wife?" snarled Zephyr.

The faerie king's eyes widened a fraction. Zephyr's shadows pressed closer, faster, swallowing the space around the spymaster and his consort, choking off his options. Thiago turned towards me briefly, and then he strode to Danaë, thrust his dagger into the air and carved a jagged portal. The void yawned open, pulling at the fabric of the battlefield itself. Danaë was freed by his command, and he tugged her into the portal after him. The leopards barely made it before the portal closed.

Zephyr's shadows retreated instantly, coiling back towards him like a tide drawn to the shore. The cocoon around me dissolved. In their place were his arms, wrapping around me like a shield. His face above mine was shadowed with worry, his breath uneven as he applied pressure to my wound.

I couldn't feel his warmth, but I tried to reassure him through the bond. *It's okay.*

His jaw tightened. He stroked my hair and cheek and leaned his forehead against mine. *It's not okay.*

Somewhere, a weary dragon roared. *Father needs my quill.*

Zephyr's arms tightened around me. *I'm not leaving you.* He turned his head briefly towards the sky, and he told a beautiful lie then. A lie I wanted to believe. *Kazimir's going to win.*

The pain flared, but I felt how the star called to me and others. It thrummed at the edge of my senses like a second heartbeat. I turned my head and saw it still lying where Maren had placed it. Gabor was there, waiting, staring at it. *He means to take it to my mother.*

Zephyr didn't move until a whinny brought Maren and Ferrith back to me. Ferrith scooped me out of my reluctant mate's arms like he didn't mind that I was fae. Even though he hated everything that lay beyond the Shrouded Woods because of what happened to Vixora. There was pity in his eyes, and tears flowed freely from Maren's as she attempted to stem the flow of my blood.

Through the haze of pain, the world blurred and spun, surreal shapes populating my peripheral vision. The sky itself was breaking apart. There were dragons, their forms outlined in the pale blue. On their backs, their riders perched like warrior queens of old, clad in shining armour and flying in formation. Feathers, beads, and ribbons streamed from their helms, and I thought that maybe it was my delirium that painted such beauty.

I thought that death had come.

I thought that I would have liked more life with him.

ZEPHYR

Liora Bramick, The Circle of Emberlight
Dragon: Satharion (Voidstalker)
Skills: high-altitude navigation, skilled in
psychic bonding, including telepathy
with her dragon and nearby allies
Known alliances: Thalindra Nightmourne,
Faerie Queen of the Court of Bones
Whereabouts: last seen in Celestiva,
The Court of Nebula
—The Dragons and Riders of the Nebula Court
(second edition)

His mate was dying, her life force slipping away like sand through his fingers. Zephyr's chest constricted painfully as he knelt beside her, his hands trembling as he cradled her face. Her skin was cold, too cold. He couldn't breathe, couldn't think, could only feel the crushing weight of helplessness.

He had been in this situation before. What use was power if it didn't save the ones he loved?

This was not how it was supposed to be. He had only just found her. To lose her now would tear him in two. But the evidence was undeniable: their mate bond was fraying. The flowing river in his mind that represented it was drying up, the currents pulling away from him. Where once her emotions had flowed gently towards him, now they were distant. He felt her fear, her pain, and her confusion like sharp thorns in his chest. It was worse still when her thoughts fragmented, fading in and out like she had dipped beneath the dark water like she would never surface.

Veda's painting depicted a queen. Surely Ysadora had to live long enough to reach that future?

No. I won't lose you. Not like this.

Zephyr lowered his forehead to hers, his shadows erratic. He could feel her faint pulse, the weight of their unspoken promises, all the futures they could have had hanging in the balance. His mind raced, going over every spell, every rune, every faerie trick he knew or herb Wylda had cultivated that might reverse the damage, but nothing —nothing—was enough to keep her alive. He would be lost without her, even with the others to depend on. He would revert to the angry male he had been when his mother and sister had died. For a moment, all he could hear was the rush of his own breath and the frantic beat of his heart.

She was asking about her father, even as she lay dying. Anger bubbled to the surface—anger at the universe, at the unfairness of it all. He could feel the pressure of it building, the need to destroy, to make his uncle feel the same helplessness that he felt right now, to make him pay.

The Binder had been an architect of Ysadora's suffering, too. If his path hadn't collided with Ysadora's, would she have been spared this? He would rather have never known his mate than for it to end this way. He would rather she live a blessed life into frail old age without him than die like this.

Then Mythros was there, nuzzling him, like he had done over the centuries in the heat of battle. The stallion became more demanding, pawed the ground, his hoof striking sparks from the stone, and snorting derisively at Gabor. His powerful chest pressed against Zephyr with enough force to make his point clear—stubborn steed. Slowly, Zephyr relinquished his hold on his mate. He laid her bleeding body in the arms of the blonde, blue-eyed mortal, who had laughed with her at Bloomtide.

He stood, sword in hand, and made a beeline for Gabor and Ysa's star, only for the sky to darken with more dragons than he had seen since his youth. More dragons than should have been possible with Faerie so broken. And Zephyr realised that the rumours of a sisterhood of dragon riders that the mercenaries had brought back from drunkards at inns and starry-eyed females in brothels were true.

They were a sight to behold. Their cries mingled with the roars of their mounts. One rider with streaming silver hair raised her hand in salute to Kazimir. Her dragon—a cosmic purple pitted with craters and vast wings—wheeled sharply to their common foe. Caldoron answered with a powerful bellow. Together, the dragon formation circled the decaying beast, driving it into submission without risking a bite. It screeched, a sound of raw fury. But it was too late. Caldoron, emboldened by the reinforcements, clamped his jaw around the white dragon's neck, his massive weight driving the creature to the ground a few metres away.

A few metres from the star, which it eyed greedily.

Cursed day. Curse it all. Zephyr sprang into action, his heart a hollow in his chest. Even dying, his mate's eyes had pleaded with him to do the right thing.

Zephyr laid his sword on Gabor's neck, and he almost flinched at the sight of his friend up close. His friend, who had made them dishes that belonged in a god's kitchen and who looked at Ysa's star in quiet repose as though a battle hadn't raged all around them. "Move away from it."

He could barely feel Ysadora now. The river in his mind was eerily calm, its surface dull, stirred only by the faintest ripples. It no longer reflected his mate's sharpness of her wit or the softness of her pleasure, the lash of her anger or the spark of her dreams.

Gabor's voice held none of the pride that had sometimes riled Zephyr. His voice was worn and quiet. "Tanuhja will make me her monster if I don't return with it. I can't escape her. If I ever meant anything to you, make this easy on me. Let me be my old self. The one who was your brother."

Zephyr understood what was being asked of him. The weight of it settled like a boulder on his chest. How many times had they fought side by side? Drunk mead and eaten together? How many times had they discussed history and females and the stars? Had he failed him?

Gabor made a desperate lunge for the star, almost as if he wanted to alleviate Zephyr's guilt.

Zephyr's grip tightened on the hilt of his blade. "I'll set you free, brother," he murmured, and struck. Sorrow tore through him like shrapnel as his blade sank deep into Gabor's chest.

His brother buckled, gratitude lighting his face as he went down, and as he lay there in those fleeting moments, his wings—mocked endlessly by mercenaries for being better suited to courtly flirtations than battle—mended and returned to their former beauty. The lacerations on his face and torso vanished, erasing all marks of his suffering. For just a heartbeat, he was whole again.

"Bring Ysa to me," he panted.

Zephyr's chest tightened, and he beckoned Maren and the blonde man over to his dying brother, Ysadora cradled between them. She was so pale now, barely there at all. There was only a whisper of life in their mate bond and her sapphire-amethyst eyes, the colour of a twilight sky— were closed.

A helpless dread settled over Zephyr. "Quickly."

Maren frowned. "Can you trust him?"

"Yes," said Zephyr, without hesitation. "We can now."

She stepped aside, her face streaked with tears. Together, Zephyr and the blonde man lowered his Ysa to the ground, and Zephyr removed the cloth that stemmed the blood from the wound, exposing his mate's stomach to the air. Then he crouched close and took her limp hand in his, his shadows warring to shield her from the world.

The bond was faint now, like a thread about to snap, his heart crushed in a vice.

Gabor placed a trembling hand on the wound, and his

breath came in laboured gasps. Though death clung to him, he gave what remained of himself to Ysadora, pouring his healing into her. Before their eyes, her wound knitted. His light spread further, suffusing her entire body. Her breathing eased. Her skin regained the faintest hint of colour. And then, impossibly, her eyes fluttered open.

Hope bloomed in him as each breath became steadier, stronger. Zephyr squeezed Gabor's shoulder.

With a shuddering sigh, Gabor's restored silver-black blended wings folded over him like a cocoon as if he were cradling himself in his final moments. His head tilted back. A ghost of a smile played on his lips before he met death with a final, peaceful exhale.

Then her family were all around. Maren and the blond man and Kazimir, who was no longer in the sky with Caldoron, relief pouring out of them as they hugged his mate and combed back her sweat-damp hair. Her father was telling her to touch the star, that it was the only way.

Zephyr's throat was tight with emotion as the river in his mind brimmed. *You came back to me.*

You are mine, and I am yours, she said simply. *The star is calling.*

She didn't wait for his counsel before deciding whether to claim its power, but the bond between them made her intention clear. Her family moved back, just a notch. He helped her sit up, his heart thudding in his chest as her hand stretched out, stalling briefly as she noticed Gabor's lifeless body, before descending to the star. Her star.

He waited a hair's breadth away, giving her room to take this step.

The light from the dark shell cast strange shadows across her achingly beautiful face. The star flared at her touch, its light shooting upward in a cascade of pure radiance, and for a moment, it was as if Ysadora had become one with it, her body bathed in its overwhelming glow. Her body stiffened for an instant, her face scrunched in concentration. Their mate bond snapped taut, a sudden rush of awareness flooding through him. He could feel her thinking, could feel the sharp spike of her magic as it met the star's power. It was as if she were being pulled apart and reassembled all at once—power, so much power, coiling through her, filling her, flooding her every nerve. He almost went to her.

No, not yet, she said.

Then came the sweet surrender as her magic merged with the star's. He felt through the bond that power had settled into her, settled into her bones like something ancient, something that belonged to her. All their possible futures spiralled through the bond, but he couldn't hold to them, only saw glimpses before they dissolved, too fragile to survive scrutiny.

The sisterhood and their dragons formed a guard around her.

It scared him that Faerie had shifted. That his mate was at the centre of it.

It scared him that the star might take more from her than it gave.

It scared him also that the Binder had convened with her. Their future would not be simple with a primordial being involved. But he would run the gauntlet of pain a thousand times over if it meant he could have her.

Her twilight eyes softened as they met his, the pain of what she had just survived still etched into her face. Then she swept her gaze over the dragons and their riders, confusion shadowing her brow, before lingering on Caldoron, who held the rotting white beast by the throat still.

The beast her mother had made, who was a fae from one of the fallen courts, and who had his own story.

Though he did not know it.

"Caldoron," said my mate as if in no doubt that he could understand her. "Let the dragon go."

He did as bidden, though his slitted eyes followed the white dragon's every movement.

Ysadora addressed the monster. "Fly home to the faerie queen, whose name is Tanuhja. Who made you. Tell my mother I am not running. Tell her I am home. Tell her I will meet her on my own terms."

As the white beast sprang into the sky with a moan, the calligrapher's daughter sank into the safety of his arms and sighed as if she could hear his chant, his prayer, his sigh.

Inkheart, Inkheart, Inkheart.

A lifeline. A promise. A shift in fate.

YSADORA

*I stand with my sisters from the Circle of
Emberlight. Even in their illustrious company, I
am the one holding the flame aloft, lighting the
way. My dragon's roar shakes the ruins.
—Ysadora's dream writing,
as seen by Cairn Everreed*

Liora Bramick came to our aid with her fellow dragon riders from the Circle of Emberlight when she felt the pulse of the star. She didn't accompany us to Ebonspire, but the curve of her smile hinted that the sisterhood's quiet influence over the flow of information was greater than anyone had suspected.

Neither did she push Father, Maren and me to return with her to the Court of Nebulas, which—as Maren had discovered—had greatly suffered with the unravelling of the balance. Liora simply told us that our paths would cross again when the time was right and that she believed one day I would ride a dragon of my own.

Father's eyebrows almost disappeared into his hairline at that.

He watched slack-jawed with the rest of us as the sisterhood took to the skies on their dragons, veering east. The dragons climbed higher, their scales catching the first light like a cascade of jewels flung into the heavens. Their riders sat tall, silhouettes stark against the sun, long braids and flowing cloaks snapping out behind them. Caldoron flew alongside them for a time, returning only when the sisterhood became specks on the horizon and dissolved into the endless expanse of sky.

Zephyr and I returned to Ebonspire with Mythros, beginning our journey a few hours earlier than the dragon, who made short work of the journey and carried Father, Maren and Ferrith as his passengers. The gatehouse remained as magnificent as ever, its spire piercing the clouds and its walls humming with ancient magic, but returning to it was bittersweet after all that had passed.

The mercenaries rushed out to greet us on arrival. Caldoron drew their attention first, and they were visibly puzzled by the addition of a mortal to our ranks. There was no hesitation, no question of my place among them. Their faces lit up at the sight of not only Zephyr's return but mine. As if they considered me family. As if they had willed my safety as much as Zephyr's, had fought and bled for both of us.

Loxley planted a smacker on Zephyr's mouth and clapped him on the back with a force that would have knocked most men over. "Took you long enough. I suppose you were sleeping on the job." But when he tried to kiss me, Zephyr intervened with a laugh.

But it was Cyprian who pulled Zephyr into a hug, Cyprian who almost choked up with emotion at the sight of his brother-in-arms and in life. "Not every day you bring a mate and a dragon and a mortal home." Then he tugged me into the same embrace before turning his charm on my family.

Sequoia merely nodded with a rare, approving smile while Wylda fussed over Father and Ferrith, instinctively knowing who felt the most uncomfortable and bridging the divide.

Mythros gleefully trotted into his stable with a flick of his tail. He thrust his head into a trough of apples like a king returning to his banquet. Caldoron seized a corner of the training ground as his own, curling up to rest with one golden eye open. He was not one for fanfare, certainly not for the displays of interest from those he considered beneath him.

I need time with my family, and you need time with yours, I told my mate through our bond.

He growled. *They are one and the same now, Ysadora.*

Perhaps, but I'll be able to soothe the prickles and hurts more quickly if they're not competing for my attention with you.

His lips curved into a smile that was both wicked and possessive. *So I'm a distraction? Fine. But when you're done, I'll be waiting. And I won't be easy to ignore.*

My cheeks heated at the memory of how his fingers had played with me on our return home. *I would have thought you were sated after our journey.*

His laughter was warm and seductive in my mind. *I'm far from finished with you.*

His charged teasing lingered between us before he reluctantly pulled his focus away from me, convening with Cyprian, Loxley, Wylda and Sequoia inside. Despite his grief, I knew he would be the leader I had come to expect him to be, filling them in on our situation, plainly stating the circumstances of Gabor's return and death, painting him as a hero for healing me without sugarcoating his betrayal.

I had my own job to do. By now, Maren and Ferrith had disappeared, but I found them in the stables, where Ferrith appeared to be tolerating Maren but keeping his distance from her.

I hesitated for a moment, my thoughts tangled, before stepping forward. "I owe you both an apology. You would never have been dragged to Faerie had it not been for me. I'm sorry for what you witnessed, for what you've been made to do because of me. And I can't promise it won't happen again, that danger won't find us once more before you make it back home. But despite all that, I'm not sorry to see you again—because I've never had friends like you. I've missed you."

Ferrith spun round from grooming a mare I had never paid much attention to before. He had washed the blood from his hair, but there was still bruising on his handsome face from where Gabor had hurt him. "Don't you do that, Ysa. Not you. Not you, who have always been so honest." He stabbed his finger in the air at both of us. "You two have been here for *weeks* without me. You left without saying goodbye. Don't say sorry for me being in Faerie. Say sorry for not bringing me in the first place."

"You can keep the rings," I said quietly. "Keep them, and everything can go back to normal for you."

Ferrith gave a bitter laugh. "Maren is *fae*. So are you. There is no normal anymore." He shook his head. "The king sent me here, you know. The king sent me here to find out what lurked in the forest because he heard about the unnatural killing at Bloomtide and my heroics trying to run after the culprit—*your mate*. And then a madwoman captured me, and all I could think of was how Vixora was killed and why you three had disappeared from Larkspur. So no. I'm not going back, Ysa. I'm sticking by your sides to make sure you are okay. Because I'm not okay." He looked at Maren from the corner of his eye, judging her reaction.

"Don't look at me like that, Ferrith Namara. I'm not going anywhere, either. Ysa can stick those whisper rings where the sun doesn't shine." She walked towards him, slowly, then quickly.

Then they were kissing like a dam had burst, and there was no stopping them. Every inch of space between them vanished, and their lips pressed together urgently as if their souls were starved for each other.

I chuckled as they toppled into a hay bale, hoping that Maren would at least tell him that my mate only killed when it was strictly necessary, and went to find Father.

I found him standing beside the bronze dragon. It wasn't often that I saw him so still, so at peace.

"He's more than my companion in battle. He's my mirror. When the world is too much, he keeps me grounded. I missed him unbearably when we were parted." For a moment, there was silence, broken only by the gentle rustling of Caldoron's wings as he shifted slightly. "I'm worried, Ysadora."

His worries weren't easily assuaged. He understood too much of Faerie to be hoodwinked. "I know."

"Even before the star, your magic outmatched mine. It seems you have no need for parchment. Neither are you limited by existing texts or spells. There is a versatility to your ink magic, Ysa, that goes beyond what I have witnessed other calligraphers perform. As though you have changed the properties of ink midcreation and can adapt to the needs of the moment. You have no training to speak of." He shook his head. "It's mind-boggling. I should stay to train you. At least to watch you for the effects of the star."

Caldoron snorted softly as if in agreement with my father's words, his golden eyes gleaming. I could almost sense the comfort between them, the way they seemed to speak without words.

"No, Father. You need to get well." Liora had links with the Court of Bones, where there was a healer gifted in mending the bones that Danaë had broken in Father's body and had healed but broken too quickly again for them to set well. Caldoron was flying him to Runeth to recuperate, and we hoped that his magic would return. I sighed. Every time I looked at a map of Faerie, I thought of Gabor.

What he did, he did willingly. Neither of us should forget that, came the velvet tones of my mate in my mind.

I couldn't always hear him, and our mate bond was still revealing itself to us, but more often than not, he reached out when my emotions flared. Sometimes, he could sense the colour of my emotions. Sometimes, I could convey whole thoughts to him, and he to me.

Like how I tire of company and want to ravage you until my name is the only thought in your head.

I blushed, and Father gave me a knowing glance. "I always wanted what you've found with him—a deep, unshakable, romantic connection. I've spent so much of my life searching for something like that, but it always seemed just out of reach. To be seen, to be understood, like you are with him." He swallowed hard. Tears welled in his eyes. "It feels too soon to part again."

"We're not parting unless you take some protective clothing from the armoury. I forbid it." I picked the lint off his cardigan and reached for his hands. "We'll see each other again. I need you."

"Be happy, Ysa. But be safe, most of all."

"Stop that. And don't worry. Zephyr is always watching out for me." I shivered with pleasure as a shadow brushed past. "Father, I never said thank you for bringing Maren into my life. She was there to guide me on my first steps into Faerie. No plan is perfect, but yours worked. And the Binder, she told me to tell you that…" I frowned, thinking back, and the universe seemed to stretch so far. "You nourished her spirit by mourning her. It rebuilt her."

He nodded, then pressed a piece of rolled parchment into my hands. "My magic failed me. After we found the star, I wrote this and hoped to find a way to get it to you."

I unfurled the yellowed paper and read.

My darling Ysa,
Light of my life.
Maren, Caldoron and I are together.

If something befalls us, go to the stone in our garden in Larkspur

to find the memories I collected for you.
Father

There was a quiet yearning in his tone as he laid bare the depths of his regret. "Will you go there? Will you place a drop of your blood on the memory stone in our garden and absorb all the memories I saved for you through the orbits? The ones I was too timid and foolish to share with you along the way?"

Was that the reason he had spent so many hours by the stone? Why I had sometimes found ink splashes there? Father was a meticulous keeper of records. Had he really hidden away his memories in a stone for me, like jewels in a vault? If he had loved me in the quiet language of preservation, his memories could map who I had been and who I might become.

I hugged the parchment to me and pressed a kiss to his cheek. "Of course I will."

THE STAR'S energy had coalesced within me. Maybe it had even consumed me. My body hummed with the weight of it, the burden of it, and yet the comfort, too. Its power was mine now. We didn't precisely know what it had done to me, and Father was worried. Zephyr, too. Sometimes, his shadows flickered, responding not just to his command but to mine. Sometimes, galaxies swirled in my mind, cascading over the edges of my thoughts. For a heartbeat, I was everything and nothing all at once, and then I met his gaze or heard his voice, and I breathed easily again.

My mate worried that the Faerie King of Silence would

seek revenge, but I wasn't so sure. I thought he might lick his wounds a while before deciding to challenge us again. By now, his remaining spies—those who had escaped Zephyr's bloodthirsty wrath during the battle—would have told him that the Circle of Emberlight was real. The sisterhood of dragon riders had risen from the Court of Nebulas, and they stood with us. Dragons were not to be taken lightly.

Neither were we. If the spymaster advanced, he would find that Faerie was a fickle mistress. The balance of power had shifted. We would meet force with force.

In the meantime, Zephyr established a routine at Ebonspire: a new normal born of necessity. The air was different, heavier, as if the stones themselves mourned the absence of another voice that would never fill its halls again. We avoided the dining hall altogether, because it held the echo of Gabor. We shared cooking duties—adding Maren and Ferrith to the roster—trained and tended to the monsters, although the wards no longer clanged to warn of new beasts roaming Faerie.

I wondered if my mother had learned her lesson.

I hoped she might leave us in peace.

Sometimes, Zephyr asked me for help in compiling a book called *The Secrets of Faerie's Veiled Beasts*, in which he recorded the monster's stories. At other times, he pushed himself so hard training with Cyprian and Loxley that I feared they might wear themselves down to nothing. Their sessions were fierce, a blur of blades to channel the loss and disquiet that haunted them all.

I sat on a knoll, my legs drawn up beneath me, watching the males spar in the forecourt of the gatehouse when Sequoia came to sit beside me. Ferrith currently preferred to train with Maren or me, but his curiosity was already getting the better of him, and there were already bets being placed on when he would relent his stubbornness. The rhythmic sound of their training, the way the fae males' respective magic clashed, was oddly soothing. Sequoia didn't speak at first; she simply settled beside me.

Eventually, she said, "I see the way Zephyr looks at you. He's happy."

It almost sounded like an accusation. I cast her a wary glance. "His home has seen battles and betrayals since I arrived. He made it a sanctuary and look at it now."

Sequoia tutted. "It's your home, too. Ebonspire was a battleground long before you arrived."

"I have a horrible sense of foreboding that our road will only get harder from here."

"So what? You think that will make him love you any less? Once you are his, Zeph will protect you always. That's just how he is. He's like that with me, even after we ended. Don't fight his instincts. He can survive anything but losing those he loves."

Wylda came out to join us. "This looks cosy. Are you two finally getting along?"

Sequoia snorted. "I wouldn't go that far."

The three of us leant together, at ease somehow, despite everything.

Sequoia stared across the plain, her dark skin lit by the dying embers of light. "You know, Zephyr was so close to beating Thiago on the battlefield. It'd make our lives easier if he claimed that court."

But that wasn't Zephyr's dream. His dream was far grander. It had started with his bewilderment at the practices of the Court of Silence and continued with his pity for the monsters. But now it was more. His dream wasn't just about survival or power—it was about restoration. He wanted to breathe life back into the fallen Court of Lore, to rebuild its halls and archives, to rekindle its purpose. He dreamed of a Faerie where every culture, every court, was cherished for its unique magic and traditions. A realm where the old wounds between courts could heal. For my mate, peace wasn't just the absence of war. It was the flourishing of all Faerie life.

I shared that dream. Maybe Zephyr felt my musings through our bond because a wisp of shadow caressed my cheek so gently I might have imagined it.

"Enough about the males." Wylda nudged me. "Tell us everything about the Circle of Emberlight. I can't believe you had all the fun. Do they look as sexy as Zephyr said they did? Were they competent riders?"

There was a rumble of laughter in my head, and I wondered for the umpteenth time how often my mate tuned in to my conversations. *I did not tell Wylda a damn thing. I should come right up there and—*

Girl talk. Get back to your boys' games.

Oh, you'll pay for that, Inkheart. Just you wait.

I nodded. "Liora said many of the sisterhood originally had their first exposure to dragons as aids to the calligraphers in the Order of the Glyph. They were simple scribes and attendants and were never allowed to ride the dragons. The bond between dragon and rider was considered something…too sacred, too dangerous for most. But then the Order burned. That was when the sisterhood was founded—it grew from the ashes because the survival of the Court of Nebulas depended on it."

"So they had to learn how to adapt," said Wylda. "Just to survive."

Sequoia sighed. "We know a little something about that."

We sat there talking for a while as the sun went down on Ebonspire, and Maren joined us for a while. I thought that it felt good to be building something new amongst so much that was broken.

When training ended, Zephyr and I went to the bath chamber where Veda's painting of me spanned a wall panel, and we looked at it together, his body curled around me: the dark-haired violet-eyed faerie queen, her hands stretching out to the stars.

Then we washed each other with slow, sensual strokes, taking turns to pay attention to every inch of each other's bodies. The water flowed over our skin like a caress, the warmth and slick skin heightening our pleasure. There was no rush, no urgency, only the quiet intimacy of knowing each other in this way.

Afterwards, he carried me to the bed chamber, and silken shadows teased me, featherlight, causing trails of goosebumps on my skin, and I gasped without him even touching me. His stormy eyes never left mine. When his fingers trailed down the central line of my body, from my collarbone downwards, I called his name and begged him to enter me. He did, driving deep and hard, finding a rhythm so sweet that I never wanted it to end. Our mate bond sang like the sweep of a violin bow across strings: tender, beautiful and strong.

He slept then, and I went into Rowena's garden, where the scent of irises and roses mixed with salt waves. I dipped my quill in pale blue ink distilled from veilstem, chewed a toffee that my mate had brought me, and wrote a letter to Elowen. The luminous droplets glimmered as I wove them into the breeze.

I told Elowen about what had transpired with her parents and mine and that I hadn't forgotten her. I told her about my star and how it had changed me and that I wasn't sure if it was for the better. I told her about the sisterhood of dragon riders and an ancient stone in a garden in the mortal realm that captured a calligrapher's memories, where Zephyr would take me in the morning. I wrote that Maren would return with me to see her baker mother and Ferrith would visit his alcoholic father, and then we would return to Faerie, because we were each other's chosen family. I wrote that I wanted her to be a part of what we had created at Ebonspire, that Ebonspire was different from the Court of Silence and that her voice was needed.

I told her we would come for her when the time was right and not to be afraid.

That she should look for dragon's wings and inky shadows and more letters on the wind.

Then I gazed out over starlit Faerie, buoyed by the promise of a future yet to unfold.

ACKNOWLEDGMENTS

To readers who love romance, adventure and wild worlds, who know that a book is more than paper and that books should be discussed but never banned.

To my reader group, thank you for your encouragement, support and sense of fun.

To my beta readers Debbie and Sherry, who have been there since the beginning of my fantasy writing journey and whom I appreciate as much as a cat appreciates naps.

To my book team, Fay, Trish and Toni, whom I trust beyond measure.

To my friends and family, both online and in real life, who sing at my side, widen my perspective, and bring laughter and levity.

To Mum, for the romance books hidden in the drawers of our childhood home, artfully cut fruit platters and homemade curries, and Dad, for teaching me about boundaries long before I realised I needed them. Gibran wrote of bows and arrows. I am lucky that together you formed my bow.

To my children, H, R & N, who miss me when a deadline approaches and bring me tea and hugs.

To my husband J, who is my comfort, the centre of my world and dreams of travelling the world on my book dime. Anywhere is home if you are with me.

Thank you, now and always.

SHARE YOUR READER LOVE

I hope you enjoyed *Garden of Ink and Ancient Stone*. Please take a few moments to leave a review online. Reviews are so appreciated. They tell authors which stories resonate and help readers discover our work.

If you are a book blogger and would like to feature my books, please get in touch at www.NilluNasser.com.

N. Z. Nasser

xoxo

STAY IN TOUCH & GRAB YOUR SHORT STORY

Come and be part of my tribe and join my facebook reader group at <u>Nasser's Book Nymphs.</u>

To receive a free short story and keep up to date with my news, sign up for my fantasy newsletter at <u>www.nillunasser.com</u>.

Here's a coupon for the first time you make a purchase in my online store at <u>www.nillunasser.com</u>: NILLU15.

TOWER OF BONES AND DIMMED STARS

INK OF THE FAE, BOOK 2

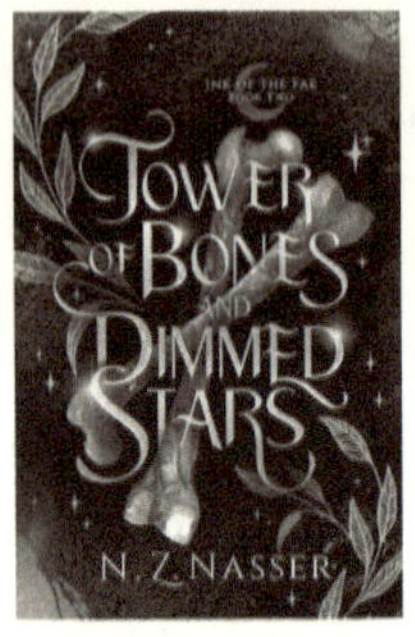

Ysadora is safely at Ebonspire, testing her volatile magic after the meteor's touch. Life with Zephyr is a dance of careful courtesy punctuated by fiery passion as if they still tread the ballroom floor. Finding a new equilibrium for their friends under one roof is no simple task, and the endless schemes of Faerie don't allow her to catch her breath.

Her father's dragon carried him to the Court of Bones to heal his broken body. But without the dragon, Ebonspire is vulnerable to attack, even with Zephyr's gift for shadows and his dungeon of monsters. Especially when the cunning Faerie King of Silence finds out they have stolen from him.

But Ysa has allies beyond the gatehouse. There's the Binder, who remains elusive. There's the Circle of Emberlight, which believes Ysa is their leader. There's Elowen, the Faerie King of Silence's daughter. And there's Ysa's dark-hearted biological mother, who yearns for a reunion.

To shield their loved ones and remake Faerie, Ysa and Zephyr must leave the gatehouse and reclaim the fallen court—and dragons—her father abandoned long ago.

ABOUT THE AUTHOR

N. Z. Nasser is a writer of fantasy fiction. Her stories are about women who change the world, filled with magic and rooted in friendship.

A lover of barefoot walks along the beach, she is glad to have left behind her career in the civil service and to never wear heels again. Whether she is writing in her garden office or wrangling laundry, she is happiest with a cup of tea at her side.

She lives in London with her husband, three children, two cats and a fox-mad dog.